That Winter in Venice

CIJI WARE

THAT WINTER IN VENICE. Copyright 2015 by Ciji Ware.

All rights reserved under International and Pan-American Copyright Conventions. By payment of the required fees, you have been granted the non-exclusive, non-transferable right to access and read the text of this book, whether on screen or in print. No part of this text may be reproduced, transmitted, down-loaded, decompiled, reverse engineered, or stored in or introduced into any information storage and retrieval system, in any form or by any means, whether electronic or mechanical, now known or hereinafter invented, without the express written permission of Lion's Paw Publishing / Life Events Library / Life Events Media LLC. Please respect this intellectual property of the author, cover artist, and photographer.

The characters and events, real locations and real persons portrayed in this book are fictitious or are used fictitiously. Any similarity are not intended.

Cover design 2015 by The Killion Group, Inc.
Cover and colophon design by Kim Killion.
Photo credit: Jim Zuckerman www.jimzuckerman.com
Formatting A Thirsty Mind Book Design

ISBN: 978-0-9889408-4-0 — ebook editions;
ISBN: 978-0-9889408-5-7 — print version

Additional Library of Congress Cataloging-in-Publication Data available upon request.
    1.Women's fiction 2. Costume Design. 3. Costume Designers 4.New Orleans Mardi Gras celebrations 5. Venetian Carnival celebrations, Venice Italy. 6. Climate Change. 7. Rising Waters 8. Urban flooding. 9. Vanishing wetlands and barrier islands 10. Environmental journalism. 11. 21st century—Contemporary Fiction. 12. Romantic Fiction.

e-Book Edition © October, 2015; Print Edition © October 2015

Published by Lion's Paw Publishing, a division of Life Events Media LLC, 1001 Bridgeway, Ste. J-224, Sausalito, CA 94965.

Life Events Library and the Lion's Paw Publishing colophon are registered trademarks of Life Events Media LLC. All rights reserved.

For information contact: www.cijiware.com

PRAISE for Ciji Ware's Historical and Contemporary Fiction

"Ware once again proves she can weave fact and fiction to create an entertaining and harmonious whole." *Publishers Weekly*

"Vibrant and exiting…" *Literary Times*

"A story so fascinating, it should come with a warning—do not start unless you want to be up all night." *Romantic Times*

"A mesmerizing blend of sizzling romance, love, and honor…Ciji Ware has written an unforgettable tale." *The Burton Report*

"A romantic tale of intrigue…a compelling story line and fascinating characters." *The Natchez Democrat*

"Ingenious, entertaining and utterly romantic…A terrific read." JANE HELLER, *New York Times & USA Today* bestselling author

"I read straight through…" MARY JO PUTNEY, *New York Times* bestselling author

"Oozes magic and romance…I loved it!" BARBARA FREETHY, #1 *New York Times* bestselling author

"Fiction at its finest…beautifully written." *Libby's Library News*

Also by CIJI WARE

Historical Novels

Island of the Swans
Wicked Company
A Race to Splendor

"Time-Slip" Historical Novels

A Cottage by the Sea
Midnight on Julia Street
A Light on the Veranda

Contemporary Novels

That Summer in Cornwall
That Autumn in Edinburgh
That Winter in Venice
That Spring in Paris — coming early 2017

Contemporary Novellas

Ring of Truth: "The Ring of Kerry Hannigan"

Nonfiction

Rightsizing Your Life
Joint Custody After Divorce

THIS NOVEL IS DEDICATED TO:

CHERYL POPP
Journalist, event producer, and my intrepid traveling companion to Venice during Carnival

and

CAROL KAVALARIS
Interior architect, entrepreneur, CEO, and my favorite consultant on leaky palazzos

and also to

VENICE, ITALY and NEW ORLEANS, LOUISIANA
Sister cities in so many ways, matchless, beloved, and eternal—let us pray…

SERENA ANTONELLI

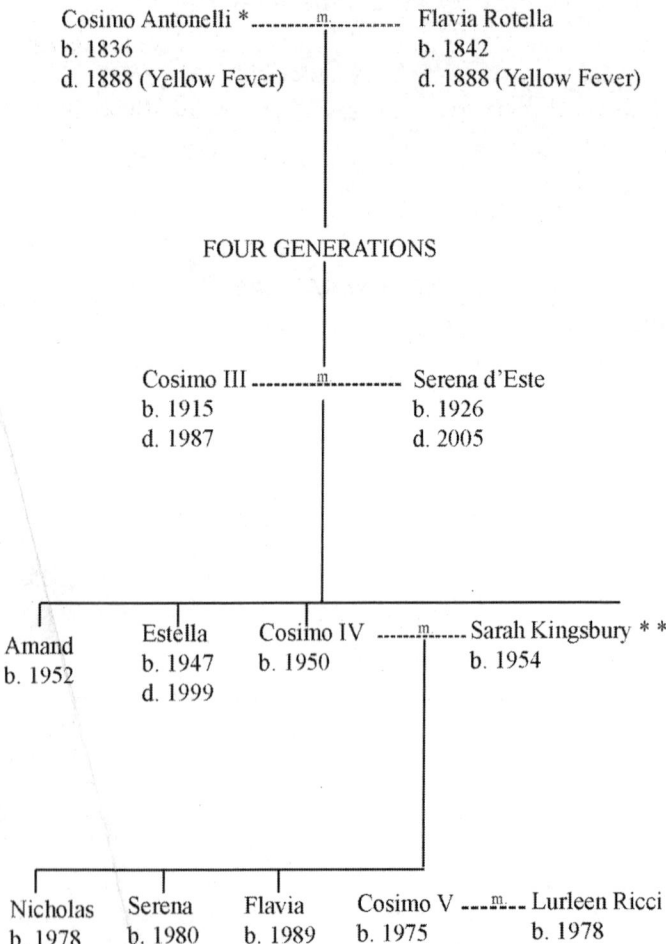

Cosimo Antonelli * ....m........ Flavia Rotella
b. 1836   b. 1842
d. 1888 (Yellow Fever)   d. 1888 (Yellow Fever)

FOUR GENERATIONS

Cosimo III ....m........ Serena d'Este
b. 1915   b. 1926
d. 1987   d. 2005

Amand   Estella   Cosimo IV ......m...... Sarah Kingsbury * *
b. 1952   b. 1947   b. 1950   b. 1954
               d. 1999

Nicholas   Serena   Flavia   Cosimo V ---m--- Lurleen Ricci
b. 1978   b. 1980   b. 1989   b. 1975   b. 1978

* Commedia delle Arte performer in Venice. Cosimo Antonelli emigrated from Italy to New Orleans in 1849 at age 13 with his parents fleeing the Revolution of 1848.

* * Sarah Kingsbury Antonelli's 2nd cousin is Antoinette Kingsbury Duvallon whose son is Kingsbury Duvallon, Jack Durand's best friend and husband of Corlis McCullough.

JACK DURAND

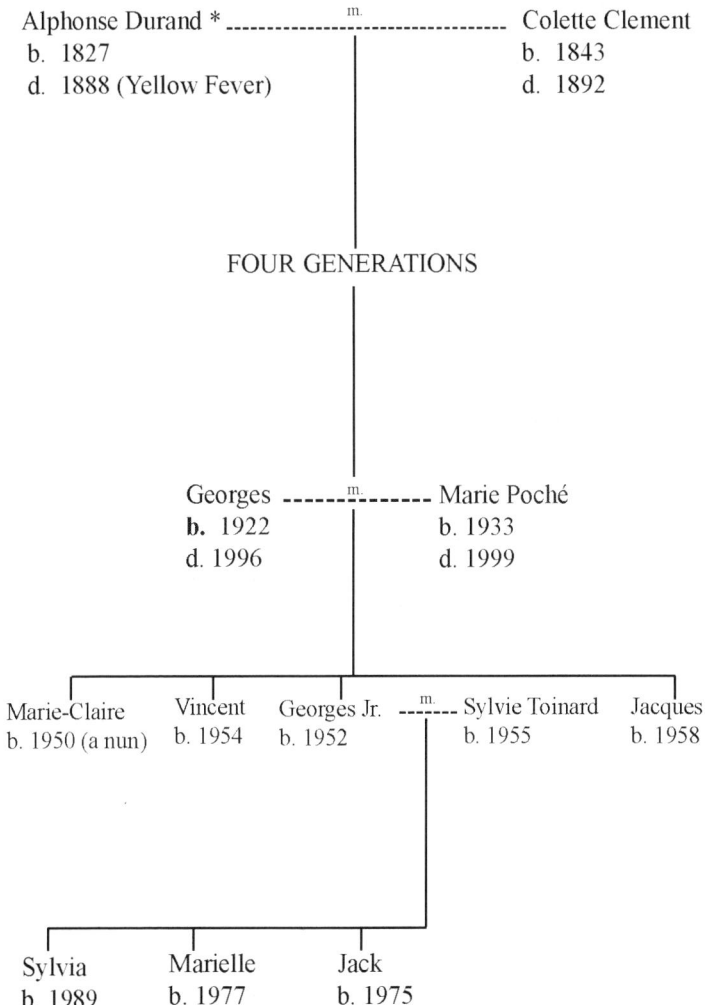

Alphonse Durand *	m.	Colette Clement
b. 1827		b. 1843
d. 1888 (Yellow Fever)		d. 1892

FOUR GENERATIONS

Georges ----m.---- Marie Poché
b. 1922   b. 1933
d. 1996   d. 1999

Marie-Claire   Vincent   Georges Jr. ---m.--- Sylvie Toinard   Jacques
b. 1950 (a nun)   b. 1954   b. 1952   b. 1955   b. 1958

Sylvia   Marielle   Jack
b. 1989   b. 1977   b. 1975

*A government functionary regulating water traffic on the River Seine.
The Durands arrived in New Orleans in 1851 after a *coup d'état* by
Louis-Napoleon Bonaparte and his subsequently becoming Napoleon III.
The dictatorship and new regime that resulted forced the Durands to flee France.

The only way to care for Venice as she deserves it is to give her a chance to touch you often—to linger and remain and return.

Henry James, *Italian Hours*

Venice, Italy November 4, 1966

A PRAYER FOR VENICE

Life giving water, death-dealing flow,
the acqua alta seeps past ancient pilings on reed-wrapped
islands where five-hundred-year-old palazzos wheeze and
groan, clinging to foundations that sink with each day's tides…

Beauty and sorrow, courage and corruption swirl through
her canals like the Adriatic Sea, bringing to *La Serenissima*
the rotting waste of careless souls—and the last, desperate
chance for a clean lease on life in the sad, salty cycle of this
water-ringed city.

Listen to the rush of the tide sweeping into the Venice Lagoon.
Before it's too late, listen…listen…
or the next six-foot wall of water will drown
the Queen of the Seas…

— Anonymous

PROLOGUE

Memo to: John Reynolds, Managing Editor, *Times-Picayune*
From: Jack Durand, Senior Environmental Reporter
Re: Global Rising Waters Conference
  Venice, Italy, January 3-10

John:
As I prepare to cover the conference, these parallels between New Orleans and Venice, Italy leap out at me.
To wit, both cities have:

- *World-renown annual Mardi Gras/Carnival celebrations*
- *Frequent Hurricanes/Acqua Alta*
- *Wetlands and barrier islands—damaged and/or disappearing*
- *Serious threats of rising water drowning both cities within 50-100 years*
- *Gigantic flood containment projects: levees, canals/mobile gates*
- *History of engineering decisions influenced by "special interests"*
- *Significant water traffic and commerce in two key national seaports causing widespread environmental destruction*
- *Historic health threats: plague/yellow fever*
- *Significant crime and reputations for crooked police officers*
- *History of high-level governmental corruption and graft (both city Mayors recently indicted for nefarious deeds)*
- *Major cathedrals/basilicas: St. Marks/St Louis*
- *Catholicism as a leading religious and cultural factor*
- *Unique boats: gondolas/pirogues*
- *Love of music: opera/jazz*
- *Famous musicians: Vivaldi/Armstrong, etc.*
- *Noteworthy cuisines: i.e. Gumbo/Pasta*
- *Tourist meccas threatened by overwhelming numbers of visitors*
- *Similar "Let the Good Times Roll" revelry lifestyles*
- *Bottom line: Irreplaceable cultures…*

So what do you think as we approach the 10th anniversary of Hurricane Katrina? Do we have more than just a conference about rising waters and climate change here? I'm reachable by text or email. Due back in the office January 11th.

Cheers,
Jack

(If Dr. Lauren Hilbert should call, please tell her I'm on assignment overseas. Thanks).

CHAPTER 1

Three days after New Year's Eve and a month after Jack Durand's thirty-ninth birthday, the seasoned newspaper reporter glanced up at the display board in the main terminal of the Louis Armstrong New Orleans International Airport. He scanned the departure listings, looking for Delta's 4 p.m. flight to JFK where he would connect with Air France to Paris and then fly on to Venice for the 5th Annual Global Rising Waters Conference. Was it possible this was his fifth time covering this *same* story?

His sister Marielle, who'd volunteered to drive him out from town, pointed down a long corridor.

"Delta's on Concourse D, isn't it? I'm pretty sure that's where all their flights leave."

"Yep…that's it. D. I better get a move on."

"You've got a few minutes more," Marielle protested, and then turned her head at the sound of laughter. "Look at all those people taking selfies over there," she exclaimed, pointing toward a cluster of new arrivals jostling each other in front of a larger-than-life statue of New Orleans' favorite trumpet player for whom the airport was named. The molded figure forever blowing his fiberglass horn stood sentry in front of a colorful mural depicting other musicians parading down a street. "Those tourists have been here for less than five minutes and already I bet they're posting on Facebook," Marielle declared.

The gaiety and celebration of the visitors, along with the revelers painted on the wall to Jack's right had an unnerving, surreal quality compared to the searing memories of Hurricane Katrina that he stashed away in the farthest corner of his brain. Merely walking into the airport conjured up the sight of aged and dying people on stretchers littering this very floor for which the terminal had been the last stop on a horrific exodus from a drowning city a decade earlier.

Think about something else...

Every time he entered these walls, now, he felt as if the storm victims featured in the gut-wrenching stories he'd reported from this place had become ghosts that would never completely fade from his consciousness. He took several deep breaths and fought against an on-rush of haunting images of that terrible time.

Given his mood this day and the events of the past week concerning a certain lady doctor, he wondered why he even bothered to drag himself across land and sea to yet another rising waters conference. Whatever resolutions and findings-of-facts that resulted from the meeting this year would undoubtedly be dismissed by the Climate Deniers and ignored by the politicos and policy makers, to say nothing of his alleged ladylove who pointedly changed the subject whenever anybody mentioned Katrina or global warming. If only he could simply head for Venice, Louisiana, down near the mouth of the Mississippi, and spend the next week fishing—alone.

Fat chance of that anytime soon...

Breaking into his gloomy reverie, he searched the terminal for the nearest "pre-check" TSA line, a status he'd earned, thanks to all the business traveling he'd done in the last ten years as a "wetlands expert"—whatever that meant these days, he thought, fighting a pessimism he found difficult to contain at times. Sure enough, he spotted the battery of screening machines that all travelers had endured since 9/11.

"Well, kiddo," Jack said, giving Marielle a hug with his free arm while balancing his computer bag on his opposite shoulder, "you take good care, y'hear? And thanks for the lift to the airport."

"Glad to do it. It was great trapping you in my car for forty minutes so we could catch up a bit...but you *still* didn't answer my question about Lauren."

"Gotta go, sweetheart," Jack replied with a shake of his head. "That's a discussion for another day."

His thirty-seven-year-old sister cast him a sharp look.

"Listen, Jack...you can't avoid figuring this out much longer. You're pushing forty, for pity's sake! If she's not the right one for you, you gotta—"

But suddenly Marielle stopped needling him, and instead, pointed excitedly to a knot of people standing nearby.

"Oh, glory..."

"*What?*" Jack asked, instantly wary of the direction the conversation with his sister had been headed.

"Look who's right over there!" his sister exclaimed. "Serena Antonelli! We used to be great friends, but I haven't seen her for the longest time. And it looks like every single member of her family is with her." Marielle smiled at her brother. "Have you ever met her?"

"Don't think so," he replied, glancing at his watch.

"She and I were at Tulane together. We even lived in the same dorm, but I hardly ever saw her after freshman year because I pledged my sorority and she practically slept in the Theater Department. She's really nice, though."

Jack had hardly known that Tulane *had* a theater department, given that he spent every waking hour at the engineering school studying hydrology whose intricacies took every brain cell he possessed to master.

"I guess she didn't get very far as a movie star in Hollywood," he noted dryly, hitching his computer bag higher on his shoulder and preparing to take his leave.

Marielle frowned at him. "Serena's a costume designer, not an actress, and she's done very well for herself, Mr. Big Shot," she retorted. "I heard that she worked in Las Vegas doing costumes for that glitzy Marco Leone show out there before she eventually came back to New Orleans after Katrina to help out her family. I've been meaning to drop by Antonelli Costumes a million times, but just never made it that far down Canal Street."

"Is the company still in the CBD?" he asked, referring to the Central Business District where a number of banks and other commercial enterprises were headquartered. Katrina had wiped out many smaller firms there that never returned to the city.

"Yeah, they're still headquartered there. A couple of friends of mine have had costumes made by them for Mardi Gras since the storm, but I heard their family business has been on the skids."

Jack's gaze shifted fifteen feet to Marielle's right and was arrested by the vision of a tall, willowy woman with lustrous dark brown hair pulled back into a smooth ponytail fastened with a black ribbon at the nape of her neck. Her long legs were clad in classically cut navy trousers, a modern version of Katharine Hepburn in an old Spencer Tracy movie. She sported a thick, cream-colored turtleneck sweater and a heavy navy anorak with fur trim around the hood that she'd slung over her arm. Everything about her was chic and understated, Jack thought with a surprising blaze of interest that he quickly tamped down.

"Man, she's nearly as tall as I am," he noted. "From the winter clothing she's got on, it looks as if she's headed to Alaska."

"New York is my guess. Somebody told me that she got a Master's degree in costume design at Yale," Marielle said over her shoulder, taking a few strides toward her former classmate. "Maybe she's got a job doing costumes on Broadway!"

Before Jack could stop her, his sister called out, "Serena!" across the space she was traversing. "Serena

Antonelli! It's *me*! Marielle Durand...well, Marielle Claiborne, *now*!" She waved enthusiastically at her school friend to draw her attention.

"Wow...Marielle! Hi!" Serena replied as Marielle reached her side. "Married, huh? Congratulations! Do you still live in New Orleans?"

That was the question everyone asked if they hadn't seen each other in a while. A hundred thousand or so had never returned to the city after August of 2005, creating a diaspora in the wake of Hurricane Katrina that stretched across America and beyond.

"Yeah, we still live here. I married a veterinarian that I met rescuing pets during the storm. Ever meet Doctor Phil...Claiborne, that is?"

"No, but that's wonderful! What part of town are you in?"

"We built a new house on one of those reclaimed lots in Lakeview we got for a steal. It was the only way we'd ever own a place, that's for sure." She gave Serena a hug. "Imagine! You and I *finally* running into each other after all this time!"

Jack observed a startled, pained expression flash across the face of Marielle's friend, and then, after a moment's hesitation, the young woman embraced his sister in return.

Serena turned to introduce Marielle to the various people encircling her, including several dark-haired, thirty-somethings who shared her Italian-American good looks and were probably her siblings, along with a man and a woman in their sixties whom Jack assumed were Serena's parents. They apparently had all come to bid Ms. Antonelli farewell, Italian family style.

Jack remained where he was, checking his cellphone for emails, while Marielle chatted with the Antonellis for a few minutes. When he didn't approach, she beckoned her brother to come join her. Jack forced a polite smile, waved, and shook his head in the negative. He pointed to the line snaking through TSA. As usual, he couldn't shake the gloom of simply *being* in this airport again and didn't feel like being sociable. However, Marielle refused to take no for an answer. She sprinted to his side and virtually dragged him over to the group while she made effusive introductions every step of the way.

"Meet my famously elusive brother, Jack Durand," she began. "Jack, this is Serena Antonelli…her little sister Flavia who I can't *believe* is as tall as we are, now. And this is Nicholas, her brother, and his partner, Gus LeMoyne, *and*…" Marielle paused for breath, "this is Mr. and Mrs. Cosimo Antonelli."

As the introductions proceeded, Serena Antonelli's dark eyes held his gaze and he marveled at their intense color. If he had to describe them for a story, he'd call them…molten chocolate. Her ink-black lashes made them seem even darker, and for some strange reason, he had a visceral urge to run like hell from her penetrating, empathetic stare.

Gesturing with his boarding pass he said, "I'm sorry to say hello-goodbye, everyone, but I've got to get to my gate. Can't miss this plane," he apologized again, addressing the Antonelli family in general and avoiding Serena's friendly expression.

Marielle chimed in, "Hold on a minute, bro! Guess what? You and Serena are on the same flight to JFK! Amazing, right?"

Serena's smile broadened. "Marielle just told me that you're going on to Venice, too. The Air France flight? For an environmental conference, is it?"

Jack nodded, not sure whether to groan or be glad. "What better place for a get-together on flood waters and climate change than Venice, a city inundated like clockwork every November."

"And on through the winter, I'm told," Serena agreed. She pulled up her left pant leg, revealing a trim ankle sheathed in knee-high rubber boots. "I've been duly warned," she added with a grin.

Marielle chimed in excitedly, "Serena just told me that she's going to assist *the* most celebrated costumer in Italy during Carnival there. Sort of like a two-month Master Class in Mardi Gras, am I right?" she added, turning to her friend for confirmation. "She'll be there the exact same time *you* are, Jack. Maybe you should stay on in Venice and go to one of the famous balls they hold there every year?" She turned toward Serena. "Tell him about the one you're working on. This is *such* serendipity!"

Jack was growing more uncomfortable by the second due to his sister's obvious eagerness that he meet, fall in love with, and marry *anyone* except his assumed girlfriend.

Serena flashed him a smile that lit up her amazing dark eyes with glowing enthusiasm.

"The people I'll be working for also put on an event each year called—not too surprisingly—*Il Ballo di Carnevale*," she said and Jack could tell by her fluid pronunciation that she spoke excellent Italian.

"Doesn't that sound *fantastic?*" Marielle exclaimed.

Jack was ashamed to admit that what was fantastic on this third day in January was heading out of the country after a holiday season he'd just as soon forget. Meanwhile, Marielle appeared oblivious to her brother's melancholy musings amidst the hubbub of the crowded airport. She beamed at him encouragingly, and then turned to address Serena.

"So what's your seat assignment?" she asked her friend eagerly.

Serena glanced briefly at Jack, who looked away, and she gave an embarrassed laugh.

"I've got an aisle seat somewhere," she answered with

a shrug. She pointed to the crowds surging through the security zone. "Gosh, this is such a zoo. Jack's right. We've gotta go, everybody."

Jack nodded, gave his irrepressible sister a last, swift hug and said a brief farewell to everyone, including Serena. With a wave over his shoulder, he set off for the security gates. He peeled off to the left of the milling hordes, happy that he was in possession of his U.S. State Department-approved Global Entry Pass that also guaranteed him pre-approved security check-in status and a faster line. The newspaper had secured it for him, thanks to his being the publication's sole remaining globetrotting environmental reporter. He always tried to keep the bitterness out of his voice whenever he apologized to people that the paper only published three times a week now—in his view one of the *Picayune's* dumbest post-Katrina management decisions. He'd done his best to adapt to the Digital Age, but the mere thought of having to file five online blogs a week, in addition to his regular in-depth reporting, only darkened his mood today even more.

Out of the corner of his eye, he saw Serena pause to kiss each family member on both cheeks as she bid farewell to her clan. He flashed his credentials at the TSA minions and hurriedly advanced toward the X-ray machines.

Then, Jack Durand relaxed. He'd be at the gate and on board the plane long before the stunning Ms. Antonelli traversed the regular security line winding its way at glacial speed through various checkpoints.

He did not need any more complications in his life, he thought with a touch of regret. Given the situation with soon-to-be Doctor Lauren Hilbert, he certainly had enough facing him as it was.

CHAPTER 2

"Mama...honestly, I've got to *go!*" Serena insisted gently, removing her mother's clinging arms from around her neck.

"You fly safe, y'hear?" her mother cautioned, and her daughter could see the tears brimming in her eyes. "Let us know when you arrive safely."

"I will, Mama," she replied with studied patience. She turned toward her brother Nicholas. "I'll text Nick as soon as the plane's wheels touch down in Venice," she added with a knowing look in his direction. Her parents both refused to learn how to use their cells phones for anything other than making emergency calls.

Sarah Antonelli had lost one child due to the cruelty of Mother Nature and her remaining children bore the weight of her constant anxiety that she would somehow lose another. The middle-aged matriarch had been sober for a few years, after a long struggle, and had become hyper-vigilant about all sorts of potential threats to her surviving offspring...terrorists, suicidal pilots, and amorous Italians being merely a few of the many dangers she feared might imperil her eldest daughter's safety.

Nick said, "Mama, I'll make sure you'll be the first to know Reenie's living it up in the city she's named for."

Sarah Antonelli cast a sharp glance at her husband and then at Serena.

"That was your father's idea to name you after *La Serenissima*...I wanted to call you Margaret after the matriarch of the Kingsburys of Covington."

"Yeah, yeah, yeah," grumbled Cosimo. "We've heard *that* before. My mother, Serena D'Este, was a great lady and *she* was the one named for Venice, since her people came from there. And, if you'll remember, Sarah, it was my turn to name a kid."

"You named your first-born after yourself," she retorted. "When we had a girl, Nonna Serena was my mother-in-law! What choice did I have?"

Before her parents' bickering could blossom to a full-fledged argument as it so often did these days, Serena blew kisses all around and strode to the end of the line that was slowly snaking toward a battery of X-ray machines. When, twenty minutes later, the woman in front of her flatly refused to be electronically stripped naked, Serena barely could suppress a groan of frustration.

"I want to be patted down," the woman insisted loudly. "I've already battled cancer. I don't need a bunch of radiation to give me *another* dose!"

The TSA official gave the passenger a pained look and yelled, "Female pat down! Number three station!" to no colleague in particular while Serena nervously glanced at her watch. At the rate she was going, she was going to miss her plane! A vision of Jack Durand sprang to mind. She'd seen him zip through the pre-check line and speculated that he was probably already sipping a highball on board. He'd certainly seemed less than enthusiastic to learn they were on the same plane to New York and then both traveling on to Venice.

What did I do to offend the guy?

She recalled Jack's standoffish manner with a prick of annoyance. Whatever was going on with him, he had made it plain to everybody, including his own sister, that he wasn't a bit interested in the rather startling coincidence they were two New Orleanians both headed to the same place at the same time, but for wildly differing reasons.

Hadn't Marielle called her brother "the elusive" Jack Durand? That was all Serena needed to know about the Pulitzer-Prize-winning journalist to be more than happy to give him a wide berth.

Celebrated…elusive…unobtainable. No more of that *in my life!*

Serena frowned and craned her neck to see if a female TSA agent were anywhere near the vicinity to give the passenger in front of her an electronic once-over.

Sweat began trickling down between Serena's breasts, thanks to the bulky turtleneck sweater she was wearing that wouldn't fit in her suitcase even if she sat on it to try to close the darn thing. She inhaled deeply, reminding herself silently that she'd be glad for its warmth when the plane's air-conditioning created a deep freeze somewhere over the Atlantic.

Tapping her right, stocking foot with impatience while her rubber boots made their way on the conveyer belt without her, she glanced over her shoulder at her fellow passengers who all wore scowls at the long delay. She hated having to wear the damn boots on the plane, but there was no way they would fit in her suitcase either.

Where was *that security pat down person, for pity's sake?*

It was another ten minutes before Serena was beckoned to put her arms over her head and get zapped inside the airport security machine. She dashed to collect her belongings that had piled up at the end of the luggage conveyor belt and headed for her departure gate at a dead run.

When she got there, a solitary airline agent pointed to her watch.

"Is your name Antonelli? Sorry, but we gave away your aisle seat assignment five minutes ago. We thought you were a no-show."

"The damned TSA!"

The agent held up her hand and plastered a fake, "Believe me, I've heard that before" smile on her face. "But you can still make the flight, if you hurry." She handed Serena a new boarding pass. "It's a center seat, but at least you're on your way to New York."

Jack looked up from his seat on the aisle as the last, harried passenger arrived, red-faced and panting from both exhaustion and frustration over nearly missing the flight.

The seat between him and the passenger on the window was blessedly empty. His fellow traveler had also opened his laptop and had been typing away just as Jack had been for the last twenty minutes. Until now.

He groaned inwardly. The plane's door at the front slammed shut, and none other than Serena Antonelli was stomping in his direction in her rubber boots, her glance scanning the seat numbers as she continuously consulted her boarding pass.

She gave one more look at the number above his head and down at him sitting on the aisle— at which moment their eyes locked. Her lips formed into a straight line and her lids fluttered shut.

Opening them, she said, "Just your luck. Sorry."

"You're sitting here?" he asked unnecessarily.

"*Sorry*," she repeated with an edge of sarcasm, "but don't blame me. It took me forty minutes to get through TSA and by the time I arrived at the gate, they'd given away *my* aisle seat."

She glanced around for a place to stow her carry-on wheelie. Every overhead compartment was stuffed to the gills. A flight attendant, noting her dilemma, marched determinedly to her side and declared her bag would have to go in the regular baggage and be claimed at JFK before she headed for her connecting flight to Europe.

Meanwhile, Jack stood up, balancing his laptop at a precarious angle, to allow her to squeeze into their row. With barely an inch to spare, she stowed her smaller flight bag under the seat in front of her and fastened her seatbelt over her heavy coat consigned to her lap. She sank back, closing her eyes a second time, and ignored him as if he were radioactive.

Well…maybe I am.

Serena wished that someone could hit her on the head so she'd be totally unconscious until she landed in New York and could make her escape.

She'd tried to sleep during the two-and-a-half-hour flight, but ten minutes into it, she was burning up in her hot sweater, despite rebelliously having thrown her anorak on the floor under her feet. She knew without looking that there was nowhere to stash the cable knit pullover, even if she ripped it off and sat in her bra next to the Almighty Jack Durand. Her traveling companion had started tapping on his keyboard the instant he regained his damned aisle seat.

So what if the guy at the *Times-Picayune* was considered a God for his searing coverage of Hurricane Katrina, and now, his daily blogs since the paper only published three times a week? He was obviously one of those hotshot journalists full of his own importance and too above-it-all to lower himself making the casual acquaintance of a college chum of his younger sister's.

She had only been vaguely aware of Jack Durand's existence as an upper classman at the engineering school during the time when she and Marielle had been fairly good friends. How he'd ended up as an environmental reporter and a specialist in climate change, the vanishing wetlands, and the perils of rising sea levels to coastal communities like theirs, she had no idea. She doubted that he'd ever set foot in a theater on the Tulane campus, so their paths hadn't crossed. She'd always hung out with creative types, ignoring even good-looking guys like Jack Durand who had calculators in their shirt pockets.

Engineers?

Bor-ing!

At the end of four years, she and Marielle had pretty much lost touch as their interests had widely diverged…she as a theatre major and Marielle doing pre-vet.

Her eyes still clamped shut, she heard the drinks cart rattle to a stop beside their row.

"Something for you, sir?" asked a chirpy flight attendant.

Even with her lids closed, Serena could tell that Jack Durand's broad shoulders, chiseled features, and full head of longish brown hair had obviously cheered up this hardworking woman's workday no end.

"Bourbon, please, and a small water."

Of course he'd drink bourbon. What good ole' southern boy doesn't?

"Your wife is sleeping," whispered the attendant. "Can I get—"

"She's not my wife, but—"

Serena's eyes flew open and she said quickly, "I'll have a spicy tomato juice with a slice of lemon. No vodka."

The attendant smiled with satisfaction. Serena speculated the woman had just been checking to see if her handsome passenger was spoken for, despite not wearing a ring on his left hand.

"Certainly, miss. Here you go."

The pert young woman turned to give her warmest smile to Jack.

"Now, you be sure to let me know if you need anything else, will you, sir?"

Serena could barely keep from rolling her eyes. Instead, she took a sip out of her plastic cup, set it down on the tray she'd flipped out from the seatback in front of her, and closed her eyes once more.

It was only another hour and a half flight to JFK and

then she'd be rid of the man. Despite their being on the same connecting plane to Europe, those airbuses were huge. What were the odds of them ever being seated next to each other for a second time?

Zero.

The serendipity that Marielle noted about her brother, Jack, and Serena being booked on the same flights to Venice stops *here*, she thought grimly, and pretended to fall asleep.

Serena Antonelli appeared to be out cold. Jack took another deep draught from his bourbon and water and stared at his computer screen. For the last ten minutes, he'd attempted to absorb the agenda for his conference scheduled to commence in Italy in less than twenty-four hours. He'd checked out a few sessions that might have some new information he could use in his blog, noted the time scheduled for his talk on the disappearing Louisiana wetlands, and chose the field trips he wanted to take, touring various flood-prevention facilities in Venice—both built and under construction—in and around the city of some 150 canals.

He glanced out the plane's window at inky darkness as they flew through the night toward New York. Ever since Katrina, he avoided looking out airplane windows during the daytime. It reminded him too much of a few helicopter ride-alongs he'd taken with the U.S. Coast Guard over sections of the city like the Ninth Ward and Lakeview, submerged in ten feet-plus of water in the days following the storm.

He dared a quick glance to his left at the sister of one of New Orleans' best known Caucasian victims of the 2005 hurricane: Cosimo Antonelli V, the eldest son of the

Cosimo IV whom Jack had just met at the airport—and the scion of the Antonelli Costume Company. The younger Cosimo had been thirty-years-old that unforgettable year, and about to become a father for the first time.

The poor guy's house on 40th Street was one of the first washed away that Monday morning when the 17th Street Canal burst its perimeter and a wall of water engulfed the neighborhood of million dollar homes. One of the newspaper reporters told him the couple had been found at the top of a set of pull-down stairs, obviously trying to get up to their attic when the water thundered through their home.

Jack reached for a gulp of bourbon and tried to banish the image from his mind. He knew only too well how little the rest of the nation was aware of the destruction of that upscale region, or that nine thousand homes were mortally wounded in the neighborhoods near Lake Pontchartrain, with 42 percent of all deaths in the storm that of white citizens. The predominantly African-American Ninth Ward, with its terrible loss of life and property, was a full-blown tragedy, for sure, but so was Lakeview and other regions of the city that hadn't received as much media attention during those awful days.

For a moment, he allowed himself to ponder what the reaction of his own two uncles must have been when they first learned what had happened to the canals flanking Lakeview and saw the devastation on the ground.

Vincent Durand, a hard-drinking, crusty, retired river barge captain, was never a man likely to dwell very long on any role he and his fellow Levee Board members may have played in the disaster that day.

On the other hand, Jack's Uncle Jacques, whose namesake he was, grew very quiet whenever the events in Lakeview came up in conversation. Jacques Durand steadfastly remained mum about what he'd observed as a junior employee in the U.S. Army Corps of Engineers that had rebuilt the canals back in the Eighties. Jack surmised his elderly uncle knew a lot more than he let on about the chain of circumstances that ultimately resulted in the disaster in many neighborhoods twenty years later.

"Mistakes were made back then, obviously," was the most Jacques had ever commented about the tragedy when asked about it by his nephew. "But, Jack, you can't change the past. You can only try to do your best in the present."

Case closed.

Well sort of, he mused, taking another sip of his drink. News organizations and a few citizens' commissions around the state had long focused on figuring out who or what was ultimately responsible for the terrible loss of life and property on August 29th, 2005. Hearings had been held, fingers had been pointed, but thus far, nobody important but the mayor had gone to jail. Now that it was ten years later, probably nobody would.

Taking a last sip of his drink, he reminded himself, as he had so often this last decade, that he covered the environment and the future of the planet, not petty politicians and bureaucrats whose past sins were too numerous to keep track of.

Even his editor at the paper was known to shrug and say with amused cynicism, "Hey, it's Louisiana. What do you expect? We're a Third World country down here and practically a Failed State."

Jack glanced at the sleeping woman whose right elbow nearly touched his left one. Given a number of factors, not the least of which was the implicit deadline Dr. Lauren Hilbert had laid down New Year's Eve, his gut told him it was probably best to steer clear of the lovely Serena Antonelli…on her way, as was he, to the most romantic city on earth.

CHAPTER 3

As soon as the plane rolled to a stop at the gate at JFK, Serena busied herself pulling her wedged-in, fur-trimmed anorak off the floor and her carry-on bag from under the seat. This, in turn, allowed time for Jack to rise from his aisle seat, offer a perfunctory farewell, and be swallowed up by fellow passengers anxious to claim their baggage and be on their way.

She prayed that the bag the flight attendant had insisted ride in the belly of the plane would turn up at baggage claim, along with her large suitcase filled with clothing and art supplies that she had not been allowed to check straight through to her flight to Europe. She'd packed not only her drawing instruments and special sketching paper, but everything she thought she'd need for her two-month stay as Allegra Benedetti's visiting assistant during the lead-up to the magnificent *Il Ballo di Carnevale*, a dinner and ball held every year for wealthy visitors during Venice's legendary Carnival festival.

Carnevale!

Serena could practically hear her grandmother's Italian inflection of the word. Her late *nonna*, Serena D'Este Antonelli, was the principal reason her granddaughter had a fairly decent grasp of the language, along with a passion for the art and culture embedded in the northern Italian heritage claimed by her father's family. Serena had embarked on an incredibly exciting quest, she reminded herself. All she had to do at this point was locate her bags and get herself to the Air France check-in.

The Delta baggage claim area was packed with people when she came down the escalator. She caught a fleeting glimpse of Jack Durand on the other side of Carousel 5 as she planted herself in a spot where she hoped she could grab her two remaining suitcases on their first go-round and make her way to the International Terminal. She was determined to allow plenty of time to go through even tighter security to get her bulky luggage on her night flight to Paris and then transit to Venice.

Lost in her thoughts about what lay ahead, she was startled by the raucous buzz that reverberated in the large hall, signaling that the baggage was about to disgorge down a steep chute and slide into the bumper guards that ringed the carousel. Impatiently, she watched suitcase upon suitcase lurch forward and pile on top of others and wondered at the mad scramble and rudeness of her fellow passengers climbing over each other to liberate their luggage.

Suddenly, she saw her largest bag appear at the top of the chute and then become stuck until a few more suitcases pushed it down the conveyor belt, only to be wedged far from the bumper guard where she could attempt to make a grab for it. She watched helplessly as it rumbled by her, pinned by equally large bags on either side.

She glanced up and saw Jack Durand easily yank a medium sized wheeled bag from the masses of similar suitcases. Hands on her hips in frustration, she impishly stuck her tongue out at him as he happened to look up, and saw him laugh.

Just then, the bag that had been taken off the plane and stowed below appeared ten feet from her, but it, too, was wedged in an inaccessible position for her to grab it, or risk being crushed by either anxious travelers, or the luggage itself.

Basta! she muttered, and resigned herself to waiting until some of the crowds had thinned out and her bags came around again.

"Can I give you a hand?" She turned and was startled to see Jack grinning at her. "I'm on that eleven-thirty-five Air France night flight to Paris that goes on to Venice, remember? You can relax. We have plenty of time."

Serena started to laugh.

"What?" Jack demanded.

"It's very nice of you to offer, but—well—a little bit surprising. At the New Orleans airport and on the flight just now it sure looked as if you definitely preferred to lone wolf it to Italy."

Jack gave her a startled look in response to her candor and then grinned at her again.

"Sorry. I had a lot on my mind...but given what I saw happening to you just now, I thought I should behave like a southern gentleman and help a lady in distress."

Serena cast him a doubtful glance but merely murmured, "You have no idea."

"And besides, I can never resist a good-looking woman who sticks her tongue out at me," he added with a straight face.

"Yep, that's always been part of my fatal charm."

Jack blinked and then grinned at her yet again. In the next instant, he shifted his gaze and pointed to the left end of the curving carousel. "Uh-oh. Isn't that your bag coming around again? The big ole' one with the New Orleans Saints luggage tag?"

"Yeah. That's it! But watch out! It's—"

Jack made a lunge for it, pushing away a large box.

"Oompft!"

"I warned you. It weighs a ton. I had to pay extra."

Jack somehow managed to get it over the lip of the bumper guards and onto the carpeted floor.

"They should have charged you as much as your plane ticket for this thing! What the hell do you have in there?"

"Art supplies. Another heavy coat. A picture portfolio.

I'm staying two months, you know."

"Working for that Carnival costume designer, Allegra…?"

"Benedetti. Allegra Benedetti. You've heard of her?" Serena asked, amazed.

"In fact, I have. When I'm in Venice for this conference this time of year, there are always pictures of her and the ball she sponsors in the local papers. She's a very attractive blond."

"What an excellent memory," Serena noted dryly. "I'm going to be half her assistant, half student."

"Marielle said you had a Masters from Yale in costume design. That doesn't sound very much like you're a student anymore."

"When it comes to the genius of Venetian costume designers like Allegra, I'm a student," Serena said firmly. "And hugely lucky to have gotten her to take me on. Oh! Look!" she cried, "There's my other bag!"

She successfully nabbed it as it passed and together, she and Jack soon had her luggage piled on top of a cart.

"Well, thanks," she said uncertainly as a silence bloomed between them. She turned to go and then hesitated because Jack was gazing at her with almost a puzzled look, as if mulling something over.

Then he said, "Look, we both have the same three-and-a-half hour layover, so why don't we make our way to the International Terminal, check in all this stuff you've got here, and have a bite of supper together."

Serena regarded him soberly.

"Are you sure? You looked pretty reluctant even to say hello to me when Marielle introduced us, and you kept yourself mighty busy during the flight to JFK. You have no obligation, here."

"Well, you kept your eyes closed the whole way," he countered.

"I just thought you preferred to keep to yourself—so I complied," she responded. "And as it happens, that's fine with me."

Once again, Jack appeared startled by her directness.

"As I said, I had stuff on my mind, but I apologize if I...I—" He paused, considering the matter carefully. "Actually," he said, as if surprised by his own conclusion, "I'd *prefer* to have dinner with you."

"Well..." Serena replied, judging silently that it would be much easier to get herself and her luggage onto the Air France flight with a big, strapping man like Jack Durand at her side. "In that case, I accept."

She figured they'd easily lose sight of each other on their Boeing 777 once they were onboard. And as for Venice...each of them definitely had other fish to fry.

Jack had a rather sheepish expression when Serena finally emerged from the regular security line she'd endured a second time after they'd each checked their big baggage through to Venice at the Air France front counter.

"Man, I've got to apply for that Global Pass-thingy you have so I'll get pre check-in status like you!" she declared, grabbing her carry-on bag off the conveyer belt and looking over her shoulder to make sure she had all her possessions, including her boots. "Give me a sec," she added, dumping everything on the floor while she pulled on her Wellingtons.

"All set?" Jack asked when she'd reorganized herself.

"I think so," she replied, counting her pieces of hand luggage.

"C'mon. I know a fairly decent place, as airport restaurants go, over on our concourse."

"I can tell you've traveled this route a few times

before," she said, her long strides keeping up with his.

"This will be my fifth conference in Venice," he said, pointing to a restaurant sign about fifty yards ahead. "I love that city."

"I love it already, too, and I've never even been there before," she said, laughing.

Jack took a sharp right and Serena followed.

"Oh, great!" she said with a laugh. "Italian food! That should get us in the mood."

The two found a table in a relatively quiet corner and swiftly ordered a glass, each, of a chianti that Serena picked out from the menu, along with plates of pasta *Bolognese*.

"Best to keep it simple until we get there," Serena suggested. "Even airport chefs can probably manage a *Bolognese*."

Soon Jack was answering her questions about Marielle and the intervening years since the two women had been school friends.

"During the storm, Marielle was amazing," related Jack. "She hadn't gotten the grades to get into vet school, but the first thing she thought of was people's pets and how to help the ones that had been abandoned."

"So that's how she met Philip Claiborne? The veterinarian she married?"

"He'd taken care of her dog, so I found out for her that he'd also evacuated to Baton Rouge, where our family ended up for a while. Together, they headed back to New Orleans as soon as they could and launched an effort to save as many stranded pets as possible in the wake of Katrina. Now, in addition to his practice, they also run a non-profit animal rescue foundation, finding homes for ailing, abandoned or elderly pets."

"Do they have any kids?"

Jack shook his head.

"Sadly, no, though they want them badly. But they sure

have got a lot of animals wandering around their place. My dad refuses to go there. Says it's a petting zoo."

Serena ran the pad of her forefinger around the rim of her wine glass and said conversationally, "Marielle mentioned that she and Philip have a place in Lakeview, now."

She instantly felt the intensity of Jack's gaze closely observing her from across the table.

"Yes, they bought one of those empty lots there through the Road Home program. Built a house a couple of years ago."

Serena inhaled a deep breath.

At length, she said, "Well, I'm glad for them. Lakeview was...*is* a wonderful place. Good for them for doing that."

Jack remained silent and took a sip of his wine. Serena broke the hush that had fallen between them.

"You know, Jack, it's so great that Marielle's found this unique path of hers, given what happened when we first both got to Tulane."

"What was that?" he said, setting down his glass.

"About a week into our freshman year, we discovered we were both feeding the same stray cat who hung around the dorms. Your sister had already bought a carton of cat food, so I bequeathed the kitty to her care, which was a wise move, since I got home from rehearsals in the wee hours and the poor thing would probably have starved."

Jack threw back his head and laughed, and Serena observed that his entire demeanor changed in an instant.

"That's Marielle," he said, nodding. "She's even got our youngest sister, Sylvia, working for her pet rescue operation sometimes."

"How *is* Sylvia? I only remember her as a little kid that Marielle showed around campus once."

Jack hesitated and grew somber once again.

"Actually, she's not doing too well. She was in high

school when Katrina hit. She's the 'tail-ender' as my father calls her and no great student, so she didn't get into Sacred Heart and went to public school instead. She lost a lot of friends in the storm...black and white. Since then, she just can't seem to get her life together. Went to rehab for drugs at one point. She's nearly twenty-eight, now, but she still lives at home."

Serena reached across the table and gave Jack's hand a brief squeeze.

"My sister Flavia is a bit like that. She's a few years younger than Sylvia, and no drugs, as far as I know, but she still has nightmares about the storm and has no ambitions, really. She's content just sewing on feathers and beads at the shop and going to concerts on the weekends with her equally unambitious friends. There's a lot I could teach her, but she's just not interested or motivated to learn new skills. I think the storm has left a very deep mark on the younger ones. They learned early that the world might not be a very safe place."

Jack looked at her somberly.

"Well, it's not. Safe, I mean. The storm left its mark on everyone who went through it. And the hell of it is, the world is going to get even *less* safe if you live where you and I do."

Serena felt a sudden stab of apprehension as she often did when people spoke of rising waters. Flooding made her think of her brother Coz and *that* made her imagine what it must be like to drown in your own house.

Serena gazed at her half-eaten plate of pasta, distracting her thoughts about what happened in Lakeview on August 29th by noting that the *Bolognese* needed some additional red wine and a lot more minced rosemary.

Finally, she volunteered, "I was in grad school in New Haven during Katrina, so I guess I'm better at putting the reality of what could face us about this climate change stuff out of my mind…most of the time." She lifted her gaze. "It must be hard, knowing as much as you do about all this."

Jack gave a slight grimace.

"Yeah…actually it is."

"Are your parents doing okay, now?"

"'Okay' about covers it. My mother left before the storm hit. My dad's a hydrologist, retired now. During Katrina, he supervised a lot of the pumping stations in the French Quarter. As you probably know, the Quarter's on high ground and physically came through everything in relatively good shape…but …everyone has their scars."

"No kidding," Serena agreed mildly, and took a sip of her wine, gazing at him over the rim of her glass.

"What?" Jack said, staring at her intently. "You're saying something in your head that you're not saying to me."

"I was just thinking that there are many levels of Post Traumatic Stress Disorder, you know? By the time I finished my Masters and got back to New Orleans ten months later and I started working with my brother, Nick, to get our family business back on track, my mother was a complete mess. She drank plenty before Katrina, but she was much worse, after. Self-medicating, I guess. I finally insisted we have a family intervention—much to the initial horror of my siblings and father—but it actually worked and so far, Sarah Kingsbury Antonelli has been clean and sober for six years now," she announced proudly.

"That's wonderful," Jack said and Serena knew he was sincere.

"It is," she agreed, "but she still shows several PTSD symptoms, and—"

"Don't we all?" He grinned faintly. "Well, maybe not *you* since you were lucky enough to miss the big show."

"But I sure didn't miss the immediate aftermath…

which had its own set of horrors," she replied.

Jack raised a finger. "Hey! Did you say your mother was a Kingsbury? Is she any relation to Kingsbury Duvallon, whose mother is also a Kingsbury?

Serena adopted her very best New Orleans accent.

"Second or third cousins, I 'spect…a couple of times removed maybe. I only know King by his amazing reputation as an historic preservationist—and the fact he's married to that terrific reporter, Corlis McCullough at WJAZ. Do you know her, too?"

"They're both very good friends of mine."

"Wow, really? I'm a huge admirer of both of them."

Jack explained how Kingsbury Duvallon and he had known each other since their days at Holy Cross elementary and high school, and later at Tulane. King's wife, Corlis McCullough, was a journalistic colleague working now as an anchorwoman. The couple seemed to be the only island of sanity in Jack's increasingly complicated life and the only friends he felt like spending time with lately.

"King's gotten to be pretty much the leading voice for the preservation of New Orleans' oldest buildings," he explained to Serena. "After Katrina, he spearheaded a unique housing program where adventurous owners gain tax incentives by restoring historical properties that had fallen into decay or had been damaged by the storm."

He described how the two of them had reconnected when Jack abandoned a career like his father in hydraulic engineering two years out of college for a job as a newspaper reporter, specializing in water issues in Louisiana, "a state basically founded in a swamp," he concluded with a frown.

Serena said with unabashed admiration, "I love watching Corlis McCullough do her political interviews more than even seeing her anchor the nightly news—and she's terrific at that, too. In fact, I think the work they both do is fantastic! I'd say they're the closest thing New Orleans has to a genuine Power Couple these days."

Jack laughed while Serena disclosed she'd designed a costume for the good-looking reporter soon after returning from graduate school.

"My first 'celebrity' client in New Orleans," she added jokingly, "but I only saw Ms. McCullough briefly at the final fitting. She wouldn't remember me, I don't think."

"I'll be sure to tell them you called them a Power Couple. Corlis, especially, will be pleased. She hailed from LA, originally, where I guess Power Couples are a dime a dozen," Jack added, his lips quirking.

He signaled for the waiter and then asked Serena if she'd like a coffee. He ordered two decafs since they both hoped to sleep on the plane. Then he scrutinized her closely.

"You have a Masters from Yale in costume design and run a costume company with your brother. Why are you taking more training in the dead of winter in a city where the *acqua alta* will probably be up to your kneecaps the entire time you're there?"

Serena felt a surge of rising excitement as she described the work of supremely talented costume designer, Allegra Benedetti. The woman's exotic creations were known the world over, along with the work of Francesco Briggi, who specialized in historically accurate attire for museum exhibitions. Both costumers also made exotic apparel for wealthy clients attending exclusive events during Carnival season.

"What these designers produce is so far above what we're used to during Mardi Gras," she enthused. "You can see it in their designs, the craftsmanship, and their attention to every detail—not only in the Venetian Carnival end of the business—but, in Allegra Benedetti's case, on the retail side where she sells modern day, high-end women's clothing accessories."

"Like what?"

Serena was surprised he was interested, but she couldn't help voicing her delight in Allegra's accomplishments.

"She designs and manufactures beautiful brocade shoes, capes, modern gowns. Her work is *glorious*! If I can raise the level of what we do at Antonelli's, maybe we can lure back some of the Mardi Gras business we've lost to China by the sheer beauty of what I hope to create after absorbing what I can in Venice. I've already gotten a few of the important Krewes to come back to us this season with orders," she enthused, alluding to some sixty social clubs that sponsored individual parades in the annual run-up to Fat Tuesday itself. "I hope, with what I learn working with Allegra, I can really make our custom products something to be proud of—and profitable."

"So your brother Nick is holding the fort in New Orleans this Mardi Gras?"

Serena shot him a guilty look.

"Yes and believe me, that took a lot of persuasion to get his blessing for this little junket of mine." She paused and then revealed, "My brother's gay, and his partner, Gustave LeMoyne, was the one who actually persuaded him my going was a good idea." Serena offered a wry smile and then added, "Gus is a huge asset to our business, whatever my father thinks."

"They were all at the airport with you, weren't they?" Jack asked. Serena nodded. "It looked to me as if LeMoyne was one of the family."

"Well, to me he *is*. My father? Not so much." She leaned back in her chair and regarded Jack closely. "But now I want to know more about *you*. You said this is the fifth time you've gone to Venice for this conference. What's your mission this time?"

Jack tilted his head to one side and gave a small shrug.

"The gathering has truly become international," he explained. "I hope, one more time, to try to light a fire under everyone there who has some say-so over restoring wetlands and barrier islands in their particular region. Without the coastal areas around the world getting serious about doing this work, the planet's in big trouble."

"So you must know Venice pretty well by now."

"I know its geography and can find my way around without too much trouble, but my Italian is of the 'ordering in restaurants' variety, which can be a serious handicap."

"And I, on the other hand, have never been to Venice, but I speak Italian reasonably well—or so said my late *Nonna*, who taught me. So, if you and I hang out together at all, we've got *La Serenissima* nailed!" she said with a laugh.

When Jack fell silent, Serena suddenly wondered if he assumed she was angling for a rendezvous when they got to Venice and could have bitten her tongue. But then he sought her gaze and asked her in a surprisingly somber tone of voice, "What's *your* mission while you're there, Serena? Other than playing acolyte to Ms. Benedetti?"

Serena raised an eyebrow and thought for a moment.

"My mission," she pronounced quietly, "is to absorb every bit of beauty I can find in Venice and their *Carnevale* and bring it all back to New Orleans. With certain exceptions, Mardi Gras in America has become tawdry and increasingly commercialized, yet its roots reach back to the Italian Renaissance, five hundred years ago. You want to restore the wetlands? *I* want to restore Mardi Gras."

"Bravo!" he said, and Serena couldn't quite tell if he were teasing her.

"Well," she said with a depreciative laugh, "my mission—next to yours—sounds pretty frivolous in the light of the threats of climate change to everything that matters in this world. I think saving New Orleans from disappearing like a southern Atlantis might be a more worthy goal."

"You know something, Ms. Antonelli?" he said, his furrowed brow smoothing out and his lips curving into a slight smile. "Maybe I need a little *more* frivolity and celebration in my life. I feel as if I've been living in a pretty dark tunnel since our city nearly drowned."

She leaned against the table's edge and saw that his fingers were clenched as they curled around his coffee cup.

"Look, I wasn't there when Katrina happened," she reminded him softly, "but I think I truly understand what you mean. Once I got home from the Northeast, I experienced the so-called Road to Recovery and lived through most of the storm's aftermath. Our government failed us in nearly every respect…and as far as I'm concerned, that leaves me feeling…very depressed at times…very untethered."

Serena was barely aware of the clatter of dishes and the sounds of travelers' voices that surrounded them. Riveting her to her seat was Jack's look of both empathy and vulnerability. She had an unexpected impulse to tell him about her grandmother's heart attack at the height of the storm and the drowning of her brother and his pregnant wife when the canal walls broke the Monday afterward. She was positive he'd understand how it had haunted her every single day since, but Jack had let go of his coffee and had completely engulfed her right hand in his. It was warm from holding his cup…and comforting.

"'Untethered'…" Jack murmured. "That's exactly how I feel sometimes. That one word perfectly describes everything since the storm. Are you sure you're not a writer?" Then, to break the spell of their locked glances, he released her hand and looked for their waiter while Serena cast a peek at her watch on her wrist.

"Oh, Lord!" she exclaimed, retrieving her hands from

his. "Look at the *time*! We've been talking here for two hours!"

"Waiter!" Jack called loudly and leapt from his chair, digging in his wallet for his credit card.

Serena, likewise, jumped to her feet and opened her purse to fish for her share of the money they owed.

"My treat," he said hastily, shoving his card at their server without even glancing at the bill. "It's that southern gentleman thing again."

"Well thank *yew*," she said with a laugh, scrambling into her coat.

They would have to head for their Air France flight at a dead run if they were to make it on board before the doors closed on them both.

CHAPTER 4

Twice in a single day, Serena's assigned seat went to another passenger— but this time, so had Jack's. There wasn't a soul in the departure lounge except a trim young man standing behind the Air France desk.

"I'm sorry, but we gave your seats to the standbys," he said as the last stragglers were just disappearing down the narrow gangway. The gate agent's hand was poised over his computer. "I was just about to declare the flight closed."

"Oh, no!" Serena moaned under her breath.

Jack swiftly placed his and Serena's passports, plus his frequent flyer and Global Entry IDs on the counter next to their two defunct boarding passes.

"So sorry we were delayed," he apologized. "Isn't there *anything* you could do to get us on this flight?"

The gate agent glanced down and studied the documents before him.

"Ah…you are both from *Nouvelle Orleans*?" he asked, his slight French accent telling them Air France often hired their own nationals, even in New York. He smiled when he looked up at Jack. "And you are *Monsieur* Durand… from a French-American family there, yes?"

"Creole. Yes, originally from France, many generations ago."

"Ah…perhaps your family came with d'Iberville?"

Jack laughed at the reference to the French Canadian explorer who was the first to discover the mouth of the Mississippi.

"Ah, you know your history. But no, not *that* long ago. The Durands came from France in the mid-nineteenth century. The ties, however, are still very strong, as you may imagine." Then, he added for good measure, "That's why I always fly Air France to Europe when I can."

Serena remained silent, figuring Jack was laying it on as thick as he dared to get them onto the flight before the gate officially closed.

The agent swiftly typed on his computer keyboard.

"Ah...*très bien*!"

Serena's spirits lifted a notch.

"There's hope?" Jack asked politely.

Serena admired his cool, calm approach to solving their problem. If it had been she trying to sort out this mess, she feared she would have begun to scream in frustration if they didn't get on this flight. However, Jack merely kept smiling at the gate manager, so she tried to do the same.

"Not only hope...better than that. *Voilà!* First Class!" announced the attendant, punching a key that began to spit new boarding passes out of the printer below his desk.

"Oh...wow..." Serena murmured.

The gate agent gave them both a cheery smile.

"Yes, you two are certainly in luck. The plane is very full but..." He pointed to Jack's documents. "Since you are such a frequent traveler with us on our Boing 777...I will upgrade you both at no charge." He smiled beneficently at both of them. "This plane has a tiny First Class but the holidays, *c'est fini,* and the section is practically empty tonight. Here you go," he said, pushing the boarding passes across his desk. "I hope you both have a very good flight."

"We will, now," Jack said. "Much appreciated, *monsieur.*"

Serena murmured her thank yous while Jack, both their boarding passes in hand, lunged for the door that would lead them to their overnight flight to Paris and on to Venice. Their section was in the front of the plane. Only one other traveler was in "*La Premiere*" with seats that folded flat for sleeping and cushions swathed in the finest French linens. When Jack and Serena had divested themselves of their coats, sweaters, and other burdens, they looked at each other in sheer relief. Not only were they *on* the flight, but also traveling in grand style.

Serena suddenly held up four fingers.

"What?" asked Jack. "Four…*what?*"

"This serendipity thing is getting kinda scary, don't you think?"

"What do you mean…the fact we're on the same flight? We were always scheduled on the same flight. Just at the back of the plane."

"That, yes, but think about it." She held up her index finger. "One, we were both going to Venice the same day. Two, despite two different seat assignments, we ended up sitting together from New Orleans to New York. Then—three—"

"We were both booked on the Air France flight to Venice, via Paris," supplied Jack. "So, what's number four?"

"And four, we both nearly missed this flight but *both* were put into *First Class*, even though *I* didn't have the same fire power that you did with Air France!"

"So you're thinking that there may be some old-fashioned New Orleans voodoo at work, here?" She could see that Jack was trying not to smile.

"Maybe. Who knows?" she replied with a grin and a shrug.

"Well, voodoo or not," Jack replied, "if they hadn't found a seat for you, I wouldn't have boarded the plane."

Serena looked at him with surprise.

"Really?"

Jack leaned forward, eye-to-eye, and smiled, "Really."

"You *are* a southern gentleman," she teased.

"Maybe. But I must confess, I didn't really think it would come to that. Not making the plane, I mean. There's almost always room in First or Business Class on these night flights, and if you treat the attendants nicely and don't throw a fit, they generally won't leave you stranded."

"I'll remember that," she replied, laughing as she put on her seatbelt for takeoff.

Once the giant plane reached cruising altitude and passengers were allowed up from their seats, Serena announced, "And now I'm going into the bathroom and take off this sweater. I am roasting!"

"And may I suggest you take off your rubber boots while you're at it."

"Good suggestion. I wouldn't want to get Mississippi mud on these swell sheets," Serena replied, smiling. "I think they're made by Porthault and have about a thousand threads per square inch."

"I expect you know your fabrics."

"That I do."

Serena made her way up the aisle as the flight attendants brought extra pillows and blankets to the anointed.

Jack watched his traveling companion's retreating back and wondered how Lauren Hilbert would have reacted if her seat had been given away and it looked as if she wouldn't make her flight?

Actually, it didn't bear thinking about.

By the time Serena returned to her sleeper seat and stowed her stray articles of clothing, Jack was nowhere to be seen. A flight attendant paused and told her that he'd left word to join him in the small buffet bar in the middle of the business section behind them. Nearly all the passengers in that area of the cabin were already in their tilt-back seats—eyeshades on, earplugs in—with the lights lowered.

Serena found Jack sitting on a bar stool, nursing a shot of bourbon, straight up.

"I don't know about you, but that wasn't decaf they served me at the airport," he said.

"I feel pretty wired myself," Serena agreed, "considering the day I had trying to herd my family to the airport on time." She surveyed the array of tiny liquor bottles on display. "Do you suppose there's an Amaretto in this mini bar?" Spotting what she was looking for, she exclaimed, "Ah ha! Yay! *Disaronno*," noting one of the most highly regarded brands and pouring its contents into another liqueur glass.

Jack cocked his head to one side and asked, "So what I want to know, is: what were you doing in Las Vegas, of all places, after your graduation from Tulane and before you went to grad school at Yale? My sister said you lived in Nevada for a few years."

"Is this an interview?"

Jack took a sip of his bourbon.

"Sort of, I guess. It's a long flight and if neither of us is sleepy, they'll be plenty of time for you to ask me questions, too." He held his glass up in a small salute. "It's an occupational hazard, I guess, but I'm actually interested. You chose the arts. How did that take you to Vegas?"

Serena sketched a brief description of her three-year stint as costume mistress with *Cirque de Roma*, a lavish show starring the celebrated singer, Marco Leone.

"You sure do stick with the Italians, don't you?" he kidded her.

"Marco was Italian-American, like I am, several generations down."

"But, isn't he the famous crooner who had a heart attack on stage and died during his show?"

"They got him offstage and he died in his dressing room."

"Is that why you came back to New Orleans? The show closed?"

An extended silence stretched between them. Serena ducked her head and stared at her drink. Despite her best efforts to blink hard, her eyes were brimming and a single drop of moisture had spilled down her cheek.

Following a long pause Jack asked quietly, "Why the tears?"

Serena fought to control her voice.

"Because…Marco died in my arms."

"That must have been terrible for you."

"It was."

"Had you…become good friends?"

Serena took a sip from her glass and then made a very uncharacteristic decision.

"Very tactfully put, Mr. Durand. We were more than friends. We'd been having an affair for two years," she said, glancing up to study Jack's expression at her revelation. "Marco's wife, Denise—who he'd been estranged from in Beverly Hills for a decade—appeared the next day to claim his riches and, of course, I was forbidden to attend the funeral."

She brushed her eyes with the back of her hand. Jack handed her a cocktail napkin stamped *Air France*. Serena nodded her thanks.

"I left Las Vegas twenty-four hours later before the press got wind of anything." She blew her nose, adding, "So, since *you're* the media you'll know what I mean when I say…everything I just stupidly told you is off the record, okay?"

"Totally."

"My family doesn't even know." She heaved a small sigh and nodded at the empty barstools. "It must be this sense I have at this altitude that we're suspended in time and space, or something. *Promise me* you won't repeat what

I've just told you to anyone?"

"You have my word. I'm a reporter, remember?" he replied, chucking her lightly under her chin. "I don't burn my sources."

She crumpled her cocktail napkin into her fist. "Thank you." She glanced around the hushed cabin. "Maybe I should go back to my seat, now."

She couldn't believe what she'd just revealed to Jack Durand, of all people, but the low lights in the cabin as they hurtled through the night sky created a strange sense both of familiarity and intimacy.

Well, she thought, after all this time, perhaps it was a healthy sign that she'd told *someone*.

Jack put a restraining hand on her forearm.

"Don't leave. Better to cry up here, than in our section up front. You don't want to wake any snoring, rich people."

She laughed through a watery smile. He squeezed her hand.

"Tell me what happened after that. *Then* you went to Yale? Vegas to New Haven. That must have been quite a culture shock."

"Boy, was it ever," she said, and took a gulp of her drink. "I had met Allegra by then. She had come to Las Vegas for a month to see about the possibility of producing a show that would utilize her design work...a kind of Venetian *Cirque du Soleil* with Italian Carnival as its theme. It never came to anything, but because I could speak Italian, I worked closely with her while she was there, demonstrating to her how our own show was produced, costumed, and mounted on stage. As I said, she is a brilliant artist," Serena said fervently, "and we worked together extremely well while she was in Nevada. She was very complimentary when she saw the work I had done for Marco's show. She urged me to get some advance training in costume design and then come see her. Six months before Marco died, I had come to the obvious conclusion that our little duet was hopeless."

"How old were you then?"

"Not quite twenty-four. He was thirty years older, to say nothing of being the kind of Catholic who wouldn't consider divorce, though he had no qualms about having an affair, of course."

"Do you suppose you...were looking for 'Daddy'?"

Serena shot him a frown.

"You practice psychology as well as journalism, do you?"

"No. Just hazarding a layman's guess."

"I was looking for plain, old, *love*, and someone to say I had talent—which, by the way, I didn't hear much of from my father-the-costumer." Serena shook her head. "But, maybe your diagnosis was correct, as a matter of fact. Marco gave me both affection and encouragement in what I do for a living, but at least I was smart enough to know—even in my early twenties—that the relationship couldn't last. I told no one that I'd applied to Yale's three-year graduate program in advanced costume design. When he died so suddenly, I had some place to go."

"And since then? No *new* older men in your life?"

"Boy, are you nosy!" Serena responded, secretly pleased he was interested enough to ask. "No older men. No younger men, either. In fact, I'd given up dating all together when I came back to New Orleans after the storm. Everything at Antonelli's was a shambles, literally. The workshop and sales office at our place in the CBD...our own house...the family...our staff...it was one, big disaster, just like Katrina. I've only had time to focus on getting the business on an even keel and trying to...well...elevate it to a higher artistic level, if you don't think I'm being too grandiose about it all."

"No," Jack shook his head. "I can see how serious you

are about what you do."

"My other job when I came home was…"

Serena paused and took another sip of her Amaretto.

"What? What else did you take on those slender shoulders of yours?"

Jack's voice was warm and soothing. It almost felt to Serena as if he were a priest, not a shrink or a journalist, and they were in a confessional at 33,000 feet, though Lord knew how long it had been since she'd been in a real one.

"One of the main things I had to do when I got back to New Orleans after grad school was to offer support to my grieving parents and siblings in the wake of my grandmother's death and…of my eldest brother, Cosimo's death, too. You see, he and his new bride drowned when the Seventeenth Street Canal—"

"I know," Jack intervened quietly. "I work for a newspaper, remember? Your grandmother, brother and sister-in-law were some of the most prominent non-African Americans to die in the storm."

"*Nonna* Serena was an old lady. It was sad, but not surprising. A lot of elderly people couldn't take the trauma, but Cosimo Antonelli, the Fifth, was the Baby Jesus in my parents' eyes," Serena said without rancor. "And they also lost little Cosimo the Sixth, since my sister-in-law was five months pregnant. My parents' grief was so terrible, the rest of us felt they would have sacrificed the remaining three kids, just to save Coz."

"C'mon, Serena."

"No, truly," she said, tears welling again in her eyes. "I'm not being overly dramatic. It was pretty horrendous for everyone and we haven't totally recovered, even now. And we're just *one* family's story after the storm…but it was a doozy."

Jack stared into his empty glass.

"Those failing canals and levees played no favorites,"

he said. He looked up but avoided her questioning gaze, adding, "Their collapse caused misery and suffering in everyone's lives in New Orleans that day, whether a person lived or died. There isn't one citizen in our city who survived the storm who hasn't been affected, one way or another."

Serena noticed an odd, remoteness come over her companion. It was as if his thoughts had traveled back a couple of thousand miles to the city built in a swamp.

"Yep. Everyone has a story to tell," Serena commented finally.

"And the wounds still fester. I know," Jack murmured, still staring into space.

After a long pause, Serena tried to catch his glance.

"Okay. You promised. What about you? What did *you* do after Tulane? How'd you go from an electronic calculator to a trench coat?"

Jack put his hands in his lap and offered a brief description of his aborted career in hydraulic engineering.

"The minute I got my first engineering job, thanks to my Daddy's pulling strings, I knew I hated it. But I did love learning about the water surrounding us and the wetlands and barrier islands, and the habitat that environment provided all our native plant and animal life. I could see how the dredging policies that had been practiced over the last eighty years were destroying the place."

"But how did you make the switch to journalism?" she persisted.

"I touted my lowly credentials as a water guy to get a job at a local paper in the Lake Charles area where I started my long career ruffling the feathers of the Powers-That-Be in Louisiana about how we're going to end up with one, big flood plain pretty soon. I got to know all the experts in both science and engineering. I've been trying ever since to persuade anyone who will listen that it makes *economic* sense to restore the wetlands and barrier islands *first* as a way of preventing the kind of huge storm surge the city experienced during Katrina…and, by the way, Venice, too, in years past."

"How's it going for you?" she asked, taking a sip of her drink and feeling the warmth of the Amaretto prompting her to put forth questions she normally wouldn't dream of asking. "Getting the Powers-That-Be to pay attention to you, I mean?"

He looked up from his glass.

"Not. Very. Well."

"Ah. That bad, huh?" Serena impulsively asked, "Well, then, let's talk about a more pleasant subject. What about *your* love life? How's *that* going?"

The expression on Jack's face telegraphed his genuine shock she'd asked such a direct question, though he certainly hadn't hesitated to ask *her* about personal matters.

"I would be no southern gentleman if I revealed much on that subject," he said lightly.

"Oh, c'mon, Jack. Don't be coy. You haven't been a priest all these years, have you?"

She didn't see his answer coming.

"Her name is Lauren," Jack said. "Lauren Hilbert."

"Oh."

"Her family's from the Garden District and—"

Serena interrupted. "She was a big deal in her sorority and a cheerleader, right?"

Jack nodded affirmatively while she tried her best to subdue a jumble of emotions, starting with her reaction that Jack Durand had a girlfriend back home, and continuing on to the startling sensation of Jack's comforting hand on hers earlier that evening. Serena raised a finger as if to remind herself of something.

"*And*, she was Queen of Cork one year, wasn't she? Antonelli's made her a costume. I was still in grad school, but I heard about it."

Nick had told her she had been a complete pain in the ass.

"Yep, that's Lauren, Queen of the May," Jack said, and Serena thought she detected a slight edge in his tone. "She was a nurse at Charity Hospital during Katrina and—"

"Oh, God!" Serena interrupted again. "It was horrendous there, wasn't it?"

"A nightmare," Jack concurred. "She finally got out by helicopter accompanying some survivors stranded on the roof and then flew with them on to Houston. After the storm, she got into med school, there. She's a doctor, now…or almost. She'll finish her residency soon and hopes to practice in NOLA."

Jack stared down at his empty glass and Serena hoped he'd fill it up again—but he didn't.

"So now that we've had an even exchange of information," he said, "I think it's probably time we headed for our swanky bunks." He stood, signaling he was prepared to return to the front of the plane, "Sleepy? I am. I think that shot of bourbon did the trick. I'm going to head back."

Serena felt as if a curtain had fallen and the show was over. She had been dismissed. It felt all too familiar. *Why* was she always immediately drawn to the guys who were already spoken for? How dumb to think someone handsome and accomplished like Jack Durand didn't have a serious woman in his life. His attitude of indifference toward her at the New Orleans Airport had told the real story, but the further they got away from their hometown, the more she ignored her original instincts about the man. Even worse, she *knew* the signs: Marco used to shower her with attention and then withdraw suddenly, like Jack just had, when he felt she was asking too many questions or making any sort of demand.

Stop beating yourself up, Serena. You didn't misinterpret

everything *that's happened with the guy on this trip…he likes you.*

First Jack plied her with personal questions and smothered her two hands with his own on several occasions. Then, in the next second, he shut down.

He's the one who's mixed up, not you! Lauren what's-her-name is welcome to him, Serena thought. From here on out, she intended to stick to what she'd told Jack earlier: she'd sworn off any relationship except the one she had with her sketchbook!

"You go ahead," she said pleasantly to his retreating back. Jack halted and turned around as if he'd expected her to follow him. She lifted her glass, indicating she still had a few last drops of Amaretto to finish. "I'll follow along in a minute."

She took her time in the minuscule bathroom to brush her teeth and don a pair of black cotton leggings and a long-sleeved, black T-shirt. As with all but a few of his fellow passengers, Jack appeared fast asleep by the time she slipped between the luxurious sheets of her flattened seat and turned off the pin-point light overhead.

Tomorrow, she'd smile at the good-looking, quixotic reporter and be "light and polite," just as she'd learned in her Al-Anon meetings during the year her mother struggled to get sober.

No more serendipity. No more Jack Durand kicking up dust. Just Venice ahead.

And she couldn't wait.

CHAPTER 5

Jack's eyes were closed but he remained awake. His mind was reviewing every second since the moment he'd met the woman now lying in the sleeper seat a foot away from him.

He certainly could make no claim, even in jest, to being a southern gentleman. He'd behaved abominably just now, egging on Serena Antonelli to trust him with a secret he was certain she'd told no one else. Then, like a jerk, he'd shut her out completely because of his own problems that included Dr. Lauren Hilbert—but certainly weren't exclusive to the woman who was supposedly his girlfriend.

No, Jack...this feels very old, doesn't it? Keeping the fairer sex at arm's length when there could be a move toward something real.

For a few moments, he forced himself to concentrate on the hum of the mighty jet engines hurtling Serena and him through starry skies toward Paris.

What would happen when they changed planes at De Gaulle for Venice? Would he see her in her namesake city, once they left the Marco Polo Airport? He thought of all he had to do at the conference and wished he hadn't agreed to be a speaker. In fact, he wished, now, he'd given the entire trip a miss.

Damn it all!

Who could have predicted this?

He *liked* Serena Antonelli. He liked her looks, her frankness. He liked her passion for her profession...her wanting to constantly improve on her skills. He'd been deeply affected by her instinctive compassion for the job he'd had to do and the terrible things he'd seen covering one of the worst natural disasters in the country's history. She seemed to *know* him, though she really didn't know him at all, of course.

And what was it about those melting brown eyes of hers? Hypnotic eyes like no others he'd ever seen. Eyes that saw right through him.

Blessedly, the sounds of the droning engines and his meandering thoughts began to pull him down, down, into the dark of a fitful sleep.

Jack inched along in the line to get his passport stamped by Immigration officials at the Marco Polo Airport on the mainland, opposite the water-ringed city of Venice. From the moment Serena had opened those mesmerizing eyes of hers, his seat companion had exhibited a polite but distant demeanor, saying very little during breakfast as the Air France plane began its descent into Paris. Once in transit at De Gaulle for their connecting flight, he had lost sight of her as the various lines swallowed up each of them and, as expected, eventually funneled them onto their final flight and into sections on opposite sides of the cabin.

Now that he was on Italian soil in the biting cold, Jack looked for her to emerge from arrivals. Water from the canal nearby sheened the pavement in ripples that flowed in concert with the wakes trailing behind boats passing in the vicinity. A feeling of mild elation took hold when he spotted Serena's slender figure pulling two large wheeled bags through the automatic doors.

He approached at a fast pace before she could slip away.

"The *Alilaguna* boat stop is about an eight minute walk from here," he announced, steam coming out of his mouth due to the chilly air surrounding them. "Or we can hire a water taxi."

"Allegra says they charge a fortune. She said I should get on the regular orange line and get off at…" Serena consulted a note on her cellphone's screen, "…at the '*Rialto Mercato*,' the stop before the Rialto Bridge."

"I can take the same one," Jack said quickly, at the very least wishing to make amends for his standoffish behavior on board their night flight. "C'mon, follow me. My conference is being held at the Laguna Palace in an industrial section of Venice, not far from here. Then the boat will eventually take you where you want to go. Here, let me grab one of those bags for you."

Serena gave a slight shake of her head.

"No. Thank you. I'm fine."

Jack halted.

"Look Serena…I owe you an apology for the way I—"

Before he could finish his sentence, she interrupted with a faint grin.

"On second thought, here, take this one…it's the heaviest."

Serena pulled the drawstrings tight on her fur-trimmed hooded jacket and put her gloved hand on the handle of her remaining suitcase. She fell in step beside him, the wheels on their various bags carving parallel tracks in the thin layer of slushy snow.

Serena offered a modest wave when Jack disembarked less than ten minutes later from the ferry that plied the waters between the airport and the various *vaporetti* stops throughout the city of Venice.

"Maybe we can try to grab dinner one night this week," he called from the gangway, but since he hadn't asked for her cell number, nor did he know where she was staying, Serena seriously doubted his offer was very sincere.

Just as well, Signorina Antonelli...just as well.

She had the sudden thought that perhaps Jack had become distant and detached for having harshly judged her relationship with Marco Leone. He seemed a more accepting person than that, but maybe she had misjudged him?

She turned toward the bow as the boat pulled away from the Laguna Palace dock and lifted her chin into a cold breeze that bit her cheeks and made her eyes water.

No excuses for the guy...and no second-guessing by you. *It is what it is.*

Both the skies and canals of Venice were cast this afternoon in heather gray, but Serena's spirits couldn't help but improve at her first glimpses of the baroque buildings lining both sides of the water. Even in the mist that was laden with shimmering snow, she hungrily absorbed the plaster facades in muted colors of ochre, sage green, lemon, and terra cotta, most of which were festooned with lacey, ivory-hued stone balconies and loggias on the upper floors.

And the *water...*everywhere! It splashed against the boat's stout hull and surged in wavelets toward the buildings on both sides as the sturdy vessel glided down the canal, setting off a wake that fanned out behind them.

It wasn't that difficult to push thoughts of Jack Durand to the back of her mind when she considered how much she was bound to learn in her two months living here and working with Allegra in the lead-up to this year's Venetian carnival season.

Even so, as the *Alilaguna* plied its way from stop to stop, she was surprised to realize that the newspaper reporter had been the first man in a few years to ignite even the slightest spark of interest in her breast. Yes, he had a serious girlfriend, but she couldn't deny that she and Jack had connected on some deep level en route to Italy. Perhaps this was the proof she'd been secretly hoping for that there *were* intriguing, smart, sexy, *suitable* men out there in the world? Who knew when she might meet one who was actually eligible—and not in the slightest elusive?

She felt herself smiling at departing passengers as the boat pushed away from the *Ca d'Oro* stop—signaling she was close to her destination.

Snow was beginning to fall in earnest as Serena made her precarious way down *Ruga Ravano* with her unwieldy suitcases in tow. Her map indicated it was a main thoroughfare leading from the *Rialto Mercato* boat stop, via a few smaller passageways, toward a large square known as the *Campo San Polo*. Fortunately, this major landmark was adjacent to the address of the lodgings that Allegra Benedetti's office manager had secured for her stay.

Serena was grateful, now, that her feet and calves were clad in warm socks and that she had on her knee-high, rubber boots, given that water sloshing from nearby canals was now coated with a thickening layer of icy white powder. She breathed a sigh of relief at the absence of step-up-step-down bridges along the route Allegra's assistant had recommended she walk along. A pastry shop she'd been told to keep an eye out for on her left suddenly appeared, her signal to turn left down a narrow passageway with a street sign, "*Calle del Forno*," painted in black letters on the wall. A quick right turn, twenty feet further on, and she dragged her two suitcases and carry-on bag over uneven square stone pavers to the entrance to *Ca'Arvo Antico*, the ultimate destination where she would finally rest her head this night, and for two months to come. From an alley branching off to her left that led back to the Grand Canal, several inches of water were flowing alarmingly toward the front door.

Out of breath from her exertions, she paused and gave a backward glance to the passageway she'd just traversed. All was silent. The nearby courtyard glistened in a city floating under a blanket of crystalline snow.

For some unaccountable reason, the stranger in Venice felt as if she'd come home.

Jack slumped against the back of his uncomfortable folding chair. He watched as the attendees to the panel of wetlands experts he'd just moderated—"Remediation of Coastal Areas Threatened by Storm Surge"—quietly filed out of the auditorium.

The session had been standing room only, but Jack feared the audience and his colleagues must feel as discouraged as he was about what they'd heard. Each panelist, whether scientist or journalist, testified to the chronic intransigence on the part of both politicians and certain corporations about the issue of restoring wetlands and barrier islands. Neither group, they reported unanimously, would agree to make the hard decisions, coordinate their efforts, nor provide the funds required in various countries to protect against their coastal cities being inundated by future changes in sea levels.

Near the end of the session, the microphone was passed back to Jack for his concluding remarks.

"In Louisiana, post-Katrina, the state has more than 150 hurricane risk reduction projects from its multi-billion dollar master plan underway. Two billion of that money is earmarked for ecosystem restoration to bring land back to wetland areas that are disappearing at the rate of a football field an *hour*," he emphasized to his audience. "But progress is far too slow. And why is that, given the obvious threat of climate change that NASA tells us is real?" he asked rhetorically. "Here's why: heavy opposition by certain industries and the politicians that answer to them through campaign contributions. Add to that, certain unwise, manmade flood control projects, along with natural forces that every second of the day eat away at Louisiana's land masses. The question becomes, can we do enough, *fast* enough, to hold back walls of water certain to sweep in again?"

Jack noted the grim expressions on the faces of various bureaucrats and policy makers sitting in the audience with headsets clamped to their ears.

"So it would appear, ladies and gentlemen," he'd said, glancing at his notes summing up the previous hour's presentation, "that what is being done so far might…*might* provide cities like mine with a 'hold' on the status quo if—and this is a *very* big if—in the meantime we don't get another catastrophic weather event that destroys the efforts made so far to save our coastal cities by saving the wetlands and barrier islands. Perhaps the most important question of all to ask ourselves is: will the worlds' leaders simply fiddle while Rome burns…or in this case, while Venice and New Orleans and other irreplaceable coastal cities *drown*? I guess we'll just have to wait and see. Goodnight."

As the last person left the auditorium, Jack leaned forward in his chair and flicked the "off" button on his mic. He abruptly stood up, desperate to escape to the bar.

Shit! What's the point to all of this?

Restless, Jack soon abandoned his colleagues and their drinks, donned his down-filled stadium coat, and emerged into the bitingly cold air outside the large, modern building that housed the Rising Waters convocation. Snow had continued to fall and he noticed that the nearby canal water was lapping perilously close to the raised boardwalks called *passerelle* that had been erected earlier that day and stretched from the entrance to the nearest *vaporetto* stop. These temporary "remediations" for the periods of *acqua alta* inundating Venice were installed to allow pedestrians to walk above the flood tides. The waters were washing in from the wintery Adriatic outside the lagoon and past a string of low-lying, ineffectual islands that didn't prevent the sea from pouring into the city's narrow canals.

Jack's thoughts drifted to his fellow New Orleanian, Serena, working in Venice for the legendary creator of Venetian costumes and the glamorous carnival ball. He wondered how *Signorina* Antonelli was faring in the city she was named for during this rather alarming spate of bad weather?

Doing an about face, he marched back into the building and sought out an official in the Press Room.

"*Signorina*," he demanded of the PR flack at the desk in the corner, "*Prego*…can you get me the phone number and directions to Allegra Benedetti's costume workshop? The establishment where the clothes are actually sewn, not her retail shop?"

A puzzled look clouded the woman's brow, as if she found his request quite odd for a man concerned with the inundation of swamps and wetlands, but it was quickly replaced by her professional smile.

"Certainly, sir," she replied in perfect English.

"*Grazie,*" he said shortly and waited for her to hand him a piece of paper with the information he'd requested. He then turned, shoved it into his pant's pocket, and headed in the direction from which he'd come. Once outside again, he paused on the elevated boardwalk and stared at the sheets of snow falling steadily onto the water surrounding him.

Maybe I should give this some more thought…

He stuffed his hands more deeply into the pockets of his down jacket and headed back to his nearby hotel to lodgings that were so sterile in their design, the place could have been a branch of Courtyards by Marriott.

Serena looked up from the expansive cutting table positioned in the center of the low-ceilinged workshop in a wood and plaster building that had to be at least four-hundred-years-old.

"*Buona notte, signorina,*" Rosa called as she and the five seamstresses she supervised filed, one by one, out the door at the top of stairs that led down to a walkway not far from the *San Tomà vaporetto* stop.

"*Buona notte,*" Serena replied. "*A domani…*"

In English, Rosa said, "Serena…don't stay too late…you must eat!"

The American *apprendista professionale*—the "professional apprentice" as her colleagues teased her—straightened to her full height and stretched her arms over her head.

"*Si…Mamma…*" Serena replied with a smile.

Allegra's team of seamstresses had been as warm and welcoming as their patroness. Rosa Garafola, especially, had made it her mission to be sure the visiting designer was well taken care of, particularly when it came to remembering to get the nutrition and rest she needed to sustain herself over the long hours of work as *Il Ballo di Carnevale* grew ever closer.

The iron grill beyond the door clanged shut. Serena glanced through the second-story window overlooking terra cotta tiled roofs that were blanketed in a mantle of snow, a sticky, wet powder that had been falling, nonstop, since the day she'd arrived. Even in her rubber boots, she wondered if she'd be able to safely slosh back to her living quarters in such wretched weather?

Was she hungry? She couldn't decide. For hours, she had been completely focused on interpreting Allegra's sketches and its resulting paper pattern for an elaborate eighteenth century gown due an important female client attending the ball. It was Serena's job to cut inexpensive muslin dress pieces from the patterns that interpreted Allegra's drawings. Once the pieces were sewn together, Serena would then drape them on a mannequin to make sure the physical rendering for the gown was true to the designer's original vision before any pair of scissors touched the luxurious silks and satins from which the costumes would ultimately be made. The atelier's customers paid an astounding amount of money for the costumes they commissioned, along with pricey tickets to the elegant masked ball and supper scheduled for Valentine's Day—and the results *had* to be spectacular.

On the floor above the ancient building that housed not only the workshop, but also a storage room wedged adjacent to a small apartment Allegra also owned, Serena could hear her employer moving heavy fabric bolts along the rough wood beamed floor overhead. The designer was seeking silk yardage of an appropriate weight to take the elaborate beadwork that would be part of the costume's front bodice. Soon, her mentor's steps sounded on the stairway and her sleek, blond head peered around the door.

"*Perfetto!*" Allegra exclaimed, entering the workshop. She leaned the bolt of gold satin near Serena's drafting table. "And how is my American shadow doing after her first week in Venice?"

"*Perfetto*," she replied with a laugh.

"*Molto bene!*" Allegra chortled. In English she continued, "Tomorrow I want to make a tour with you of the *palazzo* where the ball is to be held. I am able to rent it this year for two days, only, so we have many things to discuss about how you can help me that night, *si?*"

"Shall we get an early start? Say...nine o'clock?"

"*Molto bene*...and now, I must leave you for a dinner engagement with the technical supervisor for the entertainment at *Il Ballo*. You will leave here soon, yes? You work very hard, Serena...and I most appreciate it, but I do not want you to overtire yourself so soon. We must preserve our strength for the hard days in February, yes?"

Serena had seen from the first day that Allegra's demeanor was as friendly and supportive as it had been when they'd met in Las Vegas. She had been saddened to learn from Rosa earlier in the week that *la Signora's* beloved husband had died of cancer recently following one of her most successful annual Carnival balls. Perhaps that accounted not only for the empathy, but *la tristezza*—the sadness—Serena had detected in her mentor's gray-blue eyes, luminous behind her stylish, square rimless glasses.

"Have a lovely dinner," Serena said, "and I promise, I'll leave soon."

She heard the iron gate on the landing close and the second gate at the bottom of the stairs shut as well. A peacefulness descended on the room filled with mannequins clad in spectacular ball gowns in various stages of completion. The hush of silently falling snow outside the windows overlooking the tile roofs turned her world opaque, cocooning her in a tunnel of concentration while she carefully cut lengths of muslin into the proper shapes dictated by the paper patterns. At length, Serena inhaled a deep breath, made a few more adjustments to her project, and sank into a nearby chair.

Only in these quiet moments alone did she allow her thoughts to drift to her seatmate on the flights from New Orleans. She found herself wondering how the Rising Waters Conference had gone, and whether Jack Durand had given the slightest thought to his Air France companion since waving goodbye when her *vaporetto* pulled away from the dock the day they arrived.

As if in response to her musings, a voice rang out in halting Italian at the bottom of the stairs, startling her out of her reverie. Someone with a distinct southern accent had broken the cottony silence by asking a passerby if this was the atelier of the costumer Allegra Benedetti?

Shocked that her contemplation seemed to have summoned Jack in the flesh, Serena sprang from her seat, ran to the door, opened it and the iron gate next to it that offered the shop extra security. She peered down at a tall, broad-shouldered figure, a blurry outline seen through the snow. Jack stood at the foot of the exterior stone stairs where the second metal gate guarded the entrance to the building.

"Buona sera, signorina," he drawled, his two hands clutching the metal bars like a man in a jail cell. "I guessed you'd be working late."

CHAPTER 6

Jack was bundled against the cold and wet, clad in a three-quarter-length parka with a woolen muffler wrapped around his neck. He sported a pair of the same high, rubber boots of a style that sat under Serena's workspace.

"Have you eaten already," he called to her, "or can I take you to a *trattoria* nearby?"

"You certainly can! Let's go to Antiche Carampane. *Io sono molto affamato.*"

"You lost me there," Jack called up to her, his booted foot resting on the step ten feet from the landing where Serena tried not to shiver from cold or the shock of seeing him, large as life. "Translation?"

She laughed. "'I'm starving.' But come on up, first," she invited, descending the stone stairs to let him in the lower gate and then instructing him to follow her cautiously, as the treads leading to the next level were slick with snow. "I have to close up shop here."

She ushered him into the work area and swiftly reached to relieve him of his muffler and coat, anxious that no water clinging to his clothing would splash on the mannequins.

"Jack, this is so wild!" she said, hanging his things on pegs recently vacated by the team of seamstresses. "I was *just* thinking about you and wondering how your conference went when I heard your voice downstairs."

"You were thinking about me?" he repeated with a surprised expression. "Well, I guess we'll just have to call that Serendipity Number Five and Six, 'cause I was wondering since I last saw you how you were getting along, especially given this nasty weather."

"How did you find me here?"

"I have my ways," he said with a wolfish grin, looking

around the room with curiosity. He moved toward a mannequin draped in muslin. "This is the spot where you work?" he asked, studying the elaborately styled gown made of plain, beige cloth that she'd been slaving over.

Serena explained that eventually, that same gown would be made of gold satin that cost a hundred and forty dollars a yard. She then went on to describe her other current projects and the various worlds that working on *Il Ballo di Carnevale* had been opening up to her.

"Tell me more at dinner," he said. "We can't have you faint with hunger."

Serena locked the shop's doors and led the way downstairs and through the second gate into the swirling snow.

"So the weather hasn't gotten you down?" he teased, taking her arm as they carefully made their way in the direction of the nearby restaurant. He held the door and once free of their coats, they were directed to a quiet table in the corner of the room.

"As long as I'm in a nice, warm restaurant, or at my B and B, or at Allegra's shop...no, this disgusting weather doesn't bother me, but I can't deny that I've been frozen to the bone every second I've stepped outside!"

After a swift perusal of the menu, Serena placed their orders in Italian with the waiter.

"So it's not been exactly like New Orleans, right?" Jack joked.

"Not exactly," she said, smiling, "especially since there's talk that the Grand Canal might freeze over! I don't think that's ever happened to the Mississippi, has it?"

"Actually it did—once—in February of 1899. The entire length of the river became a block of ice all the way down to the Gulf in what was dubbed 'The Great Cold Wave'."

"Well, speaking of which...what do the people at your

conference think of this extreme weather *here*, given it's been snowing in Venice, nonstop, for weeks?"

"They're worried, but we don't seem to be getting through to the policy makers very well."

Serena regarded him closely.

"You look a bit…down," she observed. "Discouraged, I guess, is a better word."

He nodded.

"I am tired," he admitted. "I'm tired and depressed and wondering why I keep up the fight to try to get know-nothing politicians and government bureaucrats on our planet to implement policies that have a *chance*—mind you—of saving our coastal cities from a destruction that is beginning to look inevitable. The others on the panel I just chaired today are running into the same issues all over the world. The Know-nothings and Do-nothings are in charge everywhere, it looks like."

"And we just thought New Orleans was bad," she said, amazed by the melancholic vulnerability he'd revealed.

"Yeah…that's what made the conference, so far, such an absolute downer. That—and a few other things I learned today that I don't want to spoil our dinner discussing. Let's just enjoy ourselves, shall we?" he asked, summoning a thin smile that didn't alleviate the pessimism radiating in her direction from across the table.

Serena studied his tight jaw and the pained look in his eyes as Jack took his first sip of the Tuscan *Rosso di Montepulciano* their waiter had recommended.

"C'mon, *Giovanni*," she asked quietly, using the Italian version of his name. "Why not tell me about the other things that have got you down? I told you my troubles the other day…and you were a good listener. I can be the same."

Jack took another sip of his full-bodied red wine. After a long pause he said, "I got an email from my mother today.

She sounded pretty frantic. My sister, Sylvia—the twenty-eight-year-old I told you is still living at home? Well, she's back in rehab."

"Oh, God, Jack, I am *so* sorry," Serena replied, his revelation instantly stirring heartfelt sympathy. "We went through that a couple of times with Mama. No wonder you feel blue on top of everything that's happening at the conference."

"Thanks," he murmured. "It made me wonder if I should bail out of giving my other talk on Saturday and fly home to see if I can help."

"No!" Serena responded emphatically. "Don't do that!"

Jack looked both startled and slightly askance. Serena felt color rise to her cheeks.

"What I just said probably didn't sound like what I actually meant. What I mean is that in dealing with my mother's addiction, I had to learn that I didn't *cause* what was going on with her and I sure as hell couldn't control it. Or cure it," she added. "And the more I tried to play Rescue Ranger by going into my commando-I-can-fix-it-mode…the worse things became." Then she added somewhat sheepishly, "Of course, that was *my* experience. It could be different in your family."

"But to just stand by…and to let my parents deal with everything…" His words trailed off and he stared at the breadbasket in the center of the table.

Serena smiled sadly.

"They probably can't cure someone else's addiction, either," she noted gently. "Maybe they shouldn't try?"

Jack's mouth had settled into a straight line and Serena knew he didn't like what he was hearing.

"So you think tough love is the answer?" he demanded. "Believe me, we've tried that, too, and that hasn't worked, either."

It was her turn to reach across the table and cup his hand in hers.

"Not tough love, Jack…*lots* of love, but just not expressed in the way you think."

"I don't get it."

Serena released his hand and put hers, palms down, on either side of her plate.

"Look…in the 'for what it's worth' department, what I learned when I got back to New Orleans after the storm is that people who went through the trauma of Katrina sought a lot of different ways to numb the pain afterward— or to try to avoid it altogether. My brother Nicholas, for instance, plunged into work, pushing my father aside, and practically living at our costume shop. My sister, as I mentioned, barely got up in the morning and preferred to sit and sew the same thing, over and over, all day long. And my mother…well, she didn't even try to conceal her bourbon in a teacup anymore. She was wasted by eleven o'clock every single day."

"Sounds like what Sylvia's been doing."

"People like my mother and your sister have picked a very dangerous way to try to self-medicate and block out the agony they're feeling about all that's happened to them…starting, probably, way back in their childhoods— if they weren't happy ones—to say nothing of the sketchy choices they may have made along the way, even before the storm."

Serena stared into her wine glass and continued softly.

"And then, for my mother, there was the horror of Katrina itself and the death of her *favorite* child, my brother, Cosimo, and his wife and her unborn grandbaby. At long last, Mama had a honking good excuse to drink herself under the coffee table in our sitting room with the high ceilings, silk drapes, and double fireplaces," she said, with a touch of black humor she knew a fellow New Orleanian would appreciate. "And boy, did she do it up proud."

"You sound like you're still angry."

"Do I?" Serena asked, and then nodded. "I'm sure I am…at least a little bit. As the eldest daughter, it got mighty tiresome, cleaning up after her, but in a way, I envied her for finding a method to blot out the pain we all were suffering. I might have been doing the same as she was if I'd been home for the storm…but your sister is committing a kind of slow suicide and asking the rest of you to watch her die."

"Yeah," Jack agreed with a grim nod of his head. "I think that's what's so terrible for my mother, what with Sylvia living at home and all."

"Well, I know you'll think I'm pretty hard-hearted, but eventually your sister will have to decide if she wants to live…or prefers to just push on outta here. I hope she makes the decision my mother did—to make a change before it's too late."

"It's as simple as that?" Jack asked with a skeptical expression. "Deciding whether to live or to die?"

Serena nodded. "That's what it ultimately gets down to, pretty much."

"But what if people like Sylvia and your mama won't stop using? What if they *refuse* to stop, like Sylvia said to my mother's face the other day. What if they want to just keep on doing terrible things to themselves? How can a family just stand by and let it happen?"

"Well, for me," Serena ventured, "I finally understood that I had absolutely *no* control over what my mother did or did not do. I just had to let her do what she was doing— or she would kill me too."

"Oh, c'mon, Serena," Jack said testily, "isn't that a little over-dramatic?"

"Oh, for damn sure, it's *all* a great, big drama, don't you see? And for me, I found *myself* getting 'addicted' in a weird way to all the ups and downs my family was going through because of my mother's behavior. When I first came back to New Orleans, I started acting almost as crazy as Mama was!"

"You started drinking?" Jack asked in disbelief.

"Lord no! Even crazier. I started pouring perfectly good bourbon down the drain. I'd hide her wallet so she couldn't buy more. I'd look in the toilet tank for her hidden bottles and then scream in a rage when I found them. I kicked up a lot of dust, believe me. Quite the star of my *own* little drama, I was."

Jack stared at his minestrone soup. "Before I left on this trip, I ransacked Sylvia's sock drawer about every other day, looking for cocaine," he admitted. "One day I found some and gave her hell."

"Welcome to the club," she said cheerfully. "Finally it dawned on me that if I was to help Antonelli's costumes continue its hundred-and-fifty-year-old history, *I* had to step out of the vortex—the drama I couldn't control. I had to let my mother decide whether she wanted to live or die. I stopped focusing on her and started paying full attention to the job I had to do if our family business was going to stay afloat—literally—after the storm. And then, of course, all that was followed by the recession that hit us so hard a few years later."

"But you told me coming over here that you had a 'family intervention,' for your mother."

"We sure did. It was to put her on notice that—before any of the surviving family members would help or engage with her anymore—she had to say to us, 'I want to live…despite all this terrible crap that's happened.'"

"And what did she do?"

Serena shook her head and gave a short laugh.

"She kept on drinking."

"Well, what did *you* do?" he demanded.

"Went about my business. At first, everybody was mad at *me* because we'd all gotten used to the drama, y'know? And then one day, Daddy and my brother, Nicholas, brought a big ole' case of bourbon into the house, put it on the coffee table in the middle of the living room, and said to Mama, "Here! Have at it. We're done with this too, just like Serena.""

"And what happened then?"

"She drank it all. Every last drop in every last bottle."

"Jeez…"

"It just about killed each one of us to completely ignore her when she did this, but, as I said, the counselor urged us to go about our business, spending most of our time at the shop. We all tried to keep busy and away from the temptation to pick her up off the floor, or put her to bed when she was soused. No one made excuses to her friends anymore when she didn't show up at dinners or her bridge club. It was the hardest thing any of us ever did. She'd either live or she'd die, and it got down to *our* survival, too. It was *her*—or us."

"Wow. That must have been pretty rough."

"Oh…it was."

"Well, I saw her with you at the airport when we left, so I know she didn't die."

"I guess she hit bottom the day she thought she was having a heart attack and I handed her the phone to make her own 911 call to be taken to the hospital. When she was there drying out that last time, she finally got the DTs so bad, she sought help on her own and slowly pushed past a lot of the horror of losing her eldest son whom she did, truly, think was the Baby Jesus…and I say that—now—with the greatest love."

"But the change couldn't have just *happened*—" Jack said, ever the reporter. "What made the difference that time?"

"In rehab that time, she slowly began to get out of herself by helping a couple of people she met at the AA meetings who were *way* worse off than she was. She started being grateful that she still had her other children after she met a few women who'd lost everyone in their family to the storm."

"What a story."

"Well, trust me, it hasn't been all lovey-dovey ever since, but the only way out of the morass was to learn to savor the good things *still* present in our lives."

"Like what?"

"Everything and anything," Serena replied with a shrug, "even down to a beautiful sunrise on the Mississippi, or a dog who wags his tail every time he catches sight of me coming up the street to the shop in the CBD. *Gratitude*, Jack. That's what saved my mother from the dark pit, and I dearly hope it keeps working for her."

"Simple as that?" Jack repeated.

"Simple, and complicated, too. And by the way," she added, "gratitude sure saved *me*."

"From the dark pit of loving a married man?" Jack asked, his gaze riveted on hers.

Serena was startled to hear him mention her former lover. She took her time considering his question.

"No," she responded slowly, "not so much that. Marco actually did me a world of good in some important ways. He built up my shaky confidence. He told me I was pretty—even though I'm so tall—and that I was genuinely talented as a costumer. And given that my mother and father had been missing-in-action most of my life running the costume business or drinking, Marco's kindness and the attention he paid me, and…I guess you could call it 'love'…made me feel appreciated for the first time in my life."

"I see. But you said 'gratitude' saved you. From what?"

"The darkness that descended when Marco died so suddenly and I had no way I could outwardly mourn him. I got completely stuck in that grief, and on top of it, losing my grandmother, whom I adored, and my brother and his wife soon after, and in that horrible way. The final blow was watching my mother simply sink under everything that had happened to us, to say nothing of the terrible state New Orleans was in for such a long time. I thought for a long while there was simply no way *out* of that pit." She paused and captured his glance. "Well, *you* surely understand what I'm talking about. You were on the front lines in that storm and the recovery efforts. You witnessed what it did to everyone. What it probably did even to a lot of the reporters who saw such terrible things."

Jack gave a slight shrug.

"I was affected, sure," he admitted, "but I had a certain insulation being an *observer*. It put emotional distance between me and everything I was having to look at and evaluate before I wrote about it for publication."

Serena regarded him closely and took a deep draught of her wine.

"You know what?" she said, setting down her glass decisively. "I don't really believe you were as detached as you say you were, but never mind. For *me* the only path out of that big ole' dark hole was to literally count the good things I had left…the most important of which was that I still had my *life*. Whatever talents I possess, I could use to celebrate that life through Mardi Gras and Carnival and all the things that beautiful dreams and fantasies are made of."

She smiled at him across the table to lighten the mood between them that had grown so serious. She raised her glass in a toast.

"That's what I'm concentrating on now. Here's to creating beautiful fantasies, like coming to Venice and sitting in a place like this, cozy and warm and well fed, with the snow coming down and sipping some very good wine while I gaze across the table at your handsome face."

She waited for Jack to respond, but he remained silent, toying with his fork.

Serena laughed self-consciously.

Damn! Why did she always play her hand before the man played his?

Oh, that's right, she chastised herself, almost laughing aloud at the ironic situation she found herself in. Jack Durand was spoken for. Southern gent that he is, he *shouldn't* respond. He already has a woman in his life.

"Well, that sure was a big, ole' long speech I just gave," she apologized. "Sorry. And I certainly have no right to be telling you what you could do about your sister's drug addiction, or how I thought you must have secretly been wounded by Katrina."

Without warning, Jack reached across the table and seized her hand with such strength this time that he nearly knocked over her wine glass.

"Don't be sorry for saying what you just have to me," he said, as a peculiar buzz of electricity shot up the arm attached to the hand he was holding. "You've given me a lot to think about, is all. Both about Sylvia in rehab—again—and about how I've dealt with the aftermath of the storm these last years, which is to deny it had a very big impact on me."

"But maybe I overstepped—"

Jack overrode her, countering, "And you're right...I *am* really discouraged about what was said on the panel I chaired today. But, I guess I should be grateful that there are still other folks—besides me—who are trying to wake people up in time about the climate change stuff and its further degrading the coastal wetlands. You've given me a different way to think about some things."

His expression had lightened and Serena was relieved

he seemed to shake off some of his gloom.

"That's the spirit!" she teased, relieved that she hadn't offended him about such personal matters. "For me, gratitude always tends to make things seem a bit brighter." Serena gave the hand that held hers a gentle squeeze and marveled at how warm and comforting it felt to be touching him. "Look, you're grappling with much bigger problems, right now, than I am—worrying if I can translate Allegra's brilliant designs into something a rich person coming to the ball will happily pay for. I think it's definitely okay to feel blue, sometimes, about the sorry state of the world, *including* the polar ice cap melting."

Jack held her glance for a long moment and Serena had the strangest sense he was silently giving thanks that they were having dinner together this night. He released her hand and signaled for the waiter to prepare their bill.

"We're in *Venice,*" he said, finally, "and you've just convinced me I shouldn't do my usual Rescue Ranger thing, as you describe it. I only have a few more days here and then I leave on a couple of field trips to inspect the latest plans to hold back the water, here, in the next fifty years." He flashed a grin. "I think I should make the most of it. Why not celebrate that I'm in *La Serenissima* with a beautiful woman named Serena? I think it's definitely another example of serendipity. Aren't we up to Number Seven by now?"

Serena couldn't repress the broad smile she felt spreading from ear to ear.

"If you say so," she replied, tilting her head at a jaunty angle.

He'd called her *beautiful*. She was perfectly aware that she had begun out-and-out flirting with a man who was once again paying for her dinner and had a serious girlfriend back home. Well, at least he wasn't a married man, she congratulated herself.

A voice in her head sang out a warning.

Serena! You're doing it again…falling for a guy you can't have!

She answered herself silently that she and Jack were enveloped here in snowy Italy…out of time, out of space. Her attraction to the man sitting across the table from her was unmistakable, but at least this time, going in, she knew for an absolute certainty that it couldn't come to anything, so her heart was safe, wasn't it? Given the special circumstances of where they were, how could she resist a good, old-fashioned *fling*—or ignore the attractiveness of this sexy man, to say nothing of the perfect conditions surrounding them and how long she'd been celibate? If he asked her out again, she'd say yes, and let whatever happened after that…happen. After all, this was Venice! Jack would soon go back to the lady doctor, and she'd go back to Antonelli's costumes. They traveled in two different orbits in New Orleans. They'd only see each other across the field at a Saints game in the Superdome. No *problema*. But meanwhile…

"Look Jack," she proposed, "let's just have some fun while you're here, shall we? For once, let's both just *forget* about Katrina, and everything that went with it for a while, agreed?"

Jack nodded emphatically, asking, "Are you free for dinner again, on Saturday following the presentation of my grandiose scheme to get the U.S. Government to restore the Louisiana wetlands?" Then, he hastened to add, "You can show up afterwards, of course, if you don't feel like hearing me drone on."

Serena fished her cellphone from the depths of her purse.

"If I can get all my work done, I'd *love* to hear your talk Saturday about saving my hometown. And I'd love to have dinner with you again," she assured him, noting their date on her electronic calendar. "But you'd better take my phone number this time, *signor*...and text me with the time, place, *vaporetto* to take, and how I find you in that huge convention hall."

CHAPTER 7

The next few days for Serena were a whirlwind of production meetings with the staff tasked with putting on the ball, coupled with back-to-back conferences with Allegra's most important and demanding international clientele, some of whom were only now getting around to ordering their costumes.

In the cramped, upstairs workshop in *San Tomà*, a district conveniently near Serena's lodgings, her main job continued to be taking Allegra's dazzling sketches and subsequent paper patterns and then laying out and cutting corresponding pieces of cheap cotton muslin to confirm the size and proper drape of each costume for individual customers. The addition of her efforts had markedly speeded up the process for the team of five, full-time seamstresses—plus Allegra supervising—to construct the beautiful clothing in either vintage or expensive contemporary fabrics made of silks and brocades.

Much to Serena's surprise, the day following her dinner with Jack, she heard her cellphone ping with a text message from him. He had wound up his last meeting that day and would she like to join him for a late supper? Or if she'd already eaten,

> **…a nightcap at Ancora, a couple of minutes' walk from your studio? Drinks and small plates liberally dispensed at a late hour…**

Texting him to pick her up downstairs at nine-thirty, she found herself inordinately pleased and surprised that he wanted to see her in advance of their scheduled date on Saturday when she would hear him speak at the conference.

So...he feels the same...whatever-it-is...that I do!

Proof of this came when Jack volunteered over small servings of *tortellini al pesto* that night to serve as her personal guide on a series of what she came to call "Giovanni's Midnight Magical Mystery Tours."

"But Jack," she protested, "it's late and you have to be at your conference every morning this week, to say nothing of the seventeen costumes I have to cut muslin for in the next five days!"

"You said we should just have fun, didn't you?" he demanded, taking her arm as soon as they emerged from the restaurant and leading her through the snow along the raised walkway toward the *San Tomà vaporetto* stop. "So what if we two burn the candle at both ends for a while? It's Venice!"

"It's Venice!" became their mantra — and justification — for every minute spent together from that evening onwards.

Later that same night, they disembarked from the boat on the opposite side of the Grand Canal and Jack ushered her along the temporary gangways laid throughout the stunning but water-filled Piazza San Marco. She marveled at its size as big as several American football fields and anchored by the magnificent Doge Palace on one side. The grand Basilica San Marco stood to its left, and at right angles, the iconic clock tower faced the canal whose royal blue face, studded with gold stars, took her breath away.

She was startled when Jack wrapped his arm under her chin and around her shoulders for warmth, pulling her against his chest and halting their forward progress. Just then, a mellow, booming sound rang out from the enormous bell as two bronze, mechanical statues holding stout hammers, repeatedly struck its ancient, metal surface.

"Oh...how...amazing," she murmured, acutely aware of the feel of his body against her back.

"Timed it just right," Jack said smugly.

She gazed up at the beautiful clock face with its roman numerals and signs of the zodiac, along with a carved winged lion above her head.

"You sure did," Serena answered, barely above a whisper. Jack's cheek rested against the side of her head. She turned in the circle of his arms to face him. "Thank you," she said softly.

He leaned forward, hesitated, and then disappointed her with a kiss her on the nose.

"You're welcome."

Serena's gaze was nearly level with Jack's, their lips only inches apart.

"Well, to be honest," she declared in a moment of unbridled candor, "that was a bit…underwhelming."

Jack stared back and then lowered his head, his cool lips meeting her uplifted ones, his arms tightening around her shoulders until his long, lingering kiss left no doubt he'd discarded the notion of holding himself in check.

"I've been wanting to do this all evening," he muttered, pressing her lips once more, their kiss deepening and leaving her breathless. Finally, Serena pulled away and gave a slight shake of her head.

"I admit it," she whispered, "Venice is having her way with me," she warned. She leaned toward him to return the kiss, parting her lips in an open invitation that Jack seized with abandon.

Just then, a blast of wind and snow rained down on them from the tower's roof, startling them apart.

His voice sounding hoarse, Jack said, "I guess that's a message from Saint Mark, himself, saying I'd better get you home."

The next night after another late supper, Jack hired a private water taxi, complete with fur blanket and a flask of Amaretto. The looks they had exchanged when she'd first entered the restaurant signaled clearly that neither of them had forgotten a second of their passionate kisses under the clock tower. However, Jack appeared to renew his determination to maintain perfect decorum during their meal while they exchanged news of their respective activities that day. Once on board the boat he'd hired for the evening, he wrapped Serena in the fur throw and went forward to speak to the captain, apparently ordering him to crisscross several canals in order to point out his favorite churches from the water.

Just before midnight, the taxi throbbed in a low idle as they neared the *Basilica di Santa Maria della Salute*, a domed and columned beauty built in the seventeenth century with Palladian echoes, constructed on the tip of the *Dorsoduro* section of Venice.

"Come to the bow and have a look," Jack said, seizing her arm to steady her as she made her way outside the cabin.

Serena's breath caught as she absorbed the magnificence of the church looming high above their heads, the gigantic construction bathed in falling snow.

"Oh...*wow*."

She suddenly wondered aloud if any of her ancestors had ever worshipped there.

"This church was *built* on the concept of gratitude you were talking about," Jack explained, "which is why I especially wanted to show it to you. It was commissioned by Venetians as a visible means of giving thanks for having survived a plague that had killed one third of the population here."

"Worse than Katrina...or 9-11," she murmured.

Jack nodded and pointed at the enormous dome that

glistened in the full moon peeking through a hole in the storm clouds.

"That design is an engineering feat that defies logic, don't you think? Like New Orleans, the entire edifice is built on a cluster of small, swampy islands. The Venetians laid down more than a million wooden pilings hauled from Croatia, mind you, and somehow pushed each of them down about thirteen feet below the water's surface. Then they constructed wooden platforms on top of the stakes to support the entire stone and marble structure."

"But it was built five hundred years ago! How come all that wood hasn't rotted by now?"

"They say the constant flow of salt water around and through the wood petrified the pilings and platforms overtime, turning them hard as stone."

"It looks much taller than any historic building in the French Quarter," Serena replied, awed by the sheer size of the dome soaring above them. "It has a bunch of Titians inside, doesn't it?" she asked, her gaze scanning the structure's staggering beauty and symmetry. "I seem to remember something about that from my art history classes."

"That's right," he replied with a nod of admiration. "Titian's the most represented artist in the church...and even painted the ceilings, much as Michelangelo did in Rome's Sistine Chapel."

"Well...before I leave, I hope I get time to go *inside* all these fabulous sights you've been showing me. But given the hours I'm working, I have my doubts." She smiled at him happily. "These late-night tours you're providing are very appreciated, *Signor* Durand." She leaned forward and lightly kissed him on each cheek. "Thank you."

She thought for certain he would kiss her back, but instead, he turned to the driver, ordering him to return to the *Traghetto della Madonnetta* gondolier dock where he walked her back to her hotel door and bid her a chaste goodnight.

Well, what did she expect, she chastised herself? Jack had had second thoughts. He was committed to a woman back home. His kiss twenty-four hours earlier fell into the category of a "slip," she lectured herself. It was just Venice. Everywhere they looked provided a backdrop more romantic than the previous one. Jack was now silently letting her know the obvious: from here on out, he planned to maintain a safe distance. They were destined to be just friends, and certainly not lovers.

Despite these logical conclusions, she walked up the steps from the small lobby to her bedroom with an unwelcome and uncomfortably familiar feeling of deep disappointment.

The next evening, Jack texted an apology that an Italian colleague insisted on having dinner with him to review the plan for introducing his talk later in the week. Serena, too, was deluged with work, and in the late afternoon on Thursday, Allegra had invited her deputy to go with her to the Fortuny fabric company on the island opposite the *Dorsoduro* known as the *Giudecca*.

The snow had let up, but the wind still whipped their faces as they disembarked at the *Palanca vaporetto* stop. The two women walked a hundred yards in bitter cold to the brick entrance of a company that manufactured and sold magnificent silks, brocades, and printed fabrics that had graced the castles, palaces, and Park Avenue apartments of its fantastically wealthy patrons since its founding in 1919.

"*Buon pomeriggio*, Allegra," the firm's manager, Giuseppe Ianna, bid them good afternoon, as they quickly shut the showroom door against the winds blasting behind them. After introducing Serena, Allegra lost no time specifying from which of the colorful bolts displayed, floor-to-ceiling, she wanted additional yardage. Then, she arranged to have the material safely transported to the workshop by Fortuny's private water taxi.

Dusk had descended this wintery season by the time they bid farewell to Signor Ianna and boarded the boat back to the *Dorsoduro*.

"Join me for supper at *Trattoria San Tomà* and then we can work for a few hours afterwards when the shop is quieter," Allegra suggested. "I want you to do some preliminary sketches at my direction, based on my notes from the client I saw today."

Serena was gratified that Allegra would trust her with actually designing one of the gowns, based on her mentor's ideas.

"Let's hope I come up with something you like," the younger woman said, a flutter of nervousness invading her chest.

"I have every confidence you will, *cara*. I find I get more work done in the later hours, don't you?"

"Yes, of course," Serena agreed, overjoyed by the opportunity that Allegra was giving her to work side by side. She also felt a twinge of guilt that she had been meeting Jack instead of getting a dose of much-needed sleep after everyone else trudged home following her twelve-hour workdays.

Over a plate of *papardelle con scampi*—a dish made with wide, flat noodles and spicy shrimp that *Nonna* Serena d'Este had also cooked to perfection—Serena listened intently while Allegra fretted aloud about the *palazzo* where the ball would take place.

"A few years back, the high waters almost made it impossible for my staff to do the load-in with all the decorations and food for the party," Allegra related over her bowl of *gnocchi*—little potato pillows mixed with chunks of salmon and dotted with poppy seeds. "And the year my husband was so ill, the water rose so high…well," she said wearily, "there were moments I never thought we'd be able to sound the trumpets from the loggia and open the doors to our guests."

"Rosa told me briefly of your loss," Serena murmured. "I am so sorry. It must have been terribly hard for you to celebrate Carnival with a happy heart after that."

Allegra stared at her plate for a moment and then looked up.

"It is important to keep dreaming, though, no matter what happens in life, my dear Serena," she said, gazing steadily at her dinner companion. "After all, you suffered a similar loss, did you not? And yet, you have moved forward…following your passion for costume design, *sì*?"

"You knew…about Marco and me?"

"I knew that *look* I saw you often give Marco when I was with you all in Las Vegas. And I could tell he cared for you, despite the differences in your ages. When I read he had died so suddenly, I almost wrote you, but then…I thought it was not my place." She cast her a melancholy smile. "I am so sorry for what you must have suffered afterward, *cara*. That is something I understand very well."

"Thank you," Serena replied softly, ducking her head.

Why did speaking of Marco's death never fail to bring tears to her eyes, even now, she wondered? The same thing had happened with Jack when the subject was broached.

And then she realized the probable reason: both of them had offered her their sympathy and understanding— not judgment—though with Jack, she had only understood that later.

Serena used her napkin to swiftly swipe the moisture from her eyes and steered the conversation to the subject of the rented *palazzo* where Allegra had held the ball for two decades.

"And with all the snow this year," Serena ventured, "how might that complicate matters and what can we do to prepare? I imagine it eventually melts if the weather warms up a bit, am I right? But doesn't that increase the dangers of more flooding?"

Allegra heaved a heavy sigh.

"It's got me very worried again this year. As far as I could learn, the *palazzo*'s owners didn't take further measures to seal the areas inside, below the water that sprung new leaks in the last year. Of course, it is horribly expensive to remedy these kinds of problems, so I didn't really expect—"

She gave a resigned shrug to indicate there was not much she could do except install pumps during the period that the *palazzo* was rented to her company.

"You know, Allegra," Serena suggested, twisting the last of her wide noodles around her fork. "I have a friend from New Orleans speaking at the Global Rising Waters Conference going on here this week. He's invited me to come hear his talk Saturday night—that is if you don't want me to work on some special project. I could ask him if there's anyone he's met in Venice who is an expert in water sealants and such. Perhaps there is something temporary we could do to stem any further leakage into the lower floors?"

Allegra's look of hopeful relief was palpable. She reached across the table and patted Serena's hand wrapped around her glass of red wine.

"Do you speak of that very handsome young man I once saw walking toward the entrance to the atelier? The night I left you working so late, I heard him in a funny accent asking a passerby if my workshop was nearby."

Serena nodded and felt warmth infuse her cheeks. She

hoped Allegra would think it was the wine.

"He's just a new friend. I met him on the plane flying here. He doesn't speak much Italian," she explained.

"I understood well enough that he was looking for *you*," Allegra teased. "By all means, *cara*," she urged with a wink behind her high-fashion Luxottica lenses, "you must certainly find out if this young man has any ideas that could rescue us from the kind of near-disaster that almost befell the last *Il Ballo*. How nice for us both if he became our savior."

Just then Serena's phone pinged, letting her know a text message had arrived. She pulled her phone out of her handbag. Jack had sent specific instructions to guide her to the location where his talk would take place Saturday night.

There will be guest credentials in your name. See you soon!

Serena looked up from her phone. Given Jack's remoteness the last time they'd met, she was sorely tempted to text back that she couldn't attend his presentation with the excuse she had too much work. But now, she'd just gone and offered to enlist Jack's help with the seepage problem at the *palazzo*. The thought occurred to her that she could always just send him an email requesting that he contact *Signora* Benedetti directly and make an excuse about declining to meet him again…

And not see him anymore?

Suppressing a sigh, Serena texted back her thanks for providing directions, adding that she'd come to the Laguna Palace by 8p.m. if work allowed. She wondered if Jack was merely fulfilling his obligation to follow through on his previous invitation to have dinner with her after his speech?

Oh crap! She'd decide tomorrow whether or not to go…

Jack was once again seated in an uncomfortable folding chair on the side of the dais that faced the large hall where he was soon due to deliver his keynote address. Sitting next to him was his Italian counterpart whose specialty it was to recommend steps that could be taken to rebuild the outlying barrier islands that ringed the Venice Lagoon surrounding the city. Maurizio Pigati was also going to be Jack's guide when they visited the underwater mobile gates whose construction was nearly eighty percent complete—and had been mired in controversy and allegations of corruption for the last three decades. If the mechanics ultimately proved viable, seventy-nine huge metal flaps would hydraulically rise from the seabed between the lagoon and the Adriatic to protect Venice from up to six-foot tidal surges like the ones that had inundated the city as recently as 2007 and slightly lower flows in 2013.

Jack gazed into the maw of the auditorium that now was filled to near capacity. Wetland experts, water engineers and government bureaucrats from around the world had dutifully assembled to hear his talk on the lasting impact of Hurricane Katrina and the subsequent rebuilding efforts along the Mississippi, Lake Pontchartrain, and some coastal areas in the decade following. Jack and the tech guy had just checked the laptop computer plugged into the Power Point projector. With any luck, all was in readiness.

The overhead lights dimmed and Jack's Italian colleague rose to the podium and made his introductions in English. Some in the audience adjusted their headsets to be able to hear a translation of the evening's program presented to a larger-than-expected international audience.

Just as Maurizio concluded his remarks, a door opened at the back of the hall, spilling light from the lobby. Serena Antonelli, clad in her fur-trimmed parka, slipped into a seat in the last row.

She came!

Jack had figured it was fifty-fifty, given her workload and the mixed signals he knew he had been sending her. He had almost taken her into his arms again and kissed her breathless the other night as they stood bundled in the bow of the water taxi, gazing at the beautiful basilica known by locals simply as "*Salute.*" Perhaps some ancient shred of Catholic conscience had prompted him to keep things uncomplicated between them as long as he still had not resolved the situation with Lauren. After a decade together, on and off, he owed their relationship at least that much.

Nevertheless, he was startled, now, by how the mere sight of Serena entering the hall lifted his spirits. After all, he reminded himself, she and her friends and family and all the other surviving citizens of New Orleans were the *reason* he had continued to report on these confounded environmental battles. It was for them he was trying to present irrefutable scientific facts to persuade the American policy makers that the best, most economical way to halt future high water surges in Louisiana was to save the wetlands and barrier islands *while* building multi-billion-dollar projects like Italy's massive gates.

He glanced at his notes and hoped that his address to the assembled global experts could expiate to a small degree the sins of avarice, incompetence, and weakness committed by those associated with the New Orleans canal and levee failures of 2005.

Without warning, a vision assaulted him as it so often had. In his mind's eye he once again saw a young father-to-be urging his pregnant wife up the pull-down stairs that led to an attic just as thundering water smashed the house's wooden exterior walls and knocked the helpless couple into its swirling depths.

Whatever I say today…whatever its impact…this is for you,

Mr. and Mrs. Cosimo Antonelli, and everyone like you…may you rest in peace.

Serena sat at the back of the hall, transfixed by the images flashing on the screen and the passion and expertise displayed by the tall, dark-haired speaker gripping both hands on the podium. She sat rigidly in her seat as Jack spoke of events that had unfolded in the past decade since the onslaught of Hurricane Katrina against one of America's most celebrated cities.

She gasped involuntarily when a video clip taken from a helicopter flying low over the Lakeview section of New Orleans showed in sharp detail the floodwaters swamping the houses there, including her poor brother Cosimo's home on 40th Street, which she located immediately in the middle of the screen.

Soon, she couldn't even *see* the screen because of the tears that had filled her eyes and spilled down her cheek. She barely swallowed a sob at Jack's concluding plea for "experts, thought leaders and decision makers to present the urgent case to governing authorities from all the coastal regions of the world to take the urgent, necessary measures to save the planet's wetlands and islands."

Many heads were bobbing agreement in the audience as Jack was winding up his presentation.

"We must somehow persuade those elusive, self-serving, head-in-the-sand Powers-That-Be to restore these native features of our landscapes—or face the consequences. Louisiana and the U.S. Federal government has had to spend some one hundred *billion* in relief and restoration because of what was washed away—and all they really did was simply replace what Hurricane Katrina broke. We must also halt any more misguided, mismanaged manmade canals, levees, shipping channels, and oil dredging projects. *Unless* these enterprises devised by man are done properly and with scrupulous oversight, they are bound to create even further havoc on the planet. I submit that the most economical way forward is to repair as fast as we can what man destroyed: restore the wetlands and barrier islands—or else."

Looking spent, Jack bowed his head for a moment. Then, he lifted it, gazed at the audience, and said in conclusion, "Haven't we humans done damage enough? I speak this night for Katrina's one thousand, eight hundred and thirty-six *known* victims who can no longer speak for themselves. Thank you and good evening."

Serena glanced at the audience members sitting nearest her and was amazed to see she wasn't the only one with moisture brimming in her eyes. In the next instant, the hall erupted into tumultuous applause. Jack didn't acknowledge the accolades, but rather, made a grab for his notes and walked off the dais. Several in the crowd surged forward to speak to him, but he shook his head and pointed to the back of the hall, determinedly threading his way through the throng. When he arrived where Serena sat in her aisle seat in the last row, he reached for her hands and pulled her to her feet.

"You were brave to come," he said in a low voice. "I'm sure what you just heard and saw was hard to witness again."

In response, she threw her arms around his torso and quietly sobbed against his chest.

"You are...so good at...what you do," she said between gulps for air, doing her best to stop crying. "*So* good."

And then she buried her head against his suit jacket and held him even more tightly as if clinging to a life preserver in a sea of dangerous, churning water.

In the end, Jack remained twenty more minutes in the auditorium speaking to the many audience members who wanted to congratulate him and arrange to be in touch at a later date. Meanwhile, Serena announced she would head for the *gabinetto* to blow her nose and repair her makeup.

Bundled up again against the onslaught of more snow that had turned to sleet, they boarded a timely but crowded *vaporetto* and were literally forced to put their arms around each other to keep warm. The open-air boat plied its way to the *Ca' Rezzonico* stop in the *Dorsoduro* section of Venice where Jack had made late dinner reservations. He took her arm and they sprinted through blinding snow down a narrow passageway toward *Campo St. Barnaba*, a large square anchored by a massive church and ancient water well positioned in the center of the paved expanse.

By this time, Jack was relieved to see that Serena had regained her composure and laughed as they slipped and slid on the slick pavement. They were both nearly breathless by the time they approached an iron gate that led to a courtyard sporting some two-dozen wooden tables where patrons ate in the open air in the fine weather. Tonight an ingenious folding roof and heaters shut out the cold. The continuing sleet and snow once again made their progress slow going.

"You can hardly get a place to sit down here in the summertime," Jack noted as they walked under a sign, *Casin dei Nobili*, next to a shop whose windows were filled with both painted and stark white plaster carnival masks.

"A sign of the season," Serena noted, tilting her head toward the colorful display.

"They sell these things to the tourists all year around."

"Like we sell Mardi Gras beads on Bourbon Street."

"Tons of the mask shops, now, are owned by Chinese

who import their fake look-alikes from the Far East at a fraction of the cost. They're slowly driving the genuine Venetian mask-making artisans out of business." He pointed at the store window filled with fanciful masks, tri-corner hats with colorful eighteen-inch ostrich plumes, as well as menacing masks with *papier mâché* noses a foot long. "Mario Belloni, here, is one of the last of the genuine Venetian artists left, and that's because he not only produces fabulous creations like these, but he also teaches mask-making to anyone who'll pay the fee."

"I've heard about the Chinese taking over so many of these shops from nearly everyone working in my atelier," Serena nodded grimly.

Cutting short their unhappy exchange, Jack kicked aside a pile of snow pressed against a wooden door and opened it. Inside the restaurant's small interior space that served diners in winter, a rush of welcome warmth greeted them. Soon, their friendly host seated them, plainly delighted to serve anyone willing to brave the storm. The diners ordered a lentil soup to fight off the chill, and then Serena followed Jack's lead and asked for the homemade spinach ravioli with a dark, short rib *ragout* sauce, richly laced with red wine.

"A glass of local red to go with?" Jack asked, reassured to see Serena's dark eyes were crinkling at the corners and she seemed free of the wave of emotion that had burst forth when he'd strode to her side after his talk.

Truth be told, he had very nearly lost it himself when she tucked her head under his chin and sobbed into his chest.

She completely understands...she gets it. She gets me...

Pushing intruding thoughts of Lauren to the far recesses of his mind, he focused on watching Serena sample the first morsel of ravioli and loved the way she closed her eyes, chewed slowly and then swallowed, a little moan of pleasure escaping her generous mouth.

"Oh…dear…heaven," she said, poking her fork into her second plump, square pillow of pasta. "*Nonna* Serena would have wanted to murder this chef for creating something this good."

By dinner's end, the bottle of *Amarone della Valpolicella* was drained, coffee drunk, and Jack noted that Serena had a dreamy look in her eye as she sipped her small glass of Amaretto. Nearly all the patrons had departed, but the owners showed no signs of wanting to hurry them along.

Serena set her empty glass of the almond-flavored liqueur on the table just as Jack finished the remnants of his own. He glanced out the window and pointed.

"Look outside. It's basically a whiteout. This has to be the most snow and one of the coldest winters on record. I think someone is going to have to dig a path from the restaurant's front door so we can make it to the *vaporetto* stop."

Serena nodded with a look of alarm.

"We'd better get going. I wonder if the boats have stopped running because of all this?"

The restaurant owner, who had overheard their conversation as he retrieved the signed bill, nodded.

"*Si*…I think you will have to find your way by foot in the snow if you live in the *Dorsoduro*. *Il servizio di vaporetti è sospeso.*"

Serena translated.

"He says the boats have definitely stopped in this bad weather."

Jack addressed their host.

"*La Signorina* lives near *Campo San Polo*. How long do you think that will take if we walk from here?"

"Not too bad," the proprietor said with a shrug, "if you go the most direct way. Here, let me show you on the map."

Jack and Serena charted a zigzag course over innumerable bridges, down narrow alleyways, and through countless squares until, at long last, they finally reached Serena's lodgings around the corner from *Calle del Forno* off the square known as *Campo Meloni*. The pair was covered with fallen snow and their feet were numb in their rubber boots.

"It must be close to one a.m.," she speculated, her words visible in the cold air as they approached the courtyard near the front door to *Ca' Arco Antico*.

Both chilled to the bone, they entered the tiny vestibule and stamped their rubber boots on the interior doormat to shake off the snow. The husband and wife proprietors of Serena's guesthouse had obviously retired for the night and an absolute stillness enveloped them standing in the small, checkerboard foyer that led to the marble staircase and the rooms upstairs.

Jack and Serena exchanged glances as a pulsating undercurrent passed between them. Serena briefly lowered her eyes and when she looked up again, Jack was still gazing at her and gave a slight shrug, as if to say he had no control over events as they appeared to be unfolding.

"Perhaps I'll have to beg that couch?" he suggested in a whisper, casting a glance at the gold, brocade love seat intended for guests waiting to check in at the minuscule front desk that was little more than a table with a telephone on it.

"It'll be torture," she whispered back. "You're two feet longer than it is."

"I am?" he said, leaning closer.

He lowered his head and began a long, intimate exploration of her lips. His mouth tasted deliciously of brandy and the frigid temperatures they had just endured in the forty minutes it had taken them to get to her place. He released her, and took a step back toward the front door. Then, as if abruptly changing his mind, he pulled her toward him again, framing her face with his large hands, and kissed her once more, blotting out any sensible thoughts of her original plan to avoid intimacies with another man she could not have.

"God…you are delicious," he murmured, "but then, I found that out under the clock tower."

He took her in his arms once more as if everything had already been decided between them and began to nuzzle his lips beneath her ear, then in the hollow at the base of her neck, and worked his way back to her mouth.

"Delicious…" he repeated.

"I knew if I kissed you, you would be irresistible, so…" she whispered into his ear, letting go of defenses she'd built up since she'd last felt a man hold her like this, "as you can see…I'm not. Resisting, that is."

Jack gave a low chuckle. "Well, that's good to hear. I was beginning to feel like a teenager hoping for just one more kiss…when all I want is…is…"

"I can guess," she murmured, "and you are most welcome to come upstairs with me if you don't want to sleep on that tiny couch pushed against that wall over there."

Without further discussion, Serena took Jack by the hand and led him toward the grey, marble staircase that led to the first room on the landing identified by a brass plaque declaring it the *Canaletto* suite. Every few steps he halted and drew her to him, leaning again the gold brocade-covered wall while kissing her under her ear once more and cupping a breast through her heavy winter coat.

"If you keep doing that," she hissed, her breath ragged, "I'm going to start screaming and wake my fellow hotel guests."

"Can't have that," he mumbled, but didn't remove his hand.

Somehow, they made it to the top of the stairs where Serena paused for breath and pulled out a large, bronze key from her purse. Her hand trembled as the metal rattled in the keyhole and finally turned the tumblers, allowing her to open the heavy, carved wooden door. Once in her room with the door closed, they fell onto her gold silk covered bed where they stretched out on the mattress, face to face.

"I think we should take off our coats," she giggled, feeling flushed all over.

"Yes, now that we're inside and up here, I'm hot as blazes," he agreed, "and in more ways than one." He rose to his feet, divesting himself of his down parka. "And besides, I need to say something."

Here it comes...

Serena recalled how Marco had set the perimeters of their affair just before they'd fallen onto a tackier version of a bed like this one at the Las Vegas Venetian Hotel.

"If we...make love," he began, gazing at her stretched out on the bed, "and believe me, there is nothing I'd rather do in this moment, in this beautiful place...we will definitely be crossing into some serious territory."

"I...know," she replied, wondering if she should sit up to hear these pronouncements. "There's Lauren..."

"That's not what I was thinking...but of course, that's part of this."

Serena pulled herself up by her elbows and leaned her back against the silk upholstered headboard.

She patted the edge of the bed. "Before we totally lose our heads...why don't you sit down?" she said. "Tell me what's on your mind." She was not a sweet, naïve young thing anymore, she reminded herself silently. She wanted Jack to be absolutely clear on that fact. "What would you like to say?"

CHAPTER 8

Jack perched on the side of the bed and took Serena's hand that was nearest him.

"I'll be leaving in less than a week and most of the time, I'll be on assignment for the paper...writing about those Venetian water gates I talked about in my speech tonight."

"Yes...?"

"I don't want us...I don't want *you* to think that if I can't see you after...after tonight, you'll think it was only an...impulsive interlude."

She realized, suddenly, that neither one of them felt like making the beautiful evening...the beautiful *week* they'd spent together...into a one-night stand.

"Look, Jack, I'm a big girl and I might as well admit that I'm hugely attracted to you. Having said that, I can also see I must have become mighty used to making do with crumbs instead of having the whole cake. I think I understand what you're trying to say, here. Perhaps we should just—"

"I want you, Serena..." he interrupted, moving the hand he held to press it against his lap and his full-blown erection, "and I think this tells you how much, but I also think it might ultimately spoil things for us if we make love before I—"

"Decide how you feel about the lady back home?" she filled in, folding both hands in her lap and staring down at them.

"I know how I feel about the lady back home," he said sharply. Serena looked up and saw him shake his head in frustration. "That sounded harsh. What I mean you to understand is, if we're starting something serious—which is what this feels like—I want it to be right, you know what

I'm saying? And, just parenthetically, I want you to know that Lauren and I haven't..."

Serena could see he was searching for the way to say something in a most gentlemanly fashion.

"You haven't what?" she murmured.

"We haven't been...intimate for five months, now."

"Really?" She looked away, knowing she hadn't been able to keep the skepticism out of her voice.

"Really," he repeated firmly. He seized her chin between his fingers and gently turned her head to meet him eye to eye. "She's been in Houston at Med school and in December, we had a hell of a lousy holiday season. That said, there's no denying that...she and I certainly have been through a lot together, and—"

"Katrina!" Serena exploded, pounding one fist against her silk-clad mattress. "I *hate* that storm! It's bonded people and screwed them up at the same time! Fine! I agree. You two have a lot of history together. If you haven't worked it out with her, I don't think what we were about to do is a very good idea, either." She pointed to the small, gold silk settee pushed against one wall at the far end of her large room, a virtual twin of the one downstairs. "Be my guest, as it looks as if it isn't going to stop snowing any time soon."

Jack eyed the formal sofa and nodded.

An unreasonable rage had continued to boil inside her chest, but she forced a smile in an attempt to communicate that she wasn't mad at *him*.

"You're being honorable and I'm being noble," she said, somehow managing a chuckle that lightened the atmosphere. "But, man, are we missing one, all-time great, romantic opportunity!"

Jack's expression revealed his relief that she had stepped back from any further outburst. Then he startled her by seizing her hand and slowly inserting her index finger into his mouth, sending an avalanche of sparks up her arm and down her spine. Then he returned her hand to her lap.

"You are absolutely right: we sure are missing out here," he said, his voice husky with the same longing she couldn't hide. "But we've both had a fair amount to drink tonight," he added, one side of his mouth quirking upwards. "You might not feel the same about the 'romance' part in dawn's sober light."

"It's my choice how I'll feel," she said stubbornly.

"Yes it is…but *I* feel I owe it to you, most of all, to officially break it off with Lauren before you and I launch this mad gondola into the waters of the Grand Canal, you know what I mean?"

Serena tried to hide her disappointment and salvage her pride with another dose of humor.

"*Now* you decide to be sensible. But you're right."

"Yes…we both are."

"Do you want to use the bathroom first, or shall I?" she asked, relieved as well as disappointed that they both were being so levelheaded.

"You go first, but before you do…come here," he said gruffly and pulled her into his arms once more. His kisses soon became instant messages, telling her how much he regretted being such a gentleman after all.

"This is totally nuts," she whispered. "We're here, in Venice, in my beautiful, Fortuny-festooned bed, kissing like…well, like crazy people!"

"I know," he said, looking miserable. "All I want to do right now is pin you on that mattress and—"

"Now you just stop that trashy talk," she whispered, bestowing a flurry of small kisses beneath his right ear. "But, if whatever has happened between you and me is to have any truth to it, your instincts, just now, are right." She pulled away and shook her head sorrowfully. "We *should* be sensible."

"It's killing me."

"Me, too. Maybe you should sleep on the couch in the lobby, after all? No one's around until daybreak."

It was Jack's turn to shake his head. "No. I want at least to be in the same room with you."

She leaned forward to cup her hands on either side of his face. "Okay. Let's give our noble intentions a whirl. And now I'm going to brush my teeth," she announced and quickly rose from the bed.

Serena slipped into the bathroom where she donned her skin-tight flannel leggings and T-shirt that hung on a hook near the shower stall. She savagely grabbed her toothbrush, making the decision, as she gazed at her flushed reflection in the mirror, that she'd take her make-up off in the morning.

After Jack's turn using the facilities, he emerged from the bathroom, walked across the room to stand by the window and peered out. From the bed, Serena observed him gaze down at the narrow *Traghetto della Madonnetta* and, at the alley's end, the tiny slice of the Grand Canal.

"Mist and fog, now, too," he announced over his shoulder. "And there's no let up…it's definitely still seriously snowing out there." He crossed the room and once again sat on top of the covers by her side. "Sleepy?" he asked.

"No."

"But tired?"

"Exhausted."

He began stroking her hair and Serena felt her tense body beginning to relax.

"Serena, I want you to know that I've loved every minute of the time we've spent here together."

Lying on her back, Serena smiled up at him, basking in the warmth beaming at her from above.

"Me too," she agreed. "Work and play. And Venice. What more could we ask for?"

"Oh, I could think of a few things, but I'd better say goodnight." He leaned over her and kissed her on each cheek, European fashion. "Sweet dreams, *Contessa*."

"Ah...promoting me to nobility for being so noble tonight. I like that." And in that moment, she couldn't bear for him to leave her side. Before he could pull away, she threaded her arms gently around his neck. "If I promise to be your good little *Contessa*, would you please sleep beside me tonight? You can be on top of the bedspread with an extra duvet that's stored in the closet over there to keep you warm. And besides, look at how short that couch is."

Jack smiled but shook his head doubtfully.

"I don't know if that's such a great idea."

"We slept this close on the airplane coming over," she cajoled him. "Surely we have the willpower to do it again."

Jack heaved a resigned sigh.

"Fortunately for you," he informed her, "that nightcap I consumed just before we left the restaurant is taking its toll...and you've just made me an offer that's hard to refuse. Turn over on your side and I'll get the blanket."

Jack rummaged in the mirror-fronted armoire for the extra white, down-filled duvet, and deposited it on the bed. She heard, rather than saw, him divest himself of his clothes, all but his underwear, she surmised. Then he extinguished the two wall sconces and the elaborate, gold-flecked Murano glass chandelier hanging over their heads.

"Ready or not, here I come," he announced and lay down on the bed, pulling the duvet over the length of him. He shifted his weight to snuggle against Serena's backside, spoon-fashion, with sheets, blankets and a silk coverlet adding to the safety barrier separating them. He kissed her right shoulder.

"No fair," she murmured.

"Just saying *Buona notte.*"
"*Buona notte, caro…sogni d'oro.*"
"Translation, please?"
"Sweet dreams. Literally, 'May you have golden sleep'."
"Golden sleep…" he whispered into her hair. "I wish you golden, *golden* sleep, too, *Contessa.*"

Serena barely nodded, gently lulled to a state of semi-consciousness by the wine she'd consumed, the soothing warmth of Jack's arms around her ribcage, and his whispered endearments in her ear.

At dawn, Jack rose and for the first time, took in the sight of the room's cascade of gold brocade curtains flanking the tall, balconied window and the matching brocade spilling from a gilded, ornately carved wooden crown attached high on the wall above the bed where Serena lay sound asleep.

She does look like a Contessa…a Sleeping Beauty I could awake with a kiss…

With a hollow feeling of regret, he donned his clothes and stadium coat, and then tapped out a text for her cellphone. In it, he reassured her that he would call her in two days when he got back from visiting three sets of massive, moveable gates being built underwater that were engineered to hold back any future storm surges into the Venice Lagoon. That is, if their builders could ever get all of them to function correctly in concert, he considered with the cynicism of a reporter long accustomed to promises never kept.

Within minutes, he tiptoed from her room, down the staircase, and slipped out the front door even before proprietors of the guesthouse could suspect that he'd stayed the night.

Serena put her cellphone on silent mode and hurried into Allegra's main office just off the *Calle Frezzaria* behind the *Piazza San Marco* that was currently filled with about nine inches of tidal water. Several teams—nearly thirty people in all—from the costume atelier, the ball production group, and Allegra's retail store managers had assembled for an emergency meeting.

"I called you all together here," Allegra began, speaking slowly in Italian for Serena's benefit, "to get your thinking about a problem that has developed."

Those present exchanged worried glances, which served to heighten Serena's apprehension.

Allegra explained that the previous week, she'd received a letter from a city official who made sudden, insistent demands that certain repairs be made at the *palazzo* she had rented "in order to assure the 'safety of the event,'" she related. Her look of skepticism signaled to everyone that what was happening might simply be an old-fashioned Italian hands-out-for-a pay-off ploy.

"I have not been able to reach the *palazzo* owners who are residing in their other home abroad," Allegra explained, "but clearly, we must find a way to satisfy these officials and comply with the red tape in a manner that will not eat up all the profits from the ball—most of which I use, as you well know, to pay those of you in this room, along with nearly three hundred temporary workers that help us create *Il Ballo di Carnevale* each year."

Serena arched an anxious eyebrow at Rosa sitting next to her. The head seamstress nodded in silent agreement that their employer had never been involved in producing the extravagant night of entertainment solely for profits. Allegra's business had prospered throughout financial ups and downs, subsidized to an extent by her costume sales and rentals and the success of her retail stores that sold luxurious women's clothing accessories. *Il Ballo* was the manifestation of her own dream, an event to delight and dazzle the senses in the spirit of the original *Carnevale*. Serena had become convinced, now that she was working in Venice, that her mentor created the fantasy that was the ball purely for the love of her city and its history.

"Our first step is to assess in more detail any legitimate claims of damage wrought by flooding over the years, as well as the unusual amounts of snow this year," Allegra continued. "If the lower floors of the *palazzo* weren't properly repaired in the aftermath of these previous extreme winter conditions, and if the waters rise again just prior to the ball…this could seriously threaten *Il Ballo* itself."

Everyone listening to her description of the possible dangers to their enterprise exchanged troubled glances.

"Even though I don't own the *palazzo*, we must learn the extent of what we may be facing and make a plan to fix anything that could thwart our holding this event," Allegra urged, as those surrounding her began to nod in the affirmative. "I'll need all of your help and any personal contacts you may have with government officials, as well as the names of any friends and family members in the business of repairing water damage."

Her words settled heavily in the room as her staff absorbed the ominous portent of her solemn pronouncements.

Allegra then cast a glance at Serena, announcing to the assembled, "Our American colleague, Serena Antonelli, may have some connections that could be of significant help evaluating the problem, and perhaps even provide a way to approach certain high-level bureaucrats within the Ministry involved, yes, Serena?"

Serena felt all eyes upon her and quickly lowered her gaze to the notes she'd been taking. She had totally forgotten even to bring up the subject with Jack, given their highly charged dinner date and the discussion that followed in her bedchamber. She struggled to compose herself and marshal her Italian vocabulary.

"M-my American friend is a trained hydrologist and environmental journalist," she began. Then to Allegra she said, "Right now, he's on a field trip for several days with some high-level Italian colleagues, learning about the most recent advances in the construction of your mechanical water gates, but I will find out from him the names of people he knows that might be of help in a practical way to repair any damage—if the *palazzo* owners will agree—and see if he has any useful contacts within your government to help…ah…facilitate any permitting that may be required."

Serena felt guilty for having promised, before Jack even knew of her request, that he might reach out to his Italian counterparts. Fortunately, Allegra appeared satisfied by Serena's answer and instructed her office assistant, Francesca, to start phoning a list of construction workers and Venetian officials she'd already been told by friends and colleagues might also be of help.

Serena leaned back in her chair and tried to remember exactly when Jack had said he'd return from visiting the three water gate locations on the barrier islands on the far side of the lagoon. Hopefully, she'd hear from him as soon as he returned since most outlying areas he was visiting were unlikely to have reliable mobile phone service.

Jack stared at his cellphone in frustration. No text message from Serena appeared despite his frequent messages to her informing her that he had returned from inspecting the vast project known as MOSE, short, as he had learned on his trip into the lagoon, for the Venetian

Modulo Sperimentale Elettromeccanico. He had spent the entire time inspecting the three sets of hinged gates built on the sea floor that were planned to be operational by 2016 to keep unusually high tidal surges from swallowing up one of the most beautiful cities on earth. On this latest research trip, he'd been told that date was likely to be bumped once again, perhaps two to four more years down the road.

He was bursting to tell Serena that the same sort of red tape, corruption, and sheer incompetence that he'd reported on regarding New Orleans' efforts to hold back the waters at home were mirrored almost exactly in the thirty-year project he'd surveyed with Maurizio Pigati and Stefano Fabrini as his guides.

The biggest obstacles were not the engineering challenges of building the gates, which Jack determined were actually going to work, but "getting past the political partisan bickering and sheer graft in this city," as he'd written his editor at the *Picayune*. The most recent web of alleged bribes and kickbacks involved the diversion of MOSE funds to Venice's mayor to finance his recent campaign for office.

Jack had to wait to dispatch his email to his boss until he returned where there was Wi-Fi at Chioggia, a coastal town in the province of Venice at the far end of the lagoon. He'd described a row of eighteen mammoth metal gates connected to concrete housing structures with pivots that allowed them to rise and lower from the seabed, according to weather conditions. A modified version could possibly work in Louisiana and so he'd also sent his editor at the newspaper iPhone pictures he'd snapped of the entire operation.

Meanwhile, not only were there no text messages from Serena, there was nothing in his laptop's Inbox from her either, nor had she answered any of the voice calls he'd made.

Perhaps she'd concluded that his gentlemanly behavior when last she saw him was just a further example of what she might have imagined were his deeply-felt ties to Lauren, or—even worse—that he fit the description his sister had given him at the New Orleans Airport on the day they'd met.

Elusive, Marielle had called him to his face. Well, maybe he had been like that in the past...

When Lauren had slammed out of the restaurant New Year's Eve, declaring she'd take a taxi home, she'd shouted over her shoulder, "You're just a fucking commitment-phobe!" so loud, he figured half the Garden District had heard her.

Was he? Was he always in the act of seeking an escape route from the ties that bind?

For a brief moment, he allowed his mind to ponder his on-again-off-again decade-long relationship with Lauren Hilbert and wondered if—should he and Serena draw even closer—he would eventually have the same feeling of suffocation he'd experienced over the years with Lauren and several other women he'd known who also had made it clear they'd like him to ask for their hand in marriage?

Did he have a problem with commitment, or had he just not met the right woman?

Unsettled by these thoughts, Jack thrust his cellphone into his inside coat pocket and bolted for the door of his hotel room. Maybe he had felt cornered by certain women of his acquaintance in the past, but right now, he sure as hell wasn't looking for the exit where *La Contessa* was concerned.

Where was Serena? And why wasn't she answering him?

Striding down the hotel's hallway, Jack pushed the button to summon the elevator. He watched various floor numbers flash over his head as dozens of images of Serena drifted through his mind, memories he hadn't even realized he had stored after such short acquaintance. He pulled out his cellphone once again.

No messages.

What if she'd met some handsome Italian who was drowning in that woman's smoldering dark eyes, just as he had?

What if—?

He dialed her number for the seventh time, but his call went straight to voicemail. His watch noted that it was late, even for Italians to have supper. Even so, he punched a button to re-summon the elevator, hoping the damn snow had finally tapered off.

Serena folded her arms on top of a pile of crunched-up muslin left on the cutting table and allowed her head to sink down, closing her eyes in complete exhaustion. Allegra had approved of the sketches and pattern she'd made of her very first design for her mentor, but she was just too tired to cut the cheap fabric to first test her conception on a mannequin.

The sewing crew had finally gone home for the day following a marathon of work. Squeezed around the room, several additional mannequins clad in eighteenth century costumes in various stages of completion offered evidence of how hard the team had been working during the week.

Serena's eyes still closed, she finally had a moment to consider the thought that had constantly been present, despite the last two days of frenetic activity: Jack hadn't called.

Despite her previous resolve to keep a safe distance from devilishly attractive but unavailable men like Jack Durand, he'd constantly been in her thoughts since they'd chastely spent the night together. She found herself fighting a crushing sense of disappointment that she hadn't heard from him when he returned from his field trip to see the MOSE gates. The only explanation was that he'd had second thoughts—again.

And how was she going to explain to Allegra why she couldn't petition "her friend" for help regarding the leaking *palazzo?*

Deciding it was time to have something to eat before returning to her lodging, she reached below the table for her voluminous leather purse and pulled out her cellphone to see what time it had gotten to be.

Just then, she heard an insistent banging on the metal gate downstairs. Glancing at her right hand, she was shocked to see that when she'd absently put her mobile phone in silent mode during another staff meeting yesterday, she'd never changed it back! Having completely forgotten she'd silenced it herself, she'd simply expected it to ring if anyone called during the hectic day that followed.

Meanwhile, the banging on the gate had grown louder and she heard a voice shouting in a distinctive southern drawl, *"Prego! Prego! La Signorina Antonelli è qui?"*

She experienced a rush of happiness that nearly took her breath away. Bolting from her chair, she dashed to open the door and its gate on the upper landing that guarded the workshop's front entrance.

"Jack? *Giovanni?"* she cried. She pushed the gate outward, hurtling herself down the snow-slicked stone steps and fumbled at the latch of the lower gate. She flung it open and, without pausing to think, hurtled herself into Jack's waiting arms.

"*God*, am I glad to see you!" he exclaimed, and she felt him scattering kisses on top of her head, on her ear, and finally on her lips. "I thought maybe you'd thrown your cellphone into the canal."

"No…no," she said, trying to catch her breath. "My *stupido telefonino* has been in silent mode for almost two solid days, can you believe? I turned it off in a meeting yesterday and forgot to—"

"Jesus, Mary, and Joseph, Serena!" Jack exclaimed, hugging her to his chest, "I've been trying to reach you for hours. I thought maybe you were deliberately not taking my calls."

"You swear too much for a boy who went to Holy Cross," she said, tilting her head so she could nuzzle her lips beneath his ear.

Jack crushed her even harder against the front of his parka, kissing her passionately at the foot of the stairs that led up to the open door of the costume workroom. Meanwhile, the snow had turned to rain, pelting down on them in sheets.

"C'mon you madman," Serena declared, breathless. "Everyone's gone home for the night, but I can make you a cup of coffee, and—"

"I just need a cup of *you*," he mumbled into her hair, damp from the rain. "God, Serena, you had me going crazy!"

"You me too," she muttered, pushing the gate closed behind him. "C'mon…just let's get out of the rain." Frantically, they continued to kiss nonstop while moving, step-by-step, toward the beckoning warmth of the shop tucked under the eaves above the ground floor.

"You kiss great on stairs," he whispered as they arrived on the landing.

"Thanks to you, I'm getting a lot of practice," she mumbled, flashes of the way they went up the stairs at her lodgings a few days earlier flitting through her brain.

Once inside the door, Jack kicked it shut, turned her around, and pushed her back against its smooth wooden surface while he began a torturous journey nibbling from the base of Serena's neck to her lips where his kisses told her without words how much he'd missed her.

"I've just spent two days away from you regretting every second of my decision to sleep on top of that bedspread," he said hoarsely.

"Not thinking like such a noble gentleman tonight, are you?"

"No," he replied emphatically, his breath against her cheek, "especially when I couldn't get hold of you. And when I arrived back in Venice and you didn't answer at all, I haven't known *what* to think."

"You aren't thinking about Lauren, I take it?"

An arc of electricity pulsed between them.

"I have been, actually," he replied, "and here I am at your doorstep."

"It's just Venice," she scoffed gently. "We both had better watch out."

Jack pulled away, holding her by both shoulders.

"No," he said soberly, measuring each word. "It's not just Venice. I don't really know what it *is*...but it's something you and I should pay attention to, seems to me. Speaking strictly for myself, I've never felt like this before...this...compulsion...to find my way back to someone. Back to *you*," he amended.

Serena stared into Jack's eyes, startled to see a glint of moisture. Then she thought *he's just soaking wet*.

"Come. Sit right there," she commanded, pointing to a seamstress's chair surrounded by the chaos of bolts of cloth, tubs of beads, and piles of feathers. "But first, take off your coat...very carefully, if you don't mind. And anything else that's wet. Just hang your stuff on the pegs behind you so we don't get water on any of the costumes. I'll heat up some soup I think we have left over from lunch."

Serena discovered a few slices of bread and cheese in

the tiny kitchen alcove at the back of the shop, and put together a semblance of supper on a tray. Within minutes, she'd brought out two mugs filled with steaming minestrone as she began to describe the avalanche of work that had faced her all week.

Before she could even finish her sentence, Jack carefully placed both their soup cups on a nearby bench devoid of spangles or fabric, and then pulled her into his lap. His shirt was still damp, but all Serena noticed was the warmth of his chest pressed tightly against her ribcage and the side of her left breast. She clung to him, threading her fingers through his dark, damp hair, her every move revealing how glad she was he had arrived at her door at the moment crippling doubts about her feelings—and what she had begun to imagine were his—had started to overtake her.

"Jack…Jack," she said in a low voice, "it is *so* good to see you."

"Likewise…" he murmured into her ear. "Ah…*La Contessa*…who needs minestrone to warm up when I have you?"

He slipped a hand beneath the front of her sweater and sought to touch her breast beneath her bra. Again, bolts of electricity shot through her solar plexus and her breath caught.

"You are a devil, you know, to do that," she said, inhaling deeply to steady herself.

"Do what?" he teased.

"Make me all sparkly like this."

"Just how warm *is* my welcome?"

"About as warm as I feel yours is…" she replied, deliberately shifting her weight on his lap.

Jack chuckled and whispered, "Ah, so you've noticed my rising ardor, have you? Would you be offended if I told you I mastered enough Italian to secure a couple of condoms, just in case they might be called for one of these nights?"

Serena reared back, feigning shock.

"In a Catholic country? Now how did you do *that*?"

"I asked my new friend Maurizio who took me out to see the MOSE gates…and he kindly gave me several from his private stash."

"I hope you didn't name your intended quarry!"

"Of course not! A gentleman never reveals such information."

"Well, Maurizio sounds like an *amico simpatico*, for sure," she said, smiling. She kissed his nose. "And here's what *I* can contribute tonight," she announced, throwing caution to the winds. "There's a daybed upstairs. At the moment, it's covered with bolts of Fortuny velvet, but I'm sure we could…"

Jack leaned forward to kiss her once more, his lips and tongue insistent, asking silently, urgently, if she wanted him as much as he wanted her. She responded with an audible sigh and fiercely kissed him back, reveling in the touch and taste of him and the pleasure that was cascading down her spine. Finally, he lifted his head and smiled, his eyes boring into hers.

"Who needs a bed," he asked, his fingers seeking the button on her jeans, "when my lap is so handy?"

"And who said trained engineers have no sense of creativity?" Serena murmured.

"Ah…but I'm also a writer and I think we've both come to the same creative conclusion," he said, inserting the palm of his hand beneath her waistband.

"And that is?" she said, swallowing slowly.

"That making love right here on this nice chair is an inspired idea."

"Don't you want the rest of your soup?" she managed to gasp as his fingers caressing her abdomen moved steadily lower.

"First… *you*. Soup, later."

And I want you, too, Giovanni…her heart cried out, *however foolhardy this might prove to be.*

CHAPTER 9

Long before the seamstresses were due to arrive at the costume shop, Serena and Jack awoke in the daybed on the floor above the workshop. At some point during the previous evening they'd finally climbed the ancient flight of stairs to sink with exhaustion onto the piece of furniture that she jokingly called "The Fainting Couch."

"C'mon, *Contessa*," Jack suggested as pale shafts of snow-laden light filtered through the upstairs windows. "How about some breakfast?"

They held hands descending the steps from their tiny sleeping quarters and got dressed in the clothes they'd abandoned the previous evening. Jack retrieved his shirt from the back of the chair near Serena's cutting table.

"Here, let me help, Casanova," she said, fastening the top button for him and then handing him his coat from a peg on the wall.

"Well, I'm mighty flattered to be called that by a bona fide Italian," he declared, pulling her close, his parka nestled between them. "I guess you could say I had a lot of inspiration."

Serena gazed at him for a long moment. "Well, for me, anyway, last night was…wonderful. No, *amazing* is a more apt description."

Jack nodded slowly. "In actual fact," he said, brushing the backs of his fingers gently along her cheek, "it was a show stopper for me, too. You should also know that it was unlike anything I've ever experienced."

"Really?" she murmured, arching an eyebrow.

"Really."

"I guess we sort of 'forgot' about waiting until after you officially settled things with Lauren," Serena said with a look of chagrin.

"Yeah…so much for *that* New Year's Resolution. When you rushed toward me down the stairs in the rain, any thoughts other than wanting you, big time, flew right out of my brain."

Serena cast him a rueful look and admitted, "Me, too, you."

"But I want you to know, Serena, making a clean break—which I should have done months ago—will be first on my list when I get back home." He pulled her close again and kissed the top of her head. "But let's not talk about anything except what a total sex pot you turned out to be!"

"You, too, *Giovanni*…" In a move she was beginning to recognize, his kisses began at her ear, moved across her cheek, and migrated to her lips. "Uh-oh," she whispered.

"Here we go again, right?" he muttered.

Serena pulled away and gazed at him regretfully.

"We'd better get ourselves right out there into the snow and cool off, *Signor*."

"Otherwise…" he mumbled, nibbling her earlobe once more.

"Otherwise, very soon, you're likely to run into a bunch of inquisitive seamstresses. And besides, I completely forgot that I have something important to discuss with you."

Jack took a step back, a guarded look in his eye. Serena immediately sensed his unease and cast him a reassuring smile.

"I need you to help Allegra and me with something. I'll explain over a *caffè latte*. Let's get out of here before anybody arrives for work."

Bundled against the cold, they trudged through a foot of snow piled against one side of the embankment and entered a local café. Over strong coffee and plain biscotti,

Serena explained the latest dilemma facing the producer of the upcoming carnival ball. She quickly outlined the extent of the flooding at the rented *palazzo*, along with Allegra's problem getting the ball's venue into a condition that would satisfy the Venetian bureaucrats in the various ministries responsible for the building's safety and historic preservation.

"I meant to ask you before you left if you know any people through the Rising Waters Conference who could smooth the way with the government pests who are making some outrageous demands on poor Allegra. She only rents the building each year from absentee owners, but the bureaucrats say it's up to her to make it 'safe for habitation' if she wants to hold the ball there. Given that situation, is there any way you could also help us find workers experienced with making the *palazzo*'s lower floors watertight—since apparently, there's some leaking and damage?"

Jack nodded slowly, and she could see him turning over various strategies in his mind.

"As it happens, I met a few people on the trip out to inspect the gates that might actually be able to help. I'll call them before we leave here."

"You *will?* Oh, Jack, that's wonderful of you! Allegra will be so grateful, and so will I—"

"Sweetheart, it's you I'm grateful for," Jack intervened, leaning toward her across the minuscule round marble table that separated them. He raised his hand and gently touched her bottom lip. "So sweet…such a tender, generous lover you are…"

"As you've noted, artists need inspiration," she murmured, "and last night provided plenty of that from you, *Giovanni.*" As Jack lowered his hand, Serena raised her wrist and showed him her watch. "Time to go. Will you come with me and speak to Allegra about the next steps we should take at the *palazzo?*"

"Absolutely. *Andiamo, cara.*"

"Yes, let's go. Your Italian is getting so much better," she teased him.

"But before we vamoose, give me ten more minutes to make a couple of calls."

During the night Serena and Jack had spent at the costume shop, another storm had moved in off the Adriatic, dumping even more snow on the entire city. She gazed at the continuing flurries through the windows at the café, listening with rapt attention while Jack contacted by mobile phone several people he knew through the conference. To her relief, they immediately pledged to help him sort through and find solutions for the problems of the leaking *palazzo*.

"You are amazing!" she said admiringly when he hung up from talking to a contractor who supplied him with both cost estimates for labor and materials, along with the promise of a work crew that could arrive on site as soon as they received the go-ahead.

"I guess they liked my speech the other night," he said with a modest shrug. "The costs are only guesstimates, mind you. The guys first must see the actual building, but flooded basements are not a new problem here in Venice, as you can imagine."

"At least we have some ball park figures to give Allegra, to say nothing of a list of warm bodies who might be able to do the actual remedial work. As for those bureaucrats and inspectors…?"

"I'll call a few other folks I know after we see Allegra."

The pair paid for their breakfast and piled on their coats once again. Serena led the way tramping through the slush to the *San Tomà* stop where they boarded the boat that would take them to *Piazza San Marco* and Allegra's central office near her retail stores in the heart of the tourist section of the city.

By the time Serena and Jack walked into the door at *Il Ballo*'s headquarters, they both were covered in nearly an inch of cold, white powder. One of Allegra's staff promptly took their coats and another supplied them with more coffee.

"Come, come," bid Allegra from the top of a circular metal stairway to the floor above where she had a private office and her large, slanted drafting table. "Welcome to Purgatory," she joked as they entered her lair, gesturing to the piles of sketches and file drawers. "I am delighted to meet you, Jack, and am so grateful for anything you can do to help us with these *molti problemi*."

Jack quickly explained that he'd just spoken with several Italian friends of his in the field of construction and hydraulic engineering.

"Maurizio Pigati said he and a few colleagues of his are happy to offer whatever expertise and supervision they can—gratis—given that *Il Ballo di Carnevale* has brought thousands of tourists and virtually millions of euros to *La Serenissima* in the last twenty years."

"That is so kind of them…and you," she murmured.

"Of course, there still will be the costs of actually repairing the leaks," Serena hastened to add, "and at this stage we can only guess what that will be."

She offered Allegra a sheet of paper filled with calculations that she and Jack had hastily assembled while they were at the café having breakfast.

Allegra gazed from her American 'shadow', as she had

taken to calling her new assistant, to the handsome, dark-haired fellow sitting opposite her desk and shook her head in amazement.

"I am astonished and grateful beyond words and think your friend, here, Serena, is nothing short of a savior."

Jack held up a warning hand.

"We can only see if there is some solution available…some temporary measures to get you through February. Please understand that until Maurizio and his group survey the problem, he isn't even sure he can do much, but at least we will all try our best for the sake of your enterprise, Mrs. Benedetti."

Allegra leaned forward, both hands on her desk, and said earnestly, "We must do what we can. The cost of the laborers and materials to make the necessary repairs are just part of the price of putting on the ball. I'm sure that the *palazzo*'s owners will be happy, too, to have the free advice of your experts, so *mille grazie*, Jack," she assured him with a warm smile. "And do call me Allegra," she added.

"And why won't the owners shoulder some of the costs?" Serena demanded.

Allegra heaved an audible sigh and said, "They know *I'll* pay. I've been doing it for twenty years, now. They know I have no choice if I want to hold the ball. The owners are always away in winter when the flooding occurs," she added, shaking her head in a classic Italian gesture of "This is Venice." Then her expression grew grave once more.

"Something else is worrying you?" Jack asked.

"Besides solving the obvious problem of the *palazzo* potentially flooding even more than it has, there are the Venetian building and permitting officials I've been dealing with," Allegra explained. She rubbed her thumb and forefinger together, indicating the manner in which much of the business between entrepreneurs and government officials was often conducted in Italy.

Jack offered Serena's mentor a nod of understanding.

"I have a few other friends of mine who know about such things," he said obliquely. "I'll find out what they can do to quiet the barking dogs. Can you share with me the names and titles of these officials who've been pestering you?" he asked with a wink.

"Of course," Allegra replied and directed her assistant to print out a list with the appropriate contact information.

Jack took a last sip of his coffee and set his cup on the desk while Allegra scanned the list that her assistant handed to her and passed it over to him.

"Well," he said, rising to his feet and giving Serena's shoulder an affectionate squeeze. "I'd better be off and meet with Maurizio and Stefano, who insist they have 'friends in high places.'"

"Let's just hope they do," Serena said fervently.

Jack spent the next two days in Venice skipping the concluding sessions of the Global Rising Waters Conference, and instead, joined Maurizio Pigati surveying the site, along with a young, volunteer Italian engineer and contractor in his mid-thirties named Stefano Fabrini that he'd also met on the trip out to see the MOSE gates. Jack disguised a smile when he met up with the younger man who was the epitome of a sexy Italian. Of medium height, broad-shouldered, with a muscular physique, aquiline nose, a full head of dark blond hair, the charismatic *Signor* Fabrini had a habit of whistling at every half-way attractive female they encountered on the way to the *palazzo*.

Both Stefano and Maurizio Pigati were graduates of the same polytechnic college—though fifteen years apart. The Venetians had swiftly gathered a few additional colleagues to analyze the seepage problem and seek ways to prevent any more water leaking into the building.

Meanwhile, Jack figured the best way to extend his stay in Venice in order to help with the projects—to say nothing of staying close to Serena—was to persuade his editor, John Reynolds, to allow him to file a story about getting his hands dirty in the actual work of trying to remedy the results of storm surge in this most celebrated of water-locked cities.

In his email to his boss, he emphasized the pressing need to get the job done in time for Carnival. To his amazement and pleasure, he not only received a thumbs-up from Reynolds to follow developments at the *palazzo*, but also was granted two extra days to report and update on a story he'd done two years earlier about the construction of the massive MOSE Project.

"I agree," Jack had answered his editor. "Both pieces form perfect, cautionary tales for New Orleans, given the sorry tale of New Orleans officials—both corrupt and legitimate—who have squabbled for decades over how best to strengthen our own city's defenses against the next big storm surge."

Encouraged by Reynolds' positive response, Jack dug out of his electronic files an email he'd sent his boss on the eve of his departure from New Orleans for the conference. He reminded his editor of the startling parallels between the two cities with hopes that Reynolds might even assign him additional stories. Inhaling a deep breath, he pushed the Send key and sent a silent prayer into cyberspace that his marshaling these facts once again would keep him in Italy a while longer.

As I wrote in an earlier emailed memo before I left NOLA, Venice and New Orleans both have:

* *World-renown annual Mardi Gras/ Carnival celebrations*

* Frequent Hurricanes/Acqua Alta
* Wetlands and barrier islands—damaged and/or disappearing
* Serious threats of rising water drowning both cities within 50-100 years
* Gigantic flood containment projects: levees, canals/mobile gates
* History of engineering decisions influenced by "special interests"
* Significant water traffic and commerce in two key national seaports causing significant environmental damage
* Historic health threats: plague/yellow fever
* Significant crime and reputations for crooked police officers
* History of high-level governmental corruption and graft (both city Mayors recently indicted for nefarious deeds)
* Major cathedrals/basilicas: St. Marks/St Louis
* Catholicism as a leading religious and cultural factor
* Unique boats: gondolas/pirogues
* Love of music: opera/jazz
* Famous musicians: Vivaldi/Armstrong, etc.
* Noteworthy cuisines: i.e. Gumbo/Pasta
* Tourist meccas threatened by overwhelming numbers of visitors
* Similar "Let the Good Times Roll" revelry lifestyles
* Bottom line: Irreplaceable cultures…

Now that I'm actually here in Venice, I'm more convinced than ever that some of the above might provide a new angle for our 10th anniversary coverage, or at least provide a sidebar or two? Something to think about, anyway.

Cheers,
Jack

John Reynolds' answer by way of a phone text told Jack he'd pushed his editor about as far as he could.

All right, already, Durand! You made your

> **case! Spend some extra time looking into the match-ups you mentioned. I'll talk to the brass about our anniversary coverage and pass along your list, but no promises. They're already considering alternatives and so I'll have to get back to you about how they intend to deal with August 29th this year.**

The good news was that Jack's two-day reprieve had been increased to two more weeks to research the leaking palazzo and the MOSE gates stories, as well as nose around on subjects that related directly to catastrophic flooding and corruption in both cities.

> **…but don't screw around, Jackie Boy…and get me some decent photos, capisce? I want to see people, not just buildings and machines. Make these human stories, got it?**

Jack's heart went into overdrive at earning Reynolds' okay to stay on in Venice another two *weeks*! He wrote back to his boss that he'd look more deeply into the history of the thirty-year delay getting the Venetian floodgates operational and the most recent hiccup involving the arrest of the Mayor of Venice on charges of malfeasance in office. He hastened to assure his editor that he'd also dive into the hands-on efforts of the local volunteer Italian experts to stem the liquid seepage at the *palazzo* in the lead up to the ball and send along pictures to document their efforts.

There was a third reason Jack rejoiced that he was staying on in Venice. His antennae had instantly become aware of building engineer Stefano Fabrini's obvious appreciation of the "lady bosses" with whom his convention colleagues were now working on this pro bono project. It was especially apparent that whenever the two women arrived on the scene, Stefano's practiced flirtations went into high gear.

As for Jack, any niggling thoughts that he should do the honorable thing and distance himself from Serena until he'd officially broken off with Lauren seemed ridiculous. A day after the project began, Jack managed to get Maurizio alone and grilled him about Fabrini, who seemed particularly drawn to Allegra's American assistant.

"Oh, Stefano fancies himself a bit of a charming Casanova," chortled Maurizio. "You know the kind. He passionately loves the *signorina* he's with…until someone else catches his roving eye. Mrs. Benedetti recognizes the type, I'm sure." Maurizio, a man Jack judged was in his early fifties, shrugged and smiled knowingly. "I was exactly the same way at his age, which is why my *sposa* and I don't quite make the perfect, romantic couple these days, *capisci?*"

Later that afternoon, after spending the day in waist-high rubber waders working alongside Stefano in the lower floors of the leaky *palazzo*, Jack texted the news to Serena that he'd be in Venice another two weeks and that his editor needed professional-quality photos to go with both newspaper stories.

Serena texted back that she and Allegra had made a short but choppy trip across the water to Fortuny's showroom on the Island of *Giudecca* to secure a few more needed bolts of luxurious silks and velvets. On the trip over, Allegra had assured that her staff photographer would be glad to contribute images to Jack's newspaper. Problem solved.

Then the words *Fortuny's showroom is heavenly!* next appeared in the message app on his cellphone.

Can't wait to take these ideas back to Antonelli's! And btw: SO happy you can stay 2 weeks!! Dinner 10p.m. at Trattoria S. Tomà?

Si, bella... he texted in return, relieved to see that Stefano had not persuaded her to have dinner with him, as he suspected he might have by now under the guise of discussing problems at the palazzo.

At their late supper that evening, Serena again expressed her pleasure that his newspaper assignments would prolong his stay in Venice.

"It's fantastic you'll be here a while longer!" she enthused. "Maybe you can drag out your research and interviews long enough to be my date for the ball?" she added with a teasing but hopeful smile, her fork full of risotto half way to her mouth.

"Well, at the rate we're going, you never know," he replied, reaching across the table to squeeze her hand. "So far, Maurizio can't seem to pin down those government officials who were giving Allegra such a rough time. But at least, we've finally determined where the water's seeping in."

"Did Stefano and Maurizio figure out the best way for the construction workers to keep it from filling the lower floors whenever a heavy tide rolls in?"

"Not yet," Jack admitted. "There are all sorts of sealants on the market these days, but this is an historic building, so they'll have to get approval from the building's owners and the Powers-That-Be before they actually apply anything."

Serena gave a small, worried moan while she chewed. "Venice could be underwater by the time we locate the owners in Morocco and those Venetian officials make any decisions."

Jack nodded. "And, our guys also have to consider what may happen if we get another five or six inches of snow or rain right before the ball."

"I just hope your friends can figure it out in time," she responded with an anxious frown. "I haven't dared tell my mother I'm working in a city where I haven't taken off my rubber boots a single day! She might take to drink again if she knew about the floodwaters we've had to wade through all this time," she added with a smile, though Jack could see she was only half-joking. Then she asked, "By the way, what do you hear about your sister Sylvia?"

"She's still in rehab, but my mother says that, alone, is good sign."

"It is," Serena said, her encouraging smile filling him with hope.

"I guess it was a smart move that I didn't try to ride to the rescue," Jack acknowledged ruefully. "I've got you to thank for that."

Serena ducked her head and then replied, "Fingers crossed Sylvia will see there's so much more to life staying sober. As for Sarah Kingsbury Antonelli," she added with a smile, "I just tell her everything here is just fine—and it is, except for the endless snow. Thank heavens she doesn't use Google to check on the weather."

"Speaking of the Kingsburys," Jack mused. "I should get in touch with King and ask him if he has any experience with sealants used in historic buildings."

"Oh, please do…that would be great!" Serena replied. "After all, I've sort of worked it out and I think my mother and King's mother, Antoinette, are second cousins, one removed, or something like that—which probably makes your best friend King and me third cousins."

Well," Jack replied, raising his glass of wine. "This makes…what? Serendipity number one thousand?"

Serena smiled in recognition of their on-going joke. Then she grew pensive.

"Too bad King Duvallon isn't here right now," she said, staring into her wine glass. "After the storm, he must have dealt with a lot of water damage in those old buildings." She looked up at Jack with an eager nod. "Yes, do please call him soon," she repeated.

The next day, Jack sent a lengthy email to King describing the situation in the lower floors of the waterlogged palazzo and asking the historic preservationist for recommendations about products that would both be effective in keeping water out and, hopefully, pass muster with the local Italian permitting authorities. Within an hour of receiving Jack's electronic SOS, King replied that it would take some research to determine if conditions in Venice differed in significant ways from the work he'd done in New Orleans, but he'd get back to him as soon as he'd gathered any useful information.

※

Every day during Jack's extended stay in Venice, he and Serena met late in the evening after their hard days' work, rendezvousing at various small *trattorias* that Jack knew. Their action-packed days spent working on their respective projects were heightened by nights filled with romantic walks beside the canals and through snow-covered squares toward their ultimate destination—a golden, silk draped bed and the wonder of perfectly matched passion that each, now, acknowledged they urgently felt for the other. Every night, Jack set his cellphone alarm to rouse him before sunrise from a deep sleep with his arms around Serena. And each morning, he rose swiftly, dressed for the cold, and silently padded the one flight downstairs, slipping out from the guesthouse unnoticed.

Yet, simmering just below the surface, Jack sensed their mutual recognition that not only were they falling in love while the clock was ticking in the shadow of his imminent departure, but that the ghost of Lauren Hilbert had not entirely disappeared for either one of them. Even so, neither had the heart—nor the courage—to broach the subject and spoil the perfection of the beautiful snow bubble that had encased their limited time together.

Then, during the second week of Jack's lengthened assignment in Venice, he suddenly confronted some additional and very disturbing parallels between *La Serenissima* and New Orleans that he couldn't ignore in the way he had the unfinished business with Lauren.

Following several interviews with reluctant subjects about the decades of delays associated with the mammoth MOSE project in the Venice Lagoon, Jack spent an afternoon reading online about the June, 2014 indictment of the Mayor of Venice. The not-so-Honorable Giorgio Orsoni and several cronies had been accused of bribery and diverting public monies linked to the construction of the enormous metal barriers designed to prevent the mayor's own city from flooding.

Jack's eyes widened in amazement when he read that an alleged 34 million euros in pay-offs had supposedly been given to certain favorite contractors who also had been "supporters" in Orsini's latest re-election campaign.

Do these politicians never learn? Jack thought with disgust, recalling the trial of New Orleans Mayor Ray Nagin on charges of corruption, post-Katrina. In Nagin's case, the accusations of public malfeasance resulted in a conviction that same year—in 2014—of a jail sentence of ten years in Federal prison on twenty felony counts, including bribery, wire fraud, and tax evasion, among other crimes.

Jack quickly pulled up an online account of the Nagin trial as a sinking feeling invaded the pit of his stomach. He scrolled through the material, sensing that here was a crucial aspect to the New Orleans part of the story he'd pitched to his editor. With an increasing sense of dread, he confronted a line of inquiry he'd yet to thoroughly explore regarding the corruption-riddled construction delays and under-engineering of projects during many, long decades in his own water-rimmed city.

And if I do explore it, what if it leads right back to my own doorstep?

Could the tortured tale of the bribery of Venetian government, construction, and engineering officials connected to the Venetian MOSE project mirror some of the Big Easy's efforts to keep rising waters at bay? When it came to committing malfeasance and fraud, how similar to the Italians' behavior was that of NOLA's bureaucrats, administrators, levee board "watchdogs," and certain members of the U.S. Army Corps of Engineers?

What if digging into the long history of the failure of structures designed to keep Gulf and river waters out of his hometown could be laid at the feet of those who made the crooked deals for under-engineered projects—or failed to report those who *did*?

Uncle Jacques Durand worked as an engineer in the Corps office during those years...and he has ducked every question I've ever asked him about it!

And then there was Jack's Uncle Vincent and the levee board.

Hoping against hope his reporter's instincts were wrong, he quickly searched his laptop computer for a particular file of his own and stared at the glowing screen.

CHAPTER 10

Jack scanned through the last section of his Pulitzer-Prize-winning story written three years before Hurricane Katrina had changed New Orleans forever.

Holy shit! This is unbelievable! My subconscious *must have written this stuff…*

He scrolled back to the top of the file and carefully re-read, paragraph by paragraph, his bylined, multi-part article that had appeared in the *Times-Picayune* eerily predicting a disastrous storm that unfolded almost exactly as he'd forecasted it would. However, it was his own conclusions at the end of the piece that gripped him with a sense of foreboding unlike anything he'd ever experienced.

The Big Money involved in huge state and federal construction projects often spawn Big Corruption. Add to this the minor foot soldiers in public service that might stand in the way of the tsunami-like wave that Big Money channels into the building of levees and canals.

The views and opinions—and even solid engineering facts—known by these underlings are often swept aside by the incoming tide of irresistible greed on the part of certain corporate interests, along with government officials who control these subordinates' professional futures.

And thus, the underlings—who know better—fail to blow the whistle on their unethical bosses and, tragically, under-engineered projects get built despite so-called "public safe-guards" that politicians claim are in place.

The "minor foot soldiers" in the tale of the New Orleans' canals collapsing might very well include the likes of Jacques and Vincent Durand, his elderly uncles whose earlier careers were enmeshed with projects designed to strengthen the city's defenses against storm-driven rising water.

The very waters that crashed through the walls and swept away Serena's family...

Jack leaned back in his chair and drew a shaky breath, his mind racing toward the many lines of inquiry he'd have to conduct back home, none of them pleasant. Then, instead of contacting Serena about where he wanted to take her to dinner that evening, he texted her that he had to work late.

He spent the rest of the evening making further Internet searches to refresh his memory about the details of the Nagin corruption trial that a colleague had covered for his newspaper. Then, he scrolled through scores of pages of local accounts, as well as national publications that chronicled a cast of dirty American scoundrels who had robbed private and governmental recovery funds for their own, personal use. Finally, he ran another probe on the web about state and federal post-Katrina efforts initiated by several Blue Ribbon panels to understand exactly *what* had caused the colossal failures of levees and canals, and why, in the minds of some experts, the recently *rebuilt* structures still had deficiencies.

The parallels with Venice are so obvious, he thought, with a rising sense of anger and dismay. Without a doubt, some local, regional, and federal officials, along with their lowly lieutenants in both countries, had blood on their hands.

Jack typed in a new search term that pulled up documents specifically relating to the U.S. Army Corps of Engineers' structures that had collapsed in the wake of Hurricane Katrina. After twenty more minutes clicking through a number of reports, he knew unequivocally that there was no dodging the issue.

How could he, in good conscience, write this story

about criticisms of Italian attempts to stem coastal flooding without sitting down with his uncle, retired Army Corps engineer Jacques Durand, to press him for an unvarnished account of the history of repairs and "design adjustments" made in 1982 on the 17th Street and London canals? After all, these catastrophic failures to stem Katrina's storm surge had wiped out major sections of Lakeview, the same suburb where Serena's brother, wife, and unborn nephew had drowned.

As for Uncle Vincent, Jack had long described him to his friends as a good ole' boy that had enjoyed many a delicious free lunch with his fellow levee board members. He and his cronies were famous for skipping—or giving short-shrift—to scheduled inspections of the levees they supposedly oversaw in favor of another glass of bourbon and branch water on the house. Jack couldn't in good conscience file a story on the threat of another catastrophe back home without grilling the elder Durand about his role in the way levee board business was conducted prior to 2005.

Given the amount of digging these assignments were going to require to meet his editor's deadline, there was no ducking this. He'd better head back to New Orleans on the double. Maurizio had the *palazzo* project well in hand, and once the best sealant and cover coating were decided upon, his team could effect a "fix," if only a temporary one.

Unbidden, a vision of the good-looking Stefano Fabrini leapt to the front of Jack's raft of gloomy thoughts. He had caught the handsome Italian casting increasingly warm, interested glances in Serena's direction whenever she came to the *palazzo*. Fabrini would also be at the ball, no doubt. If Jack weren't in attendance, the lothario would probably even offer to escort the visiting American, if given half the chance.

But surely, what Jack and Serena had begun in Venice

would make the transition back home, wouldn't it?

Jack stared at his computer screen, overcome by a sudden stab of fear. If his uncles Jacques or Vincent had played a role in the sorry saga of how the two canals had caved in and swept away Cosimo Antonelli V's family, there would *be* no future with Serena—the issue of his relationship with Lauren Hilbert notwithstanding.

Jack remembered all too clearly holding Serena sobbing in his arms after she'd seen the aerial views of her brother's neighborhood inundated by water. How could she give her heart or ally herself to a man whose family members might be a direct, or even indirect, cause of the worst tragedy her own family had ever endured?

Jack stared, unseeing, at a diagram of the two canals bordering Lakeview, Louisiana that he'd pulled up on his laptop, full screen.

Before—or if—he could ever propose to Serena that they spend a lifetime together, *first* he had to uncover two truths: what did his uncles know, and when did they know it?

It was long after midnight when Jack used Serena's second key to slip upstairs, unseen, to the *Canaletto* room at her lodgings. He stood quietly beside the gold colored brocade coverlet folded neatly at the bottom of the bed and gazed down at her dark, shoulder-length hair fanned across the pillow. Her hand was curled, childlike, under her chin. A small frown furrowed her forehead above arched eyebrows and lids that disguised the liquid brown irises that so beguiled him.

From her steady breathing, he sensed the extent of her exhaustion from working fourteen-hour-days at the atelier assisting with some fifty costumes Allegra had designed for the ball since the first of the year. Her deep sleep was also occasioned by her other job: toiling at the main office, helping her mentor with anything and everything connected with producing the grand event that was fast approaching.

And then there had been his nights spent with her, here, in this beautiful, silk-draped bedroom, exploring not only their bodies, but also craving to truly know one another, heart and soul.

Jack was grateful that the moment for the two of them to discuss in specific detail what he intended to do about Lauren Hilbert and what might develop between them after that had never seemed to present itself. Given what had developed in front of his computer screen this day, he'd felt compelled to book an earlier flight back to New Orleans. Gazing down at Serena, now, he despaired of finding a way to tell her about the role his uncles may have played so long ago, a chain of possible events that had risen before him, tonight, like long-dead corpses floating in a canal.

In the thirty-six hours before he would board Air France's flight out of Marco Polo Airport, he still had a couple of interviews to complete about the sins of the Mayor of Venice. Then he would leave Venice—and Serena—to fly home to face Lauren.

...And God knows what else, he reflected, a feeling of dread burrowing deep inside his chest.

He took in the sight of the woman he knew, now, he loved deeply. How could he possibly say goodbye without warning her what might lie ahead? Yet, he shouldn't tell anyone about his suspicions until he was sure of his facts, or risk unfairly slandering members of his own family. And if the worst happened: his uncles became part of the story he was assigned to tell for his newspaper, journalistic ethics would forbid him revealing, prior to publication, the source of his explosive information to anyone, including the woman he wanted to make his wife.

Serena's peaceful, sleeping form and the potent combination of her beauty, humor and kindness that he'd observed in her everyday actions only served to depress him further. There had never been anyone like this woman in his entire life, he thought as a sense of despair swept over him.

That's why I could never commit to marriage with Lauren or anyone else, for God's sake! Somehow I knew to wait for this.

Serena Antonelli had a flair not only for exquisite costume design and the management of the atelier, but also an amazing talent for friendship with Allegra, her co-workers—and *him*—to say nothing of the way she stirred both sexual and emotional sensations in him that he'd never before felt.

You are one in a million, my darling Serena, he thought, shocked to feel moisture fill his eyes.

The damnable problem was…he knew, now, with absolute certainty that he wanted what *she* wanted! For the first time in his life he could see himself with a wife and children and a future that they'd both glimpsed during this time in Venice.

But, given what you learned tonight, that's a long, long way off, pal…

If—for *whatever* reason—he couldn't step up to the plate with a woman like her, wasn't it better that he just go home and let things gently taper off, as they had so often in his life? He knew without question that what the two of them had been experiencing in Venice could certainly end in a life-long commitment.

But what if Jacques and Vincent…

He'd begun to think in circles. It all came back to the truth that if either of his uncles had contributed to the deaths of Serena's brother and his wife, he, Jack, would have to let her go.

Serena stirred and burrowed more deeply under the covers. Jack wanted nothing more than to crawl in beside her…knowing she would awake and fiercely pull him to her.

Steeling himself to remain where he was, he was paralyzed by the thought that if he simply dropped off the radar once Serena returned to their hometown—and because of the journalistic constraints surrounding his job—didn't tell her *why* he'd had to take such an action, he would be wounding her far more grievously than anything Marco Leone had ever done to her.

Even so, until he could chase down all the facts that potentially linked his investigations in Venice with past events in New Orleans, it was probably kinder, and the better of two lousy choices, to take a quiet step back *now*, while he still could. As Lauren had only made too plain: a woman in her thirties had a biological clock ticking so loud, a man Jack's age could hear it in his sleep. There was no doubt in his mind he would officially break it off with Lauren as soon as he saw her again, but the mere thought of pulling a disappearing act on Serena—even if it turned out to be an act of mercy—was abhorrent.

But face it, Jack! You don't have any choice at this point.

He continued to gaze at Serena, grateful she was spared the storm of thoughts swirling in his head. He would think of a non-confrontational way to make an exit. He would figure out how to leave her in Venice without promising a future together until he could be sure they could even *have* one.

Jack felt moisture fill his eyes again, knowing his only way to let her down gently was simply to play the elusive role he was famous for—and which she was bound to believe. Hopefully, she'd eventually surmise that if he'd broken it off with her, it certainly wasn't because of anything she'd done wrong. Actually, *he* hadn't done anything wrong, either, but that wouldn't matter, would it? It was a classic case of "bound by circumstances," but she certainly would never trust him again.

God, what a mess!

Jack did a silent about-face and retreated down the stairs, slipping out the front door of *Ca' Arco Antico* as a light dusting of snow once more began to fall, with a promise of more to come.

Serena awoke the next morning, surprised to see that the covers on the other side of her bed were smooth and obviously not slept in. She glanced at the door to the bathroom. It remained open. The shower wasn't running, nor was the light on.

Jack had never showed up.

More than a little puzzled and then concerned, she grabbed for her cellphone that was charging on the other side of the room. The little red dot told her there was a text message.

Worked late. Solid day of interviews ahead. T-P deadline dictates early flight Tuesday. 6:30 at the Danieli tonight, okay?

Serena stepped out of her rubber boots in the ladies cloak room and slipped on a pair of sexy little sling-back heels she'd brought with her in her leather tote. Checking her heavy coat, gloves, and cashmere scarf with the waiting attendant, she reentered the spectacular lobby of the Danieli Hotel, marveling at the soaring, cream-colored ceilings studded with gilt entablature.

A broad staircase with crimson carpeting flowed down from the base of a series of arches on the floor above. A couple of masked, costumed figures in Italian Renaissance attire the color of red wine gazed down at her from the balcony, just two representatives of the legions of revelers bedecked in all manner of historical regalia that appeared without warning everywhere in Venice during the run-up to Fat Tuesday.

In the lobby itself, waist-high stone columns scattered around the massive public space held four-feet-high displays of flowers fanning out from carved stone vases that appeared to be from Roman times. She quickly located the elevator that whisked her up to the Danieli's famed *Ristorante Terrazza,* its floors also blanketed in the same crimson carpet as the hotel's lobby, but on this level were spectacular views of the Grand Canal in every direction.

Jack was already seated at an intimate table-for-two that was clad in creamy linen and overlooked a broad window and the snow-covered terrace outside. The gray, chilly waters of the canal were barely visible through the early evening gloom.

In fact, it seemed strange to Serena to be eating at such an early hour. Jack's terse text mid-afternoon explaining that he'd have to get up at four in order to catch his early morning flight back to New Orleans had signaled something was afoot. In a later message, he'd also apologized for not being able to come to her lodgings "due to deadlines, etc." She was unsettled by his uncharacteristic behavior and felt as if she needed to don some sort of emotional armor—but for what?

Before she took the chair that the waiter had pulled back for her, she placed her hand on Jack's to prevent him having to stand up from the table. Then she leaned down and kissed him on both cheeks.

"*Buona sera, Giovanni.* I definitely like your choice of a

place to bid a fond farewell," she said by way of greeting, sensing her eyebrow had arched of its own accord.

Jack glanced at her with an odd expression, and then quickly looked down at the menu she'd seen him studying as she crossed the restaurant to his table in this quiet corner. Without further comment, he waited for her to be seated and engaged their server, who spoke excellent English, in a long discussion of the chef's specials that evening.

Serena silently watched both men, instantly wary that an inexplicable distance had bloomed between her dinner companion and herself. When the server nodded in her direction, in rapid Italian she placed her dinner order for *orecchiette con amorini,* a traditional dish of tiny caps of pasta they both loved. Then she asked for a bottle of *Prosecco* to be brought to the table immediately. The waiter nodded and made his exit.

A brief silence ensued. Then, Serena spoke up before Jack could.

"Okay. What's up?" she asked without preamble. "You didn't warm my bed last night and you booked the earliest flight you could to get out of here tomorrow morning. And don't think I didn't notice that you actually flinched when I kissed you just now. Why?"

At that inopportune moment, the sommelier arrived and placed two flutes on the table. Both diners fell silent as the server stepped forward proffering a frosty bottle from which he poured them each a glass of Italian "champagne." To Serena, the click of the bottle being stowed in a silver ice bucket near Jack's side sounded thunderous. A few more seconds ticked by. She remained silent.

"Cheers," Jack said, finally, raising his glass.

"Not really," Serena replied, not lifting hers.

She waited, her glass on the table.

"My editor—" he began.

She held up her hand to silence him.

"Let's just not do this," she said, measuring out each word. "Let's not talk about work deadlines 'and etcetera,' okay? Just give it to me straight, Jack. Something's going on with you. What is it?"

She could see he was taken aback by her blunt assessment of the atmosphere between them.

"I should have known," he said, toying with his silver knife next to a gold-encrusted dinner plate, "that I couldn't make this easy for either of us."

"Make what easy?"

"Saying goodbye."

"Why should it be hard, unless it really *is* goodbye—and why would that be?"

When the silence grew between them again, she waited, but Jack continued to stare at his knife.

"So what's the problem here?" she pressed. "This is feeling very weird…as if my time is up and Jack Durand is heading for the exit." Jack shot her a look that was unreadable. "You're not shifting into your legendary Mr. Elusive mode, are you?"

Serena could tell by his hunched shoulders that he was a very unhappy man—but why?

"I realize that's been my reputation," he allowed, "but this time it feels…it felt…totally different."

"Well? *Is* it different *this* time or not, Jack?"

She saw him suppress a sigh.

"We can't avoid the truth, Serena, which is that I never made a clean break with Lauren—"

"Well…make it!" she interrupted. "A clean break. But what you're telling me is old news. There's something else going on, Jack. What *is* it?"

He shifted his weight in his chair and she could practically see the wheels going around in his head as he searched for an answer he thought would satisfy her.

"I guess…" he said on a long breath, "I guess I…I *do* need some time to work through all…this. Time and space to figure everything out."

"To figure out *what*, Jack? How you feel about me? I know how I feel about *you*. Nothing complicated on *this* side of the table."

He began to stroke the silver knife with his right, index finger.

"You think it's that simple?" he challenged her. "You surprise me a bit, Serena, considering what you've been through before. Don't you think you could use a break to evaluate our time here in Venice? After all, it's only been—"

"What an absolute crock!" she exclaimed, fighting to subdue a wave of woe that could easily result in her beginning to wail in the middle of the Danieli Hotel dining room. "Always hedging your bets, are you, Jack?"

Serena knew she was starting to sound petulant, but she couldn't help herself. Jack had now all but admitted he was, indeed, one of those emotionally unreliable characters that had been the bane of her adult life. Within a brief twenty-four hours he had made a complete about-face, intimating that it was she, and she alone, who had rushed into their relationship. She stared at him with bitter disappointment. What was unfolding in these beautiful surroundings was totally infuriating—and she felt blindsided.

Even so, if she were honest with herself, a tiny doubt had surfaced when he didn't turn up at *Ca' Arco Antico*. The texts he'd sent sounded an alarm bell that she'd obviously ignored, ascribing her feelings of unease as merely her old paranoia raising its ugly head. But *now…*

She felt an utter fool.

"Serena, we both knew from the start that Venice was having its way with us—"

"*I* was the one that first posed that possibility!" she

snapped. "*You* were the one who said to disregard it, but hey...I'm glad you're being so honest about your uncertainty concerning the two of us." She glared across the table at him, adding, "I just wish you'd declared that playing this exit card was your default M.O. *before* we made love at the atelier, and *prior* to my asking for help regarding the flooding at the *palazzo*."

"I wasn't 'playing' anything," he retorted.

She balled up her large, snowy linen napkin between both hands.

"Well, you know I'm the daughter of a dry drunk. I cannot deny that I've gotten mighty *addicted* to you, Jack Durand, to say nothing of your come-hither ways. Unfortunately, my faulty assumption, given everything that's happened between us, was that you felt the same. Your abrupt pullback, now, is definitely coming as a shock...but then—that's the chance we all take when we ignore the evidence, isn't it?"

"It's nothing you've done—"

"You *bet* it's nothing I've done—other than to ignore the facts!" she interrupted. "Your own sister sounded the warning at the airport. 'Meet my elusive brother, Jack.' I made the mistake of thinking, as things went along with us here, that this time it *was* different for you."

"Believe me, Serena, it's different!" he declared heatedly, and then lowered his voice to avoid garnering unwanted attention in the hushed dining room. "I've felt the exact same pull towards you, but the only sane thing to do at this juncture is for me first to deal with the situation with Lauren and—"

"And *what?*" she hissed, unable to hide her exasperation.

Jack hesitated and then replied with resignation, "See where we are with everything."

"Oh, puh-leez," she declared with undisguised sarcasm.

"This is just nuts!"

"You're probably right, and believe me, I'm well aware that I've had this particular character flaw of push-pull in the past."

"I thought you'd gotten over it," she replied softly and heard the catch in her voice.

Jack paused as if carefully debating his next words. Then he said, "So had I."

Serena's mind was racing with five different notions for how she could make an exit without causing a scene.

"I-I can't stay," she said, finally.

"Yes you can. Let's have a nice dinner. I *want* you to."

"You can't have what you want this time," she bit back, desperate to make her departure before the tears spilled down her cheeks. "Please give me back my key."

She carefully shook out her linen napkin and began to fold it in neat squares while she watched Jack dig in his pocket and place the key to the front door of her guesthouse between them on the table. After another long pause, Jack spoke first.

"Well, at least I hope you know that I'll do everything I can to help you with the seepage issue at the *palazzo*."

"Oh! What a comfort! You care about *seepage*?"

She flung her napkin at his chest.

"Serena…this isn't the way I—"

She cut him off.

"Now, here's some honesty back from *me*." She raised her right hand. "I swear upon Saint Mark and all the other holies around here that I will *never* again—as I did those years in Las Vegas—allow myself to pine an instant over an emotionally untrustworthy guy who can't—or doesn't chose—to be a central part of my life!"

She grabbed the key off the table, rose from her chair, and glanced toward the exit.

"Serena, look, I am so sorry for all this…"

She shot daggers down at him and continued as if he hadn't spoken.

"Trust me, I will soon recover from this *coitus interruptus* because the man I want is someone who also *pines* to be with me, like I do with him—you know what I'm saying?"

"I *do* pine."

"There you go again!" she protested. "Push-pull."

Before Jack could reply, Serena seized her purse from the floor and then rose to her full height beside their table.

"And by the way, what we're arguing about is not over future promises to each other or—God forbid—the 'M Word,' *marriage*, if that's what's triggered this insanity, though marriage is very much something I want in my life one day," she declared. "It's about knowing—without a single doubt—that the guy in my life *is* the guy in my life. That he has my back under any and all circumstances…and that I have his!"

She turned, but before she could take a step Jack pleaded, "Serena, please don't go. Maybe I should explain to you—"

"Any more of your 'explanations' will just make this worse!" she exclaimed over her shoulder. Then, she turned to face him again. "But I do want to thank you for warning me now, rather than when I got back to New Orleans, that you'd pull something like this. And if Lauren Hilbert ever gets wind of what happened between us here, you can just sing her that old song."

"What song?" Jack asked, looking as if he were actually trapped in the lowest rung of Dante's *Inferno*.

By this time, she was seething with anger at the notion that Jack had calculated he could avoid a scene simply by playing the "I-have-to-deal-first-with-Lauren-Hilbert" card. The plain fact was he simply was exhibiting his well-documented 'too close for comfort' emotional claustrophobia.

"Oh, you know that tune," Serena replied with a brittle

smile. "'*It was great fun…but it was just one of those things…*'"

"That's not how this was and you know it!"

"Do I? I'm sure Lauren will forgive you for this minor 'slip' because it sounds to me as if the long-distance toe dance you two have had going—where you've kept each other at arm's length for *years*—is exactly what both of you really *want*."

"It's not what *I* want, but—"

"*Jack*," she warned in a low tone of voice. "What's just happened here is not what I wanted either."

For some strange reason, she'd suddenly grown very calm. She put her purse's strap over her shoulder as if she were merely departing for a brief visit to the ladies room to refresh her make-up.

"Then why won't you sit down?" he urged, adding, "*Please*."

She ignored his request and replied quietly, "I'm glad you finally played it straight and told me tonight that you needed a break. What I need, though, is to put a period at the end of this particular sentence."

She realized she startled him by coming around to his side of the table, bending down, and lightly kissing him on both cheeks as she had when she'd arrived earlier. He *had* done her a favor, she told herself, fighting the lump in her throat that had grown the size of a *ravioli*. Knowing Jack during this brief, intense time had shown her that she could feel love again. It had demonstrated there was a possibility that there existed someone out there with whom she might want to share a life.

It just wasn't going to be Jack. And that fact nearly cut off her breath.

She stood back and drank in the sight of his face, handsome as always despite his expression of—what? Pained relief? Locking glances, she lectured herself to be thankful she'd only known him less than a month and that he'd awakened her from the beautiful, romantic, *impossible* dream that was Venice before she'd totally lost her heart and soul.

At least, she prayed that was true. Certain memories she'd shared with him, though, would last her a lifetime. But, she would get over this, she vowed silently. She'd done it before.

Gratitude, Serena. Feel thankful you are still able to experience such wonderful feelings of joy…and let it go this time…

"Serena, can't you just sit down and we can—"

"Goodnight." she murmured, firm in her resolve to get away from the table with her dignity intact. "Safe travels home, *Giovanni*. And thank you for recruiting Stefano and his crew. We can take it from here."

The disconcerted look on Jack's face at the mention of Stefano Fabrini morphed into a genuine grimace, although she hadn't a clue why that should be.

With a small shrug, Serena turned and—in an admirable display of poise, she thought—slowly walked out of the roof-top restaurant just as the waiter arrived at the coveted table by the window to serve their favorite first course, *orecchiette con amorini*.

CHAPTER 11

Jack recalled his flight back to New Orleans as one of loneliest twelve hours of his life. Fortunately, a text message with an invitation to dinner at the Duvallons his first night home awaited him as soon as he landed at Louis Armstrong International.

After their meal, King invited him onto the wrought iron gallery of his home that overlooked Dauphine Street in the Lower French Quarter.

"Here," King said, handing Jack a brandy. "I 'spect getting back to New Orleans feels like quite a change after all that snow in Venice you described tonight. It's amazingly balmy, here, for late January, don't you think? 'Bout fifty degrees this hour, the weatherman said."

"Is Corlis joining us?" Jack asked.

"She will in a minute. Since I did the cooking tonight, it's her turn to stack the dishes in the dishwasher," he said with a lazy smile.

Jack had always admired the rather egalitarian marriage between Louisiana's celebrated crusader to save historic buildings and New Orleans's best-known TV anchor. Both were busy people, just like Serena and him…but before his thoughts drifted too far in that direction, King bid him to take a seat in one of the wicker chairs.

"You said you wanted to ask me something?"

Jack nodded, deciding to get right to the point.

"Do you know—or have you ever met—Serena Antonelli?"

"From the costume company Antonelli's?" King asked, nodding affirmatively. "I know who she is, of course, but haven't met her, I don't think."

"Do you know that the two of you are cousins?"

King laughed. "Our family's been here so long, I'm cousins with practically everyone in New Orleans."

"Her mother was a Kingsbury."

"Yeah..." King said, looking thoughtful. "Actually, now that I think about it, I've heard Serena's name mentioned over the years, but my magnolia mama was never close to the women in her family. Too much competition, I guess."

Jack knew well the troubled relationships King had endured within his complicated family circle, so he merely nodded and made no further comment about Serena. However, King was clearly intrigued that Jack had asked about her.

"So...I take it *you* know her. How did you meet?"

"On the way to Venice."

"Well, well," he chuckled. "And did you see her while you were in that most romantic of cities?"

"Dinner a few times," Jack replied noncommittally, but King had caught the scent.

"And—?" his friend demanded in a teasing tone.

"She's a terrific, talented lady, but as a result of meeting her, I've got something else I've got to ask you."

King stopped smiling at the seriousness of Jack's tone and gazed at his friend with his full attention.

"Shoot."

Jack inhaled a deep breath. King was a few years older than he was and when it came to politics and public scandals, the crusader was deeply knowledgeable about where most of the bodies were buried in New Orleans.

"Do you have any first-hand information about the role either of my uncles may have played back in the day regarding the construction or maintenance of the Seventeenth Street and London canals?"

King looked startled by the question and then narrowed his gaze.

"Why are you interested in that subject after all these years?"

"Before I can answer that," Jack replied, "I have to stress that this is one of those 'Cone of Silence' conversations," he added, making an arc in the air above his head with both hands. "I'm actually violating journalist ethics naming a potential source on my story to anyone outside the *Times-Picayune*, but I *have* to talk to someone who'll understand what I'm up against, and you are my first and only choice."

King, for many years a lawyer who specialized in land use and saving the city's historic housing stock, grew grave.

"Look, Jack, I'll consider whatever you want to tell me privileged information. It won't leave this balcony, guaranteed."

King was his best friend. Corlis and her husband were the most trustworthy people he knew. Jack decided to come clean.

"I'm interested to find out if either of my uncles could legitimately—or even partially—be blamed for the canal and levee collapses because I learned that Serena Antonelli's brother, Cosimo, and his pregnant wife lived on Fortieth Street in Lakeview where they—"

"They drowned when the canals gave way," King intervened. "I read about it in your newspaper when it happened. Did you cover that story?"

"Thankfully, no. I was too busy on my environmental beat talking to scientists who were trying to figure out whether it was the wind or the water that caused so much damage during Katrina."

"But the role your uncles may or may not have played in this sorry history of the canals and levees is important to you *because*…?"

King let his sentence dangle and looked at Jack expectantly.

"Because I fell pretty hard for Serena Antonelli and it matters if my uncles had a hand in her brother's death."

"Whoa," King responded.

"Yeah...whoa...*big* time." Jack raised a warning hand. "It has obviously occurred to me that it would be a total non-starter if my family, in *any* way, was responsible for what happened to her brother, his wife, and their unborn child."

"That's mighty heavy," King agreed, his sympathy a welcome respite from Jack's thinking these thoughts on his own. "So, how did you leave it with the nice lady in Venice?"

"I didn't tell her about the possible connection, if that's what you're asking."

"It is. And why didn't you tell her?"

"I figured I should find out first if there *was* a connection—and then...deal with it. Complicating everything is that if my uncles *are* involved in this story, I can't tell anyone until my editor and I decide how the information will be used—and published."

"So when it occurred to you there might *be* a connection, you abruptly came back to New Orleans, leaving Serena—whom you've just told me you fell for hard—with no idea of this possible linkage between your families?"

"That is correct, and you're too damn smart."

Ignoring Jack's aside, King asked, "So, assuming she fell just as hard for *you*, she still thinks everything is a 'go' between you two, am I right?" Jack nearly winced in the wake of King's stern, disapproving look.

"She did until our last few days together...but not any more," Jack replied glumly. "I didn't call or see her for two days before I left, and she sensed, right away, during our last dinner together that something had gone wrong between us. Now, I 'spect, she just thinks I've cooled down on how I feel about her—and probably concludes it's because I'm a commitment-phobe, or something."

King remained silent as a sign he wanted Jack to explain himself more thoroughly before rendering any opinions.

"Just before I left Venice I told Serena that I'd have to resolve my on-off relationship with Lauren Hilbert before she and I could—"

"*That* was your excuse for not telling her what was up with you?" interrupted King.

Jack nodded sheepishly. "I had to give her some reason I was pulling back until I knew what the story is with my uncles. Serena thinks I've simply gone into my famous 'Keep-'Em-At-Arms-Length' mode."

"Everybody around here knows you do that, so maybe she already heard about your M.O.," King agreed mildly. Then he demanded, "Why didn't you just tell her your worries?"

Jack shifted uncomfortably in his chair.

"I didn't want to malign my uncles until I really know if they had anything to do with the canal failures that killed all those people in Lakeview. It's not fair to them, either, to speculate to outsiders about any accusations until I dig out the facts about all this. So…I just kept my distance from Serena my last two days there…and then I left."

"You did a proverbial about-face, did you? Smooth move." King cast Jack a sour look. "Corlis did that kinda thing to me once, years ago, and then I reacted like a total ass because I didn't understand how this 'don't fry a source' thing worked with you reporters and it all nearly derailed us, *permanently!*"

"Jesus, King—"

"Well, I'm just saying that if you really think she's the one, you gotta trust that she can handle whatever it is you ultimately find out—and journalistic ethics be damned."

"It just doesn't work that way!" Jack shot back with

frustration. "And besides, how *could* she handle it, as you say, if it turns out—"

"Well, maybe it's time to find out what's real between you?" insisted King with a wave of his hand. "And what about Lauren?" he pressed. "How much does Serena know about that torturous tale?"

"I told her some of the history between us," Jack replied, knowing he sounded defensive.

"And is Lauren still in the picture?" King challenged.

"Lauren went off in a huff New Year's Eve."

"Ah…yes. I think Corlis and I would have heard if the almost-a-doc had found a diamond engagement ring under the Christmas tree," King commented blandly. "She obviously didn't, so she was plenty pissed, right?"

"That's about the size of it," Jack acknowledged. "By the time New Year's Eve rolled around, she was one unhappy lady. She jumped out of my car parked in front of her house on one occasion during the holidays and then on New Year's Eve, she stormed out of the restaurant while I was paying the check and she took a taxi home. She wouldn't answer her cell phone the next day before she left to go back to Houston, so nothing between us got resolved."

"And then you left for the rising waters conference in Venice, right?"

"Yeah…right after that. I was introduced to Serena at the New Orleans airport by my sister and—well—things…ah…unfolded from there," Jack admitted, feeling worse by the minute.

"Boy…you are surely in one, big mess!"

"I know that, King!" Jack exclaimed, "but can we get back to the heart of the problem? Do *you* or your father know—or have heard about—stuff my uncles may have been involved with regarding that canal and the levees? I've asked Jacques and Vincent about it a couple of times over the years and they both clammed up tight."

"Well, I know that your Uncle Vincent and the levee board members did a lot more drinking than inspecting the levees," King said with a shrug. "And I have no idea what the levee inspectors knew over the years about the integrity of the canal walls that were engineered by the Corps."

"When I ran an online search before I left Venice, I read about some vague accusations about the engineering of the walls back in the eighties when Uncle Jacques was working in that unit," Jack said, "but I only had time to scratch the surface. Even so, I got the feeling that benign neglect was the least of their sins on the levee board, and the Corps has been a target of criticism from Day One since Katrina."

"It's Corlis who probably knows more about all this than I do," King said. "Her TV station did a big series after the storm looking into what specific canal walls and levees failed—and why."

Just then, as if on cue, King's wife appeared at the door.

"*What* do I know more about?" Corlis asked with a big smile as she stepped onto the gallery with a snifter of brandy in her hand. A stunning brunette given to wearing well-cut slacks and matching sweaters, she smiled at her visitor, adding, "I've been meaning to ask you. How watertight were those windows in my old condo during the downpour the night you got back from Venice?"

Jack had bought Corlis McCullough's flat on Julia Street in the Central Business District when she'd married King and moved into his house in the French Quarter a couple of years before the storm. Several windows in the Julia Street building that faced the street had blown out of the 1840-era building during Katrina, which Jack had subsequently had repaired.

"King's window guy did a great job back then," he replied, referring to one of a cadre of building experts his friend had on call in his campaign to preserve some of the oldest structures in the city. "The new seals came through just fine. But I was just asking King what he knew about my uncles Jacques and Vincent and any part they may have played in the canals that failed in Lakeview."

Corlis arched a quizzical eyebrow, and asked, "Is this just idle curiosity on your part—or something else?"

"No," King replied for his friend, "and if he tells you anything more regarding the story he's working on, you have to promise it doesn't leave our gallery here, right Jack?"

Jack nodded and Corlis, too, bobbed her head.

"Ah…the old not-revealing-your-sources problem. Know it well." The veteran broadcast journalist raised her right hand and promised complete confidentiality, furrowing her brow in thought. Then she smiled faintly. "You're asking a very interesting question, actually, especially coming from *you*."

"I sure wish I *didn't* have to ask it."

"Well," continued Corlis, "nearly ten years ago, now, I was part of the investigative team at WJAZ that was able to confirm that the Army Corps had *not* followed the recommendations by an outside design firm regarding the flood walls."

"Yeah…I did come across that in my preliminary search."

"Right," Corlis confirmed, adding, "And did you see the report that showed that the outside consultants had specifically said that the pilings supporting those massive structures should be driven to a depth far deeper than the Corps ultimately sank them during the so-called 'improvement project' back in the nineteen eighties?" She heaved a sigh. "Whether your Uncle Jacques was part of the decision not to go down to the recommended depth on the Seventeenth and London canals when he worked for the Corps…I just don't know."

Corlis fell silent, appearing to be turning over something in her mind.

"What?" King prompted. He laughed and said to Jack, "I know my wife's look when she's dredging that steel-trap memory of hers."

Corlis shrugged. "I'd have to look at my notes or look at the tape again, but I seem to remember, now, that Jacques Durand refused to speak on the record to one of our other reporters about the role he played as a junior engineer way back then. I do remember someone on our team tried to interview him for the five-part TV series we did on 'Accountability After the Storm.' Yes!" she said, snapping her fingers. "I remember seeing some news outtakes we never used in the final series where he flatly refused when a reporter tried to ambush him entering Corps headquarters. Said he couldn't remember back all that time and that he had enough to worry about, post Katrina."

Jack nodded grimly and disclosed, "I once asked him point blank, myself, about what he knew about those efforts in the eighties to shore up the existing walls, but he quickly sidestepped the question that time, too."

King raised his brandy glass.

"Hey, look…before you two string up the poor guy, you gotta remember that he must have been a young engineer in his mid-twenties back then. He may not have even been shown the recommendations by that outside firm. He probably just worked on whatever section of the project he was ordered to by his higher-ups."

Jack gazed beyond the second-story gallery railing at the high-rise buildings towering over the French Quarter ten blocks away.

"But what I need to find out is if Jacque at least *knew* what was going on back then. The scuttlebutt, you know what I'm saying? The corners being cut—"

"*If* he had any access whatsoever to what was going on," King cut in.

"Or if," Jack overrode his friend, "as an accredited engineer, he had any notion that what he might have been asked to help plan back then was fatally flawed and could ultimately result in such horrifying death and destruction."

"When you accepted this assignment, didn't you realize you'd be put in the position of investigating your own family?" Corlis asked with a questioning look in the direction of her husband.

"The piece has just sort of evolved out of my coverage about the rising waters conference," Jack explained. "The big wigs at the paper are in the midst of planning the tenth anniversary coverage. Nothing's been put in concrete, as yet, as to how the *T-P's* going to handle it all."

King amplified for his wife's benefit.

"And complicating matters even further, while our buddy, here, was in Venice, Jack met a woman from New Orleans whose rather prominent brother, sister-in-law and unborn child drowned in Lakeview."

Jack stared off into space and murmured, "All of a sudden, what roles my uncles may or may not have played in the failure of the canal walls present a big problem. A personal one."

Corlis took a moment to absorb what had just been said.

"Holy sh—" she began. "You met Serena Antonelli in *Venice*?" she asked, incredulous. "She's gorgeous! And nice, to boot."

"You are too quick for your own good," Jack said sourly.

"Young Cosimo Antonelli and his wife's death had WJAZ crews sitting in pontoon boats near the roof of their house for days! Poor Serena wasn't in town for the storm,

I don't think."

"No, she wasn't," Jack confirmed, briefly explaining Serena's time at Yale and the professional reasons she'd gone to Italy on the same day he had. "She said Antonelli's had designed a costume for you, Corlis."

"I'm a huge fan of her work!" Corlis replied. "And who could forget that horrific story about how the eldest Antonelli son of Antonelli Costumes drowned trying to get his poor, pregnant wife up to the attic when the canal wall collapsed." The veteran reporter shook her head sadly at the memory, and then glanced at King. "I wonder how the family's costume company is doing? They were on the ropes, I know, after the storm. Serena had just come back to town to help get the enterprise back on its feet when I met her briefly at a fitting for the costume Antonelli's made for me."

"Jack, here," volunteered King with a wink to his wife, "apparently got along *very* well with Ms. Antonelli and now worries that his uncles could be in some way responsible for what happened to the canals that flooded Cosimo Antonelli's Lakeview house."

"Oh. Wow," Corlis said, nodding soberly. "That could definitely complicate a budding friendship, no doubt about it."

"Gee...thanks," Jack replied.

"Which brings up another dicey subject," Corlis said. "What about your *other* friend? I haven't heard you mention Lauren Hilbert even once tonight."

"Jeez, Corlis," Jack complained.

"And by the way," King chimed in. "When *is* she due to come home to New Orleans?"

"Some friends you two are," Jack grumbled. "If you must know, I had an email today that announced she's arriving in New Orleans this weekend. She's just completed her internship and residency at the hospital in Houston and is waiting to hear where she'll get her first job."

Corlis glanced at King and then said in her best faux New Orleans accent, "Well, then, do y'all want to come here to dinner Saturday night?" Her tone grew teasing. "King can make us an ole' crawfish and shrimp boil and we can amuse ourselves watching you two fight it out as to what happens next."

Corlis had always been polite whenever the four of them had been together, but Jack had long assumed that Lauren was not on her list of favorite people and had known for quite a while that they'd never be close. Even so, he'd always felt that both she and King had made very effort to support his relationship with Lauren—until tonight, when they'd heard about his meeting Serena.

Just then his cell phone suddenly made a familiar sound. He pulled out from his pocket and couldn't keep a grin from spreading across his face.

Corlis peered over Jack's shoulder and clapped her hands.

"It's her!" she told King in a hoarse whisper.

"Lauren?" King asked, looking confused.

"No! Serena Antonelli!" she hissed, grinning, and poked Jack in the arm.

Jack, too, was staring at his cellphone's caller I.D.

"Amazing," he muttered. It was the first communication from Serena since he'd left Venice. He nodded sheepishly at his hosts, pushed the On button, and said into the phone self-consciously, *"Ciao, bella! Va bene? No?"*

Serena sounded in Jack's ear as if she were in the room next to the balcony where the three of them were stationed looking down on Dauphine Street.

"Your accent is improving," Serena declared, quickly apologizing for calling so late. "It's very early morning here and another storm off the Adriatic yesterday caused serious flooding again in the *palazzo*."

"God…I'm so sorry to hear that. Can I—"

"No one that Allegra called to help us has shown up, literally to stem the tide," she added hurriedly. "Even that nice guy that your friends hired to supervise getting the seepage under control—Stefano Fabrini—isn't answering his cellphone today."

Jack felt an instant stab of relief that, even though it sounded as if Serena had Stefano on speed-dial, she spoke of him so casually. He was even happier to hear that the guy had apparently let her down.

Well, not really. She sounds so stressed out.

"Jeez, Serena, that's terrible. Glad you called."

Serena interrupted briskly.

"Do you know anyone else here I could call? *Il Ballo* is fast approaching and Allegra is desperate."

Jack felt the eyes of King and Corlis boring into his back as he walked to the far side of the gallery. Meanwhile, he clicked over to his contacts and gave her the name and telephone number of another of the hydrologists who had taken him on a tour of the MOSE project in the Lagoon.

"If Stefano doesn't get in touch, I'm sure Paolo Bronzoni will get you somebody," he assured her. "He was the guy who came with Stefano and Maurizio Pigati that first day to inspect the problems at the *palazzo*. I'll text Paolo myself as soon as I get off the phone." He paused and lowered his voice. "Otherwise, how is everything else going?"

He felt an acute awkwardness invade their conversation and could tell from her momentary hesitation that she felt it as well.

"Oh…okay, I guess. It's Pressure City around here, trying to finish all the costumes and get ready for the ball, in addition to the absolutely appalling weather we keep having. But, hey…it's Venice in the winter, right?"

He detected the sarcasm in her voice that made him think she would never have called him if he weren't the last card she could play to help her employer. He heard her sneeze.

"Are you okay? Sounds like you have a cold."

"I think the damp, mold, and sogginess here finally got to me. Listen," she said abruptly, "thanks so much, but I've gotta go." He heard a paroxysm of coughing. Then Serena choked out in a rasping voice, "I'll give Paolo's number a try. Thanks. Bye."

Before Jack could engage her further, the phone clicked in his ear and she was gone.

Both King and Corlis were regarding him with blatant curiosity. Jack actually felt his face grown warm.

"That was…Serena," he explained unnecessarily.

King said to Corlis, "Turns out her mother is a Kingsbury."

"No kidding? That means she's your cousin, King! That'll help when I try to get on her schedule the next time I need a costume," she said with a twinkle in her eye. "The costume Serena designed for me when I was Queen of Cork a few years after Lauren had the honor was gorgeous, remember, King? I actually *looked* like a champagne bottle. Serena made me a green, sequined fish-tail evening gown with a fantastic hat that had a three-foot high froth of white ostrich feathers, like bubbles, spurting sky-high!"

"You're kidding?" Jack murmured. "I remember that costume on you. You looked like a million bucks in it."

"As I said before, I only met Serena at the final fitting, but, boy, is she good at what she does!"

"So how is she doing over there?" King prompted.

"Serena? Not great," Jack replied. "I could tell she's got a bad cold. She's in the midst of helping her boss throw a big, annual ball, as she does every Mardi Gras season."

"You mean *Carnevale*…" Corlis corrected him.

"Yeah…Carnival it's called over there. The *palazzo* where it's held has some serious seepage issues that are getting worse because of the terrible winter they've been having. And now, another storm is rolling in off the Adriatic."

Adopting a bad Italian accent once again, Corlis turned to her husband.

"Oh, King…I woulda so love-a to go to that some day…get away from all the ticky-tackiness of Bourbon Street and take part in some real, Renaissance-style revelry."

King smiled indulgently. "Maybe we'll go there some day, sugar, especially given that Serena is my second or third cousin, once removed."

"Absolutely!" chortled his wife. She looked over at Jack slyly. "We've just *got* to get to know this woman better. She sounds fabulous."

But Jack warned that the weather in Venice currently was a far cry from temperatures in New Orleans this season.

"So far, there's been constant snow four inches thick on the canals of Venice," he said, "and I'm really worried that her cold sounds like it's borderline pneumonia."

"Sounds to me like you care a lot about a seriously nice local girl far from home!" Corlis replied gleefully. "I hope she hasn't moved to Venice permanently."

"No, she's only there for Carnival season," Jack replied.

"Do you think Lauren knows her from Tulane days?" she asked with feigned innocence.

Jack shot her a look and then replied slowly, "Serena and my sister Marielle were friends there, so Lauren might know *of* her. They're all about the same age, but they haven't met, far as I know."

Jack pushed thoughts of the interlocking relationships so typical of New Orleans far from his mind.

To King he explained, "Serena and the woman she's

working for have got some big problems on their hands. Water from a new storm is apparently pouring into the lower floors of the *palazzo* they rent each year as the venue for the ball. Before I left, I got some Italian colleagues to try to patch up the damage from last year, but it sounds as if they couldn't get their hands on the right materials."

"Or the rising waters are higher than normal," King suggested.

"Making things even worse, when I was there, the Italian building authorities were giving them a hard time…asking for what, basically, sounded to me like minor league extortion just to get the paperwork involved approved in time for the event."

"Sounds just like New Orleans," Corlis chimed in.

"And if the weather continues as bad as it's been forecast for over there, *Il Ballo di Carnevale* might have to be cancelled, which would be a big disappointment for the four hundred folks who've bought tickets—to say nothing of the money already spent on it by the woman who sponsors it."

CHAPTER 12

Serena stared at the cellphone she had so brusquely disconnected. The caller ID, "JACK DURAND," disappeared from the screen, leaving her with an unwelcome feeling of bereavement and a sense that she had all but childishly hung up on the guy.

For a moment, she remained standing on the floor below Allegra's event headquarters where she'd sought some privacy when she'd dialed his mobile phone. With a sigh, she headed back up the flight of stairs to the production office where every desk was occupied and a low, urgent murmur of Italian filled the air.

Allegra called from her office on the floor above, "Serena…can you come up to Purgatory for a moment? *Grazie, cara.*"

Serena mounted the metal spiral stairs and entered Allegra's inner sanctum, impressed by the paperwork stacked neatly on her boss's desk that related to various aspects of producing the ball, designing the costumes—and her employer's main source of revenue—manufacturing her elegant clothing and women's accessories for the retail end of her business.

"Would you be free for an early dinner?" asked Allegra, looking up from the mountains of paperwork. "We can go over some things I've had on my mind before I forget them," she said with a wave at the piles on her desk.

The rest of the day went by quickly and just as the doors were opening, the two women were seated at a small, table tucked into the corner of *Alle Testiere*, an Osteria on *Calle del Mondo Nova*, ten minutes' walk from the events office. Once drinks had been ordered, Serena was astounded when Allegra patted her hand across the white linen tablecloth and asked, "Tell me about our 'hero', *Signor* Durand. He has left Venice, no?"

Serena stared at her water glass, composing a reply. From the day Jack had departed, she had been determined to put their brief idyll behind her *"as just one of those things"* and immerse herself into the myriad preparations for Carnival and the ball. Thus far, she had been utterly unsuccessful at doing this, but at least she thought no one else had noticed her distress. Try as she might, she'd found herself thinking about Jack every waking hour. It was not a good sign that her highly intuitive employer was asking about him.

"Yes, he left ten days ago," she managed, finally, her throat tight.

"And you are quite sad, no?" Allegra pressed.

Serena paused and then answered resignedly, "Yes, I am, damn it!"

"Tell me," Allegra said, her expression one of total sympathy. "I have been where you are…and at least I can offer my sympathy, *cara*."

Serena swiftly alluded to the wonderful days she'd spent with the newspaper reporter from her hometown, followed by his abrupt departure.

"And I can tell that you are mystified by that, no?" Allegra asked, observing her quietly.

"More like haunted by how strangely it ended," she admitted, "but here's something even stranger," she added, shaking her head. "I don't regret a moment of our time together. I'm angry at him—and yet I'm not."

"He adores you. I could tell the second I saw him calling your name outside the costume shop."

Serena looked up, confused. "Then why do you suppose he called it off the way he did?"

"Perhaps he didn't call it off. Is it possible he meant what you just told me he said? That he just needed time to deal with that other woman you mentioned...the *dottoressa*...?"

"Maybe..." Serena said doubtfully, "but my instinct says that's not the main or only reason. Before our last dinner, I'd already felt confident he would deal with officially ending his relationship with Lauren Hilbert that had been in a state of disrepair, anyway, for months before we met. No," she said, shaking her head once more, "there is something else going on and I haven't a clue what it is."

She folded her napkin, heaved a sigh, and fought the tears that began to rim her eyes.

"I swore I would *not* obsess over this whole thing and just look at me!" She cast a worried glance at her dinner companion. "And I don't want this stupid turn of events to in any way lessen my focus or distract me for why I've come to Venice."

The empathy radiating from Allegra made it even harder for Serena to maintain her composure.

"Feelings are important, too," Allegra said gently. "Knowing you've met your soul mate, Serena, even if you cannot be together, means you're *alive*! It means you have heart! You love. You risk. You *dream*!" She gave a shrug. "Sometimes you win, sometimes not. But if you truly love someone, you *never* lose. You have that love you felt to keep close to you for all your days. It will keep you warm on the days, like now, when you have to work very hard at the profession you've chosen."

Serena knew instinctively that Allegra was speaking from her own experience, but she hesitated to ask about her mentor's previous losses in love since she hadn't volunteered anything further about herself. Allegra offered a rueful smile.

"Never fear. I will be keeping you so busy from now to the night of *Il Ballo* and its aftermath, that you will forget this Jack Durand for a while—if only for a few weeks. That should help a bit."

Serena managed a shrug of agreement and immediately felt her spirits raise a notch.

Bless dear Allegra. I will *get through this,* she reminded herself for the hundredth time.

It was such a relief to have someone to talk to... someone who understood how it felt to have come so close to feeling that she was, at last, in a safe harbor, only to have the boat sink beneath her feet.

Allegra pulled her large, leather-bound notebook from her handbag and made room for it on the restaurant's table.

"We still have much to do if we are going to be able to create the magic of Carnival in Venice, despite the skies weeping so. Today, I had yet *another* inspector from yet *another* department in Venice telephone me." She handed her companion a slip of paper with several lines of writing. "Can you try again, Serena, to get hold of Maurizio Pigati or Paolo Bronzoni to see if any of them knows who this government man is and what he actually does? And perhaps you can also learn what that young engineer... Stefano?...has to say about the water that continues to seep into the *palazzo*, despite all our efforts."

Serena nodded and leaned back in her chair while she waited for Allegra to pay their bill. Then they both donned their rubber boots and heavy jackets and made their way back through the waters that swirled over some of the boardwalks. They caught the *vaporetto* at the *San Marco* stop and made the quick trip across the Grand Canal to *San Tomà*. Soaked to the skin, they finally arrived at the costume construction shop and trudged up the stone steps for a few more hours of work.

As the next day's pace intensified, Serena routinely checked to make sure she kept her cellphone nearby—and turned on. When it rang, however, she was startled out of deep concentration on the project she'd been working on for more than an hour. Her sudden lunge for her phone, buried beneath papers on the corner of the cutting table, set off a fit of coughing, a residual souvenir of the serious cold she'd been fighting for a week.

"Hello?" she gasped, choking down another spasm.

"Serena? That you, *bella*?"

Her caller ID announced that Stefano Fabrini had finally responded to her various attempts to contact him.

"*Sì*...where the heck are you, anyway?" she demanded, trying to reign in her irritation after two days of constant telephone and text messages. Fortunately, Jack's other colleague, Paolo Bronzoni, had returned her call immediately and was scheduled to meet her tomorrow morning.

"I'm in Verona," Stefano replied cheerfully, "on the mainland." Serena heard a burst of Italian in the background and music in the distance. "I'm at...my *Mamma's*...fixing a leak in her roof. I so apologize, *cara*, for not—"

Another eruption of muffled, but rapid Italian could be heard, and to Serena's ears, the speaker definitely did not sound a day over thirty.

"Well," she replied briskly, "we've got more than just a leak to worry about at the *palazzo*. A full foot of water has come into the bottom floor since last night. Can you come help us? Today?"

"*Subito!*" Stefano replied instantly. "Would three o'clock this afternoon be suitable? I'll bring my crew with some pumping equipment and we'll see what else we can do, okay, *cara*?" He paused and lowered his voice. "You cannot know how much I look forward to seeing you again."

Despite not wanting to fall for his smooth talk and long-delayed promises of help, Serena couldn't help feeling relief that she had been given a reprieve from having to admit to Allegra that Jack's friends weren't going to come through for them.

"Are you sure you can get here from Verona by three?" she pressed, growing worried once more that Stefano might not show up on time. "I've got so much to do. I'd rather you just give me a realistic estimate of when you can get to the *palazzo* so I can meet you there and not waste time."

"It's a little more than an hour's drive," he declared. "*Si, si,* I can be there by three." He paused, lowered his voice, and said with a throaty chuckle, "And *cara*, it will give me nothing but pleasure to see you. Perhaps, afterward, I can take you to dinner?"

Serena made a face at the phone, ignoring his invitation.

"When I couldn't get you on the phone, I called Paolo Bronzoni and he says he'll come to the *palazzo* tomorrow morning, nine o'clock, sharp."

"Excellent!" Stefano exclaimed. "By then, we'll have the water pumped out and we can consult with my old colleague what we might do next to keep the water out *permanently*—or at least until after *Il Ballo*."

Appeased somewhat by these words, Serena leaned back in her chair and heaved a sigh, giving a thumbs up to Allegra, who had just walked into the costume shop and had been listening intently to Serena's side of the conversation that had been in half Italian, half English.

"Okay, then," Serena said emphatically. "Show up at three and Allegra will definitely consider you the hero of *Il Ballo*."

"Ah…" Stefano purred into her ear. "It is your hero I wish to be."

"*Ciao, Signor Fabrini,*" she said firmly.

"*Ciao, cara,*" he echoed, in response to which Serena was sure she heard a young woman's voice declare, "*Bastardo!*"

True to his word—and much to Serena's amazement—Stefano and two burly men with a large piece of machinery she could only assume was the Italian version of a sump pump, were waiting for her when she arrived at the *palazzo* with the key that Allegra had provided that would let them into the lower floors.

"No *Signora* Allegra?" Stefano inquired, looking pleased by that fact.

"Mrs. Benedetti is too busy," Serena replied shortly. "She sent me to handle this."

"*Brava*," he said with a smile and a wink.

Within an hour, the pump had been activated and was droning away, sending the water out an upper window through a long rubber pipe.

Stefano bid his workers adieu and turned to Serena, who was shivering in her coat and blowing her nose into a tissue.

"*Cara*," he said with genuine concern. "You have a...a...how you say in English? A *testa fredda*...?"

"A head cold. Yes, I do, and it's a doozy."

"Doozy? What means this word?"

"Really bad," she translated. "It's gone to my chest as well. I should get back to work where it's vaguely warmer than this drafty pile of plaster."

"No!" he declared, taking her by the arm. "I live only a short distance from here. You will come to my flat. I will make you a hot drink with Amaretto and lemon juice and take care of you."

"There's absolutely no need for that," she protested. "I have piles of work to do and—"

"If you don't rest and recover, you won't be able to do *any* work, *cara*, and might not even be able to go to *Il Ballo*. You understand what I'm saying? This...how you say…this very, very wet weather makes a disease of the lungs for people not used to it. Just come with me and get warm for a bit, at least."

Stefano reached up and felt her forehead with the back of the fingers of his hand.

"*Febbre*, I think," he pronounced.

"You think I have a fever?" she asked, alarmed. Serena felt her own forehead. Sure enough, it felt warm to the touch, the only part of her body that was. She *couldn't* get any sicker than she was! Allegra was counting on her.

"*Si*. Let me at least get you something warm to drink before you return to your work."

"All right," she agreed reluctantly. "As long as you promise me that your place is truly nearby?"

Despite feeling flushed, she was actually starting to shiver even more in her thick coat and the cashmere scarf wound three times around her neck.

"*Si, si*. Just a two minute walk."

"Then, yes, make me something warm to drink, and then I must get back to the atelier," she insisted. "The sewing ladies will wonder where I've gotten to."

For once, Stefano wasn't stretching the truth. His flat was a mere one hundred yards beyond a nearby bridge and down a narrow alleyway. Surprisingly, his living quarters were very neat, if spare, except for an unmade brass bed positioned in a corner of the large, principal room. Once Serena had shed her coat and rubber boots, she headed straight for a small sofa on the opposite side of the tall-ceilinged chamber.

"Here, *cara*," he said solicitously, handing her a woolen throw, "wrap your beautiful body in this and rest while I make you my special potion."

Serena sank back on the feathered cushions and pulled the small blanket up under her chin, wondering if her host intended to pour a double dose of spirits in his medicinal offering to render her helpless in the wake of his amorous supplications? Within minutes, Stefano returned with a cup that warmed her hands and smelled deliciously of Amaretto, lemon juice, and honey.

"Drink…drink it all," he commanded.

She took a sip and judged it contained a reasonable amount of her favorite liqueur, so she did as he bid and drank a good portion in one go. She loved the sensation of the warm liquid sliding soothingly down her scratchy throat.

"Wonderful," she murmured. Within minutes she felt the lulling effects of both the spirits seeping through her veins and the luxury of being wrapped in a cozy cocoon.

Before she knew it, she was fast asleep.

Jack fought against the depression he always experienced whenever he came to the New Orleans Airport lobby. Once again, he saw in his mind's eye the canvas stretchers where many frail, elderly citizens of his hometown had breathed their last during Katrina.

It was ten years ago, Durand. Get over it!

The traffic on I-10 had been a bear and he was running late. According to Lauren's phone text, her plane was already on the ground. He sprinted toward arrivals where travelers on Delta emerged from the security area and paused to catch his breath. A second later, he heard a familiar voice call out.

"Jack! *Jack*, over here! Finally!"

He turned and took in the sight of Lauren's nearly white-blond, chin length hair, pulled smoothly off her pale forehead by a black velvet headband. A Burberry trench coat over her arm, she wore trim jet-black slacks topped by a white cotton turtleneck, the perfect choice for a chic, budding young female surgeon who'd just departed from the temperate winter climes in Texas. She swiftly walked to his side.

"Hi, you," she said, flashing him the coquettish smile she'd perfected as a cheerleader at Tulane.

"Hey…Lauren…" he replied, and felt an acute awkwardness as she embraced him with fervor. Her pale coloring and short stature felt so foreign and were the diametric opposite image of the woman he'd left in Venice. He pulled back from her quickly, asking inanely, "How the heck are you?"

"Better, now, that I see you actually made it here to pick me up." She smiled at him, dimples winking, and a sure signal that she was in one of her few cheery moods. She linked her arm through his, and added, "C'mon…let's get out of here so I can tell you my fabulous news!"

Jack had nearly reached the Garden District turn off of Highway 10 by the time Lauren finished describing to him in great detail the job offer she'd received from the Ochsner Medical Center, along with her enthusiastic plans to move back to New Orleans by the end of April.

"That's a great achievement," he said—and meant it. Ochsner's was on a par with the Cleveland and Mayo clinics and getting a berth there was a definite coup. Even so, the half-expected news filled him with nothing but dread.

Lauren kept up her chatter about the new position she'd been offered as he sped down the off ramp and turned in the direction of the impressive Hilbert house on Poydras Street. His thoughts strayed to his sister, Marielle, wondering what she'd say when she found out what he was about to do. Marielle had never held much affection for the young woman sitting in the passenger seat. In fact, she'd dubbed her "the All-Sorority-Sister-All-The-Time" and avoided her when she could.

Ironically, Marielle, herself, had been the one to introduce them and in their early acquaintance, he'd found in Lauren a rare breed of southern womanhood: a female on a professional path of her own. After her stint as an RN at Charity Hospital before and during Katrina, and her eventual acceptance at med school in Houston, she had become as intensely focused on her medical career as *he* was on his journalistic one, which had worked well for both of them. They knew a lot of the same people and they'd mostly enjoyed each other's company as she'd progressed from nurse to med student to intern to hospital resident, residing in Houston ninety percent of the time. However, a palpable, free form tension had slowly built between them the last few years and had ultimately flared into two memorable arguments—one right before Christmas when, in Lauren's words, they needed to discuss the "What's Next?" factor. That was the chat that had ended with her leaping out of his car and slamming her front door in his face.

And then there'd been New Year's Eve…

"Hey," Lauren said sharply, bringing his thoughts crashing back to the uncomfortable present. She pointed out the window as he pulled up in front of her family home. "I thought we were going straight to your place? I told my parents I'd be arriving Saturday so you and I could—"

Jack made no reply as he turned off the engine and shifted in the driver's seat to face her.

"We have to talk."

Lauren returned his gaze with a measured look, as if she'd half expected him to suggest they remain in the car and hash out their rocky time together over the holidays. Since this was nothing new in their relationship, her tone became that of a doctor dealing with a difficult patient in the ER.

"But I thought we'd do this on Julia Street, Jack...and a few other things as well," she added, her annoyed expression morphing into a come-hither countenance that he imagined wouldn't last long when he told her what was on his mind.

Jack paused, gathering his thoughts around the words he'd been planning from the second he'd received word Lauren was coming to New Orleans for the weekend. Before he could begin, however, her eyes narrowed. Her flirtatious manner a forgotten memory, she pounded the dashboard on the passenger side.

"Don't you dare!" she cried with shrill emphasis. "I can see it in your face. Don't you *dare* tell me you're breaking up with me! Not now! Not after all I did to nail a job in New Orleans, and everything, and—"

"Look, Lauren," Jack interrupted, his hands gripping the steering wheel.

This was going to be a scene, just like New Year's Eve. Just like all the other times they'd had disagreements. Lauren would first get angry; then start to cry, and—he'd give in, just to keep the peace.

Not this time, little lady...

He took a deep breath and plunged ahead.

"I'm really happy for you about getting a position at Ochsner, and I have enormous respect for what you've done as a med student."

"Well, now," she almost purred, a look of stark relief smoothing her brow, "that's much better."

Doggedly, Jack continued, "Getting a spot at Ochsner is an incredible achievement, Lauren, and I think you'll be a great fit there. But, you and I *aren't* a good fit anymore. Look at how it ended with us last month. How it's been for *six* months—a year, or more, actually—since we've had a single, happy moment together. If you honestly think back, we haven't had very many in the last few *years*, not really."

Lauren took a few moments to absorb his last words. Then, she inhaled a deep breath and appeared to take a tactic other than exploding with anger, followed by tears, which this time he couldn't really blame her for. Surprising him, she gave a small shrug and flashed her dimpled smile once again.

"Every couple has its ups and downs. Ever since the storm, you hold on to things too much, Jack. You've got to put Katrina behind you. Sure, you and I have had some bumps. We've been living in two different cities for ages, so what could we expect? But, now we've made it *through* all the bad stuff. You're still a Pulitzer-prize winning journalist, and I'm now a full-fledged doctor. What's past is past. We have our whole future ahead of us, now that I landed a job here in town."

Jack shook his head.

"We've been in this relationship for a decade and there's plenty of evidence it just isn't going to work, long term. At least not for me. I'm sorry that I didn't face it sooner and tell you what I've been feeling for quite some time, now. Letting things slide as I have wasn't an honorable way to behave and I truly apologize for my part in this."

Lauren's response to these words didn't appear to be affected in the slightest by his heartfelt regret for not admitting the truth for longer than he cared to acknowledge.

"And you think *this* is honorable?" she demanded, making no attempt to disguise her fury. "You think that you haven't, until this very moment, led me to believe—"

"Oh, hell…cut it out, Lauren!" he exclaimed, banging the steering wheel with a fist. "I did *not* propose marriage to you at Christmas, remember?" he demanded. "Nor the Christmas before that! Stop making up this...this...*fantasy* of yours that we've always gotten along well, except for a few, minor bumps in the road. You know as well as I do we haven't felt comfortable in each other's company or wanted...no, *pined* to be together during these long absences with you in Houston. The unhappy truth is we never really pined for each other in the slightest degree, even when you were living in New Orleans before the storm!"

"That's not true!" Lauren protested and assumed a familiar, wounded look as if she were about to burst into tears. "Everyone thought we were a great match! My whole family expected you to give me a ring by New Year's. So did *I*! But typical you...you said nothing about our future and did even less!"

What a steel magnolia this woman is. Now it's all my *fault. Well, for once I'm not giving in to her manipulation, just to act like a so-called gentleman.*

"The fact that I wasn't prompted to propose by this time should have told you something," he replied evenly. "It sure did me." He deliberately held her gaze. "I think we were a convenience for each other, I'm ashamed to say. We spent just enough time in each other's company during our busy lives that it kinda, sorta worked for us for a while. It just doesn't work for *me* anymore. I want more. You can't build a lifetime together acting and reacting, as we do whenever we're around each other for more than a couple of days. Surely you've felt it, too?"

Lauren's brow smoothed and she looked at him with laser-like perception.

"You want more, do you? Does that mean you've *found* more?"

Jack was startled into silence by her powers of lightning speed deduction.

"There's someone else," she stated flatly, no hint of tears. "You've been cheating on me. When did it happen?" she demanded. "Before Christmas? Thanksgiving?"

Before he could offer an answer, her voice went up a few decibels.

"*Venice?*" she shouted. "Did you take someone with you to Venice? Is that it, you bastard? You never even told me you were going again to that stupid conference! Am I going to run into this creature all over New Orleans, now that I'm moving back?"

"I didn't *take* anyone to Venice, but there *is* someone else—not that it relates to you and me in the slightest."

Should he tell her the full story—that he met Serena for the first time at the airport and that they'd *spent time* together in Venice?

Lauren's bitter, high-pitched laugh cut short his thoughts.

"I don't believe you!" she yelled. "I think you've been sneaking around behind my back for a long time. *Who is she?*"

Jack inhaled a long breath and disclosed, "You guessed correctly," he acknowledged. "I got to know her in Venice."

"Oh, that's rich! Now that I'm moving back to New Orleans, you decided to find yourself a girlfriend who lives even *farther* away from where you live! How perfect for you." She snorted with disgust. "You are a head case, Jack Durand! A genuine, diagnosable commitment-phobe!"

"So you've said before," he noted, his jaw clenched, "but, look, Lauren," he continued, deciding in the next instant to extend the olive branch. "I totally understand how my being the one to raise the subject of the proverbial elephant-in-the-living-room we've had going here for quite a while is infuriating. And my not asking you to marry me over the holidays—when everyone we know expected me to—was disappointing for you, I know. But just so *you* know, the woman I met is still in Venice and I'm here, and we left it like that."

"Really?" Lauren snapped. "How sad for you."

Ignoring her sarcasm, he continued, "But meeting her and…enjoying her company made me face the fact that you and I were living a lie and I wanted to straighten it out. I wanted to face the truth that…I wasn't ever going to ask you to marry me."

Jack realized his words cut Lauren to the core, but they had to be said.

"What I don't get," Lauren retorted, her lips puckering in the pout he knew so well, "is what you expect from the person you're with, whether it's me or some Italian bombshell!"

"She's hardly an 'Italian bombshell' and—"

But Lauren wasn't listening.

"You're always busy chasing a story around here, or on the road. And there I was, studying for a medical degree in another state. How could you expect me to give you any more than I gave? I had to listen to you always moaning about how much mud is silting up the mouth of the Mississippi and what dolts the politicians were, and about how Katrina was the greatest American catastrophe, ever! You were a boring, broken record and I didn't want to hear about it anymore! How much attention did *you* lavish on our relationship?"

"Not nearly enough," Jack admitted, shocked by her assessment that he knew contained some grains of truth. He took a deep breath to steady himself, determined to finish what he'd started. "That's what I'm trying to tell you, Lauren. I take responsibility for my part in screwing us up."

Her mood shifting once again, Lauren seized his hand off the steering wheel and held it in a death grip.

"So maybe we can fix this," she said in a tone that

sounded more desperate than conciliatory. "Now that you know what you did to mess us up."

It's as if she played no part in this. God, I want this to be over!

"No, Lauren," Jack replied more determined than ever he was speaking his own truth. He detached her hand from his, gently laying it in her lap. "I'm afraid I am, in fact, officially ending things between us. You know and I know our relationship was already broken beyond repair."

"I *didn't* know that," she said in a low voice, clasping her hands and staring down at them.

Jack wasn't sure if she was now crying crocodile tears, or was genuinely struck by the finality of his words—and perhaps truly saddened by them. He leaned forward, hoping they could close the book gently, for once.

"I want to thank you for the world we shared for a while…especially Katrina and its direct aftermath. And you know what I think? You'll make a great doctor."

"Plastic surgeon," she replied, her lips settling into a thin line with no trace of tears. "I'm going to be working with the best guy in the South." She cast a steely gaze across the space separating them in the front seat. "So, are you going to go back to Italy and *marry* this girl?" she demanded.

Jack paused and then gave a small shake of his head. There was no need to hurt Lauren's feelings any more than he already had.

"Who knows if I'll ever marry anyone at the rate I'm going." He cast her a lopsided grin, hoping to lighten the atmosphere. "I do know though, that *you* want to get married and have kids, so I'm probably doing you a big favor telling you before it's too late that I'm not your guy."

"Better late than never," she retorted acidly. Lauren reached for the handle to open the door, looking back over her should. "And by the way," she said, her voice laden with a venom she must have been saving for one of her famous exit lines, "don't flatter yourself that I'll be pining over *you*, because I won't!"

"Good for you," he complimented her with a sincerity that surprised him, and then felt a pang of remorse when he remembered Serena had said to him at the Danieli Hotel restaurant that she wanted the man in her life to long for her as much as she longed for him. He and Lauren had, indeed, made a holy mess of their relationship. Could he be any different with someone else? With Serena?

"Let me help you with your luggage," he said to Lauren's back. He was suddenly overcome by a weariness laced with impending relief that his former girlfriend would soon flounce up the path to her family's front door and storm, one last time, out of his life. Why in the world had he been with her such a long time, he wondered? It was a question he needed to answer before he involved himself any more deeply with someone else. Even the beautiful Ms. Antonelli.

Jack still had Lauren's two suitcases in hand when her mother flung open the front door, all smiles, only to see her daughter dash past without a word of greeting and sprint up the elegant, curving front staircase.

Avoiding Adele Hilbert's bewildered gaze, he deposited his burdens just inside the black and white tiled foyer and returned to the front porch.

"Well, hello there, Jack," Mrs. Hilbert said, her puzzled expression deepening. She turned in time to see Lauren disappear on the landing above. "It's so nice to see you after this long while. Is anything wrong? I have some sweet tea cooling in the refrigerator. Are you hungry? Can I make you something more substantial? That was so kind of you to collect Lauren at the airport. I must have misunderstood. I thought she was arriving Saturday."

"No, she came today. And thank you, Mrs. Hilbert, for your hospitality, but I'm on deadline for the paper, so I can't stay."

For a brief moment, the pair exchanged glances in silence while Jack struggled to invent his own exit line.

Finally he said, "I'm sure Lauren will tell you why she's upset. Please let her know I wish her all the best."

And before Lauren's mother could reply or grill him for further explanation, Jack walked swiftly down the manicured path to his car and sped away.

Retracing his route to the I-10 in the direction of downtown New Orleans, Jack expected to feel like a heel about what had just transpired. Instead, the weight of the world had strangely and miraculously been lifted from his shoulders—that was, until he thought about his next onerous assignment: interviewing his two, aging uncles about their pasts.

CHAPTER 13

If Jack were a betting man, he figured that the answers from at least one of his uncles probably doomed him to a life he'd described to Lauren during their unhappy conversation in his car.

Everlasting bachelorhood.

Upon several days' reflection, one thing he knew for sure. If he eventually concluded he wasn't fit to marry Serena Antonelli, he wouldn't marry anyone. He was no monk or martyr, he thought, turning down Julia Street and hoping for a lucky parking place near his brick-fronted building. The block-long collection of row houses was another landmarked structure, thanks to the efforts of King Duvallon and his New Orleans Preservation Alliance. Scoring a spot near his front door, he mused that, as his future life rolled on, he was sure to encounter other women who could offer some amusement or temporary distraction, but he had come to realize with dreaded certainty, there would never be anyone for him except *La Contessa*.

At his desk in his home office, he dialed Jacques Durand's number, allowing it to ring into the double digits until voice mail picked up. His efforts to reach his other uncle produced the same result.

It was nearly four o'clock, and not worth heading back to the office.

He answered pages of email, made himself a drink, and sat numbly in front of his TV set watching Game 3 of the NCAA's March Madness contest.

March Madness just about describes my life perfectly, he thought morosely and took a deep sip of his bourbon and water.

Serena's cough began to tickle the back of her throat again, despite the muffler wrapped tightly around her neck. She wore the scarf to ward off drafts penetrating the antique glass windows not far from the large cutting table in the middle of the low-ceilinged room at the atelier in *San Tomà*.

Unable to suppress it any longer, a hacking cough took hold of her again as it had been doing for the past week. Rosa, her friend and stalwart head seamstress, swiftly handed Serena a cup of steaming tea that she'd kept steadily brewing in the back of the workshop for the staff this dank, chilly day. It had been one that had followed many others in monotonous succession for weeks.

"*Mille grazie*," Serena gasped, and then nodded in the direction of the paper pattern pieces sprinkled with notations to guide her as she cut the muslin and prepared to pin and drape pieces of an eighteenth century-style skirt over the bamboo panniers that extended a foot-and-a-half from either side of the nearby mannequin's waist. "Do you think these are okay?" she rasped.

Rosa studied Serena's interpretation of Allegra's latest creation for a wealthy female CEO coming for *Carnevale* from Silicon Valley in California, and nodded.

"*Perfetto, cara*. Let me sew them up for you. You rest for a bit."

Serena stared out through the window at the snow-laced mist clinging to the tile rooftops nearby. She had to chuckle at the memory of Stefano Fabrini's obvious attempts to use her pesky cold as an excuse to awake her from the couch where she'd fallen asleep the previous day and lead her directly to his bed. When she had demurred to make the trip, he had not been in the least threatening, but rather sweet and almost childlike in the way he used every wile to attempt to persuade her to let him make "wonderful love to you that will cure all your ails!"

"You mean 'ills?'" she'd teased him.

Then she'd pointed to her throat, which actually had begun to throb with pain, and protested he might become as sick as she was. She'd asked if could she please just fall back to sleep on his comfortable silk couch which was barely long enough for her to stretch to her full length.

Virtually unable to sit upright, she'd spent the night on Stefano's sofa and reluctantly called in sick the next day, promising to return to the workshop as soon as she could crawl out of her own bed, which she had twenty-four hours after that, still with her hacking cough a constant companion.

However, in her feverish dreams the night she'd remained at Stefano's flat, she found herself on the embankment between a building and a bridge that arched over a small canal. Jack stood in the shadows while Stefano was offering her a hand to mount the mist-swathed bridge. Serena longed to disappear into the darkness with Jack, but woke up with a start just as she reached for his hand, only for him to fade into nothingness. Swimming to consciousness, she was assailed by a piercing emptiness when she realized it was morning and Jack Durand had become, indeed, only a figment of her imagination. The next thing that swam before her bloodshot eyes was the view of her host rising from his bed in his very brief underwear.

Stefano was in the bathroom when his cell phone began to vibrate in its silenced mode.

"Your phone!" she'd croaked.

"Let it ring," he answered.

Fifteen minutes later, it had vibrated against Stefan's wooden bedside table again—and again, he didn't answer it in her presence. Serena had repressed a smile, guessing that, perhaps, the young lady in Verona whom Serena had overheard vociferously protesting Stefano's coming to her rescue at the leaky *palazzo* was determined to get hold of him.

Serena had to admit that for a moment that morning she'd been sorely tempted—given her dream and the unrelenting melancholy she'd battled since Jack's departure—to surrender to Stefano's romantic overtures. His constant wheedling and flattery continued when he handed her a perfectly made cup of *espresso* that he'd produced in his minuscule kitchen. She longed for human comfort, if only for the temporary solace his lavish attentions might offer. Why couldn't she just be like a guy, she thought wistfully. Why couldn't she just seek a nice warm body as attractive as Stefano's for a night or two to help her forget her troubles? But she knew it wouldn't work…not really…and the insistent and repeated ringing of his mobile phone on his bedside table signaled it would be foolish of her to try this tactic. Instead, she dutifully bid him a grateful and chaste farewell before she headed back to her own lodgings and slept the entire day and night away.

A modern Casanova…but an awfully charming one.

Within the hour of Rosa helping Serena stitch the latest muslin version of the creation next in the queue of customer's costumes, Allegra arrived at the workshop to see how her American assistant was feeling. She had also come to check on progress for costumes being made for the last of her very best—and wealthiest—clients. In less than five days *Il Ballo di Carnevale* was due to take place.

As for Stefano Fabrini, Serena had to admit—lothario or not—the handsome young Italian had been a Godsend both to her and Allegra, commandeering a crew not only to pump out every drop of moisture in the leaking areas of the *palazzo*'s lower floors, but also to search for a solution to the disintegrating foundations that allowed more water to seep in, the second the pumps were turned off.

"We just need Stefano to keep us dry until after the ball," Allegra sighed. "The weather report just announced there's yet a *new* storm brewing in the Adriatic that's expected to dump more sleet and snow on Venice. I doubt there's any pump invented that could keep up with that much extra water flowing into that building."

"Oh, no," groaned Serena before a paroxysm of coughing took hold. "Just what we don't need," she gasped.

The next morning, Serena came to event headquarters after her latest early-morning conference with Stefano at the *palazzo*. She mounted the circular stairs and knocked on the doorframe of Allegra's office.

"Now Stefano's problem is getting permission from the city's historic landmarks commission to apply a new type of sealant that he says 'might' keep the *palazzo*'s walls more water tight—that is, if he can even obtain such a product to ward off disaster during the next storm that's due to hit full force tomorrow. Apparently, the best ones are made in the U.S."

This day, Allegra, too, had swathed her throat with a warm scarf. Over night she'd come down with the same cold her entire staff had been battling for weeks. She regarded Serena closely. Another coughing fit had seized the younger woman and she'd turned her back until it had passed.

"*Cara*, we should both probably be resting in bed, or perhaps in hospital," Allegra said with black humor. "Your work assisting the pattern-maker is done. I insist you go to your lodgings and rest for today."

"Absolutely not," Serena insisted, fighting off more coughing that practically made her gag. "Rosa is making all of us pots of her special tea. Everyone is sick, so I'm not infecting anyone. I'll drink my tea and help the others with the endless beading still left to do on the costumes draped on those mannequins at the workshop. I'll be fine. In fact," she said, forcing a smile, "I think I'm actually on the mend, now."

It was midnight by the time Rosa and the last seamstress left for the night. Just as she heard the gate close on the other side of the door, her phone pinged. She had to smile to see that Stefano had sent her a text.

Cara...I am below stairs hiding in the shadows from Rosa, but I've come to walk you home.

"Why the hell not?" she said aloud, texting him back that she'd be down in a minute. She reached for her anorak and ubiquitous muffler that she wrapped tightly around her neck.

The broad-shoulder Italian stood at the foot of the stone staircase, his hands shoved into his cognac colored leather jacket. Her heart flipped over and all she could remember was a rainy, sleet-filled night when she'd run down these very steps to throw herself into Jack's arms. It had been the first night they'd made love...

"*Signora* Benedetti makes you work too hard," Stefano scolded, linking her arm in his as soon as she'd shut the downstairs metal gate.

"She tried to make me go home at noon," Serena defended her mentoress. "It's just that there is so much to do in the little time we have left. How did it go with those bureaucrats at building department?"

"I will explain it all over dinner."

"Thank you, but I've already eaten." She declined to tell him all she'd had was a cup of soup. She continued to lean on his arm as they tramped through the accumulated snow piled along the narrow canal that led in the direction of her guesthouse near *Campo San Polo*. "But I am happy you came to walk me home while you tell me the latest."

"*Cara...I think* you are one of those women who play...ah...how you say? Hard to achieve?"

"Hard to get?" Serena replied with a laugh. "That's right, Stefano...but no worries. I can see you're irresistible to lots of women, so you have plenty of female company and you and I can just be friends, which I think will be much more long lasting, *si*? Now, tell me what you've learned today when you called on the authorities who are making such impossible demands on us."

"You make me so sad, *La Serenissima*," he complained, his full lips in a genuine pout, "but, alright. I will tell you what happened today." He slipped an arm around her waist as they continued to walk toward her lodgings at *Ca'Arco Antico*. In Italian he said, "They demand proof that any new sealant we suggest using won't destroy the centuries-old plaster."

Serena shrugged.

"Well, at least that's a legitimate issue. The bureaucrats need proof that anything you put on to fix the situation won't make it worse." She suddenly had an idea how she could get proof that a particular product had already proven its worth. "I think I know how to get them an answer they may accept."

"If you can do that," Stefano said with a grim expression she'd seldom seen on his normally cheerful countenance, "you are a genius, dear Serena."

Her thoughts sped first to Jack, and veered quickly to Jack's best friend—her third cousin, once removed—Kingsbury Duvallon, the celebrated historic preservationist back home. Silently, she determined she'd simply call him directly, without Jack Durand serving as intermediary, to find out if the revered New Orleans Historic Preservation Alliance had ever found an acceptable product that might keep the lower floors dry, at least until the ball was over. As she and her Italian escort made their way toward the front door of her guesthouse, the snow had begun to fall again in earnest. With lightening speed, he seized the key from her hands and opened the door that led to the small hotel's foyer.

Serena prepared herself for the kiss she knew he would attempt to bestow. Mounting a pre-emptive strike she said firmly, "*Buona notte, Stefano. E mille grazie, mio amico!*" she emphasized.

He gently seized both of her shoulders between his large hands and cast her a doleful look, refusing to give up.

"*Bella, bella*...let me come in with you to keep you warm tonight. Our walk in the snow has you shivering again."

Serena was, in fact, trembling from the cold, despite the warmth of her anorak. She was also tired and sad. She wondered if Jack was following the alarming Italian weather reports? If he was, he hadn't made any further attempt to get in touch about their current snow emergency.

What do you expect, Serena? You practically hung up on the guy!

Still and all, he *could* have reached out to her one more time and he hadn't, she thought with a startling flash of anger. Ashamed to admit it, she was sorely tempted to allow the increasingly ardent and totally charming *Signor* Fabrini to have his way with her. It would serve Jack right!

That way leads to disaster, and you know it! And besides, your life is complicated enough, you dope!

Sensing her indecision, Stefano drew closer.

"You might, at least, consider letting me come upstairs with you, *sì?*" he said with a broad smile just bordering on triumphant.

"*Tristamente, no,*" she rejected him gently in Italian. She pointed to the scarf around her neck and said in English, "I'm still *very* sick. I don't want you to catch this terrible cold. Allegra and I need you to stay well, so you can be our hero and fix the *palazzo* in time for the ball!"

She kissed two fingertips and touched the side of his cheek, stubbled with a rather sexy day's growth of beard.

Stefano's gaze grew smoky with his hope that he would ultimately wear down her resistance.

"You are so kind, *cara,* to have a care for my health. I will do anything to help you and *Signora* Allegra. Perhaps you will invite me to this outrageously expensive *ballo*. I can be your… how you say… *escorta… accompagnatore?*"

"My date for the ball?" Serena replied with a smile. "Unfortunately, I will be working like a fiend that night…and I'm sure Allegra will want you monitoring the basement. I will ask, though, that you be given a complimentary ticket and at some point, come upstairs and have supper. Perhaps we will have a dance at the disco together before dawn breaks. Would that please you?"

She retrieved her door key from his hand, bid him goodnight, pushing him playfully out the front door, and firmly closed it behind her. She turned and mounted the marble staircase to her room with the brass plaque that read in elegant script *Canaletto*, wondering briefly why she was being so noble when nothing would soothe her sore heart as much as to be enfolded in the ardent embrace of such a drop-dead, handsome Italian.

Or would it?

It was long past the usual hour that Jack's colleagues at the *Times-Picayune* departed for the night. He squinted tiredly at his glowing computer screen as the first page appeared of a long document that Corlis McCullough had generously sent him from a web citation in the files of WJAZ. It was merely one of the myriad official, public reports and original documents obtained by the TV station through the Freedom of Information Act. He'd been scrolling through them all day to glean the known facts about the collapse of the 17th Street and London canals a decade earlier.

Fighting off the day's fatigue, he was determined, before he quit for the night, to tackle a history of the U.S. Army Corps of Engineers' work on supposed improvements both to the city's canal walls and the gigantic "Mr. GO" construction—an acronym that stood for Mississippi Gulf River Outlet. The man-made channel designed for tankers was a little-used, 72-mile shortcut from the Gulf of Mexico to the Industrial Canal in New Orleans. Over the years, the canal had allowed salt water to seep in and destroy the wetlands, the very barriers in times past that had kept Gulf water surges from inundating the city.

Jack prayed that this document, going back to the nineteen eighties when his Uncle Jacques Durand was a wet-behind-the-ears junior engineer, would finally answer the questions: what did Jacques know about the inferior construction history of the two canals—and when did he know it?

Corlis had emphasized that she had worked on a different aspect of the "Katrina Aftermath" story ten years earlier, "but I remember that we'd used the Information Act to secure some of these documents, which therefore are available for all to read—including you! Ten years ago, I only briefly thumbed through the ones that didn't relate directly to my assignment. Let me know if you hit pay-dirt, which I suppose you're hoping you don't," she'd added in a sympathetic postscript to the attachments she'd sent over by email.

Jack initiated a global search for his uncle's name, along with the dates Corlis thought might match up with what the reporter was looking for. He physically held his breath for the second it took the search engine to pull up all references to "Jacques Durand" buried within the scan of the original document that was now more than three decades old. He blessed the forgotten government minion who had been tasked with electronically converting all this material and filing it in the Corps' database. His eyes raked a dozen or so pages that his search turned up. Twenty minutes later, he reared back in his chair.

"Bingo," he muttered. And then, "Oh, shit!"

There on the screen was the scanned signature *Jacques Durand, Engineer,* one of several signatures at the bottom of the final specifications for making the 1982 improvements to the 17th Street Canal walls.

Jack made a quick calculation. In 1982, his uncle was twenty-four years old. Just as King Duvallon had speculated, Jacques was a very junior engineer who had, curiously enough, been asked to sign off on the nuts-and-bolts requirements of a very large, publicly funded project.

Did his uncle *know* what he was signing back then, Jack wondered? Was he aware that the specifications listed in this document were much *lower* than the recommendations of an outside consulting firm—cited, as he'd seen earlier, at the back of the report? Had he seen the consultants' urgent advice that had recommended much deeper pilings to hold the walls in place than those that were ultimately sunk into the sandy soil?

Without warning, the familiar vision that Jack all too often imagined in his mind's eye rose before him once again: many feet of water, pushed by the storm surge, inexorably bearing down against the walls' lower extremities and exerting enormous pounds-per-square-inch pressure. He could easily imagine it eating away at a structure that—this document proved—was sunk a paltry ten feet below the land's surface, instead of the recommended forty. And when that water ultimately punched through the bottom walls, it rushed like a locomotive into the yards and past the jungle gyms and garden swings of million-dollar houses that lined the waffle-iron street grid that was the New Orleans suburb of Lakeview.

Jack closed his eyes against the recurring image of Serena's brother rushing to the side of his pregnant wife, urging her to quickly scramble up a narrow, retractable stairway to the attic. But the waters were quicker than Cosimo Antonelli's urgent pleas that she hurry. In agonizing seconds, the black waters rose, turning Lurleen Antonelli's nightgown into a billowing parachute that could do nothing to save her. The force of the water swept both husband and wife the last few feet toward the enclosed attic where they drowned in its swirling depths.

What if that had been *him*, trying to save another Antonelli…trying to save Serena?

Just then, Jack's cellphone rang, jolting him out of this disturbing reverie. He punched the phone's answer button.

"Hey, buddy," King began. "Working late again?"

Without a pause, he asked Jack if he had been paying attention to the latest news bulletins on CNN about the rising waters assaulting Venice, Italy that week.

Alarmed to hear this, Jack replied, "No, I've done nothing all day but dive into all the documentation that Corlis emailed me. I didn't realize how late it's gotten to be." He glanced at the array of muted TV sets strung against the newsroom's far wall. "It's on CNN, even? Do they say how high the tides are?"

"Well, it's morning in Venice right now and all I can say is that I hope that nice lady you met is staying dry. Last

I saw, there's a four-and-a-half-foot high tidal surge from a big, ole' Adriatic storm rolling through that poor place. All the historic preservationists around the globe that report into my list serve say they're plenty worried about this one."

Jack felt his chest tighten and fretted that Serena was not only threatened by flood waters, but she had sounded so congested when he last talked to her, she might have pneumonia by now. How would she get herself to a clinic or hospital in those high waters, if she needed to? Unbidden, his thoughts flew back ten years to Charity Hospital and the poor patients stranded on the rooftop awaiting rescues that, for some, came too late.

There was a long silence between Jack and his best friend, and then King said, "Just so you know, that very same nice lady rang me up."

"Serena did *what*? Is she okay?"

"I thought you'd be interested," King chuckled. "She wanted to know my opinion about using this new mineral-based waterproofing product that some building engineer told her about. It's actually a liquid-applied invention and made in America. Turns out, it's the one we slapped on, big time, on scores of old buildings around here after the storm."

"Did it work?"

"Damn right, it did! We put it on structures made of two-hundred-year-old plaster. You know, the stuff we've got all over the French Quarter."

"You're kidding me! Serena Antonelli called *you*?"

"She sure did. Told me to turn on CNN. She said she figured that since she and I are second or third cousins, once removed, on the Kingsbury side, she didn't need a formal introduction."

"So, what did you tell her?" Jack demanded, highly incensed that Serena hadn't gotten in touch with *him* in such a dire emergency.

"I told her that the brand of sealant she'd heard about is a mighty fine product and that it's a pre-mixed, advanced liquid rubber that dries fairly quickly after it's applied."

"What did she say to that?"

"She was thrilled to hear that the beauty of this stuff is that it turns into an extremely quick-drying waterproofing and crack-isolation *membrane*. I also pointed out that it provides a thin, continuous barrier to protect the walls and floors from further water damage."

"And besides your technical mumbo-jumbo, does it look halfway decent *when* it dries?" Jack demanded, still flabbergasted Serena had called King instead of him. She must feel well enough by now to despise him.

King paused, considering, Jack surmised, whether he should be offended or amused by his best friend's testy tone.

"Well…" he drawled, and Jack knew immediately that King was enjoying every minute of this conversation, "I told her about another thing she probably needs in order to get the sealant past the Italian historic preservation authorities, to say nothing of those pesky government permit department bureaucrats she says keep hounding them over there. It's another American product called ArcusStone, a durable limestone plaster made in Texas outta…well…ground-up *limestone* and water, plus a bunch of patented polymers and colorants. It's applied over the weatherproofing to provide a natural stone or 'Venetian' finish."

"Ah…the aesthetics of historic preservation," Jack murmured.

"Exactly! Once the ArcusStone stuff sets over the sealant, it dries looking exactly like vintage plaster coating. Given how big that ole' *palazzo* she's trying to keep from drowning is, she'd better have a *lot* of both products on hand."

"You say they're both made in America," Jack retorted. "How's she going to get the stuff over there? The ball's just days away!"

"That was a hurdle," King agreed. "But if we can get the materials over there PDQ, those two products will make it all look just like the original—only pretty damn water-tight."

"So, now what? Did Serena think the authorities would grant permission to fix the problem this way? She's running out of time and the government officials have been...difficult," Jack added, thinking of the demands of local bureaucrats that bordered on near-extortion, according to Serena.

"Like some New Orleans building officials, you mean?" King noted dryly. "She asked me to put what I'd said about this stuff not hurting the buildings and looking so authentic in an email sent from the New Orleans Historic Preservation Alliance I represent. She and the engineers she's working with immediately took my letter to the...*Condono Edilizio* and the...*Ufficio Catasto* in Venice—whatever they are—" he concluded, fracturing the Italian even worse than Jack would have.

"The permits and records offices, you mean," Jack supplied.

"Yeah...those places," King continued. "Serena hopes that might convince the petty functionaries over there that these two products will fix them up, fine, and won't destroy the historic character of the building."

"So you've already sent the email?" Jack confirmed.

"If I do say so myself, I composed a brilliant epistle on the Alliance letterhead under my signature. I also sent a print copy with my real John Hancock via air express, after I copied her the electronic one, so she had it right away. Then I ordered up a great deal of both the sealant and ArcusStone material that will be drop-shipped to Venice tonight, out of the distributor in Baton Rouge."

"Holy shit, man...you did all that so fast—and you paid for it?"

"Yep. Anything for the family, ya know."

King's words were a private joke between them, given Duvallon's dicey relationship with parents who had passed off the birth of a son as legitimate when King's godfather was actually his biological sire.

"Serena's boss will reimburse you, for sure."

"Not a problem," King replied.

Meanwhile, Jack felt a huge wave of relief. Despite the horrendous weather assailing Venice, perhaps Serena and Allegra at least had a slim chance of pulling off these repairs in time for the ball. He grudgingly admitted to himself that Serena had been smart to deal directly with King, who obviously had expedited everything.

"So you think they can make the deadline?" he asked.

"This gal Serena is one smart cookie," King replied admiringly. "She said she was taking my documentation to the port authorities, too, so they'd let the stuff into the country and be good-to-go as soon as the government folks and the *palazzo*'s owners granted permission to use it on the building. It's going to be a cliff-hanger, for sure, but, yes, I think she and her boss have a chance of getting that ole' palace fixed in time."

Jack remained silent for a moment, digesting everything King had disclosed. Then he said, "Given the way business is done in Italy, don't you think that precious shipment should be escorted by someone reliable when it's off-loaded from the plane into Customs at Marco Polo Airport?"

King chuckled into his ear.

"Yeah...my thoughts, exactly! And from what you've told me, Serena might never receive it, otherwise, or have to pay a fortune to persuade the port officials to release it—

even if it makes it that far."

"To say nothing," Jack added, a bubble of anticipation gurgling in his gut, "of getting the Venetian building and preservation folks to say 'yes' to your proposed fix."

"Right you are," King agreed. "I think Serena needs some heavy reinforcements, kinda like the cavalry showing up, don't you? You feel like coming with me and forgetting all the business of not seeing her until you know the absolute truth about what your uncles did, or did not do?"

Now I know what at least one of my uncles did.

But rather than wait for Jack's answer, King yelled, "Hey, Corlis, darlin'…you really serious about wanting to go to that version of Mardi Gras over there in Venice, Italy?"

Corlis' uncharacteristically girlish squeal carried all the way to Jack's eardrum pressed again his cellphone as she shouted, "You betcha, baby doll! I'm owed about a year of vacation time from WJAZ."

King asked Jack, "Wanna double date? You think Lauren's up for going to something like this?"

"Lauren and I broke up. Officially."

"Yeah," King drawled. "I think I heard that."

"Then why'd you ask?" Jack grumbled, figuring Lauren had been mighty pissed off and had since complained about him far and wide. Few juicy tidbits like that escaped Ace Reporter Corlis McCullough in a gossipy town like New Orleans.

"Just checking to see if I heard the story straight," King replied with an innocent air. "Musta been mighty unpleasant for you, I bet."

"You got that right. But it's over, thank God."

"So you're free to go over there, ride shotgun with us on that shipment, and help me help my cousin save the day?"

Even though Jack couldn't see through the phone, he

could tell his best buddy had a wolfish grin on his face.

"You bet," Jack agreed, a sense of elation sweeping over him that was a welcome relief from the gloom that had enveloped him the entire time he'd been back in New Orleans. "But can you please make it look to your long, lost cousin as if *I also* had a hand in helping you save the day?"

"Buy you some cred? You betcha," King replied, "and I'm glad to see you're beginning to have a clue how to court a lady."

Oh, hell...

In the excitement of the moment he'd pushed aside the ultimate import of what he'd just uncovered.

"I can help out, but I can't court the lady until I find out whether my Uncle Jacques *knew* the specs on the Seventeenth Street Canal were far below what was recommended by the outside experts when he signed off on the plans."

"Oh, shit. You found *evidence* that Jacques was definitely involved back then?"

"Just before you called, I found his signature on the 1982 documents Corlis sent me that okayed a deeply deficient, under-engineered plan to shore up the existing walls. The same walls that failed during Katrina and killed Serena's brother. It couldn't be any worse, King. Keep that under your hat, by the way—even to your wife. I have to talk to my editor and get some guidance about all this since I'm related to the guy."

"Tell her," King advised shortly.

"Tell Corlis? I'm not telling *anybody* else but Reynolds and you about all this. I'm telling *you* because I'm going a little crazy, knowing this stuff, and you're the one person who's always had my back. Even so, I need your word you won't say anything to anyone else either, even to Corlis—whom I also trust completely—but she's a competing journalist and would ethically have to tell her boss at

WJAZ, especially with the tenth anniversary coming up."

"I see your point and you have my word, but I meant tell *Serena*. At least tell her the basics of what's going on with your story for the *T-P* and let *her* decide whether she wants to have anything to do with you, or not."

"I can't do that until I know why Jacques was willing to sign off on those specs back in 1982," Jack replied stubbornly, adding, "and it also will affect how I have to handle writing this story for the paper. It may turn out that I have to step away completely and let somebody else take the byline—not that that would alter how Serena will feel about the Durand family."

"You don't know that, for sure," King said sharply. "You don't know how she'll feel about *you*! Stop feeling her feelings *for* her, for God's sake!"

"I gotta get all the facts straight, King! Maybe there *were* extenuating circumstances, and maybe she'd be understanding about it all, but I have to talk to Jacques before I say anything to Serena. It's the way it has to be done in my business."

Jack could sense King's frustration at hearing his answer but all his friend replied was, "I don't care about all that. I say, tell her." His advice was met with silence. "Okay, then," King said with a sigh. "Your call. My lips are sealed. But, get to our place in an hour, and we'll go out to the airport from here."

"What about airline tickets?"

"Got 'em in the works. Eleven p.m. flight, I'm hoping. Email me your passport number when we hang up, okay? You can pay me back, later."

CHAPTER 14

By some miracle, Jack got his editor, John Reynolds, to answer his cellphone, despite the fact that it was after business hours. He tersely explained the high waters flooding into Venice and the threat to the city, to say nothing of the unknown fate of the carnival ball he was highlighting in one of the two stories he'd been assigned.

"I dunno, Durand. I can certainly see how this is impacting the stories you're writing, but can't you just follow the news feed, or call your sources over there? Two trips to Venice in a month looks bad on the expense side of the ledger, you know what I'm saying?"

"I've got to go," Jack insisted, trying to keep the desperation out of his voice. "I've got to see what's happening for myself."

He honestly felt his reasons for going to Italy again were sound journalistically, but another emotion he'd never experienced before was the engine propelling him to board the plane with King and Corlis that night.

He *had* to see Serena again, even if he was forced to masquerade as Mr. Elusive in front of her until he knew for certain whether Jacques had willingly or innocently signed off the canal walls' faulty design.

Holy crap! I am actually physically pining for this woman!

There was an unmistakable ache in his solar plexus and a tightness gripping his chest, none of which were probably anything other than stress, he assured himself. But, whatever was plaguing him, he had to be with Serena again—even if he knew it might be for the last time, other than seeing her in a crowded room in New Orleans some time. He winced at the thought of catching a future glimpse of her across a busy street in the Quarter…or in the Central Business District where her costume shop was…or, even worse, on Julia Street where he lived in a district of popular art galleries.

King was partially right. Serena should decide for herself, once all the facts were known, but until the facts *were* known, it was more important that he help get the materials into Italy and onto the walls of the *palazzo*. At least he could do that much for her.

"Look, Reynolds," he was amazed to hear himself saying to his editor, "I feel getting back over there is so crucial that I'll pay my own flight—if the paper will pick up incidentals. I can sleep on a friend's couch."

There was a long silence on the other end.

"Well, if you think it's that important to both stories—the drowning *palazzo* and how U.S. products are being used to remedy the damage, *and* the piece you're doing about Venice's underwater gates…"

"I do," he cut in.

"Okay, then…but *watch* those incidentals, will you?"

"Thanks, man."

There was a long silence and Jack feared Reynolds was having second thoughts.

Instead his editor said, "You know something, Durand? I'm thinking that this piece on the leaking palace should be a separate deal to run the week of Fat Tuesday. All the stuff you've learned about the underwater gates and corrupted officials over there could be saved for a bigger story about the various schemes for holding off the rising waters in both cities, along with comparing the issues of construction, malfeasance, and incompetence in New Orleans and Venice in the last ten years."

"Yeah, the parallels are pretty impressive," Jack said, hoping this expansion might mean he could stay longer in Venice.

Meanwhile, Reynolds actually sounded as if was getting excited. Thinking aloud, he continued, "Like you said in your memo, it could be part of a two or three-section series to run this August during the week of the tenth anniversary since Katrina."

It suddenly occurred to Jack that heading up the anniversary coverage for the newspaper would mean stringing everything out with Serena for another six *months*, but Reynolds was on a roll.

"If we amplify what you've been working all this time, sum up all major water abatement projects in both places, add in a comparison of efforts to save and restore the wetlands and barrier islands in Louisiana and Northern Italy—throw in a sidebar about *both* mayors being arrested—and then position it right, it *would* be a perfect series for the anniversary!" Reynolds repeated. "Even better, the bosses upstairs would have a problem solved and think I'm justified in granting you this extension and pouring more expense money into the *palazzo* story to run during Mardi Gras week."

Instead of feeling elated, Jack felt nothing but dismay about waiting such a long period for the expanded story to run. How in the world could he put off leveling with Serena for all that time without breaking the journalist code of never revealing any facts about a story to outsiders until it was published?

"You think the brass is willing to back up editorial if we find more skeletons in our local closets?" Jack demanded.

"They'd better," Reynolds replied, sounding grim. "I ran that memo of yours by the guys upstairs last week and they liked it pretty well. And let's face it, the suits sure as hell haven't come up with anything better for our Katrina coverage, so I definitely think I can persuade them to go for this!"

In the intervening silence from Jack's end, his boss

growled, "Look, Durand, I'm doing you a big favor. You get to go back to Venice and you'll get a big byline during the tenth anniversary coverage. What more do you want?"

"I appreciate what you're saying, but—"

"No buts!" he declared, sounding exasperated. "That's the only way I'll agree to you going back to Italy on the company clock."

Jack knew that his tone bucked no argument. "Right. Got it."

"I'm getting beat up by the bean counters around here on every nickel and dime editorial spends. And keep it under your hat about what you're doing. We don't want the *Advocate* or anybody else to get wind of the Katrina angle you've developed."

"Okay, but—"

His editor didn't let him finish his sentence before cutting in again, "And absolutely *no* lounging around Italy more than three or four days, this trip, you hear? File your story a.s.a.p. about helping stem the tide in the flooded building in time for Venetian Carnival, and hightail it back here. You'll have plenty work left to do on the New Orleans chunk of the story. I think you're about six hours ahead of us over there, so we can run your *palazzo* piece on Fat Tuesday, here, or the day after, you got that?"

"Got it. But what if we fail to stem the leaks because the stuff doesn't work, or the bureaucrats stand in the way of even letting us apply it to the walls?"

"That's a story, too," Reynolds reminded him. "We'll go with it, either way. And you'd better produce some pretty explosive stuff for the Katrina series to justify all the time and money you're spending, okay? And have the friggin' anniversary pieces in perfect order by August fifteenth so we can fact-check every last word with the company lawyer, you got me?"

"Got it," Jack repeated gloomily.

"And you still gotta crank out your weekly blogs from now to August, got that, too?"

"Yep."

"Then, goodnight."

"Goodnight."

"And travel safe, you hear?" Reynolds added to Jack's complete astonishment.

At least, his editor was still of the old school of journalism where, if a reporter got his facts straight, he'd back him to the end against the pressure of the advertisers and politicians who hated reportage that gored their ox. Even so, the minute Jack hung up, an avalanche of doubts assailed him.

Maybe he shouldn't go? As his editor had said, Jack could probably find out most of the information he needed over the phone and Internet. And surely King could mastermind getting the sealant and plaster coating products into the country on his own? Paolo and Maurizio and — yes—Stefano could supervise properly applying the materials on the walls and deal with the Venetian bureaucrats.

Good God, he thought, he was spending his own money when the damned newspaper should be picking up the entire tab for this work! Not only that, Serena had called King for help in this dire emergency, not him. She probably wouldn't even speak to him once he got to Venice.

What the hell am I doing?

Jack didn't have to think very hard to come up with the answer. He was the classic fool in love and acting like a crazy person. It was not his usual M.O., that was for sure, but something told him that he was powerless to do a thing about it. There was no avoiding the fact he longed to be with Serena Antonelli—truly *pined* for her, he would have to admit—and he was willing to risk everything just to see her again.

"*Attenzione!*"

Allegra called for quiet among her assembled *Il Ballo* production team and office crew. The core group, numbering nearly thirty, sat and stood around a big table, prepared to go over the timeline for the upcoming event. Commencing in the early hours the next morning, they would load their catering equipment into the *palazzo* and set up for the cocktail party, a seated dinner to be held on the upper floors, as well as install the theatrical gear required by the *Cirque de Soleil*-type entertainment scheduled to take place throughout the glittering evening. A disco for the more energetic guests would be created on the ground floor where everyone was scheduled to enter the *palazzo* from their arriving water taxis.

"That is, if the waters aren't too high and the dock's still floating there," someone commented nervously.

Before Allegra could continue reading from her list of assignments, those present heard a loud knock at the open door. Serena swiveled in her leather chair and stifled a small scream.

Framed in the doorway stood Jack Durand, flanked by an equally tall, broad-shouldered man and a good-looking woman clad in a full-length fox fur coat. Both Jack and his male companion were swathed in raingear and tall rubber boots that were still slick with moisture. Jack nodded to his now-silent audience and addressed Allegra as he advanced a few steps into the conference room.

"Good afternoon, Mrs. Benedetti," he began, a satisfied smile pulling at the corners of his mouth. "There is a boat with a lot of drums of sealant and bags of special limestone plaster from America tied up not too far from here."

He made a slight bow and then gestured to his companions who remained standing in the doorway.

"May I introduce you to the cousins of your American colleague, Ms. Antonelli? This is Kingsbury Duvallon, of the New Orleans Historic Preservation Alliance, and his wife, Corlis McCullough, a broadcast journalist. Do we have the permission of the local authorities to take this material to the *palazzo* and see if we can seal out that water in time for the ball?"

Since most of Allegra's team understood English to varying degrees, a rousing cheer went up, followed by a buzz of excited conversations. Their leader cast a dazzling smile in the direction of the surprise visitors and held out both hands in greeting as she rose from her chair at the end of the conference table.

"In America, don't you say, 'the cavalry has arrived?'" Allegra declared, turning to Serena for confirmation.

However, her second-in-command could only stare at Jack while Allegra embraced him and then, in turn, kissed Corlis and King on both cheeks, European style.

"The warmest of Venetian welcomes to darling Serena's cousins from New Orleans. *Bravi*! And I can't believe you've come back to us, Jack...or that you three have wrought such a miracle. *Grazie! Mille Grazie!*"

Jack responded with a depreciative shrug.

"I persuaded my editor that a story about a traditional, fifteenth century *palazzo* and a carnival ball trying to literally keep its head above water after the series of storms you've been having was a worthy subject for the Mardi Gras-loving citizens of New Orleans to read later this week."

Allegra laughed. "Then you are doubly welcome back to Venice, *caro*."

But Serena could see that Jack had begun to frown.

"What about the authorities, though?" he asked. Gesturing in the direction of his male companion he added, "King, here, whom I hasten to tell you is the man who truly wrought this miracle, managed to talk us through your

Customs. Fortunately, the engineer, Paolo Bronzoni, was there to help translate and had a launch waiting to get the sealant materials and us away from the airport before any more demands could be made on us. However, my question to you is, can we go ahead and use everything we've brought from America to try to fix the building that I understand you don't own?"

Allegra bid them to join the group gathered around the large conference table. She pointed to a stack of papers resting near her place at the head.

"The Preservation Alliance's letterhead worked wonders with the historical landmarks commission here. They put pressure on the city's building permits and inspection department officials to agree to your scheme, and between all that and your friend Paolo—who must have waved a magic wand somewhere—we just received the permission an hour ago to do the work, even without the *autorizzazione* of the *palazzo*'s owners, who live mostly in Morocco and don't embrace the *telefonino*, the mobile phone. This morning the project was officially declared *una situazione di emergenza*."

"An emergency situation," Serena supplied automatically, still staring at Jack, not quite believing what was standing ten feet away.

She hadn't heard a word from him in days, or he from her. She had almost persuaded herself that she was, at last, making a measurable amount of progress forgetting their time together in January. Seeing him, now, instantly erased any belief she may have harbored that she was slowly getting over the pangs of remorse that had burrowed into her heart from the moments she turned her back on him at the Danieli Hotel.

Allegra formally introduced her American visitors to her employees. A ripple of recognition and admiration rose when she recited King Duvallon's achievements saving from demolition a major historic building on Canal Street in New Orleans' French Quarter that had once been owned by the city's Free People of Color back in the nineteenth century, adding in rapid Italian, "and this is also the man who lead the effort to restore damaged and aging structures all over the city following the devastation of Hurricane Katrina."

While this recitation was going on, Serena dared glance again at Jack who briefly met her gaze and then looked down at his knee-high boots. Was he deliberately avoiding her, Serena wondered?

"And now, my dear American saviors," Allegra said gaily, "shall I ride with you to the *palazzo* and show you where to unload those wonderful products you've brought with you?" She seized the pile of correspondence from the table, turned, and smiled at Serena with a twinkle in her eye. "You are responsible for keeping these precious documents in hand."

"Fine," Serena said, nodding. "I won't let them out of my sight."

"Oh...but you are to come with us, *cara*, for I fear I will need you to translate to the workers waiting there what means this 'ArcusStone' and instructions for applying it. Also, there are a few other terms that will need explanation in these letters from our friends, here, as well as the nonsense written to me from the officials at the *Condono Edilizio* and the *Ufficio Catasto. Andiamo.*"

"Let's go," Serena translated Allegra's last command, wondering what, exactly, a trip to the *palazzo* with this group would mean for Jack and her...

A long, wooden boat sat deep in the water beside a canal not far from Allegra's office. The vessel was laden with the heavy materials that had been air-shipped from America and was under the protection of Paolo Bronzoni who stood like a sentry in the stern. Meanwhile, Allegra proposed a change of plans. Corlis and Serena should depart on foot, directly to the nearby costume rental shop. Snow had begun to fall again, and the mist was so thick upon the water that it would be slow-going up the Grand Canal to the *palazzo*.

"As there is so little time before the ball," explained Allegra hurriedly to Jack and King, "I want Serena and Corlis to choose costumes for themselves and for you two, also, since they know your sizes. Meanwhile, I'll take back all those papers I gave to Serena and we can get started immediately on applying the sealant. Between you men, Paolo, and me traveling together to the *palazzo* by boat, we can surely figure out the English-to-Italian instructions for applying the products you've brought."

Jack took a few steps toward Serena, but before he could say anything to her privately, she turned and seized Corlis by the hand to guide her back toward the costume rental shop one alley over from Allegra's main office.

Corlis called over her shoulder, "See you back at the *Pensione Accademia* at six, okay, King?" She halted dead in her tracks and asked Serena, "Do you know where that *is* and how in the world I can get there, later?"

Serena laughed and then dug into her coat pocket with nary a glance in Jack's direction.

"Before we're through, I will give you a quick lesson in how to read this map. You are definitely going to need it!" She handed Corlis a fold-up map the size of a playing card. "This proved to be a Godsend when I first arrived."

Jack felt cut to the quick. Hadn't she said *he* was a Godsend, showing her "his" Venice, including their "Magical Midnight Mystery Tours?" Why hadn't he spoken to her the minute they walked into Allegra's office? He had wanted nothing more than to enfold her in his arms, but it had been simply a matter of too many people in the room for such a momentous encounter, to say nothing of everything else going on regarding attempts to repair the *palazzo*'s lower floors. She obviously felt he'd deliberately avoided her, and now, she was obviously avoiding *him*.

He watched Corlis tuck the miniature map into the pocket of her fur coat and the two women headed off once more into the snow-laden mist without a backward glance.

"Get on board, buddy," ordered King, who had taken in the entire scene. As Jack passed him to step into the stout vessel, his friend mumbled. "I'd say you have some pretty tall fences to mend."

Allegra was already standing near neatly stacked piles of bags labeled *ArcusStone*. She gave Jack a brief, sympathetic glance as he passed by. However, she didn't engage him further, but, instead, turned to King and swiftly fell into an animated conversation about the tasks that lay ahead.

Allegra's assistant, Francesca, was waiting for Corlis and Serena upstairs at the costume rental shop that was tucked away down a narrow alley to the left of the *Piazza San Marco*. At the top of the stairs was a floor where racks of glittering costumes made of bejeweled satins and sequined silks filled a cramped area. Nearby were several large fitting rooms with wine red velvet curtains where customers were allowed to try on a vast array of finery from which to choose.

"Wow, wow, and *wow*..." breathed Corlis as she caught sight of a large glass case full of dazzling headdresses, also sparkling with faux jewels and a rainbow of plumes, along with a spectacular collection of costume jewelry and elegant masks fashioned for both men and women.

"Allegra insists that her four hundred guests be dressed in proper, period attire," Francesca explained, "so over the years, she designed and had all these beautiful costumes constructed, as Serena well knows by now," she added with an appreciative smile aimed in her colleague's direction.

She gestured toward a male mannequin bedecked in midnight blue satin knee breeches, white silk stockings and black buckled brogues. The handsomely tailored three-quarters jacket was made of the same deep blue, but in velvet, embellished with silver lace on the wide cuffs. Two rows of sterling silver buttons marched up the jacket's front and flanked a white satin, intricately embroidered waistcoat with a froth of lace bubbling at the throat.

"I think that would suit *Signor* Duvallon quite well, don't you?" Francesca inquired. "As it seems to be in his size, it would look splendidly on a man of his stature, *si*?"

"Oh, yes," Corlis agreed, clapping her hands. "He'll far outshine me in that outfit, for sure."

"Ah…but Allegra wants *you* to try on this," Francesca said, pointing to a deeply cut bodice made of golden satin, overlaid with gold tissue organza and studded with closely aligned pearls.

Hinged, umbrella-like bamboo panniers, two feet wide at the hips, supported the gown's billowing skirt made of the same, rich fabric, à la Marie Antoinette.

"It's a court gown," Serena chimed in. "It comes with a set of gossamer wings attached to the back, as well as an elaborate, jeweled and feathered headpiece worn on quite an impressive eighteenth century white wig."

"OMG…" Corlis murmured. "It's exquisite! Allegra selected this for *me*? This must rent for a pile of euros! She doesn't even know me."

Francesca smiled softly. "She already considers you and *Signor* Duvallon good friends for all you have done to make it possible for us hold the ball this year. She wore this costume herself the year…the year her husband passed away. It is very dear to her."

Corlis was led to a dressing room and, after several long minutes, appeared completely transformed, with the organza wings creating a sense of magic.

"Oh, Corlis," Serena declared on a long breath. "You look fantastic in it!"

"I am honored to wear it," Corlis said, with a grateful glance in Francesca's direction. "Please thank Allegra for me when you see her later, will you?" She gently touched the beadwork just below the curve of the tight-fitting bodice. "This is incredible! What an amazing world you've chosen to be part of, Serena."

"I know," she agreed. "I'm humbled every time I walk into this place."

"Well, you're no slouch yourself, missy," Corlis replied over her shoulder as she retreated toward the dressing room to remove the gown that fit her so perfectly. "I think the champagne costume you made for me comes close to these."

"Oh, no!" scoffed Serena, "but thank you for the kind words. Wait until you see the ideas I'll be taking home with me," she called to the closed curtain where King's wife had disappeared to put on her street clothes once again.

Serena turned, smiled at Francesca, and shifted to Italian.

"I know how busy you are right now. We don't want to take any more of your time. I think these two costumes for my cousins are perfect. Can you have them sent to the *Pensione Accademia* when someone has a free moment?"

"What about a costume for Jack?' Corlis prompted, reentering the room.

Francesca pointed to a hanger with a long, flowing robe made of heavy burgundy-colored velvet decorated with gold braid trim on the neckline and sleeves.

"As a working journalist during the ball, *Signor* Durand will be required by tradition to wear a *caftan*."

Corlis gave a laugh and winked at Serena. "Hey, he'll be the most comfortable of all of us! Even so, I'm glad I'm off duty from WJAZ and am allowed to wear that magnificent gown Allegra picked out for me." To Francesca she said, "Can you also send Jack's costume to the *Accademia Pensione*?"

"Of course," Francesca replied and gave instructions in rapid Italian to a member of the staff.

Corlis leaned near Serena's ear and disclosed, "The *T-P* is so cheap these days, Jack paid his own way here, so we're taking pity on him and he's sleeping on our couch."

Serena refrained from telling Corlis how her time with Jack in Venice began by his offering to sleep on *her* sofa at *Ca'Arco Antico*. She began to ponder the reasons for his surprise return to Venice, other than the obvious one: to help his friend King help Allegra make the *palazzo* habitable in time for the ball—and thus complete his story for his newspaper.

"And you, *signorina*?" asked Francesca, breaking into Serena's meandering thoughts. "Allegra hopes you would enjoy wearing her beautiful Seas of Venice gown. Since you're here, do you have time to try it on?"

"Me? Wear *that*?" she breathed almost in a whisper.

"What's the matter?" Corlis said with alarm, looking from one woman to the other.

"Nothing," Serena hastened to reply in English. "In fact, it's wonderful! But I can't believe that Allegra wants *me* to wear this to the ball," she said, pointing to a mannequin surrounded by a three-sided mirror. "I think it may be her masterpiece!"

The reflecting glass offered a view from every angle of a frothy, sage green, strapless gown. Its contours were fashioned in waves of silky fabric to simulate the restless Adriatic that so often pounded Venice mercilessly, yet had provided the city sustenance and protected its citizens from marauders from the time of Attila the Hun. Within the folds of delicate cloth were sewn brilliants of tourmaline, faux emeralds, and man-made crystals that sparkled with the gown's slightest movement.

"Come," urged Francesca. "I will help you into this myself."

Serena disappeared behind the red, velvet curtain cloaking the dressing room Corlis had used and eventually emerged clad in the tight-fitting "mermaid cut" gown. She had quickly pinned her dark hair on top of her head while one of the staff clapped long, dangling aquamarine and clear crystal earrings on her earlobes, along with a matching necklace that skirted the iridescent silk bodice's daring décolletage. Francesca added the final touch with a matching silk "fascinator" styled hat that featured wisps of sage, royal blue, and purple tulle mimicking ripples on the water.

As Serena turned slowly in front of the three-paneled mirror, Corlis ventured in hushed tones, "I think you and that gown are the most beautiful creations I've ever seen. Your boss must think you're something very special, Serena Antonelli."

"She's been extraordinarily kind, despite all the trying situations that have weighed on her this season," Serena replied. "I'm totally amazed she'd want me to wear this gown."

"A Grace-Under-Pressure gal, huh?" Corlis declared, linking her arm with Serena's as if they had been friends of long-standing, which Serena suddenly felt as if they were.

"Like *you*, Ms. McCullough," Serena said with a smile. "I once saw you on TV, knee-deep in water, reporting during the worst of Katrina."

Corlis shrugged and squeezed her hand, saying only, "C'mon…get dressed and let's go get some soup, or something, to warm up. Then you can show me how I can find the way back to my hotel on that swell little map you gave me. Jet lag just kicked in. I'll need a nap before long."

Serena nodded affirmatively and pointed to her purse sitting on a nearby chair, asking Francesca to hand it to her. She fished out her cellphone and checked for text messages. Then, she glanced up at Corlis.

"Can you survive if we first stop by the *palazzo* on the way back to your hotel and get something to eat there? Allegra had to return to the office and wants me to report on progress so far." She glanced again at her cellphone, adding, "She says that the inspectors announced that they will be at the *palazzo* tomorrow afternoon. Talk about cutting it close!"

"Yikes!" Corlis responded, and then turned to thank the young women who had helped them with their costume selections. Francesca assisted Serena out of her tight-fitting gown and arranged to have it sent to the workshop near *San Tomà* where several staff members would dress for the ball.

"It's actually happening," Serena murmured. "*Il Ballo*, I mean."

Francesca made the sign of the cross.

"Let us pray to San Marco this miracle will, indeed, come to pass."

***

"I hate to spend the money, but I think we'd best take a water taxi to the *palazzo*," Serena proposed.

They were standing in the lobby of the Hotel Monaco that wasn't far from where they'd tried on their costumes. Serena knew the concierge could get them a boat even in weather as dreadful as what they could see through the front windows facing the Grand Canal.

"My treat," Corlis declared, and in a few minutes, the two women had boarded the sleek vessel that looked like it might be a Chris-Craft plying the waters of Lake Tahoe.

"Prepare to pay a ransom of euros," Serena warned.

"I'm on vacation," Corlis answered breezily.

From the boat's cozy, heated interior, Serena strained for a first glimpse through heavily falling snow of the *palazzo* that fronted the Grand Canal. Just beyond the *San Tomà vaporetto* stop, Serena spotted the fifteenth century structure, with its mullioned windows and a wide loggia embraced by pointed, half-circle arches that created a lacy effect on two exterior floors.

As the building drew ever closer, Serena said to Corlis, "I've always thought that it has the look of a miniature Doge's Palace, which you'll see when we show you *Piazza San Marco*."

Corlis heaved a happy sigh and murmured, "Everywhere I look, it's all so beautiful!"

"Even in sleet and snow," Serena agreed with a laugh.

Fortunately, the heavy weather had abated somewhat as the boat drew near the dock. The *palazzo*'s Venetian Gothic style was reinforced by their view of an open front door, allowing them a glimpse of the baroque interior staircase. It rose in double ramps on either side of the ground floor to the magnificent rooms above.

"During the ball, you'll be able to get a good look at ceiling frescos and decorations by Tiepolo, Guarana, and Zanchi," Serena disclosed. "Back in the day, this place welcomed Tsar Paul of Russia, and Josephine Bonaparte, along with Joseph the Second of Austria. You and King will be in good company," she teased.

"Wowie, zowie," Corlis exclaimed in awe. "I wonder if I have any Italian blood in me? It would be terrific if I could claim to be related to the incredible people who created such a stunning city."

"Well, since King and I are cousins on the Kingsbury side, I'll give you bragging rights to the Venetian Antonellis-by-marriage, how's that?"

"That'll work!" Corlis replied with a grin, just as they prepared to step from the boat onto the bobbing dock that led to the impressive front door.

"I'm glad to see the waters that were flooding this room yesterday appear to have receded quite a bit," Serena said over her shoulder as the pair approached the wide entrance.

"Maybe they've done it!" Corlis exclaimed. "Do you think that by now, they've pumped enough water out of the lower floors to begin applying the sealant?"

"Looks like it. See? There are no supplies on the dock, so they must have been able to take them downstairs. I'll bet they're using them right now. *Bravo*, the boys from NOLA!"

Serena halted at the arched entrance where workers were erecting a cutout sunburst to frame the huge door. She whipped out her cellphone to text Allegra the latest good news that at least the ground floor where guests would arrive was no longer awash in water. She'd report on any other findings as to the floor below the waterline after she inspected the work done thus far.

And where was Jack, she wondered? Downstairs helping the men who were doing the actual work of repair, or off to interview someone in the government for his story for the newspaper about Venice's big water gates—and how they'd survived this latest storm?

No business of yours, Serena Antonelli! The man barely said hello, earlier.

Her job, she reminded herself sternly, was to stay focused on helping Allegra get through the next forty-eight hours.

CHAPTER 15

Both Jack and Stefano Fabrini heard women's voices and then the sound of their booted feet on the section of the stone staircase that descended to the ground floor. The room, some of which was embedded below the waterline, had been drained of moisture by means of a cluster of ubiquitous pumping machines and whirring fans. The thick coat of the American-made sealant had been applied and the fans were at full speed to hasten the drying process.

Jack quickly headed for the door, hoping, at last, to be able to talk to Serena privately. He couldn't really fathom what he was going to *say*, but he had to speak to her…had to make some sort of connection. He sprinted toward the exit that led upstairs, annoyed to realize that Stefano was following in his wake.

Before Jack could say a word, the Italian engineer hailed Serena just as she arrived at the door.

"*Buona giornata, cara*! I am happy to see that my…how you say… *attenzione*…has made your sickness of the throat better, yes?"

Attention—to what? Jack wondered with irritation. He thought he detected a flicker of exasperation flash in Serena's eyes.

"Yes, thank you, Stefano. My cold and cough are much improved, thanks to your recommendation of hot Amaretto, lemon and honey."

"And sleep," he added with a slight smile tugging at his lips. "That did you a world of good, did it not?"

"Yes," she replied evenly. "Staying home from work in my own bed a full day brought me back from the dead." She turned toward Jack and asked, "So, what's the latest I can report to Allegra? Is the sealant doing what it's supposed to?"

"Yes, I'm happy to say," Jack answered, wondering exactly what other cures for a cold Serena and Stefano may have shared. "Paolo and King just gave the go-ahead to mix up the ArcusStone coating material as soon as the sealant is dry enough."

"Wow…that's great news! Let me give Allegra an update," Serena exclaimed and then began texting furiously.

"Listen," Jack proposed, "why don't you, Corlis, and I have something to eat while we're waiting to see what the interior walls look like, once the coat of ArcusStone has been applied?"

Serena looked up from her phone and Jack felt her measuring gaze. She hesitated and then shook her head in the negative.

"Sorry. Can't," she replied shortly, returning her gaze to her cellphone where she continued texting her employer. "I have to take some pictures on my iPhone to send to Allegra, and then head back to the workshop. I've been out of the office for hours and I've got a zillion things I have to get done before tomorrow."

Meanwhile, Stefano stepped forward and took Serena's arm, guiding her further into the lower room dotted with noisy fans and speaking in high-speed Italian. Jack could only conclude that the son-of-a-gun intended to show her in more detail the work that had been accomplished that morning, and—Jack had no doubt—assume most of the credit.

Corlis leaned toward Jack and said in a solemn undertone, "Houston, I think we have a problem."

Jack nodded grimly and pointed toward the bowels of the soggy building.

"That would seem to be an understatement," he replied.

The following day, Serena could never have described to outsiders the thousand-and-one details that went into producing an event like a glamorous ball attended by hundreds of guests arriving by water. It involved not only providing some three hundred period rental costumes to customers—all on the same day—but also the responsibility for shepherding virtually hundreds of behind-the-scenes helpers with scores of tasks to perform. And all that was in addition to having to set up four individually decorated rooms for the formal, seated dinner. Then there was a rehearsal for a two-hour show that featured everything from opera singers to flamenco dancers, to a scantily clad female rock-n-roll musician with a guitar covered in shimmering mirrors. And, to top her list of "To Do" items, there was the circus performer she'd had to track down who blew up a big, red balloon, somehow got himself *inside* the rubbery sphere, and could bounce along a raised runway among the guests!

"It's always been a crowd favorite," Allegra had insisted. "The man travels all over Italy doing his act, but you must find him and try to persuade him to be here this year."

She had.

Given the task of supervising the back-stage aspects of the musical performances that would start after dinner concluded, Serena felt as if she were suddenly in Las Vegas again, setting up wardrobe racks, make-up stations, and writing out the order of each performance in Italian. She posted the sheets at various locations in the *palazzo* so the singers, dancers, and musicians could enter and exit in timely fashion.

"Is the trapeze hung yet for the aerialist where guests enter?" Allegra said over her mobile phone from upstairs in the building where she was supervising the load-in of the food and catering equipment. "He's due in a half hour and can be quite the diva at times."

"Done," Serena replied. "The electrician finally got the spotlights and smoke machines working and the sound check went perfectly."

A corporate event was being held in the *palazzo* two days after the ball, which meant, given the flooding to date, Allegra's organization had only one day to load in, set up, and then would have to vacate all their equipment within twenty-four hours. There had been a myriad of minor glitches all morning that Serena had managed to handle, choosing not to bother Allegra with any problems she could solve on her own. Even so, the pressure on everyone was intense and it was beginning to take its toll in mild hysterics on the part of some members of the staff.

Just then, her phone pinged again with a text from Corlis asking how things were going.

Serena typed furiously, apologizing that she'd had to cancel a dinner rendezvous the previous evening with the visitors from New Orleans, including Jack, and had worked far into the night.

> **It's madhouse here. Four waiters are out sick and a couple of the staff now have the same cold I've been fighting.**

Corlis responded:

> **Look for us tonight and good luck!**

Serena sent a quick reply:

> **I'm the one wearing a mask…ha-ha.**

Jack would never be able to spot her now, and there

would be nearly forty members of the working press there, all in red velvet caftans. If she weren't so crazed with all she had to do, she'd probably want to scream with frustration that this might turn out to be the most miserable Valentine's Day in her life.

Serena forced herself to return her concentration to the remaining tasks connected with the musical show. At the rate the dinner prep was going on the floor above her and the latest cold blast of snow falling outside, they were going to need more than good luck to get through this night.

A minor miracle would be nice.

Allegra and Serena were soaking wet from the combination of sleet and falling snow by the time they sped back to the costume workshop near *San Tomà* to don their own costumes.

After toweling off, Serena had scarcely been laced into her tight-fitting organza ball gown when Rosa announced, "Just got texted…your water taxi's waiting for you, Serena. Yours, *Signora* Benedetti, is scheduled for an half-hour from now."

Serena and several of the women from the costume shop who were helping out behind the scenes at the ball would be among the first to arrive. Allegra would make her grand entrance as Queen of the Carnival Ball at ten p.m. and greet the mass of costumed guests making their way into the entrance of the *palazzo*.

Serena forced a cheery smile despite the butterflies beating against ribs constricted by her tight, boned bodice.

"*Ciao* everyone. See you there!"

"You look beautiful as The Seas of Venice," Allegra said, nodding at Serena's exquisite sage green silk gown and giving her hand a squeeze. "Wait until the gentlemen from New Orleans see you tonight," she added with a wink as she took a mask from Rosa and held it to Serena's face.

Well, one particular gentleman would probably not even spare her a glance, Serena thought bleakly, and then forced her mind to the millions of chores ahead.

Once Serena boarded the water taxi adjacent to *Campo San Tomà*, it took less than five minutes to travel the Grand Canal to the fifteenth century *palazzo*, now lit by floodlights bathing it in gold and purple.

The snow had finally let up and she felt a little thrill ripple down her spine when she caught sight of the twinkling lights illuminating the points of the gilded sunburst that had been attached to the frame of the wide entrance door near the landing dock.

A pair of liveried pages in white satin knee breeches and three-quarter length, cuffed coats assisted her out of the boat, greeting her with *"Buona Sera, Signorina,"* displaying the deference of a paying guest. Water splashed perilously close as one page guided her along the gangway and through the front door—then turned, and sped back to the dock to greet the next arrivals. A few feet past the arched entrance, she halted and stared with a sense of relief—mixed with disbelief.

Only hours earlier, chaos had reigned throughout the five-story building when she'd left for the costume workshop to get dressed in all her finery. In the remaining time before the witching hour of nine o'clock, Allegra's team had wrought the miracle they all had worked so hard to help her achieve. Her dream, her vision, her *genius*, thought Serena, had somehow been made manifest within the walls of the five-hundred-year-old *palazzo*.

Within the high-ceilinged room, eight raised pedestals, ten-feet-high, six-feet-wide—four to a side—provided a colonnade between which guests entered the large entrance hall. At the sound of celestial music echoing in Serena's ears, her upturned gaze swept the platforms swathed in cream-colored silk that now supported wraithlike dancers swaying on each one, ethereal figures clad in full-length, snowy-white, diaphanous organza, white make-up, and flowing, platinum wigs. Suspended by invisible wires that Serena knew anchored each performer safely to the ceiling, the otherworldly creatures beckoned to the guests like ghosts in a dream amid swirls of mist pumped into the room by unseen machines sequestered behind the forty foot lengths of white silk that lined the walls.

In the center of the room, suspended twenty-five feet above the limestone floor on a thick, silver rope, a muscular aerialist—his naked torso glistening with sprayed-on glitter Serena had left with the make-up artist earlier in the day—dazzled the spectators with death-defying contortions above the heads of the costumed, milling crowds. She spent the next twenty minutes making a quick survey of the backstage elements and confirming with the stagehands that all was well before checking with the bartenders that their two stations on this floor had all the supplies needed.

Guests had begun to pour inside the building in droves, their magnificent costumes adding to the sparkling décor. If frost and frigid temperatures reigned outside the *palazzo*, inside, Allegra's imagination had created a winter wonderland of light, music and pure fantasy.

For several moments Serena stood absolutely still, drinking in the spectacular scene. Then, she pulled her thoughts back to the many more assignments ahead and chose the stone staircase on the right, intent on checking on the caterers due to serve some four hundred five-course meals to guests who had practically paid what nearly amounted to Serena's life savings in order to attend *Il Ballo di Carnevale*.

Suddenly she heard trumpets blare and turned on the landing in time to see the Queen of the Venice Carnival Ball float through the front door in a floor-length confection of rose silk organza with a boned collar, etched in gold braid, that fanned around Allegra's smiling face in a style reminiscent of Elizabethan times. Head seamstress Rosa Garafola had sewed the dress in complete secrecy. Not even Serena had seen it before tonight.

The applauding crowd below parted, allowing Allegra to make her stately way toward a raised dais at the far end of the room near the double staircase where Serena gazed down from the floor above. The tall, imposing figure of Neptune—his trident by his side—along with his court, all dressed in silver and crystal, bowed deeply and welcomed the mistress of the evening into their midst.

It was exactly ten o'clock. The ball had officially begun and a long night lay ahead.

"The Cupid Room never got any wine!" hissed Francesca in Serena's ear. "And I'm not dead sure they ever got their main course!"

"You're kidding?" Serena groaned. Some of Allegra's favored guests had been assigned the Cupid Room with its magnificent Murano glass chandeliers. Heavy pale peach silk drapes that hung floor-to-ceiling framed a twenty-foot tall mirror that was illuminated by massive silver sconces, their candles casting an aura of romance throughout the space the size of a hotel lobby. "I'll talk to the caterer."

"Too late," Francesca replied with a grimace. "They've already started to serve dessert in there."

"Oh, glory…that's not good. Let me see if I can at least

get the wine guy to remedy his part of the fiasco."

Serena had found it exhausting to try to move swiftly in a gown whose mermaid styling required her to take tiny steps when all she wanted to do was sprint from one problem area to another. Her mask was also an impediment, but she knew from observing the other members of the staff that wearing it was an absolute requirement.

She was kept so busy solving various glitches that came up during the subsequent five hours that she didn't have time to search for Corlis or King in their carnival finery, or even try to catch a glimpse of Jack consigned to his floor-length velvet caftan. And besides, someone forgot to count the photographers, so there were many more than thirty members of the media milling about, all similarly dressed and masked. Figuring out which one he was would waste her precious time and energy. And for what?

She moved with as much speed as she could muster upstairs to the top floor where the caterers were headquartered to see about getting a case of champagne sent to the Cupid Room when she suddenly had a thought. She was certain that Corlis would have described to Jack the distinctive, one-of-a-kind gown Serena was wearing?

Surely, he wasn't trying to avoid her entirely?

Jack had hardly been able to eat a bite of the food supplied to members of the media in a room off the massive *piano nobili* at the right of the stairs. His itchy mask with its long, *papier-mâché* nose was created in a style worn centuries earlier by Venetian doctors hoping to keep their distance from plague victims they attempted to treat. Its uncomfortable contours were driving him absolutely crazy, to say nothing of the difficulty he'd been having seeing through the eye slits.

Not only that, he was roasting in the full-length, velvet journalist's caftan that had been assigned him. All evening, he'd been searching for Serena, but he'd had to shift his head, not just his eyes, in order to spy anything other than what lay straight ahead of him.

A voice beside him chortled, "Trying to spot that magnificent creature in the sea-green gown?"

Jack recognized King's voice before he was able to swivel his head to see him face-to-face and he knew he was being royally ribbed.

"If you must know, yes."

Corlis, standing next to her husband, volunteered, "How can you have missed her?" That 'Seas of Venice' costume is tight as a second skin. I have no idea how she can do her work in it, but she sure looks fabulous, don't you think?" she added, pointing her organza-clad arm toward a far corner in the gilt and frescoed ballroom.

Jack painfully shifted his gaze once again and was rewarded with a view of a stunningly beautiful, dark-haired woman in a gown that looked like shimmering sea foam. Her lush curves and small waist, along with the sparkling gems she wore in her upswept hair, on her earlobes, and around her neck literally left him speechless. That is, until he saw a tall, masked figure that had to be Stefano Fabrini, hovering at her side.

"Oh, *sh*—"

Corlis quickly intervened.

"No expletives allowed, Jack," she joked, having also caught sight of the familiar figure buzzing around Serena as she turned away from Fabrini to have a word with a livery-clad headwaiter. "I don't think she's paying that Italian Romeo a bit of attention, do you, King?"

"I'm not so sure," King replied and Jack could tell he was

grinning behind his mask. "Better go check it out, Durand, and pronto, if I were you. The night isn't getting any younger." To Corlis he said, "The dancing is starting downstairs in the disco, can you hear? Want to give it a whirl?"

Serena returned to the post where Allegra had assigned her following dinner: the spot where the performers made their exits. By the time the show had reached its conclusion, she almost chuckled out loud to see where Stefano had drifted off to—the same man who had rarely left her side all evening despite her terse, repeated explanations that she had work to do.

Clad in tight-fitting breeches and sporting a bulging codpiece at the apex of his groin, he was currently leaning with one hand braced against a gilded window frame and whispering into the ear of a buxom lady with a loud Texas accent. If he was trying to make Serena pay more attention to him, his actions were laughable. Even so, they did remind her—as if she needed any more evidence—that, charming and good-looking as he was, he was what they called in Las Vegas 'a serious player," and of absolutely no romantic interest to her.

And *where* was Jack? Here she was, surrounded by more beauty than she'd ever experienced in her life and the man she yearned to be with on Valentine's Day was…

Right in front of her!

"Serena…?"

Standing in her path was a tall, dark-haired figure in a regimental journalist's caftan, his face obscured by a mask with a monstrously long nose.

"Jack?" she ventured. "I…I wondered if…well, I wondered if you were even here."

"I can understand why. Every damn media person at

the ball was given the same ridiculous get-up I'm wearing!"

Serena suppressed a giggle.

"It's a tradition around here," she explained. She peered at his disguise, adding, "I don't think your *maschera nera dal lungo naso a becco* does you justice."

"My what?"

"Your *maschera*...mask with the long nose. *Lungo becco*...it means 'long nose...long 'beak,' if you will.'"

Jack fingered the proboscis that extended at least eight inches from his face.

"No kidding," he said sourly.

"But your costume must be much more comfortable than this dress," Serena assured him.

"About that dress..." he said reverently, moving closer.

"You like it? *On* me, I mean? It was originally made for Allegra a few years back."

"I like it on you...off you. Yes," he said, his voice sounding slightly hoarse under his mask, "I like it a *whole* lot."

"Well, thank you," she said, and realized how prim she must sound. Her heart had begun to race and she was doing her level best to appear calm, cool, and collected. Which she wasn't. "I'm glad you came back to Venice so you could see me in it."

"The dress is beautiful, but I came back to see *you*."

She cast him a doubtful look and replied, "You had a strange way of showing it when you arrived yesterday."

"I know. I didn't know how to get you alone with all those people in the conference room, and then you seemed awfully busy."

Serene nodded. What was the point of feigning disinterest in front of Jack? She heaved a sigh and admitted, "I wanted to *look* busy because I didn't know if you ...whether you were here just because of your story for the *T-P*, or...for some other reason."

"The story is the passport that got me here, after some heavy persuasion exerted on my editor. But I'm here because of you."

"And...well...what about Lauren? Did you...sort it out with her?"

Serena suddenly felt like a jealous ninny even to ask the question, but she had to know.

"That's why I wangled a trip over here. I wanted to tell you in person that I spoke with Lauren as soon as I could. That chapter is closed, and I—"

He seized her hand and pulled her into an alcove formed by a set of deep-set windows that overlooked the Grand Canal. Their surroundings were cast in darkness, now, except for shafts of light beaming from the ancient buildings across the water.

Hidden somewhat by the twenty-foot drapes cascading to the floor on either side of the alcove, Jack removed his mask and leaned forward within inches of her face.

"I might as well admit it, Serena. I now know what it feels like to *pine* for someone else—and I don't like the feeling very much."

"I don't either," she murmured, her gaze locked on his.

"And I hated the way we were at the Danieli that night. It was even worse on the phone when you called New Orleans. I had to see you again...talk to you...touch you, and—"

Without warning, he maneuvered them both deeper into the recessed space framed by the partially closed curtains and clasped her hard against his chest. Before she knew it, he'd stripped off her silver and green mask, tossing it along with his own onto the brocade window seat nearby. A second later, he bent down to kiss her fiercely, as if he thought she might flee the ball like Cinderella.

"Oh, God, I wanted to do this from the moment I saw you in Allegra's office!"

"Liar," she whispered, staring into his eyes. "You didn't even look at me.".

"That was because I was afraid you'd never speak to me again, let alone let me..."

His lips marked a molten trail from her ear lobe to the base of her neck. Behind her closed lids, Serena reveled in the pure sensation of his broad hands on her back.

"I felt so awful after I walked out of the Danieli," she confessed, against his cheek. "It was just one, big achy feeling of misery from that second, until...just now."

"Well what about Fabrini?" he demanded, pulling away from her. "I saw the way he was sniffing around you all night! You two obviously know each other better than you did when I left."

"I love it that you sound jealous," she laughed, "but trust me, Stefano is Casanova, reincarnated. Not my type at all."

"How long did it take you to find that out?" he retorted, and Serena knew he wanted to know if they'd slept together.

"One night," she answered truthfully. "At his place. He took me there to get out of the snow."

Jack's expression turned from shock to a look that almost scared her. She placed her hand on his arm.

"Trust me, I was practically on death's door with a cold. He gave me his version of an Italian hot toddy and I fell asleep on his couch. I left the next morning, still sick as a dog, but unsullied," she said, suppressing a smile. "But given the way you'd been behaving, believe me, I was almost of a mind to succumb to his persistent invitations. Lucky for you, I didn't give in to temptation."

Jack pursed his lips, mildly mollified by this, but then asked tersely, "Well, tell me this: why did you call King for help with the *palazzo*, instead of me, and then practically hang up on me when we spoke that night?"

Serena inhaled deeply and gazed directly into his eyes.

"Because I felt you hadn't played it straight with me right before you left Venice. I knew…or at least I sensed…there was something else besides having to officially end your relationship with Lauren that was troubling when you announced you suddenly had to go back to New Orleans. Something you refused to tell me. Something you *still* haven't told me. It gave me pause. I guess I'd have to say that I stopped trusting you."

Jack hesitated a long moment and Serena could see he was once again forming his words too carefully to give her much comfort.

"I hope you'll trust me now when I say that I had—and have—nothing but your best interests at heart. Both of our best interests, in fact."

"But…?" she filled in for him.

"There was…there *is* something," he amended. "It has to do with writing this story about the parallels between Venice and New Orleans. The rising waters, the architectural beauty…the corporate and governmental corruption."

"So? I know all that already," she replied, unable to hide her exasperation.

"My editor has decided to publish the *palazzo* story separately and make the rest of what I've learned here and in New Orleans into a big deal—maybe even a three-parter to run during the week of the tenth year anniversary of Katrina."

"Well, that's wonderful! But what does it have to do with *us*?"

Again, he hesitated.

"*Jack!*" she insisted.

"There are a lot of pieces to the reporting that I can't talk about at *all*—with you or with anyone else except my bosses—until it's published. I'm dealing with a lot of questions that haven't been answered in the ten years since the storm. And there are aspects to the story I have to investigate over the next seven months that might upset a lot of people in our town. Some of what I've uncovered is pretty explosive stuff and I have a duty to protect my sources."

"I understand that, Jack," she said evenly. "But that can't be what made you suddenly distance yourself from me right before you left last time."

Jack seized her hands tightly, as if willing her to understand his words by osmosis.

"Because of the sensitive nature of what I'm going to be writing about, it's highly likely that both the paper and I will be soundly ridiculed in high places. That doesn't bother me, since God knows I'm used to it, but what I end up including in this story might even upset *you*...or your family..." he said, gazing at her with a peculiar intensity. "You know...the death of your brother and his wife and—all that stuff... is bound to be stirred up again."

"Something tells me *you're* dreading stirring it all up again."

Jack looked down at their conjoined hands and nodded.

"You are one, perceptive lady," he mumbled.

"If you think rehashing everything is going to upset me, maybe I just won't read it," she ventured softly, "though it would be hard to ignore something you'd worked so hard on for half a year." She stood on tiptoe and kissed him softly on his cheek, pulling back to seek his glance again. "Look, Jack...I understand that you have a job to do, and you can't share every aspect of it with me. And you probably have your own wounds to heal, despite your conviction that being an 'observer' somehow made you immune from the post-traumatic stress so many experienced. And are *still* experiencing," she amended, "like my mother."

Jack heaved an audible sigh.

"The deeper I dig into the events of ten years ago, the more I'm beginning to think you might be right to a degree I haven't…been able to acknowledge or accept."

"Hey…" she said, reaching up to brush a strand of dark hair off his forehead, "each of us has to make our peace with the past and reconcile on our own what happened to us individually as a result of Katrina."

"That's true, I suppose," Jack replied, not sounding convinced about something. "But maybe there are some things that can never be reconciled, and what do we do then?"

Just then, over Jack's shoulder, Serena caught a glimpse of Allegra who appeared to be a woman on a mission.

"Oh, glory…there's my boss," she said hurriedly. "She needs help with something. I've got to go."

"Where can I find you later?" he demanded as Serena lifted the long skirts of her ball gown and prepared to depart.

"How about right here, behind the curtains?" she said, with a come-hither smile.

"Even better, King's booked a water taxi to pick us up on the dock outside the front entrance at six a.m."

"I'll be there if I can," she assured him. "Did you get anything to eat? If you go up the stairs and through the door on the right at the far end of the room, you can grab one of the plates of food that never made it into one of the dining rooms. There are some comfortable chairs in the corner, back there, where you could even grab a nap."

"Can't you go with me?" he urged. "It's three o'clock in the morning!"

Serena regretfully pointed toward Allegra who was conferring with one of her many assistants.

"Still on duty," she said hurriedly, "and you've got to

put your mask back on," she reminded him.

Jack leaned down and retrieved their masks from the window seat cushion, handing hers to her and retying his own around the back of his head.

"You mean I have to wear this blasted thing a couple of more hours?" he groused.

"Tradition," she said with mock solemnity, "but buck up, *signor*...if you play your cards right, I might make it worth your while."

"Is that a guarantee?" he challenged, cocking his head to one side, a lascivious grin broadening below the lip of the mask.

Serena knew, for certain, now, that Jack was every bit as glad to see her as she was to see him. Even so, there was still a missing piece to the puzzle of his abrupt departure from Venice. But did that matter, really, she asked herself as she sped across the room in Allegra's direction? She was bound to learn what it was in good time. The main thing was, he'd come back to Venice to see her and tell her in person that he'd officially broken it off with Lauren Hilbert. Even better, there was no doubt in her mind that he'd missed her as much as she'd missed him.

CHAPTER 16

Only a handful of costumed guests, along with the musicians and Allegra's staff, remained in the *palazzo* as dawn broke sullenly across the choppy waters of the canal under a canopy of still-gray skies.

"My darling, indispensible Serena," Allegra said with a weary smile. "I now proclaim you officially off-duty." She then turned and seized a microphone from the bandstand to make a general announcement in Italian to the assembled.

"Thank you, thank you, everyone! Pack up what you need to at the moment, and the rest of you, get a bit of sleep. Be back here by noon and we will start the load out. As most of you know, there's a big corporate event scheduled for here the day after tomorrow, so we only have eight hours to remove what we've brought in."

When Allegra returned to her side, Serena asked, "Are you sure you don't need me, still?" She was certain that their leader wouldn't leave the *palazzo* until the last team member was out of the building.

"Sometime after midnight, I caught a glimpse of you in the window alcove, *cara*," she replied with a wink. "I think it is your obligation to be extremely hospitable to our saviors, don't you? Especially *Signor* Durand, who has come all this way to see you again."

Serena could feel her cheeks grow warm under her bejeweled mask that, mercifully, still disguised the upper part of her face.

"That is so kind of you to say," she murmured. "The Duvallons have hired a water taxi for six a.m., so…"

"By all means…go, *go*!" Allegra urged, pointing to an enormous mahogany clock standing against a brocaded wall nearby that showed it was nearing the hour. "I will see you back here at noon. And Serena?"

"Yes?"

"*Mille, mille grazie!* I don't think I could have managed this year without you. Between the snow, the flooding, and everyone getting sick, plus the problems with the building officials…you were a rescuing angel, and so were your friends."

"Oh, Allegra, no."

"Oh, *yes*!" she insisted, and Serena saw her eyes were moist. "If not for the miracle they wrought, we very well might have been prevented from even opening our doors last night."

"Those southern boys were pretty amazing, weren't they?" Serena said, suddenly filled with a sense of pride for what the shock troops from New Orleans and their Italian counterparts had accomplished in the nick of time.

"Well," Allegra said, giving Serena's hand a squeeze, "I hope I can persuade you all to come to Venice for a few weeks every year when the weather isn't so horrendous."

"I've loved experiencing *Carnevale*," she assured her employer, "but I, for one, would definitely like to visit you sometime when it's not so cold."

Allegra threw her head back and laughed louder than Serena had ever heard her.

"By all means, *cara*. I want one day to take you to the Lido where, I assure you, there are genuine sunbathers there in July and August. Now, go on with you!"

King and Corlis were already sitting in the sleek water taxi's luxurious cabin when Serena raced out of the broad front entrance of the *palazzo* to join Jack. He stood waiting on the dock with an anxious expression visible, now, that he was without his long-nosed mask. A gentle snow had started again, around two a.m. and continued to fall throughout the night. Serena immediately slowed down to tread carefully in her narrow-skirted ball gown along the slippery gangway where six inches of drifts had been swept to each side.

"Thanks for waiting," she said, her breath coming out in little cloudbursts.

"I got your text just before we'd figured you couldn't get free and we were about to pull away. Quick, get inside," he urged, offering her a hand into the boat. "Corlis says it's nice and warm in there."

Serena hiked up her gown beneath her long cloak and gingerly stepped on deck with a second steadying hand from the captain. She ducked her head to join the Duvallons in the enclosed section of the boat, followed by Jack, who flopped down on the seat beside her and immediately threw his mask on the leather seat. Everyone else quickly followed suit.

"At last," Jack breathed. "Whoever decided everybody in the press corps had to wear these long-nosed numbers was a sadist."

"I wouldn't take it personally," Serena said, smiling. "As you could see tonight, that style of mask is very popular generally. And for you *nosy* reporters," she teased him, "those long beaks and your caftan uniform serve as early-warning signals to guests who may be attending with women who are not their wives. The naughty ones can quickly make themselves scarce if they see one of you heading their way."

"Clever," Corlis chortled. "I hope they never decree in New Orleans that media folks all have to wear the same type of boring old costume during Mardi Gras!"

King leaned his bewigged head against the bulwark and let out a long breath.

"Man, do these Venetians know how to party," he said tiredly, closing his eyes. "Maybe it's just jet-lag, but I think they even put the Krewe of Cork to shame."

"What you saw tonight were mostly Texans and rich Europeans," Jack commented dryly. "I bet there weren't fifty Venetians in the entire *palazzo* who'd paid for their tickets."

Serena shook her head affirmatively. "It's kind of like our Mardi Gras in New Orleans. The locals have their own parties in private homes, and celebrate Fat Tuesday among themselves more than taking part in the show for the tourists you saw tonight."

"Ah…but what fun to be a tourist in Venice!" Corlis exclaimed. "What a spectacle…and these costumes!" she said, patting her silk skirt that was heavily encrusted with silver and gold beading. "I wouldn't have missed this night for anything."

"It was all pretty gorgeous, wasn't it?" Serena murmured. Now that she had sat down for the first time in hours she was suddenly fighting off a crushing wave of fatigue. Like her cousin King, she leaned back and closed her eyes.

Jack leaned toward her and whispered in her ear, "Now, no falling asleep, y'hear? We've got omelets and toasted *ciabatta* waiting for us at the *pensione*, and then…"

Serena's eyes flew open. Jack hadn't finished his sentence. He didn't need to.

To Serena's surprise, their foursome didn't immediately repair to the dining room at the *Pensione Accademia*.

"Before we eat those omelets, I gotta ditch these duds," King said, having returned from the front desk where he handed Corlis the key to their room. He turned with a slight smile tugging his lips. "And look what the management has produced," he announced to Jack. "Your very own room. Somebody unexpectedly checked out last night."

"My editor will *kill* me if I put this on my expense account," Jack protested.

"In case you didn't notice, you've also been working for the New Orleans Preservation Alliance during the last twenty-four hours," King said gruffly. "We have funds set aside for just such emergencies."

"Hey, King, that's bullshit! I can't just—"

"Yes you can, darlin'," Corlis intervened in her faux southern drawl. "And besides, King and I want some privacy in this gorgeous place, don't we, sugar? Kinda a second honeymoon."

"You betcha!" King said, grinning now. To the astonished Serena he added, "As a matter of fact…I think I'm too bushed to do anything but dive under those downy bedspreads they've got up there in our room. How 'bout you, darling?" he asked his wife. "Shall we cancel those omelets? We can call the kitchen from upstairs."

"Excellent idea," Corlis replied. She stuck out one brocade-clad foot from beneath the hem of her gown. "My feet in these eighteenth century high heels are *killing* me."

During their exchange, Serena felt her face flush to the roots of her scalp. Jack now had his own room in the hotel, a fact that greatly unnerved her. Earlier, she'd been so sure he was as glad to see her as she was to see him, but the worm of doubt that he hadn't disclosed the entire reason for his leaving Venice so abruptly last time had begun to burrow once again into her consciousness. By the time Corlis and King had disappeared up the marble staircase leading off the lobby, she felt an awkward pause bloom between Jack and her as they stood uncertainly near the hotel's front door.

"Are you hungry?" she asked.

"Not for omelets."

Ignoring his obvious inference, she glanced toward the entrance.

"Well, if we're not going to eat, I guess I should—"

"Come upstairs with me," he interrupted. "That's what you should do. Come to the room King and Corlis just arranged for us." He grasped her two gloved hands in his. "Please, Serena. I know you're exhausted. So am I, but I just want us to be together tonight."

"And tomorrow night?" she asked, daring him to meet her steady glance.

Jack paused and Serena suddenly realized she was holding her breath.

"I want that too. And the night after that…and the night after that."

"And when we both get back to New Orleans?" she challenged him.

"If you only knew how much I want you permanently in my bed on Julia Street," he said in a low voice, "you wouldn't even ask that question."

"And in your life, Jack? Do you want that, too?"

"Especially that."

Serena saw in his glance a peculiar sadness she couldn't quite fathom. In the next moment, Jack almost seemed to sway on his feet, the hem of his caftan brushing the floor in small ripples.

"You are about to drop, too," she said softly.

"Thirty-six hours without much sleep and some physically hard labor that this scribe definitely isn't used to have taken their toil, I think."

"Same here. Okay, then. It's safe to go upstairs."

Jack cast her a look saying he wasn't thrilled with her last comment as she took his velvet-clad arm, but nevertheless, he appeared grateful for her steadying presence. As if she were leading a patient back to his hospital room, she slowly guided him upstairs. Clearly, they were both too physically and emotionally spent to do anything but fall into bed and go unconscious. She'd confront her doubts tomorrow.

"I just want to sleep beside you," he mumbled, reaching for the stair railing, "even if I'm on top of the covers and you're underneath, like our first time at *Ca'Arco Antico*."

"I want to be beside you, too, *Giovanni*," she admitted. Once they reached the upper floor, she glanced at the number on his door key and pointed ten feet down the hall. "C'mon, here's our room. We can decide who sleeps where, once we're inside."

"Serena?"

"Hmmm?"

"It's eleven-thirty. Aren't you due back at the *palazzo* at noon?"

"Huh? Mmmm…oh, God! Yes!"

In the next moment, Serena struggled to sit upright in the huge bed with its gold leaf headboard and blood red brocade drapes cascading from a large, carved wood and gilt circlet, affixed near the ceiling.

"Oh, no!" she moaned. "I don't even remember going to sleep!"

"Me, neither," Jack grumbled. He pointed to their grand surroundings. "What a waste!"

Serena agreed with a rueful laugh. Her Seas of Venice gown was draped over a matching red silk sofa where she'd left it on the far side of the enormous room when Jack had helped her out of its tightly boned bodice. Seconds later, she'd literally fallen into bed and, within minutes, slipped into a sleep of the dead, as apparently had Jack.

She threw her legs over the side of the mattress and

then suddenly realized she didn't have a stitch of clothing on. Neither did her bedmate, although their stark nakedness obviously hadn't led to romance.

"Oh, hell! What am I going to put on?" she demanded. "I can't go back to the *palazzo* to help with the load-out wearing *that*!" she wailed, pointing to the exquisite creation she and Allegra both considered so precious.

Jack reached for the bedside phone and asked to be put through to King and Corlis' room. Fortunately, the pair hadn't yet gone down to a late breakfast and within minutes, a hotel staff member delivered a pair of jeans, a turtleneck sweater, and a jacket that Corlis willingly loaned her.

Meanwhile, Serena had jumped in the shower for less than five minutes. She then scrambled into her borrowed clothing, blessing the fates that she'd worn flat shoes underneath her ball gown that was currently wrapped in the woolen cloak she had worn the previous night.

"Here, eat this Power Bar," Jack insisted, shoving some sustenance into the hand not holding the bulky clothing. "It's left over from the plane. And I see you don't have your purse with you, so here are some Euros for the *vaporetto*."

"Thanks," she replied hurriedly. "You and Corlis are lifesavers. They'll be coffee at the *palazzo*, I'm praying."

Serena turned to leave.

"Dinner tonight?" he asked quickly.

She halted halfway to the wide, mahogany door studded with impressive brass hinges and shining hardware.

"I hope so," she answered, turning abruptly to face him. "It depends on when we finish getting all the equipment out and everything back to various warehouses. When do you have to leave Venice?"

"Tomorrow. Early. And my story about stemming the

leaks and contrasting *Il Ballo di Carnevale* with similar Mardi Gras celebrations like the Rex Ball is due later today." He gave a short laugh. "I guess we'll both be busy for the next eight hours."

"Can't you get the paper to let you stay a bit longer?"

Before Jack could relate the strict orders he'd received from his editor, Serena waved her hand in resignation and bolted for the door. She was late already.

Jack called out to her, "I'll text you where to meet the Duvallons and me tonight, okay?"

Serena turned, her hand on the doorknob. "I'll make a reservation at *Antiche Carampane*, and I'll meet you there if I possibly can," she suggested in a rush. "Nine o'clock okay? I know it's late if you're flying out tomorrow, but it'll give me the best chance of joining you all. Remember, it's near *Campo San Polo*? It's real Venetian. King and Corlis will love it."

"And afterward, let's go to your place, yes?" Jack said, crossing the large room to stand beside her near the door. "I can't let King pay for a second night here. This is the Bridal Suite."

Then, before Serena could say another word, he bent down and kissed her with such thoroughness, she thought she could very easily faint from lack of oxygen. Her pulse beating wildly, she nearly gave in and led him back to their magnificent red brocade bed—which was exactly where she longed to be.

"Oh...Serena," Jack groaned. "This is killing me!"

"Believe me...it's killing me too." Then, the thought of poor Allegra facing the mess they'd left at the *palazzo* floated through her consciousness. Driven by guilt that she was seriously late, she whispered, "See you tonight, let us pray," and then forced herself to pull away.

Before either of them could say or do anything else, she ran down the stairs and out the front door of the elegant

Pensione Accademia, making a beeline for the *vaporetto* that had just pulled into its stop.

Ten hours later, Jack sensed that both he and Serena were running on pure adrenaline. The pair had parted company with King and Corlis at the edge of *Campo San Polo* after an incredible Venetian meal highlighted by a plate of *il fritto misto di pesce con le moeche*—a mixed seafood stir-fry with little soft shell crabs that twice every year changed the actual shape of their shells.

"I totally forgot to ask you," Serena said as they hooked arms to avoid slipping on the icy steps of a bridge they had to cross to get to Serena's lodgings just off nearby *Calle del Forno*, "Did you get your story in today?"

"Somehow I managed to, despite the distraction of that gorgeous bed in our room that kept reminding me of what we missed last night," he said with a rueful laugh. "But, yeah. I made my deadline before I had to check out of the place. Force of habit, I guess. And were you and Allegra able to empty out all your gear from the *palazzo* in time for the next guys to set up for another event?" Serena offered a weary nod. "And by the way," he asked, "why didn't *that* group take some responsibility for the water filling up the lower floors of that place these last few weeks?"

Serena grimaced. "The head of that outfit happens to be related to the *palazzo*'s absentee owners and figured that Allegra should be the one to fix things since her event came first. Apparently, problems with high water flooding the lower floors there happen nearly every year."

"Nice," Jack said grimly, adding, "You two have sure been under a tremendous amount of pressure. Won't it be good to get back to New Orleans?"

Serena glanced around at the star-filled sky, now that

the latest storm had blown through. The stone and plaster buildings flanking them on both sides were bathed in shades of gold and gloom cast by the streetlights dotting their path. There was a hush that seemed to enfold them in a magical net of silence as they made their way down the shuttered, deserted streets. She halted and stretched out one arm to embrace the scene.

"Can you *hear* the stillness?" she murmured. "No cars. Everyone tucked in their beds. Hardly any water traffic at this hour. And even though it's so cold, do you feel how the air is light and fresh? I'm going to *miss* Venice."

"How long will you stay?" Jack asked, and he fought a sudden sense of uneasiness prompted by what might happen while they were apart.

"I'll be home in ten days. That was my original arrangement with Allegra. Two months working for her through *Carnevale* and cleanup. It's been incredible, but I'm sure I'll be ready to go home by then."

"So when can I meet you at the airport?" he demanded, determined not to let anything mar the miracle that he was standing inches away from her. He leaned down, pulled her scarf away from her neck, and kissed the hollow of her throat. Her scent was of the shampoo she used, lemon tinged and fresh smelling. He could feel the tense lines around his mouth relaxing as he pressed his lips against her cool skin. Pulling back, he said, "I want to know exactly when I'll see you next."

Even if it's after my story runs, I want a date on the calendar…

Man, was he a different guy from what he had been two months ago, he thought with a sense of bemusement that bordered on the ridiculous.

By this time, they had turned into *Calle del Forno* and had only another few feet until they turned right and reached the door of her lodgings at *Ca' Arco Antico*. It was after midnight and all was quiet in the courtyard.

"At some point, I suppose," Serena replied lightly, fishing for her key to the front door, "we'll have to talk about what happens when I get back to New Orleans."

He had a sudden wave of anxiety wash over him. Was she going to send him away, postponing any reunion until she knew about what he'd been keeping from her? He couldn't blame her, really, but his gut clenched even so.

When the door opened, she turned, smiled at him from the depths of her smoky eyes, and pointed her index finger skyward.

"Upstairs, first, *Signor Giovanni*. Chat later."

More relieved than he had ever felt in his life, Jack had barely entered the hotel's minuscule, silent lobby before he took her in his arms.

"Finally…" he breathed his relief into her fragrant hair, its scent neutralizing any cautionary thoughts that had plagued him earlier.

"Finally," she repeated, and clung to him.

Her nearness was intoxicating and neither of them could ignore the stirring in his groin.

Serena leaned back in his arms, uncertainty suddenly tingeing her gaze.

"Jack…" she whispered, her eyes searching his. "I want to be with you so much tonight. In my bed. But I also want you to know that I can tell you are still holding something back. I just hope it's only about journalist ethics, and not something that's personal—something that I should know."

Jack felt as if a stake had been run clean through his solar plexus. She was such a smart, intuitive woman and read him so well, he thought with an inward sigh.

"Can you trust me that I will tell you everything I can, *when* I can?"

"Once your Katrina stories are published, you mean?"

"Sooner, if I can," Jack assured her, "but it'll most likely be after the August 29th anniversary date. Just know that what I can't tell you is governed by the peculiar circumstances of this damned, expanded assignment I'm saddled with."

For Jack, even the thought of having to tell her someday that the Durands may have been a cause of the Antonelli's family tragedy was too horrible to contemplate.

At length, to his relief, she murmured, "Alright. That's enough for me," and slid her arms around his neck. "At least for now, anyway."

God, she was an incredible woman…but would she think he was even a decent *guy after August 29th?*

Then, as if to prove her leap of faith, she began kissing him in a fashion that was clearly calculated to speed them upstairs to her room. If tonight turned out to be the last time they could ever be together like this, Jack thought, he would risk telling her absolutely everything as soon as he possibly could. She deserved to know the unvarnished truth, even if he had to endure the pain that she might choose to walk away.

But for now…

Arms around each other, they slowly climbed the marble staircase where a tall, mahogany door with the familiar oval brass plaque appeared on the landing.

"May I welcome you back to the *Canaletto* Room?" Serena said with a crooked smile, accompanied by a hint of shyness that pierced his well-defended heart.

Once inside with the door now firmly locked, Jack took his time helping Serena remove her warm jacket she'd borrowed from Corlis earlier that day. He savored the warmth and feel of her body beneath his fingers as he worked the buttons marching down the front of the bulky garment. He tossed it on a chair upholstered in the same, golden brocade that covered the bed, and in the next moment, mirroring his actions, she reached out to help him shed his thick coat. With increasing urgency, they stripped each other of every stitch of clothing. Before a minute had passed, there was a trail of their discards extending from the door to the edge of the mattress.

"My beautiful Serena," Jack murmured, his hands skimming lightly from her shoulders to her thighs, her slender frame and long limbs responding to his touch with aching familiarity. He gently pulled the ribbon fastening her hair at her neck. He drank in the sight of the dark strands cascading down her shoulders. "This was how I wanted to say goodbye last time…to love you like this so you would know how much you mean to me…so there would be no doubts, no questioning of my feelings for you."

Jack supported her back and carefully laid her across the bedcovers, his breath catching at how lovely she looked with her dark eyes staring up at him.

"What a brunette Botticelli you are," he said, smiling down at her, her sable hair fanned across the pillow.

Serena reached up to grasp him by both shoulders and then glanced down at his waistline with a faint smile playing around her lips. Her slender fingers took gentle possession of a most tender part of him and touched him reverently.

"Ah…I think we'll have to call you Neptune *Rising…*" she whispered.

Slowly, she pulled him down so he smothered the length of her frame, her body beneath him a luxurious cushion of curves and soft skin and a heady scent of longing and desire.

And then he shut out even that thought and slowly sheathed himself in Serena's welcoming warmth.

However the fates played out this tortured tale, this night would belong to them both. By any measure, it was worth the risk.

A thick mist lay on the Grand Canal, a sliver of which Jack could glimpse out the balconied window in the *Canaletto* Room that faced *Traghetto della Madonnetta*. The narrow passageway he had gazed at so often from this window ended at a small dock where gondoliers crossed the Grand Canal from the *San Polo* district to *Sant'Angelo* on the *San Marco* side. He was due at the *Pensione Accademia* to meet with King and Corlis in half an hour. There, he would return Corlis' clothing to her that Serena had borrowed, pick up his luggage, and the trio would board the water taxi to Marco Polo Airport.

He shrugged on his heavy coat and gazed down at Serena once more, sleeping on her side, a hand curled under her chin as he'd so often seen her the times when he'd left this room at the crack of dawn. The nights they had shared in this bed came back to him in a wondrous rush of tactile memories and a sense that here was home…here were the feelings he'd always known were missing until now. Serena was all he wanted in a life's companion. All he'd ever wanted. He could only think how much his body and soul yearned to make love to this woman once more before he left, to let her know with taste and touch that after today—whatever the future held—no one else would ever lay a claim to his heart like *La Contessa Antonelli*…

He bent over the bed and brushed a kiss against her forehead.

"*Arrivederci, cara*," he whispered.

"Oh, no…it's time for you to leave?" she murmured, and pulled herself up on her elbows.

"Yes…and I hope I don't get lost sprinting to the Duvallons' hotel," he said, touching his index finger to his lips and then pressing it against her own.

"Forget that pocket map and go for broke. Use your phone's GPS," she urged, swinging her legs to the side of the bed. "It's so easy to get turned around." She glanced out the window, adding, "And especially when it's foggy like this."

He heard her pad behind him to the door and was glad, wanting to keep her close until the last possible moment. He turned and she melted into his arms.

"Fly safe," she mumbled into his chest. She tilted her head and met his gaze. "Last night was...well...pretty unforgettable. I loved..." She halted, mid-sentence. "Oh, hell, I might as well say it in case your plane crashes—or mine does in two weeks. I love you, Jack. It scares me how much."

Jack pulled her hard against him. Something had shifted in him, something momentous. Without qualm or hesitation he replied, "I love you too, *Contessa*. So much, it's pretty staggering. I'll be counting the days until you come back to New Orleans."

Serena's broad smile told him he'd given her the reassurance every woman needs after a night like the one they'd just spent together. The fireworks between them wasn't just lust, although there had been plenty of that. His feelings for her were beyond serious, Jack knew. They had "forever" written all over them—that is, if the Gods were on their side.

Who's ever in charge up there, he prayed silently in the manner of a lapsed Catholic, *please*, please *may my fears that the Durands must answer for any sins prove groundless...*

"This is just goodbye for now, darling," Jack said, and then realized with a jolt he'd never called any other woman by that endearment.

"*Addio, caro*," replied Serena. "I'll let you know my flight number and when it's supposed to land. Now go...*go* before I start to cry!"

He nodded, moisture filling his own eyes. He exited swiftly and heard the door close behind him, followed by the sound of his footsteps slapping against the marble staircase that led to the lobby and the lodging's front door. His cellphone in hand, he sprinted down *Calle del Forno* while his mind filled with strategies for a means through which he could continue to see Serena in the next few months without compromising the integrity of the story he had to produce for the *T-P*.

There has to be a way…

By the time he arrived at King and Corlis' *pensione*, it was worth the bloody fortune it cost for his phone's GPS function to guide him flawlessly down murky alleyways and across several bridges to the *Dorsoduro* section of the island where the Duvallons were waiting, dockside. In minutes, the trio boarded the water taxi that sped the three friends on the first leg of their long journey home to New Orleans.

Serena's last ten days in Venice were filled with the mundane work of reconciling invoices for materials and time spent creating the new costumes made for Allegra's numerous clients. She also helped with the task of entering notes that described new creations made that year for the rental business—and catalogued them in a pictorial database that tracked some fifteen hundred costumes already hanging in rows at Allegra's atelier where people came to make their selections for special occasions throughout the year.

Ironically, no more storms off the Adriatic smashed into Venice from the moment Jack and the Duvallons departed the city. Although temperatures remained in the low thirties, without the sleet and snow, the weather to Serena felt positively balmy.

A week before she was to leave for New Orleans, Allegra invited her to dinner at *Ignazio*, a rustic, wood-beamed tavern near Serena's lodgings with a vine-covered courtyard in summer, and a year-round menu of traditional Venetian cuisine.

As soon as their glasses were filed with *prosecco,* Allegra raised hers and said, "I've already told you I hope you will come back to Venice at any time of year, but if you want a permanent invitation to come to *Carnevale* as my guest, I've brought you this."

From her voluminous leather tote she withdrew a wine-red, velvet-clad invitation nearly the size of a file folder with Serena's name written in a flourish of gold script on the front.

"As long as I am producing this event," Allegra continued, "you—and three more guests—are to be *my* guests in any given year at the dinner and ball, including the costumes of your choice."

"Oh, Allegra…how wonderful! I'll have to negotiate fiercely with my brother to be allowed to ever again get away from New Orleans during our Mardi Gras season, but I expect, some years, I'll finish my work a few days early and escape to Venice." She stared at the beautiful invitation and then met her friend's gaze. "And perhaps, one year, you'll leave all the work to one of your deputies and come to spend Fat Tuesday with me at our Mardi Gras."

Allegra shook her head doubtfully. "I will put on *Il Ballo di Carnevale* for as many years as I am able. But I will definitely come to visit you and my saviors in New Orleans at another time of year."

"Jazz Fest!" Serena exclaimed. "Or Quarter Fest! *That's* when you should come! It's usually not too hot at the end of April and beginning May, and you'll see my city in its truest incarnation. These two musical events feature a real gumbo of sights and sounds and flavors!"

"I would adore to," Allegra replied. Then her smile faded. "And what of that special savior, *Giovanni*? How did things work out with that lovely man?"

Serena fought the flood of heat that instantly infused her cheeks. She could not think of the last night they'd spent together without a blush fanning up from her throat.

"Well…we…ah…sorted out a lot of things while he was here last time, but still…there's something he's thus far unwilling or unable to tell me that I sense is important for how it ultimately turns out for us."

"Has he given you a reason for not telling you?"

"It involves the newspaper series he's been assigned that will mark the anniversary of Hurricane Katrina in late August. I can't imagine what it is he can't tell me, but apparently, journalistic ethics require not disclosing a bunch of stuff until after the story is published."

"And why would that affect the two of you, I wonder?" Allegra asked with a puzzled expression. "What would there be about a newspaper story he's doing that could impact *your* relationship?"

"That's what I don't understand," Serena mused. She paused and then revealed, "My brother and his pregnant wife drowned in the storm."

"Oh, no…how terrible for your family," she murmured.

Serena nodded her thanks and continued, "I got the feeling from Jack he thought that his rehashing that nightmare would somehow…I dunno," she said with an audible sigh, "…would perhaps make me angry with him for stirring all that up again? I'll just have to wait and see. For sure, I don't look forward to thinking or reading about all that again."

"Jack Durand seems a caring, honest man. Just hold on to that until you know exactly what is involved down the road."

"Good advice," Serena said, raising her glass once again. "As always." She leaned into the table and added, "I will never forget all the things you've taught me, Allegra.

About the designing of costumes…and about life. I can never thank you—"

"And I can never thank *you*," she interrupted, "but I wish to try." She reached into her voluminous handbag again and pulled out an out-sized manila envelope that looked as if it could contain a chest X-ray, or something equally large.

"Here are copies of all my drawings of costumes that you cut out of muslin. You did such a wonderful job testing if my pattern pieces would translate into the gowns looking the way I envisioned, and then making some necessary adjustments. I want you to have the original sketches…perhaps spin some of them off into costumes of your own devising."

"Oh…my…God!" Serena exclaimed, her eyes drinking in the fanciful lines of Allegra's fantastic creations. The last drawing had tissue paper pattern pieces attached. It was one she hadn't worked on: The Seas of Venice costume that she'd worn to the ball.

"I can't give you the costume," Allegra apologized, "but I would love it if you made one of your own. No one who has worn it looked more lovely in it than you."

"I-I can't believe you'd do this…make me this incredibly generous gift." She looked up from the drawings to meet Allegra's gaze.

"I wanted to," the older woman replied simply.

Serena stared at the Seas of Venice sketch again, eyes shining.

"Nothing could inspire me more to bring my own family's costume firm closer to the level of beauty you have created at your atelier. I will have the drawing framed when I get home and hang it over my desk at Antonelli's! Thank you *so* very much, dear Allegra."

"*Mille grazie, cara Serena. Ora siamo amiche per sempre.*"

"Oh, yes," Serena nodded. "We *are* friends forever…"

CHAPTER 17

In the first week Jack returned to New Orleans, his editor and several of his colleagues congratulated him on his story about repairing the *palazzo* in time for Venetian Carnival in spite of the atrocious weather and rising floodwaters. Several of his co-workers took great pleasure ribbing him about the accompanying photograph that showed him clad in his *giornalista* caftan, along with the rest of the media. Only a few people mentioned the problems he described in the article of fighting the "unhelpful" Venetian bureaucracy whose byzantine ways nearly scuttled the entire enterprise.

*Too familiar a story around here...*he fumed silently.

"And great that you could bring in the local angle," John Reynolds noted in a rare compliment. "The bosses upstairs loved the fact that you and King Duvallon got American limestone products through those tricky customs officials over there." He turned to his assistant and barked, "Get Advertising on the phone. Tell them to go after some ads from those ArcusStone folks and the sealant people that Jack mentioned in his story. They should be good for a half-page ad—or two, even—this month!"

When Jack handed in his expense account, Reynolds actually patted him on the back.

"Amazing! How did you do that trip for practically nothing?"

"Friends in right places, plus I paid my own airfare," he reminded his boss.

Reynolds eyed him narrowly and then grinned.

"Did you learn a lot of Italian while you were there?"

Jack allowed himself to grin back.

"Some."

"I'll just bet," Reynolds replied. "A lot of those women in the photos you used in your story looked pretty damn sexy in their costumes. You reporters have all the fun."

But for Jack, the next few weeks of research were going to be anything but fun. Reynolds had gotten the official go-ahead from his bosses for a three-part approach to the paper's coverage of the tenth anniversary of Hurricane Katrina. Jack's expanded assignment meant that there was no way he could avoid finally getting to the bottom of his uncles' involvement in the crucial decisions made both by the U.S. Army Corps of Engineers in the 1980s, as well as examining the decades of policies practiced by members of New Orleans's Levee Board leading up to the storm.

A few days before Serena was due to arrive back in town, Jack accepted his mother's invitation to the Durand's regular Sunday dinner hosted at their family home in the Bywater section on Royal Street, a few blocks from the Mississippi. Ironically enough, his family home was in one of the few racially mixed areas of the predominately black Upper Ninth Ward to escape serious flooding in Katrina. In Colonial times, it had been mostly plantation land—that is, until the nineteenth century when many people from France—including the Durands' ancestors, he'd been told—settled there where land was relatively cheap. Shotgun houses and bungalows were interspersed with some of New Orleans's most renowned art galleries and music venues.

"It's gotten mighty too full of hipsters around here, if you asked me," his father often groused about the current mix of white and black blue-collar families who grew up there and bohemian arrivals that moved into the neighborhood in the wake of Katrina. The latter group had been driven out of the trendy French Quarter by rising prices.

On Sunday morning, Jack awoke in his four-poster bed on Julia Street in the heart of the Warehouse District with a feeling of dread about attending the family dinner. Once he'd made coffee, he filled his favorite Jazz Fest mug with the steaming brew and padded to his small office with a view of nearby Charles Street where the khaki-green streetcars rattled by.

It must be eighty degrees outside already, he thought, eyeing a stack of documents piled on his desk. He wondered what the temperature was in Venice and quickly summoned it on his cellphone's weather app. It was a breezy forty-seven. He forced himself away from the image he put on his cellphone's landing page of Serena wearing her winter anorak and sitting in the bow of a Number One *vaporetto*, heading for Allegra's office near St. Mark's Square.

After rifling through the various paper folders on his desk, he selected the ones he would need this day and filed them into his reporter's bag. At noon, he locked his door and headed for an inevitable confrontation that had the potential for ruining the rest of his life.

When Jack arrived at his family's house, his father, George Durand, Jr., was busy pulling out extra folding chairs from the storage shed at the back of the property that abutted Gallier Street. The small wooden structure stood to the rear of his parents' jaunty royal blue bungalow, built in the 1940s, with its white trim and bright blue concrete steps leading to the front door.

For as long as his son could remember, "G Junior"— as his dad was known—was the one member of the large, extended family that was counted upon to solve a mechanical problem, or simply get things *done*, and had earned the reputation as Mr. Reliable. His professional life as a hydraulic engineer was spent overseeing the health of the various French Quarter pumping stations. Even during Katrina, he and his colleagues had kept the tropical downpours from flooding this particular region beyond one or two feet deep.

Over the years as the older generations had passed away, most Durand family dinners tended to be hosted by him and Jack's mother, the former Sylvie Toinard, at the rambling wooden bungalow that had amply housed their three children while they were growing up. The house still provided a home for Jack's youngest sister Sylvia. The twenty-six-year-old, now two months out of rehab, appeared to be holding her own, as his mother had whispered in his ear before he'd wandered out of her kitchen with a beer in hand to find his uncles sitting on the screen porch.

Before any of the guests sat down at the family table, Jack was determined to corner his father's brothers, Jacques and Vincent, alone. He found them nursing their bourbons and talking about the previous football season while the women scurried about in the kitchen, preparing the two o'clock Sunday meal.

"Hey, there…how y'all doing?" Jack ventured, pulling up a straight-backed wooden chair.

After a few perfunctory pleasantries were exchanged, Jack casually brought up the fact he'd recently been assigned some stories that would probably run during the tenth anniversary of Katrina, in late August.

"You know, I'm curious, Uncle J," he began what he'd known for some time, now, would be a difficult conversation. "What do you remember about the improvements that supposedly were made on the Seventeenth Street Canal back in the early nineteen eighties?"

Jacques took a slow sip from his highball glass.

"Nothing, really," he grunted. "Just that we were supposed to shore up what was already there."

"Did they ever ask you to sign off on any of the plans?" Jack asked, knowing full well that his uncle had put his signature on the fateful documents that allowed pilings to be under-engineered, rather than sunk to a far greater depth which the outside consulting engineers had mandated back then.

"God, Almighty!" Jacques replied, shooting his nephew a hard look. "That's more than thirty years ago! What're you asking about that again, for? How can you expect an ole' man like me to remember what I did back then?"

"You're not old, Uncle J," Jack replied. "You're in your late fifties."

"Well, I *feel* old! I've been retired since the *last* time y'all wrote about the storm, remember? As far as I'm concerned, it's ancient history."

"Well, what about you, Uncle Vincent?" Jack pressed, turning to address Jacques' older brother. "You served on the Levee Board all those years. Did your inspections set off any alarm bells before Katrina?"

Vincent gazed speculatively at his nephew.

"Am I being officially interviewed, here, son?" he asked. "Is this a set-up for another of your ex-po-zays? 'Cause if it is, *no comment*!"

Jack could feel his heart speed up. He bent over in his chair and opened the briefcase he'd stowed at his feet and pulled out a copy of the document he'd located that contained Jacques Durand's signature okaying the design specs for the 1982 retrofit of the 17th Street Canal. He handed it to his uncle.

"Good God, where did you dig this up?" Vince exclaimed, peering over his younger brother's shoulder.

"Through the Freedom of Information Act."

Jack noted that Jacques' hands shook slightly as he

squinted and bent over to gain a closer look at the piece of paper with his signature at the bottom, clear as day.

"I was twenty-four-years-old when I signed that," he murmured, staring at it as if it were some ghost, come back to haunt him.

"This don't mean nothing!" Vincent scoffed. "Jacques, here, didn't have a clue what it was all about back then, did you Jacques? Nobody did."

Jack shrugged. "Well, I found some stuff that said there were some outside consultants back then who strongly recommended sinking those pilings another twenty-thirty feet or so beyond the ten feet that the Army Corps ultimately decided upon. Did either of you know about their findings?"

He handed over a page of the consultant's report with the ignored references highlighted in yellow.

Vince glared at his nephew.

"Why the hell are you rehashing all this stuff?" he demanded. "Why put your nose in where it doesn't belong?" He scowled at the offending documents. "Trying to make a bigger name for yourself, are you, now that that paper of yours is on the ropes? Think another *Pu*-lit-zer Prize for a bunch of lies and innuendoes will do the trick?" Vince shook his head, making no effort to disguise his disgust. "I bet you're just trying to line up your next job at the expense of your own family. You should hang your head in shame, boy!"

"I'm just doing the job I have now," Jack replied evenly.

Vincent Durand had never had one good word to say about the environmental movement that Jack had reported on for years. He often commented that he thought the notion of climate change was cooked up "by those California yahoos trying to sell us solar panels!"

To Jacques, Jack said, "These documents here are part

of the public record. I wanted to give you both a chance to explain. The anniversary series is trying to put all the pieces together as to why Katrina hit the city so hard when it was only a Category One the hour it actually made landfall near here. We're trying to evaluate if it could happen again."

"There's nothing I want to say about this," Jacques mumbled, handing the papers back.

"Well, *I* have something to say to you, boy!" Vincent exclaimed heatedly. "You just let sleeping dogs lie, you hear me?"

With a mounting sense of dread, Jack pulled from his reporter's bag several documents chronicling Levee Board meetings that showed the supposed watchdog group that Vincent Durand had served on for years clocked more time eating on the taxpayers' dime at fancy New Orleans restaurants than inspecting the levees they were charged with overseeing.

"That's an old story, full of lies!" Vincent sneered. "The *T-P* tried to stir that pot right after Katrina, and you might have noticed, the Orleans Levee Board doesn't even exist anymore, as of 2007!"

"That's because it was vilified, dissolved, and then replaced by new regional flood protection authorities," Jack corrected his uncle in a level tone.

"And not a single one of us serving on those boards went to jail!"

"True," Jack agreed. He pointed to the papers in his hand that outlined various conflicts-of-interest that arose because the old levee district generated its revenues from the Lakefront Airport, a marina, and a casino—enterprises that had little to do with flood control. One report characterized the U.S. Army Corps of Engineers as having been "forced to partner" with politically appointed officials like former barge captain, Vincent Durand, who had no hydraulic engineering experience, nor had ever been engaged in any aspect of the business of flood protection.

"The levees you oversaw back then, Uncle Vince, are the very levees that failed the worst during Katrina. I wondered if you could explain how this...this way of conducting the levee board's business came about over the years. Believe it or not, I'm actually trying to *understand*— with the hindsight of ten years—how all the aspects of the disaster fit together."

"I thought you were a swamp-loving environmental reporter," Vince jeered, "not some ambulance-chasing self-appointed investigator!"

Jack was getting angry now.

"This is probably one of the biggest environmental stories in the history of the country!" he retorted. "Even *you* can't dispute the fact that the conduct of the Levee Board and the Army Corps are a huge part of what happened to New Orleans as a result of Katrina."

"Now look here, boy," Vincent replied, his voice so low it was close to a growl. "I'm going say this once and then I hope you understand that you'd better shut the fuck up about all this ancient history! Nobody wants to hear it. Katrina happened a decade ago. Worry about the *next* hurricane, will ya?"

"That's exactly what I *am* worried about," Jack countered, sensing that his grip on his own temper was slipping. "I'm *very* worried. Some experts say the *new* levees and walls weren't rebuilt strong enough—and for the same kinds of corruption and conflicts-of-interest we had before."

"You calling me corrupt?" Vincent demanded, his voice rising.

"I'm just asking you questions!" Jack retorted. "Ten years later, I'm *still* trying to answer questions for the families of the eighteen hundred citizens who *died*—and for everyone else who saw this city wrecked!"

A deadly silence invaded the back screen porch. Jack could hear the traffic rattling by on Royal and Gallier streets.

Jacques' shoulders slumped and he took another large sip of bourbon, avoiding Jack's gaze. Meanwhile, Vincent's eyes had narrowed to slits in his fleshy face and his fists were curled like a pugilist, ready to throw a punch. Jack suddenly wondered what it had been like for his younger cousins Mary Lou and Michael to grow up in combative Uncle Vince's household across Lake Pontchartrain in the nearly all-white town of Covington?

Vincent raised his index finger and began shaking it at Jack.

"Katrina or no Katrina, there are alligators out there in the swamp who could eat you alive, you know what I'm saying, boy? They could do our family great *harm*, you hear me? I'm telling you: *ignore* all this crap! No one will thank you for digging up this shit! *No* one!"

Jack's heart felt like a stone in his chest as he stared at his two uncles—one silent, the other red-faced and appearing he might be close to having a stroke. However, before he could ask any further questions, Jack's younger sister, Sylvia, poked her head through the door and called them all to dinner.

"Mama says everyone's to come to the table, now."

Jacques and Vincent barely grumbled a reply, but Jack managed to summon a smile, saying, "Thanks, sweetheart. We're coming right in."

"Sit next to me?" Sylvia offered, her eyes darting from her brother to their uncles who remained silent and hadn't made a move to rise from their wooden chairs.

"You betcha," Jack replied, glad for an excuse to follow her out the door and avoid any additional conversation. "And I wonder if I could interest you in helping me out a little bit to find a present for our sister's birthday this week.

Marielle's coming up on the Big Three-Eight, you know..."

Sylvia happily linked her arm through his and replied, "Easy-Louisey! Just get her anything that has to do with animals."

"Well...that's always a possibility," he allowed, "but I was thinking about something strictly for her. Give it some thought, will you? A new dress? A piece of nice jewelry? Tickets to the Saints' game? For instance, what would *you* like? That might give us some ideas."

Sylvia's startled gaze told Jack the sad fact that she'd probably seldom been asked what she'd like. She offered him the sweetest look and squeezed his arm.

"I will think some...and call you on your cell."

"Great. Then we can go shopping together, and maybe grab lunch?"

Jack thought how wonderful it would be to bring along Serena on such a venture. She'd probably have some great ideas as well, though after his recent exchange with his uncles, his worries about the links between their two families came back like floodwaters roaring down the Mississippi.

"It'll be *fun*," Sylvia whispered, bringing his thoughts back to the Durand dining room. She nodded in the direction of Marielle and her husband who were already seated at the big, oval table where guests sat elbow-to-elbow. She squeezed his arm again. "It's great having you home, bro. Sometime, I want you to tell me all about Venice. I'd love to visit there someday."

It was the most enthusiasm on any subject he'd heard from Sylvia in an age. What would his little sister say if she knew how much her big brother loved Venice and the woman he'd met there?

As soon as the stragglers sat down, large bowls of gumbo and rice were passed around and the conversation was lively—with the noticeable exception of Jacques and

Vincent Durand who, immediately following the main meal, refused the offer of dessert. In their next breath, both made excuses to their startled wives and off-spring, explaining to the puzzled faces looking at them from around the dining table that they had a poker game starting in ten minutes at the VFW.

Two days later, Jack met his younger sister Sylvia for lunch at Herbsaint on St. Charles Avenue after purchasing a hand blown glass heart for Marielle's up-coming birthday that Sylvia had found at New Orleans Glassblowers on Magazine Street.

"It's perfect as a paperweight to hold down all those files on rescued animals that pile up on Marielle's desk," he congratulated her, and then put a second gift-wrapped box on the table between them.

"What's this?" Sylvia asked, looking pleased.

"Open it," Jack said with a smile.

His sister carefully picked off the ribbon and removed the top of the box.

"For me?" she squealed. "A *pink* heart like M's red one? I love it!"

"I bought it behind your back when you were looking at the glass candle sticks," he revealed smugly. "I expect if you're back helping out at the shelter, you have a few files on your own desk, right? I figured if you liked the paperweight well enough to give it to your sister for her birthday, you might want one for yourself."

Sylvia's eyes were luminous and she clasped her present to her chest.

"Thank you *so* much, Jackie. This is so nice of you."

"It's just a little symbol to remind you how happy I am to have you home and looking so well."

Sylvia dropped her eyes to the table and said in a low voice, "Me too, you."

"Look, Syl, I know it's been a struggle, but you are strong and brave and I'm so proud of what you've accomplished."

Sylvia looked up, her eyes full of gratitude. "It's nice to have you back in New Orleans, Jack. I missed you so much."

"I missed you too, sweetheart," he answered, thinking how much he'd worried when he'd heard from his mother she was back in rehab. "Just don't take your glass heart to work before we give the red one to Marielle tomorrow, deal?" he added with a grin. "And thanks for helping me out with this."

The waitress came and Sylvia ordered dessert, the banana brown butter tart with salted caramel ice cream.

"I'll share," she announced with a contented smile. Then she said shyly, "Marielle said she bet that you saw Serena Antonelli a few times while you were in Venice. Did you?"

"A few times," Jack murmured noncommittally, taking a sip of coffee.

"M told me how you two were taking the same flights all the way to Venice. I remember meeting Serena when Sis was in college and I visited their dorm. Serena's really a nice person."

Startled, Jack gazed across the table, imagining what sisterly gossip the two had exchanged.

"Yes, she's a very nice, very talented lady."

"Are you going to see her again now that you're home?"

Jack paused. "She's still working over there for a costumer."

"But when she gets back?" Sylvia persisted.

Jack gave her one of his brotherly smiles of

exasperation.

"We'll see." And then, making a quick decision, he added. "Sure...probably."

"Does that mean you're breaking up with Lauren?"

Jack almost laughed out loud, but forced a solemn expression on his face. Trust the women in his family to get down to basics, fast. He was on the verge of offering one of his opaque answers when he said, "Can you keep a secret for a while? Even from your mother and sister?"

Sylvia reacted with surprise, as if she were astounded her older brother would honor her with such a confidence.

"I promise! I won't say a word to anyone. *What?*"

"I've told Lauren that we shouldn't see each other anymore...as a couple, I mean. Our paths have just veered off in very different directions. It was time we faced it. I wish her well, but it's over."

"Good!" Sylvia said emphatically just as the waitress arrived with dessert. "Lauren got so mean since the storm...to you and...well...everybody else."

Jack looked closely at his sister whose opinions were so often disregarded by the entire family and asked sharply, "Was she ever not nice to you?"

"Basically, she just ignored me, except once she asked if I was still doing drugs." Sylvia gave him a crooked smile. "I was...doing drugs, I mean, but she said it just to put me down. She also said that a lot of doctors and nurses she knew got hooked like I was."

Jack could barely restrain himself from pounding a fist on the table. Sylvia was so vulnerable. What kind of bedside manner did they teach in Med school, he wondered, seething with anger. But to his youngest sister he merely said, "Well, you won't have to put up with that stuff anymore," adding, "and I'm really so happy to see you're...taking things one day at a time. That takes courage, and I want you to let me know if...well, if I can ever do anything...or you need a friendly ear, sweetheart."

He grabbed a spoon off the table and dipped into the swiftly vanishing ice cream. After a few bites, he glanced at his watch.

"You have to go, right?" Sylvia said, looking disappointed their lunch was coming to an end.

"I've got to get back and make a bunch of phone calls on my story." He smiled reassuringly at her. "But let's do this again, shall we? You pick the restaurant and I'll meet you, say...week after next, okay?"

"That'd be awesome!" Sylvia said.

"And remember, not a word about Lauren to anyone until I tell you."

"Gotcha!" she replied happily. "But let me know when I can tell Marielle and Mama, okay? They're gonna be doing the Happy Dance, for sure!"

"Really? Y'all could have told me you felt that way a few years ago, you know."

Sylvia's eyes narrowed and she took a last bite of the banana tart.

"You wouldn't have listened."

Jack paused, reflected on how much things had changed for him since the January day he flew to Venice, and shook his head.

"You're probably right." He smiled again. "But I'll listen now."

"Awesome!" she repeated, and Jack chuckled, signaling for the check. "When you give me the go-ahead to break the news about Lauren, Marielle and Mama won't *believe* that I know something about you before *they* do!"

Jack signed the credit card receipt for lunch, gave his sister a big hug, and headed back to his office.

That afternoon and into the evening, both uncles refused to answer their nephew's repeated follow-up phone calls. Jack figured Captain Vince Durand was a lost cause, but his instincts told him his namesake uncle was worth one more try in a week or two.

John Reynolds buzzed Jack at his desk in the newsroom "bullpen" and asked him to come into his office.

"When you tackle a story, you sure don't do anything the easy way," his editor remarked, pointing to Jack's factsheet that he'd turned in earlier in the day. "Are you really ready to write all this stuff?" he asked. "Including all this information about your uncles' involvement with the levees and canals?"

"That's why I wanted to give you an early heads-up about where my digging had taken me. I have a lot still to confirm, but I need some guidance, here."

"No shit," Reynolds retorted.

Jack inhaled deeply and then explained, "I wanted you to know what *I* now know about the role I believe they and the organizations they worked for played in this very big picture I'm trying to paint for our readers. I'd be lying if I didn't say that I'd preferred not to *name* my flesh-and-blood relatives as sources. I was hoping that when it comes to it, we could just say that we have on-the-record interviews and documentation from reliable sources that shows blah, blah, blah."

"Blah, blah, blah can cover a lot of ground," Reynolds groused. "The lawyers upstairs will want specifics. Can you get either or both of your uncles on-the-record?"

"I don't know, yet. I'm doing my best." Jack gestured toward the outline for his three-part anniversary series. "I've provided you what I've found out thus far because I wanted your views—early on—as to how you think we should handle some of the more explosive material I've outlined there. Especially the latest stuff I found out about specific players on the Levee Board and in the Corps."

"Well, first, you will have to *write* the three parts and we'll have each and every sentence fact-checked and lawyered up the ying-yang," Reynolds noted with a sigh, absently tapping Jack's file with a drumroll of his fingers.

"I've put what I've learned about the 1982 work that was done on the canal walls into my outline, but I still have to nail an interview with my uncle who worked in that period at the Army Corps of Engineers—and so far, he's been ducking me."

"Well, until you do talk to him, we won't know if the lawyers will say we have to quote certain sources by name—and *whose* names those have to be. Let me know what happens."

"Sounds like a plan."

His editor looked at Jack across the papers on his desk with a glance that almost seemed sympathetic. "You are one of the last honest and fearless reporters in our business, Jack Durand. Digging into all this stuff takes guts. Let's see if we can avoid blowing your family to smithereens—but I can't promise, now that you've told me about their involvement. If you find out more bad stuff, try to remember that they sure as hell weren't the only ones to turn a blind eye. Get as many of those involved to speak on-the-record as you can, y'hear? It'll give us more choice as to who we have to quote by name."

"Right. And speaking of blowing up my life," Jack replied, "I have to tell you something else that I *didn't* write in that rundown, there."

"Oh, brother," Reynolds groaned. "Shoot."

Jack briefly disclosed to his editor his romantic relationship with Serena Antonelli whose brother and sister-in-law died as a result of the 17th Street Canal collapse—the same canal that, then, junior engineer Jacques Durand had worked on so many years before.

"Holy shit!" Reynolds exclaimed, using his favorite epithet again.

"Neither Serena nor I realized the possible connection between our families when we first met and…well…before anything serious developed. Now, it's different."

"You *are* an honest guy to tell me about this," his editor said, rubbing his chin and tapping his index finger on the material Jack had given him. "For one thing…all this stuff is going into my vault, right now. All we can do—*you* can do—is to do your best to tell the story as the facts dictate. On my side, I'll try as much as I'm able to persuade our lawyers to protect the most sensitive sources."

"Thanks," Jack said shortly. "I hope we can work it that way. And if we can't…" He paused. "You can always assign someone else to work with me and give him or her the byline."

"Hey, Durand," his editor ribbed him. "If a Pulitzer Prize-winning workaholic like you is willing to give up credit on a major piece of journalism like this, you *must* be in l-o-v-e, love!!"

Jack affected a shrug, but was embarrassed and prepared to depart the inner office as quickly as possible.

Sensing this, Reynolds held up his hand.

"Look, Jack…I can only say, as your long-suffering boss—having lived through your dark moods and a few harrowing moments due to the stuff you write—I'd honestly like to see it all work out for you, buddy."

"Amen," Jack agreed and then glanced at the clock. "Gotta go. Serena left Venice today and arrives at the airport in forty minutes."

"Go! Get outta here! It's a total gas to see you brought down to the level of mere mortals," John Reynolds chuckled, a wicked gleam in his eye. "But, don't worry, Jackie boy, all these secrets you've revealed today are safe with me." Reynolds stood up and scooped Jack's documents into a manila envelope marked 'Katrina Anniversary Series/Durand.' "In fact, I'm headed for the vault right now."

"We've got everything electronically," Jack reminded him.

"Maybe, but I like to have actual paper in my control. I guess I'm a dinosaur like everyone else who's been around here prior to Google search engines."

Jack hurried back to his desk, grabbed a jacket and his reporter's bag and laptop, and bolted for the exit. For the first time in weeks, he felt some of the burden that had been weighing him down so heavily since he began the Katrina project lessen a bit.

Perhaps there *was* a way to tell the unsettling history of mistakes and oversights and the usual greed and corruption surrounding the costliest disaster in American history without blowing his own life to bits.

Just now, John Reynolds had offered him the first shred of hope that he could tell the story honestly, but not name all the names. He clung fiercely to this possibility. He had to. Serena was coming home, and all he wanted right now, was to bring her to *his* home and keep her safe from the heartache and misery that she and her family had endured the last ten years.

That *he* had endured, as well, he admitted to himself with some surprise.

The best he had to hope for was that he could tell his story, certain that his "anonymous sources" knew the truth of what really happened a decade ago, but perhaps not having to identify all of them as individuals. It was done all the time, he reflected, thinking back to the lore surrounding "Deep Throat" and the Watergate scandal he'd heard older reporters talk about when he first entered the news business.

Of course, he, Jack, would always be aware of the role

his own family members played—actions they'd taken either from fear or avarice—but he might not have to tell Serena of the dark link between their two families, and that was what mattered to him the most. He could just sketch the outlines in general terms and spare her the specific details.

Perhaps this, finally, was the way out…the way he and Serena could be together? The way a healing could begin for all concerned. If only he could be certain that he'd discovered the path to putting the storm behind him, and behind the people he cared about, once and for all.

The truth was the truth, but why make everyone suffer from it forever?

Of course, *he'd* know the secret—and he'd have to live with it in order to have *La Contessa* a central part of his life…for the rest of his life.

A voice in Jack's head reminded him that even if his relationship with Serena survived the publication of his journalism, he was condemned, regardless, to live with the knowledge of the part his uncles probably played in the destruction of his beloved New Orleans.

CHAPTER 18

Even before Serena stepped out of the plane's gangway, she felt actual butterflies fluttering against her diaphragm. She headed toward the baggage claim area with her fellow passengers, glad she'd sent all her suitcases into the plane's hold, despite the outrageous charges she faced for the extra weight. It felt strange to walk down the lengthy Delta terminal with only her handbag and heavy winter coat over her arm.

She glanced out the large windows at the line of planes waiting for the next wave of travelers. Her warm slacks and sweater, given the sultry sunshine glaring on the tarmac, made her skin prickle and she couldn't wait to shed them. Spring had obviously arrived in Louisiana, and the environment surrounding her was about as different from *La Serenissima* as could be imagined.

She fished in her pocket for her cellphone and turned it on, amazed, as always, that the device quickly adjusted to a new time zone. A text message popped up.

I'm here! Waiting for you is driving me crazy! Look for me, Louie, and his trumpet...

Her heart took a little skip. Jack had been texting her every five minutes, it seemed, from the moment she'd landed in New York and gone through Customs prior to the final leg of her journey to New Orleans. This last message mirrored the same excitement she felt at the prospect of seeing him again after more than two weeks. There were some hurdles they still have to get over, she reminded herself sternly, questions that continued to linger about certain things not said, as well as the loving things he had.

Serena managed to locate a luggage cart and waited impatiently for her bags to tumble down the chute. She suddenly remembered the moment when she'd stuck her tongue out at Jack at JFK in New York, en route to Venice, when he'd easily recovered his suitcase as her two had become wedged and impossible to grab. What a lifetime ago that seemed.

When she emerged through the arrivals door, she headed straight for the looming statue of Louis Armstrong blowing his horn, but had only taken a few steps before Jack sprinted to her side.

"Hey, baby…La Contessa has landed!"

Before she could reply, he pulled her close, scooped his hands to encase the sides of her head, and kissed her with an intensity that took her breath away. She was dimly aware of the laughter and scattered applause from bystanders.

When finally they came up for air, she whispered, "Well, *buona sera* to you too, handsome."

Jack hugged her tightly against his chest, her winter coat squeezed between them. Serena felt him take a deep breath and then exhale against her neck as if something worrisome had passed them by. Then he stepped back and surveyed the mound of luggage she'd piled onto the cart.

"Wow…did you bring back a few bulky costumes from the ball?" he teased.

"You're close. Actually, I brought back a fair amount of fabric. Who could resist Fortuny? More is being sent by slow boat from my friends at the factory."

"I've got a downstairs storage closet at Julia Street— that is, if you would like to…"

"Come home with you? Yes, please."

Jack leaned forward and kissed her again.

"My aged condo awaits. But what about your family?"

"I didn't tell them precisely what flight I was on

because I wanted just the two of us to have some time together to...well...to see where the hell we are with everything and—"

"We're in the same city again, that's where we are, thank God," he interrupted, "and without that Casanova Fabrini, sniffing around!"

Serena burst out laughing.

"Do you think there's anything to reincarnation?" she asked.

"Yes," Jack said with a grimace. "Definitely." He took possession of her luggage cart and nodded toward the exit. "Hungry?"

"Famished. The food on board was really bad."

"And let me guess what's the first thing you want to eat: gumbo?"

"Definitely. But later. What about we go to Liuzza's on Bienville for a fried oyster po'boy with a side of Rockefeller bisque?" she suggested, salivating at the thought of New Orleans' own version of a submarine sandwich. The best ones were made by an old time Italian restaurant in Mid-City that sat smack between the airport and the French Quarter. The eatery had been swamped with six feet of water, thanks to the storm, but the owners had rebuilt and the place was as popular as ever.

"How 'bout this?" Jack countered. "Let's order po'boys and the bisque on my cellphone, pick-up it all up on the way, and eat at Julia Street. We'll get gumbo, too, and have it for breakfast!"

"Hey, baby...you awake?"

Jack looked across at Serena, snuggled beneath the covers of his four-poster plantation bed that Corlis had sold him when he'd bought her Julia Street condo.

Containers from Liuzza's littered both bedside tables, along with their wine glasses, now empty. A box of condoms, with several packets missing, was also there amidst the clutter.

What a night...

"Hmmm...what time is it?" she asked.

"You'll be embarrassed," Jack replied. "It's just before noon. Good time for gumbo, though."

Serena opened her eyes, rolled onto her side, and with a smile that told him all he needed to know, reached out to splay her hand against his bare chest.

"Hmmm...gumbo. Sounds almost as delicious as you were."

"Now, is that anything a proper *contessa* would say?"

"Who said anything about being proper? Come here, you!"

But it was Jack who pulled her hard against the length of his naked frame. His immediate response below the waist answered any questions she might have about how much the previous night had meant to him.

"Ah...Serena," he breathed into her hair that smelled of the same fragrant shampoo she had allowed him to use when they took a long, hot shower together sometime after three a.m. "If only we could stay right here all day. Thank God you came home on a Saturday, though. How about I heat up the gumbo and we have it right here?"

"Eat here again?" she said with a sly smile. "That could be dangerous."

"Well, that's right. You never know what could happen."

"We were so bad, weren't we?" she said, her voice husky and inviting. "I only remember us charging up your stairs, and the next thing I knew, you'd stashed the gumbo in the fridge and the po'boys beside the bed, here, and—"

"And the rest is history," he mumbled, leaning down to

nuzzle the hollow in her throat that was guaranteed to get the colored lights spinning.

"Oh...boy," she whispered, her arms sliding around his shoulders.

This time their lovemaking was slow and languid, as if they wished to show each other how much pleasure and pure happiness they could contribute to the conflagration of heat and light that they always generated together. In a swift move that surprised and delighted him, Serena boldly straddled his thighs, the covers draped over her shoulders like a cape, her breasts a feast for both his eyes and lips.

"May I...?" she murmured, her sweet request squeezing his heart. "May I hold you...here?"

"Oh...yes indeed...you may."

He allowed her full rein to explore any part of his body she wished, until the moment came when he could stand it no longer. He swiftly rolled them both over on the mattress and gently held each of her wrists flat against the pillow where her lustrous hair fanned out against the white linen. Her dark eyes, the eyes that had so bewitched him from the very first moment, were luminous with...tears?

"Serena...what's the matter? Are you—?"

"Happy, happy, *happy*..." she whispered.

"Oh, sweetheart," he said, smiling down at her. He raised himself on his elbows and bent to kiss her on each eyelid, tasting the saltiness from her tears. Then balancing on one arm, he reached for one of the little square packets in the box on the bedside table and held it between them.

"How about a little more happiness?"

"Yes, yes, *please*..." she whispered with an urgency that nearly undid him.

When he lifted her by her waist and guided their bodies to slowly, exquisitely meld together, his heart overflowed with sensations unlike anything he'd ever know. He felt as if he, too, would weep for the joy that had come into their lives so unexpectedly when they boarded the same plane that hurtled them through the night sky on their way to Venice.

At this moment, it felt to Jack as if he were soaring again through dark space with pinpricks of crystal lights on every side, and after the heavens exploded as they were destined to, the two of them lay quietly in each other's arms, sleek with perspiration.

At length, Jack said softly, "After we have our lunch, I'll drop you at your house, if that's all right."

Their faces inches apart, Serena gazed at him, making no response, as if she were well schooled in not ever showing disappointment. The afternoon light fell in narrow shafts through the half opened shutters in Jack's high-ceiling bedroom. The airy space suddenly reminded him of the expansive room at *Ca' Arco Antico* where they had made love with the waters of Venice lapping against stone foundations a block away.

Finally she murmured a neutral, "Okay."

"I'd much rather stay right here," he assured her.

"But you're not going to do that because…?"

"Because I've got to drive down to Venice later this afternoon. Isn't it strange?" he said, smoothing a strand of chestnut hair off her damp forehead. "I'm going to Venice, Louisiana, that insane tiny town near the mouth of the Mississippi."

"I've never been there."

"Basically, it's perched in a swamp that's disappearing, acres in a single day."

"Why go there, then, if there's not much to see?"

He sensed a tension building between them. He could tell she was doing her best to sound like he was free to do as he pleased, but he wasn't fooled. This was old stuff. His job versus his life.

"I'm meeting with some fisherman early tomorrow morning who want to show me the latest ravages of the erosion cutting into what's left of the wetlands and barrier islands down there. It's so damn similar to what's happening in the Venice Lagoon, it drives me crazy!"

Serena laid her hand on his arm and her expression cleared. She leaned forward and kissed him on the nose.

"Now that I know about this stuff you've told me, it drives me crazy, too," she said. "The parallels between Venice, Italy and New Orleans are amazing. Going down to Venice, Louisiana sounds like it might make a good addition to your story."

Jack sank back on his pillow and closed his eyes as a wave of relief washed over him. She understood his world like no one else ever had and could act like a grown-up, even when it meant he'd have to leave for a while. He opened his eyes and leaned toward her.

"Thanks for saying that," he said, lightly strafing his fingers along her jaw line. "There are so many moving parts to this story, Serena…and every single fact will have to be triple-checked and lawyered to the Nth degree. You know, don't you, that if it weren't for this friggin' albatross I've saddled myself with, I'd never leave you today."

"I know…now" she replied quietly. "When you tell me what's going on with you, like you just did, I totally get it. And anyway, I have to show up at my family's place, sometime, so this actually works out fine." She threw aside the bedcovers, adding, "How about you put the gumbo on the stove, and while it's warming up, I'll turn on the shower?"

Without the slightest embarrassment, she walked stark naked down the hallway.

Jack, likewise bare-assed, headed for his small kitchen where he set the pot on low as he heard the taps go on in the shower. Moments later, he padded in bare feet toward the bathroom, unable to recall when he'd ever felt this good.

Serena's family welcomed her home with varying degrees of enthusiasm. Her mother had burst into tears at the sight of her standing at the front door, surrounded by her suitcases where the cab driver had deposited them. For several more minutes, Sarah Antonelli had sobbed her relief that her daughter had miraculously made it home safely from a trip she had considered dangerous in the extreme.

"I figured out that you had at least *twelve* takeoffs and landings flying to Venice and back," her mother said, pressing her ready handkerchief to her eyes, "to say nothing of a country filled with Mafia hit men, street thieves, and Italian lotharios!"

"Only one lothario, Mama," Serena assured her, reaching for a paper napkin from the holder on the kitchen counter to dab the continuing moisture filling her mother's eyes.

"I *knew* it!" Sarah exclaimed.

"Trust me, *Signor* Stefano Fabrini was pretty harmless."

"He doesn't sound harmless," her mother insisted stubbornly.

Jack had offered to drive Serena home, but she figured it was best to introduce the momentous changes in her life gradually to her family and especially her mother.

Her sister Flavia was her usual moody, uncommunicative self, waving her hellos with a pair of ear-buds stuffed in her head and a perfunctory kiss on Serena's cheek. Within minutes of her older sister's arrival, she'd slipped back into her room upstairs.

Cosimo Antonelli seemed happy enough to have his eldest daughter safely back home, but scowled the minute his surviving son, Nicholas, walked through the door at the end of another work day at Antonelli's Costume Company.

Nick held out his arms wide before enfolding his returning sibling with effusive hugs and kisses. He ignored his father's dark looks and drew Serena into the sitting room, wanting to know every detail of what she'd seen and done during her apprenticeship in Venice.

"Gus and I nearly went crazy without your help during Mardi Gras," he declared, referring to his partner, Gus LeMoyne, who now, Nick revealed quietly, had assumed responsibility for managing the small staff while Nick ran the business side of the operation.

He closed the door and lowered his voice.

"Flavia was a total pain, as usual, refusing to do anything but the usual scut work…but at least we've survived another year and I can't wait to hear about how you think we can up our game. Somehow, we've got to make this family enterprise into something that can actually support us all."

She squeezed both his hands. "And I have a plan to do just that!"

"Fabulous! While you were away, I put the books on Quicken—finally—and not before a big ole' fight with Daddy. He just wouldn't accept the truth that despite a killing amount of hard work, we barely broke even this year, Reenie."

Serena reached out and gave him a bear hug.

"I know the last weeks were probably horrible for you and Gus, but I promise, my absence will be worth it. I've got so many projects that will make us money, it's going to take days to tell you about them all! And wait till you see the great stuff I managed to get through U.S. Customs in New York!" she chortled, excited by the prospect of infusing their business with new ideas that would hopefully get them back on track. "Yards and yards of Fortuny fabrics—and at a nice price, thanks to Allegra's influence and charge account! I paid her back with the overtime I'd put in on everything I worked on, there."

"Wow," Nick replied with admiration.

She paused and then lowered her voice as Nick had done.

"But what *about* Daddy? Is he even going into work anymore? Mama said he just mostly mopes around here and she declared loudly so he could hear that he's been hell to live with while I've been gone."

"Well, blessed be that Gus and I have made the third floor at the shop into a very nice apartment for ourselves so I don't have to deal with his bad temper unless he deigns to come into the office, which he hardly ever does anymore."

"Oh, man," she groaned.

"He tells everyone he's been given a 'forced retirement by my own children,'" Nick said with a scowl that matched the one Serena had seen Cosimo bestow earlier that day when her brother walked into the family home.

"So you're living at work?" she asked. "Lucky you."

"Well, think about this," Nick offered with a sly grin. "There's still enough space left to build out another one-bedroom apartment on the third floor, if you ever want it. As for me, I just couldn't take Coz's nasty remarks about how disappointed he was with a son who liked men better than women and—well…you can just imagine the things he said over the last two months. Especially since you weren't here to keep his mouth vaguely under control."

"Oh, Nicky…I'm so sorry," Serena said, reaching across the sofa to touch his sleeve. "I expect, given the nuns who brought him up and rapped his knuckles all those years, his views on gays are pounded into his DNA by now. But, you know my mantra: 'acceptance of the way things *are* is the key to happiness'—and then plan from there. We have to just *accept*—not like, mind you—that's how he feels."

"Easy for you to say," Nick attempted to joke.

"Want to make a pact to ignore the mean things Daddy says, and just move forward? Let's keep putting one foot in front of the other and see if the surviving Antonellis can keep the place afloat."

"Sweet Louisiana, I hope so," Nick replied with a discouraged shake of his head. "I figure we can give it two or three more years to see if we can make a genuine comeback with this family business of ours. Frankly, a lot of days, I seriously have my doubts."

"Keep the faith, bro!" Serena exhorted, and then gave a shrug that acknowledged their father was making an already difficult task a hundred times *more* difficult. "And besides, what else are we fit to do to make a living here in the Bayou State?"

Nick threw back his head and laughed.

"Not much, that's for damn sure. Of course, you could always marry a Yankee with some big bucks to help us out! They're down here buying everything in sight in the Quarter."

"Trust me. There are no Yankees on the horizon in *my* life."

Serena thought about Jack and was sorely tempted to tell Nick how she was literally bursting with happiness. She longed to describe everything about their amazing meet-up on the plane to Venice and their love affair that bloomed despite Jack's former girlfriend and the hideous weather that rained down on them in Italy during the entire time they were there. But then, she figured she'd indulge in that pleasure when she wasn't sitting under her family's roof with ears most likely pressed against the living room door.

"Are you over jet lag yet?" he asked. "How soon will you feel like coming back to work?"

"I just got home!" she protested, and almost laughed at how little sleep she and Jack had gotten in her first twenty-four hours in New Orleans. "I might just have to grab some shut-eye at my drafting table around four o'clock, but how about I come back to work tomorrow morning, bright and early?"

Nick pulled her against his chest in another show of brotherly affection.

"Serena Antonelli, I knew there was a reason I wanted you as a full partner in this crazy enterprise we've got going."

"I'm your sis, remember?" she shot back with mock indignation. "It's in the company by-laws. You don't have a choice!" She gave his chin a gentle fist bump. "You *can't* get rid of me!"

Nick put his hands together as if in prayer, his eyes rolling skyward.

"Thank you, Jesus!"

Serena kept her promise to quickly launch a number of projects at Antonelli's costumes that she prayed would help their post-Mardi Gras sagging bottom line. The most important, in her view, was her campaign to recruit some of the sixty-odd krewes in New Orleans to reconsider sending away to China for the raft of regalia they would need for next year's parades and private celebrations. Her immediate goal was to persuade them to outfit their members, instead, from Antonelli's, a move that could boost the firm's income enormously.

In fact, springtime was the season the leaders of the various Mardi Gras social clubs decided on the next year's theme—always a closely guarded secret from their competitors. In view of this, Serena's first plan of action was to create a series of highly elaborate costumes based on the sketches that Allegra had given as her "going away" present. She was determined to make them stunning and elaborate examples of the higher art of historically accurate and/or fanciful attire. Even her younger sister, Flavia, showed a spark of interest when Serena recruited her to do the elaborate beadwork—and demonstrated some of sewing techniques she'd learned in the *San Tomà* workshop under Rosa's tutelage.

The most spectacular of her creations were featured in elaborate window displays at the front of the store. In addition, two rows of dressed mannequins from the best of their existing stock of costumes greeted customers upon their arrival at the shop and provided a path on their clients' way to the private consultation rooms where the Antonelli staff met with potential clients.

"Wowser, Serena!" enthused Etheline, their receptionist, as the installation was set up to the right of the front desk. "These new costumes totally rock!"

Much to Serena's surprise—and to the delight of Nick and Gus—secretaries and other workers in the Central Business District walking by the shop began to gather outside the windows during the noontime hour. Before April was out and Quarter Fest was in full swing, two chairmen of medium-sized krewes had decided to have Antonelli's Costume Company execute their ideas for the coming Mardi Gras season.

"Way to go!" Jack exalted at dinner a few night's later at Corlis and King's when she mentioned her amazement at the crowds that now gawked at their windows every day.

Jack's longtime friends now automatically included his declared ladylove in every invitation extended to him—having given Serena their stamp of approval in other obvious ways as well.

"How amazing," Corlis congratulated her. "You know, those costumes would offer some great visuals for a TV business story. WJAZ could do a piece about the post-Katrina rebirth of Antonelli's, now that their top designer has returned from working during Venice *Carnevale,* she mused. "We could show our viewers that the younger generation has taken up the reins, blah, blah, blah."

"That's journalese for 'the rest of the story,'" Jack informed her as a good-humored aside.

"*Love* the blah, blah, blah part," Serena joked, but then grew somber. "But, I don't know…" she continued, her voice full of doubt. "That's an angle sure to give my poor brother, Nick, heartburn in terms of my dad, who frankly isn't too happy about turning over those reins." She heaved an audible sigh and thanked Corlis for her suggestion. Now that she'd been home a few weeks, she considered her a wonderful new friend whom she had grown fonder of each time they met. "And what I just said about my dad? That's off-the-record, of course," she added, deadpan.

"But it's true, isn't it?" Corlis insisted. "You are, in fact, trying to re-launch your business, and you and Nick *are* the ones doing it?"

"And his partner, Gus LeMoyne," Serena reminded them. She shook her head in a rare show of discouragement. "And *that's* another true fact guaranteed to drive Cosimo Antonelli, The Fourth, right around the twist."

"Well, if you don't want me to send a crew…"

Jack intervened, "Look, Serena, if you're drawing crowds in the CBD, some other media outlet, including the *T-P* or *The Advocate,* will get wind of this, 'cause the story is a natural! I say, better let Corlis do it, first, so anyone else who piles in later will get most of their facts right, based on the segment she produces. Unfortunately, that's the way it works in our biz, these days."

Serena cast her hostess a plaintive glance.

"It's really nice of you to even consider doing a piece about Antonelli's and—"

"Nice, sh-mice," Corlis interrupted with a wave of her hand. "I agree with Jack. It's a great local story, and besides, I *love* costumes, as you can probably tell by now. And any new angle about Mardi Gras—New Orleans' hallowed moneymaker—is bound to go down well with my boss, to say nothing of the advertisers on WJAZ. And besides," she added with a grin, "it sure would be a nice break for me to cover a story that was fun and kept me out of hot water for a change."

"Well…a little public notice of what we're trying to accomplish at this hundred-and-fifty-year-old company would be great in terms of letting the krewes consider 'buying local'," Serena agreed.

"And that's another reason why it'd make a good piece," King interjected. "Any time we can show the world New Orleans is still on the map for locals, the better it is for preserving the place. We've been invaded by folks bent on gentrification at a bargain price, and all they really do is use this city as a second home or pure party town."

After a brief pause, Serena nodded her agreement.

"Okay," Corlis declared. "It's settled, then. How about if I come by tomorrow with a crew around eleven-thirty? I can see if the shop's lookie-loos were just a fluke last week, or if it's becoming a genuine 'happening' down there." Serena's hostess picked up the coffee pot from the sideboard, and refilled her guests' cups. "I can't promise my assignment editor will go for this—or if the piece will even pan out, Serena—but it's worth a shot, don't you think?"

"Definitely," she replied, nodding her head more vigorously to show her appreciation. If Allegra were here, Serena thought, she'd be jumping for joy over the possibility of a story that was bound to drive more business to a costumer's door. "And thank y'all for urging me to see beyond the bumps in the road when it comes to family businesses."

She rolled her eyes.

"What?" Jack asked, quick, as always, to pick up on her mood.

"Well...it seems my brother Nick moved out of the house while I was away—given the friction that exists between my father and him."

"Where'd he end up?" Jack asked, curious.

"He and Gus have built a nice apartment on the third floor at the shop to keep peace in the Antonelli household. What they did in two months' time is inspiring! I'm nearly a thirty-five-year-old woman, for pity's sake, and I'm seriously thinking of taking the square footage that's left and creating my own little nest up there."

"Well, that's an idea," Corlis said with a quick glance in Jack's direction.

Serena heaved another small sigh. "Our father is having a hard adjustment both to the idea of his gay son being with a live-in partner, as well as this changing-of-the-guard business at Antonelli's. I truly understand it can't be easy for him...but living at home at my age isn't easy either, and apparently, it's been brutally rough on poor Nick."

A long pause ensued and Serena blushed scarlet when she noticed that Corlis, again, was looking directly at Jack as if he and his Julia Street living quarters were the answer to Serena's housing dilemma. Hinting that she wanted to move in with Jack had not at all been her intention when she raised the subject of housing, and she was more than slightly mortified to see that Jack stared at his coffee cup and remained silent.

To cover the awkward moment, Serena quickly rose from her dining room chair and said brightly, "Let me help you clear the table. We've all got a busy week ahead and I told Nick I'd meet him first thing in the morning to bring him up to date on our latest orders...which, as I said, are coming in nicely, thank the Baby Jesus."

Less than ten minutes later, Jack backed out of the Duvallons' precious off-street parking spot inside the courtyard enclosed by fanciful wrought-iron gates. After a pause for on-coming traffic, he pulled onto Dauphine Street.

"I'm glad you gave the go-ahead for Corlis to do a story about Antonelli's," he said, heading for Canal Street on the other side of the French Quarter.

"I am too," she replied, stealing a glance across the front seat. "I'll have to warn Daddy to be at the shop so Corlis can talk about the 'generations' as she mentioned, but I won't tell him exactly what the thrust of the story is. He'll complain afterward, but I know the rest of us will love it, and I'm sure it will be good for business, which is the main point."

When Jack pulled up in front of his Julia Street flat, he turned off the ignition and looked over at Serena.

"I'm going to have to go into radio silence for a little while," he announced in a subdued tone of voice.

Given his lack of response at the Duvallon's table when the matter of housing came up, Serena took Jack's latest announcement as an early warning signal, rather like an alert that a hurricane might be coming her way.

"Going into 'radio silence'? What does that mean... exactly?"

Serena suddenly wondered if the old Jack had just resurfaced and he was about to become Mr. Elusive for the first time in months. In what could turn out to be a moment of colossal irony, just that week she'd finally broken it to her mother—who subsequently told her father—that Jack Durand, the newspaper reporter her family had met at the airport the day she left for Venice, had become the new man in her life. She'd even had the temerity to say that she'd brook no negative comments if she chose to spend the night with him. Her mother nervously asked her if it was "serious between you two?" Serena had smiled a wee bit smugly and had replied, "We'll see, won't we?"

Meanwhile, Jack was staring out his windshield at the balcony of his flat in the row of brick, landmarked buildings that fronted an entire block of Julia Street.

Finally, he answered, "Radio silence just means that this week I'm tackling a raft of very dicey interviews for the Katrina series."

"Well, yes, but—"

Jack continued without a pause, "Tomorrow I'll be up in the capitol grilling some politicos about past policies. After that, I have to talk my way into the Army Corps of Engineers headquarters where I remain rather unpopular after the last big hurricane stories I did. Next up is driving down river to talk to the Coast Guard. Then there are some new levee czars I have to track down, and then, hopefully, I'll nail some retired hydraulic engineers and—"

"I get it, I get it!" Serena interrupted, unable to mask her irritation at the lineup of excuses he had marshaled to say he was going off the grid.

On one hand, she completely understood he would be buried in work in order to get the stories done by the August 29th deadline. Even so, his long litany of To Do's sounded to her rather like a case of "He doth protest too much."

"Serena?" Jack's expression had become unreadable.

"No need to provide me with a laundry list," she declared. "Just say it: what you're telling me is that we won't be seeing each other much, right?"

She knew a brush off when she heard one.

"Now don't be looking at me that way, Serena!" Jack demanded. "This is about the way I have to report a story that's this big and this important. It's not about *us*! Man, sometimes I think *you're* the one with the PTSD."

Shocked by this accusation she shot back, "What are you talking about? I wasn't even here for Katrina, remember?"

"I'm not talking about the storm. I'm talking about Las Vegas."

"What does that crack mean?" she exclaimed, sensing a vein in her neck had begun to throb.

"You know what it means…that you think I'm pulling away from you."

"Well, aren't you?" she accused. "You suddenly tell me you're about to do your usual disappearing act, now that I'm home and after you made absolutely *no* comment about my eventually wanting to move out of my family's place. What am I supposed to think?"

Jack stared at her across the car with a puzzled expression and then he said quietly, "Do you know what I really wanted to say at dinner when you mentioned you might create an apartment for yourself on the third floor of the shop?"

"No, what?" she snapped. "'Great idea?'"

"Now, there you go again," he said, leaning toward her to seize her hand, but she pulled away. Undeterred, he continued, "I wanted to say, 'Hold it right there, Ms. Antonelli! No need to hire a carpenter. I want you to come live with *me*. On Julia Street.'" He pointed through the windshield. "Right there, on the second floor."

"Well, why didn't you say that?" she challenged. "Your silence was totally embarrassing."

Jack paused and inhaled deeply.

"'Cause I can't say that I want us to live together…to *be* together to anybody but you. Not yet, anyway."

"And why is that?" she demanded, unable to hide her exasperation. She wasn't even sure she wanted to move in with Jack without feeling more confident that their relationship wouldn't be an on-again, off-again nightmare like she'd had with Marco in Las Vegas—and Jack had had with Lauren Hilbert.

Jack replied in a weary tone, "Until I'm out the other side of reporting this frigging story, I've got to just keep putting one foot in front of the other while I keep my mouth shut."

"But why does that prevent you from telling *me* what's going on with you?"

"I just did tell you and it made you angry."

Serena was brought up short by his convoluted statement.

"You gave me your travel itinerary," she retorted. "What's making me angry is knowing that you only have told me *part* of what's really going on. I just know that you're leaving out something important. And by the way, Jack," she added parenthetically, "I'm not even sure I would move in with you as an alternative to having my own place at the shop."

Jack grasped the steering wheel and said, "You wouldn't?"

"Not until I understand the reasons for how you behaved just now in front of Corlis and King—your best friends! You went into radio silence with *all* of us around the table when our discussion brushed against the subject of our future together. You're not fooling me, Jack. There's still a *missing* piece!"

CHAPTER 19

Jack inhaled deeply, looking as if he had the weight of the world on his shoulders, and turned toward Serena who remained sitting stiffly in the passenger seat.

"I've never asked a woman to live with me," he said in a low voice, "and it's all I want to do at this moment." With a nod toward his front door, he added, "I'd like nothing better than to have us go up those stairs, carry you over the threshold, and start a life together."

Serena stared across the car in shock.

Had Jack Durand just proposed they get married, or at the very least, declare to the world they were officially a couple?

Not exactly, Serena judged. What he'd just said to her held too many qualifiers and was the opposite of how he'd behaved at the Duvallons twenty minutes earlier. Even so, she felt her heart soften and reached out to grasp the hand she'd rejected a few moments earlier.

"Oh, Jack…what *is* it? What's holding you back? Just tell me."

He turned and held her gaze, a look of abject misery invading his eyes.

"The part that's missing, as you put it, is that I-I'm dealing with something within my own family that also may involve the story. The rules I live under as a journalist say I can't tell you—or anybody else except my editor—about it right now. I have to work through all the issues…confirm all the facts as best I can. But you have my word that I'll explain every single background detail once the story hits the newsstands."

"I know you're trying to tell me something that will put my mind at ease," Serena said softly, "but I still don't get it."

Jack nodded. "I know it all must sound very mysterious

and convoluted, but I hope you can tell how much I *mean* what I'm saying. I want us to live together. It's just that I can't ask you to do that right now—publicly or privately. In fact, I can't even elaborate any more about it than that, period. This *hairball* of competing interests is all I ever think about—except you."

At length, Serena lifted both hands and framed his face, the stubble on his jaw line pressing against her palms. This was a far different response than Jack once gave her when they sat at dinner at the Danieli in Venice. She ducked her head, kissed him gently on the lips, and then offered a sad smile.

"Other than wrestling with my own crazy family and plotting the great comeback at Antonelli's, you're all I ever think about, either." She paused, and then asked, "Shall we go upstairs?"

"So you won't build yourself an apartment, right?" he asked, his brow furrowed.

She tempered her next words by bestowing another feathery kiss on his lips.

"It's probably a very good idea if we slowed this train down a bit," she suggested.

"Damn it, Serena…that's pretty much the *opposite* of what I want!"

Then, why didn't you say in front of Corlis and King that you wanted me to live with you? she demanded silently. The mixed signals he'd been sending out tonight were driving her nuts!

But instead of voicing those thoughts, some instinct for self-preservation prompted her to say instead, "Look, Jack…let's be logical. Clearly, we both have a lot of family and professional stuff to work through right now…so…it's probably good that we each have our own place, wherever it's located. If this is going to make sense for us for the long term, we can afford to slow down and take some of the pressure off."

Jack shot her a doubtful look, and Serena could tell his reporter's mind was considering every word she said—and how she said it. In the next second, the thought came to her that she either had to trust this man that he truly had her welfare at heart—as well as his own—or break off the relationship right now. She took a deep breath, wondering if this *was* Las Vegas all over again…or something new and wonderful? In her mind's eye she could see the whirling blur of a roulette wheel she'd passed when she walked through the hotel's casino every night on her way to the theater to perform her backstage duties for Marco's *Cirque de Roma* show.

She decided to bet every last chip.

"It's okay, Jack," she reassured him quietly. "Share all the behind-the-scenes details with me when you can—or when you're ready."

Relief flooded his handsome features and he pulled her roughly against his chest so that she found herself virtually sprawled across the car's front seat. His lips slanted over hers and he kissed her with the intensity of a drowning man who clung to the hope of finding safe harbor.

"Hey, scribe," she gasped when he finally released her. "Look how we're steaming up the windows."

His eyes were smoke signals telling her they'd be in his four-poster bed as soon as he could reach for the door handle and help her out of the car. Without further conversation, they exited the cramped space. Jack swiftly seized her hand, hustled her through the front door, and up the stairs to his flat.

A single lamp illuminated the high-ceilinged bedroom, leaving the tall, mahogany highboy and marble fireplace in shadow. A look of hunger tinged with desperation invaded Jack's expression as he took her in his arms and then slowly began removing her clothing, piece by piece.

"Oh, baby…just look at you," he murmured, pushing

her gently onto his bed. "My *Serenissima…*"

She watched, riveted by the view, as he speedily removed his own clothes and leaned a naked knee on the mattress, hovering above her for a long moment before lowering his lean body next to hers, facing her nose to nose.

"*Signorina* Antonelli," he whispered, "*La Contessa* of Julia Street."

Arching an eyebrow she whispered back, "Not yet…but maybe some day, *Giovanni.*"

During the next three weeks, Jack was in and out of New Orleans reporting his story, while Serena kept busy consulting with clients and creating costumes from Allegra's sketches and her own. He regularly kept in touch by text or phone and Serena decided that, for now, she'd have to be satisfied that Jack had told her all he could about his newspaper assignment and some bizarre connection involving the Durands.

For Jack's part, he finally told his sister Sylvia that she could let his family know he'd officially broken up with Lauren. Even so, he had yet to introduce the new woman in his life to other members of his family besides his sister, Marielle—nor had Serena brought him home to meet her clan.

Before going public beyond their close friendship with the Duvallons, Serena had determined it was probably best to put some time and distance between the love they'd declared for each other and his ending his relationship with the woman he'd kept company with for nearly a decade. Serena's other reason for keeping their respective families in the dark was Jack's current project for the *Times-Picayune*.

For several days she'd turned over in her mind the fact that Jack's father and two uncles had been involved in various professions having to do with water...his father working as an hydraulic engineer at the French Quarter pumping stations, she remembered him saying once, and one of his uncles having been a barge captain until he'd been injured on the job and retired.

She thought, suddenly, of the scandals Jack had related about public monies stolen from the Venetian MOSE water gates project. Was he worried that his own family might have somehow been "on the take" or involved in well-known cases of governmental bribery and fraud in the "Third World State of Louisiana?"

But what families with a history of many generations in New Orleans *didn't* have a scandal or two in their closets, she mused? Lord only knew what Cosimo Antonelli or his forebears might have done over the years running the family costume company in the Central Business District. How had the various generations of Cosimos dealt with demands associated with building permits, police protection, and wily competitors? Jack should have surmised that *she* certainly wasn't one to throw any stones.

The one thing she knew for certain about Jack as a journalist was that he was rock solid honest. What still had her worried, however, were the undisclosed reasons that this mysterious link between his family and the story he had agreed to write obviously troubled him deeply.

As it turned out, Corlis McCullough's TV piece for WJAZ about the "Rebirth of Antonelli's Costume Company" resulted in a colorful video profile of Serena Antonelli describing her time in Venice studying under the celebrated Allegra Benedetti. Corlis' narration focused on "New Orleans' talented master designer's plans to incorporate Italian-style carnival fashions in her newest elaborate and elegant creations for the company's local and national clients."

Much to Serena's relief, the fact that younger members of the Antonelli family were assuming more responsibility for managing the company's post-Katrina rebirth was only mentioned in a single sentence.

The next thing the Antonelli clan knew—and unbeknownst even to Jack—the *Times-Picayune* fashion editor saw WJAZ-TV's story and immediately initiated a large, pictorial spread about the glittering new "elegant and authentic" costumes now available to rent, or to be commissioned at the family-owned enterprise.

"I'll just bet that Cosimo nearly blew a gasket when he saw that 'reborn' part on TV and the emphasis in the print piece on everything new we're trying to do around here," Gus commented dryly as he tacked a copy of the article on the company bulletin board in the employees' lounge.

Sipping from a cup of Café du Monde's brand of dark roast coffee laced with chicory, Serena grinned and replied, "Well, he grunted that Antonelli's had been alive for more than a century and didn't need 'birthin'' no new babies' in his opinion, but I think he was actually pretty happy with all the notice we're getting. He liked Corlis' story on WJAZ the best, though, 'cause it showed him at the head of the conference table when she did the voice-over section about the history of the firm."

The best news was that the phone soon started ringing off the hook with various krewe captains wanting to make appointments to see what the fuss was all about. At lunch at Felix's Oyster Bar on Royal Street celebrating Jack's return to New Orleans after another week away, Serena explained she'd had a hard sell convincing potential clients "that the higher prices Antonelli's has to charge to achieve the quality that will make the costumes stand out is a *better* choice than ordering from Asia—and never being sure what the packages are going to contain when they arrive."

"And how are you doing on that score?" Jack asked, as a dozen char-grilled oysters arrived, still sizzling on the platter. "Convincing the krewes to patronize you, I mean?"

Serena shrugged. "I win some and lose some, but I've persuaded a few big fish to see things the Antonelli way and place large orders."

"Good for you," Jack chortled, stabbing his fork into a plump, crispy oyster swimming in a blistering mix of butter, garlic, and herbs and sprinkled with Parmesan and Romano cheeses.

Just then, Serena's cellphone gave its distinctive chime from the bottom of her tote bag. She fished it out and grimaced.

"Golly…it's a hospital," she noted with alarm, staring at the phone ID. "I'd better take this."

She walked outside the noisy restaurant and was gone nearly ten minutes. The joyous look on her face when she returned more than made up for the six oysters Jack had saved for her that were now stone cold.

"This is a miracle!" she exclaimed, slipping into her seat. Raising her voice slightly to be heard above the din, she continued, "that call was from the chairwoman of the big benefit for pediatric care for the poor. She's putting on a fashion show called 'Mardi Gras Madness in May' and wanted to know if the costumes she saw in the *T-P* article and on WJAZ could be used as the finale for the entire event! She said she saw me on TV and wants me, along with Corlis and a bunch of women in the media, to be the models!"

"Wow, sweetheart…that's fantastic!"

"And it couldn't happen at a better time, Jack! All the krewes will be finalizing their plans for next February. We're bound to get some more last-minute business when word spreads around town about this. I wonder if Corlis waved her magic wand once again to make this happen?"

"I don't doubt it at all," Jack replied dryly. "I can't help but notice that lady is definitely in your corner." Then he glanced down at his watch and his pleased expression grew grim. "Gotta go, sugar."

"Can't you help me eat some of these cold oysters?" she pleaded. "I'm so sorry I interrupted our lunch."

"For a worthy cause, and anyway, I ate more than my share. Turns out, I've got a pretty tough interview this afternoon"

"And you think one more oyster might lay you low?"

Serena didn't know the half of it, Jack thought as he gave her a buss on the cheek and slipped out the door almost at a dead run. He had left his car in a lot just off Canal Street and drove as fast as he dared to Uncle Jacques house for an unannounced visit.

"An ole' fashioned ambush interview," he muttered aloud to himself as he pulled in a half block away from a dilapidated house in an un-gentrified section of the Lower Garden District.

A sense of dread dogged every step as he mounted the wooden porch and rang the bell. The early May heat beat down against his back, but sweat had soaked his shirt from the minute he'd set out from Canal Street. He knew his aunt would be playing bridge with his own mother over at his house this afternoon and prayed he would finally have Jacques alone with no easy means of escape. This was one interview that was an absolute must.

His uncle's startled gaze at the sight of his nephew standing on the other side of the screened door soon became a look of apprehension, followed by one of surprising resignation.

"I figured after that family dinner, you wouldn't give in." He heaved a sigh, his shoulders sagging. "Better come in, son. I got some sweet tea in the fridge, or do you want a beer?"

"Nothing, thanks," Jack replied, following him into a dark front sitting room with only a standing lamp turned on next to a worn, faux suede Barcalounger.

"You need your hands free to write, I 'spect?"

"Why don't I record our conversation and give you a copy of the tape later, so you'll know I won't twist your words."

His uncle sunk heavily into his big chair and folded his hands in his ample lap.

"I know you won't do that, son."

Jack stared from across the couch, taken aback at his uncle's gentle tone.

"I would do anything not to have to ask you these questions, Uncle J, but once I saw that document where you were one of the engineers that signed off on the specifications for the Seventeenth Street Canal walls in 1982, I-I—well, as a reporter on this particular story, I have no choice."

"You have to follow up. I understand that."

"You do?" Jack asked, switching on his tape recorder and identifying the day, time, and subject of his interview. "And do you know what it might mean?"

"That I'll be the scapegoat. The higher-ups have been looking for one all this time in case certain stuff ever got out."

"So, do you feel the part *you* and the other engineers played back in the eighties caused the wall failures?" Jack asked carefully.

"Can't really say I know for sure, either way. All I know

is that it's long past time I come clean about the part I *did* play back then...before I kick the bucket, you know what I'm saying?"

"The colonels and various Corps commanders will come in for some tough criticism, too, Jacques, I guarantee it. But your signing that document may hold the key to the entire story of why those walls and levees gave way thirty-three years later."

"You're telling *me*?" Jacques replied, his voice so low, Jack wondered if his uncle's words had been caught on tape. Jacques looked steadily at his nephew. "Well, we better go."

"Go? Go where?"

"The Seventeenth Street Canal, right around Fortieth Street."

Jack felt his blood pressure elevate a few notches. That was the same street where Serena's brother had lived.

His uncle pushed against the brown arms of the chair whose upholstery was worn in predictable spots from long use. He pulled himself to a standing position with some difficulty. Jacques was only in his late fifties, but early retirement and a sedentary lifestyle had proved risky to his health. The portly figure rarely left the Barcalounger these days and Jack speculated that his uncle was in danger of slipping into Diabetes 2 if he ate many more servings of his wife's caramel bread pudding.

"Why Fortieth Street?" Jack asked, dreading to go near the spot where Serena's brother drowned.

"Fortieth is the stretch where I always figured that wall would one day give way."

A few minutes later, the two men climbed into Jack's car and drove out to the 17th Street Canal, repaired in the decade since Katrina to withstand "at least a Category Two hurricane, right?" Jack confirmed, pointing to the new wall. He eased his vehicle onto a grassy curb, fished his tape recorder out of his briefcase again, and turned it on. "Tell me why *you* predicted that the wall would fail...and fail here at around Fortieth Street?" he asked quietly.

"As I said before, at the time we patched it up, I didn't know for sure how it would behave or if it would ever be truly tested by a storm, but...well...just like you have, son, I read all the reports afterwards. The flood walls back then were built to withstand only seven feet of water, which was half the fourteen feet of water the original design intended."

"So why wasn't it built to the proper strength, given the recommendations of the outside consultants back then?"

Jacques shrugged, leaning against the inside of the closed car door. "Some say it was to save money and earn a bunch of 'atta-boys' from Congressional budget committees. Others thought it was because the oil and gas guys wanted the allotted money to build the projects that would benefit *them* and skimp on the others so there'd be enough money."

"Skimp on what? For what?"

"Oh, changing the flow of the Mississippi for easier access for the tankers to the Gulf...the Mr. GO Canal...stuff like that."

"With hindsight, what do you think caused the decisions to stint on the original design? Why were the recommendations of that outside consultant firm in 1982 ignored? Why didn't the Corps do what the consultants said to do: make the canal walls *stronger* than what the Corps ultimately specified?"

Jacques shook his head.

"A lot of questions, son, and a lot of reasons." He ticked off on his fingers, "Political pressure. Financial pressure. Certain people trying to grandstand themselves into higher government positions. All of that crap from special interests went into the ultimate decision of what to build and how to build it. *All* of it!" he spat.

"Did you object at the time?" Jack asked, trying his best to keep his tone neutral.

"Sure I did!" Jacques snapped. Then he shook his head "Well, the truth is, I was twenty-four-years-old, so I made a mild sort of protest, was about all."

"And what happened?"

"Got a big time push-back."

"And?"

"I signed the drawings anyway, and so did the other engineers who worked on that part of the project."

"*Why?*"

"My bosses made it very clear there was no future for me as a civilian engineer with the Corps if I didn't sign 'em. We had just bought our house and your cousin Lani was just born. The big boys in Washington, I guess, decided they could cut corners and dumb down the designs, figuring they'd get credit for saving money or please the oil and gas guys, but they sure as hell wanted some New Orleans foot soldiers' names on those bogus specs."

Jack pointed to his briefcase full of documents that he'd placed on the seat between them.

"I have a report stashed in there that shows that the Corps finally admitted after Katrina that they'd had a catastrophic failure due to under-engineering. Of course, they didn't cop to it until several independent investigations proved it without a doubt," Jack said.

Jacques waved a dismissive hand in the air and scoffed, "Those old levees and floodwalls were a system in name only—incomplete, inconsistent, and with design performance flaws any idiot could have seen. C'mon," he directed, "let me show you why," and got out of the car.

While the two men walked toward the post-Katrina rebuilt 17th Street Canal wall, Jack was amazed at how candid his uncle had grown during their conversation. He ventured to voice another shocking bit of history he'd unearthed and watched his uncle's reaction.

"Another report I've seen agreed with you, Jacques, that the Corps—somewhere along the chain-of-command—took short cuts simply to save money, and later it either covered it up or remained silent about what was in the official files."

"They knew all along that their predecessors had done bad things even before those commissions dug it all up, but they just had to have it drug out of 'em, didn't they?" Jacques gazed speculatively at his nephew and asked, "Why are you so focused on the Seventeenth? What about the other canal and levee failures? What about the Mr. GO canal and those wetlands and barrier islands you're always going on about?"

"I'll write about those, too, but—" He paused, pointing. "Look over there."

By this time, the two men had slowly made it to a rise that gave a broad view of the canal and the property beyond. Jack pointed out an empty lot in the middle of 40th Street. There was a For Sale sign, and a $14,000 figure on the placard.

"What about it?" Jacques asked, his brow furrowed. "It's no secret that hundreds of houses were washed away around here and they're just selling the land, now, dirt cheap."

"That mammoth storm surge that washed into Fortieth Street matters a lot to me, personally, as it happens," Jack said, gesturing toward the For Sale sign.

"Who lived there?" Jacques murmured, his eyes now

focused in a thousand-yard stare. "Someone you know?"

Jack took a deep breath.

"Now *I'm* the one not coming clean."

Startled by his nephew's confession, Jacques shifted his gaze and waited for the younger man to explain.

"I *love* the woman whose brother died right over there, where that sign is now," Jack said, trying to keep his voice steady. "If she learns in my newspaper story that my own uncle was part of the reason that her brother drowned in his own home, she won't want anything to do with me. Her entire family is still in mourning a decade later and probably will never truly recover."

Jacques' chin sunk onto his chest, but Jack kept talking.

"So you see…this thing I have with the Seventeenth Street Canal *is* partly personal. Sure, it's pivotal to the public's right-to-know what really happened, but I had to learn for myself the whys and wherefores of *your* involvement here," Jack said, touching his uncle's sleeve. "And trust me, I hope to God I won't have to use your name in my story. It'll be up to the lawyers if I do or don't." Despite his best efforts, his voice broke, but he managed to add, "At least, now, you'll have some company knowing and living with the truth of what happened here ten years ago."

"*Jesus H. Christ*, Jack!" his uncle exploded. "And what am I supposed to do, now that you've told me this? Go kill myself? 'Cause that's exactly what I feel like doing—and *have*, for the longest time."

"No!" Jack shot back harshly. "Cut the self-pity! You're not the only star in this little drama. There's plenty of blame to go around in this town! Those other engineers signed, just like you did."

"But what happens now?" Jacques insisted with a strangled cry. "You say you love this woman. Do you love her enough that it's worth exposing my sins to the world and humiliating your whole family like this?"

Jack ignored his uncle's attempts to induce guilt into the equation. At heart, he felt tremendous empathy for his uncle, but it was time for everyone concerned to be straight with each other.

"I hope to introduce you to Serena one day," he said. "You'd like her, Uncle J. But for now, you and I both have to suck it up and try to get the truth out to the people of New Orleans and see if they'll do anything to make things better."

"Maybe they will; maybe they won't," Jacques replied with a heavy sigh. "Probably nothing will change, whatever your story says. Just like the last time you wrote about all this garbage."

"Well, it's up to the readers and the voters, not us. Your job, which you've just done for me, is to tell me the truth. My job is to tell 'em what I believe actually happened—and try to prove it. Once we've done that, you and I have to have the courage to go on living our lives, knowing what we both know."

A light breeze had come up, ruffling the canal water nearby. Jacques resumed staring at the new wall, unseeing. In the next moment, his uncle's massive shoulders began to heave. Then, he covered his eyes as sobs tore from his throat.

"Oh, God…oh, *God,* Jack! I am so sorry. I am—"

To Jack, it seemed as if years of pent-up grief wracked his favorite uncle's large frame. He put an arm around his shoulder in an awkward gesture of comfort. The sobs continued and Jack sank his forehead against the man's bulk, fighting a well of emotion that also had him in its grip.

"I know how sorry you are, Uncle J," he said, his voice low. "Ever since I was a kid, I've somehow known that you've been sorry for something terrible that happened in your life, but I just didn't know *what.* This wall collapsing sure as hell wasn't all your fault."

"But I could have stood up to them!" he said, his voice choking. "I could have said, 'Hell, no!' But I didn't...and believe me, I've been punished, big time, living with this crap all these years. And it just got a whole lot worse, knowing what you told me today. It's that woman you met in Venice, right? Your mother told us the few things she's heard from Marielle about her. Told us you'd broken it off with that Hilbert girl. Says she's never seen you like you are when you even mention the new girl's name."

"Her name is Serena Antonelli," he confirmed.

"Yeah, that's her," he said, nodding. "Your ma's complained that you haven't even had her to the house. She makes costumes, your sister Sylvie said, right?"

"That's right."

Jacques paused as it dawned on him who Serena was and her connection with the place where they were presently standing.

"Her brother was Cosimo the Fourth or Fifth Antonelli, wasn't he?" Jacques said barely above a whisper. "His wife drowned, too...and their unborn child. I remember when all that was in the papers and on TV after the storm." The senior Durand took a step back and gazed again at the empty lot on 40th Street. "So those collapsing canal walls I signed off on were what killed *three* family members of the woman you love."

"Four," Jack corrected. "Her grandmother died of a heart attack being evacuated from a nursing home."

"Holy Mother of God! What a nightmare this is."

"That it is," Jack agreed bleakly.

Both men remained lost in their own misery for a long moment, until Jacques asked, "Are we through here? I need a drink."

Jack nodded, and pointed to the car.

"Yeah, let's go, but I gotta ask you one more question."

Jacques cast him a wary glance as Jack checked to make

sure that the recorder was still rolling.

"You save the worst for last, don't you, you guys from the Society of Environmental Journalists?"

His last words were faintly mocking.

"How do you know about that group?"

"You were the president a while back, weren't you? Hey, you're my namesake," Jacques said, giving his nephew's upper arm a gentle fist bump. "Actually, when they elected you president, it made me right proud. I've been following your meetings for years now."

Jack reared back with surprise.

"Well then, let me ask you this, Uncle Jacques. Here's the question we pose at every convention we've held since Katrina: do you think what's been rebuilt in New Orleans *now* is good enough?"

Jacques took a few more heavy steps towards the car and spoke over his shoulder.

"Well, the new Storm Surge Risk Reduction System the Corps constructed cost fourteen-and-half *billion* bucks! They got themselves new pumps, levees, power stations, water gates, and put surge barriers all over New Orleans. And then there's the *fifty* billion dollar Master Plan they've got going slated for the next fifty years."

Jack hurried to catch up with him so he could be sure his next words were recorded, and also to observe his uncle's face when repeated his question.

"But does what's been constructed in the last ten years *solve* the problem if we get a bigger storm...say a Category Three?" Jack pressed.

He needed an expert's opinion, *on the record*.

Jacques halted and turned to face his nephew. After a long pause, the older man asked, "You still got that danged recorder thing running?"

"Yep."

Jacques nodded and leaned toward his nephew. "Well,

the Corps says there've been lots of improvements... taller, sturdier floodwalls and levees... better design of the braces and pumping stations."

"Okay, okay. But what do *you* think?"

"In my professional opinion," Jacques Durand began, and then heaved an exhausted sigh. "It's still not a *system*. It's still a patchwork quilt, built by the lowest bidder, or somebody's best buddy, God help us all!"

"So you don't think the new system could take a Category Three?"

After a few seconds' pause, Jacques shook his head.

"Is that a 'no?'" Jack said for the benefit of the palm-sized recorder he held in his hand.

"It's at least a 'maybe not.' The engines that power the new floodgates might burn up with that much pressure on them, and the water will just keep coming in. It may not be enough. This is only my two cents, mind you."

"Wow," Jack murmured. "But you're an engineer with years of experience."

Jack's sister Marielle and her husband now lived in Lakeview, fairly near the empty lot on 40th Street. His heart felt like it would be squeezed right out of his chest. He put a hand on Jacques sleeve again to be sure he had his attention.

"And despite all the failures and larceny, is it true that to your knowledge, nobody was fired, or got demoted, no one resigned, and no serious institutional changes were made in the Army Corps, despite the catastrophic failures, am I right?" Jack pressed.

"Yeah, you're right!" Jacques exclaimed, bitterness clinging to each word. "The boys *really* in charge got raises, more funding, promotions, and bigger appropriations. The only thing that happened is that some of us who knew the truth—that the disaster was *manmade*—got pushed out the door, all nice and legal-like." He glanced over at Jack, eyes narrowing. "That story you wrote for the *T-P* before the storm, predicting what might happen? Well, it didn't help your uncle keep his job, I can tell you that."

Jack nodded, acknowledging the truth of his uncle's statement. Then he said, "I was worried that your bosses figured you were a source. But you *weren't* back then, Jacques! You clammed up every time I asked you about the walls and levees before Katrina. Why did they force you out? *How* did they?"

"Even though I stayed mum, stayed loyal to a fault, it didn't make a difference with the higher ups. I was closely related to you, and besides, *they* knew I knew the truth. They wanted my ass in the wringer from then on. And *after* the hurricane, it was holy hell in the Corps for me. So, after a couple of years, I made a deal with 'em. I'd keep my mouth shut if they'd let me leave honorably and pay me my pension and health benefits."

"So why are you talking to me now?" Jack asked sharply.

By this time they had reached their car parked near the grassy curb. Jacques Durand leaned against the passenger door and pounded his fist hard against the vehicle's roof.

"Because I can't live with it any more! I know the tenth anniversary's coming and it's all going to be stirred up again. I'm tired of lying and dodging bullets coming my way…especially from you."

Jack was chagrined to admit to himself that he had never, truly considered how the story he was about to write could leave a member of his own family destitute, stripped of his pension and too old to get other work in his field. He'd only worried about how Serena's family would be affected. The consequences for Jacques Durand could be equally devastating. Suddenly Jack wished he'd been a general assignment reporter merely covering murder, mayhem, and Mardi Gras.

"God, Jacques, how did we end up at *this* spot, on *this* day, I wonder?"

"I knew it would all come out one day," Jacques replied. "Look, I'm willing to stand up in front of you, my own kin, and take responsibility for what I did back then, but I'd be mighty grateful if you don't have to quote me by name."

"As I said before, that will be up to the *T-P*'s lawyers, not me." Another thought struck Jack and he asked, "If what you told me today does wind up in my story attributed to you, Jacques, what do you think will happen with your pension?"

His uncle slid his hands from the car's roof and allowed them to fall by his side.

"If you say in your article that's how silence was guaranteed—by threatening to fire the younger engineers without any benefits or recourse—I don't think anyone who knows about these kinds of deals to get rid of potential whistleblowers like me will *dare* pull the rug out from me, personally, at this point, 'cause they know the *T-P* will be watching for it. And even if they try, I'll sue the bastards!"

Hearing the first hint of a fighting spirit in his uncle's words, Jack stood by his car as Jacques reached for the passenger door handle and then paused.

"You know, don't you, Jack, that in 2008, the U.S. District Court placed responsibility for the floodwall failure on the Corps, but also said that the agency is protected from financial liability by the Flood Control Act of 1928."

"Which means they could screw up *again* and not be accountable?" asked Jack, the leaden feeling in his chest growing heavier.

"You got it, son. Now, let's go get that drink."

The two men climbed into their car and sped off. Glancing straight ahead through the windshield as the new 17th Street Canal wall disappeared from view, Jack knew his first concern should be about the repercussions for his own family, given what Jacques had confirmed this day.

Yet all he could think of was that the lawyers for the *Times-Picayune* would be the ones to decide his future with Serena. And even if the attorneys said Jacques Durand could remain an anonymous source in Jack's story, living with the truth and not telling the woman he loved about the murderous twists of fate that connected their two families would be high price he'd always pay for loving her so deeply, and wanting her to be his wife.

CHAPTER 20

"Aren't we supposed to say 'Break a leg,' or something?" King asked.

"I'm praying your joke still means 'Good luck,'" groused Corlis, "since I'm going to need it modeling my costume wearing those stiletto heels. That raised runway they've got us on feels like a death trap!"

The TV newswoman, her husband, and Serena entered the elegant lobby of the Hotel Monteleone on Royal Street and prepared to part company.

Back-stage on long clothing racks, Antonelli's latest costume creations awaited the models that would strut their stuff as part of the finale of the hot-ticket seated dinner and fashion show to follow at the hospital gala fundraiser for New Orleans's critically-ill, indigent children.

Corlis frowned at Serena who pointed toward the door where King would enter the ballroom and the two women would proceed backstage. "What if my heel gets caught again in that mermaid gown you've put me in?"

"You'll be fine," Serena assured her. "After rehearsal, yesterday, I sewed a little handle on the fish tail so you can hold it up and keep it clear of your feet."

King gave his wife's shoulders a squeeze.

"A sexy mermaid, are you? I can't wait." Answering a ping on his cellphone, he fished it out of his pocket and pointed to the screen. "Jack has texted me to hold his seat. He's just finishing up at the lawyers' office at the paper." To Serena he added with a wink, "Says he wants you not to worry. He'll be here on time."

Serena's heart gave an excited lurch. Despite Jack's newest warnings he would mostly be out of touch during these last weeks in May, he had continued to communicate with her by text or phone every day, letting her know where he was, even if he didn't tell her anything about how his reporting of the Katrina anniversary story was going.

"Okay, then," Serena said with a happy smile. "Here's where we leave you. Clap loud, will you guys?"

"Will do," King promised, bending low to kiss his wife goodbye. "See ya later, Ms. Mermaid," he added, giving Corlis' derrière a friendly pat.

Into his briefcase Jack stashed his copious notes, his tape recorder, and audiocassettes he'd guarded with his life—and snapped the lid shut.

His editor, John Reynolds, pulled out a cloth handkerchief and patted his brow in mock relief. He gestured toward the exiting lawyers in gray suits and smiled at the perky court reporter. The young woman had been brought in at the insistence both of the *T-P* house attorney and the outside law firm engaged to vet the anniversary coverage. She'd been hired to take verbatim notes on her special device. During the entire session just completed they'd combed through Part 1 of Jack's Katrina story, line by line, for liability, slander, and libel issues.

"I'm glad we got an early start with the lawyers on Part One," Reynolds pronounced, heaving a relieved sigh. "It's only late May for our August pub date, but this is dicey stuff. So far, so good." He gazed at his reporter and lowered his voice. "And I think you dodged a bullet about not having to name Jacques Durand, other than as an informed source that declined to be identified."

"Yeah…a major relief, as far as I'm concerned," Jack agreed. Silently, he thanked the fates that he'd be granted that favor, at least.

"I didn't think old Chambordeau would go for it," his editor said with a chuckle, "but I guess he and the outside lawyers feel you have enough other supporting documentation and quoted sources to just leave it as an anonymous interviewee."

"Actually, I was amazed, too, but the point is, we do have all the other documentation. Besides, the story's aim is to have our readers *understand* what kind of pressures are put on good, decent public servants like my uncle working within government agencies to come up with answers that the special interests *want*—even if those answers aren't honest. The readers need to know *how* these decisions get made not to do the job right—and then demand a change so these cities won't literally disappear underwater over the next half century or so!"

"Well, good luck with *that*," Reynolds said with a sour expression.

"All this is so fascinating," offered the freelance court reporter moonlighting from her day job. "It's way more interesting than sitting all day in divorce court."

By this time, she had packed up her equipment and cast an "I'm available for a cocktail" smile in Jack's direction.

Reynolds shot her a hard look.

"And, just so you know, Judy, *nothing* about what you heard here leaves this room, right?" the editor said gruffly, in response to which the woman merely ducked her head and nodded.

"And that reminds me," Jack said, grabbing his briefcase with its precious cargo and handing it to Reynolds. "Can you store this in the vault? I've got to change into my tuxedo in the men's room. I'm due at the Monteleone for that children's benefit in half an hour," he added for the enlightenment of his audience of two. "A couple of friends of mine are involved and I promised I'd show up."

"Oh…right," said the young woman who'd been chastised by his boss. Her slight pout at not being invited out for a drink had morphed into a speculative look. "I got an invitation for that event, too, but the tickets were too pricey for my budget." She picked up the case containing her court-reporting device, turned abruptly, and headed for the door, calling over her shoulder, "Have fun, tonight, y'hear?"

Twenty minutes later, Jack slipped into his seat next to King and ordered a Bourbon Old Fashioned. He was feeling a tremendous sense of relief that Part 1 of his story was pretty much buttoned down and could run in August without publicly naming or shaming his uncle. Jacques' anonymous story, however, helped lay out the reasons—learned in the subsequent ten years since the storm—why the walls of the 17th Street Canal and some others were virtually programmed to fail. The retired engineer had done his duty to come clean, and Jack had done his by being straight with his editor and the lawyers about his personal connections to his crucial "source."

But no sooner had their drinks been served then Jack's spirits took an immediate nosedive. Out of the corner of one eye, he spotted none other than Dr. Lauren Hilbert. Her blond, shoulder-length hair was pulled off her forehead with her signature velvet headband. She had on ice white stiletto heels that must have cost five hundred dollars a pair, and a lemon yellow suit which had "Mardi Gras Madness in May" written all over it. The hem of its pencil-thin skirt skimmed just at her knees, showing off her shapely calves to good effect. She'd make a dandy lawyer's wife, Jack thought, or perhaps the spouse of a hedge fund guy...but surely she could no longer imagine herself married to a lowly reporter?

Thank God she's not my problem anymore.

In the next moment, he was not so sure. Her program in hand, Lauren turned and scanned the ballroom, her gaze eventually resting on their table. He watched her take in the sight of King and him sitting with empty seats on either side of them. For a dreaded moment, Jack thought she was going to approach, but blessedly, she moved on in the direction of the premium tables for high rollers positioned at the front of the room.

"Dodged *two* bullets today," he muttered under his breath.

King, who had seen everything, shook his head.

"Don't bet on it," he replied. "It's Lauren, remember."

"Yeah," Jack said. "I remember. Hail that waiter over there, will you? I need another drink."

Backstage, two-dozen women were chatting excitedly as the fashion coordinator called for silence and climbed on a chair to give them final instructions. Corlis and Serena stood in their ornate costumes at the end of the long line of other models dressed in outfits from top women's retailers in town. The climax of the show would be the spectacular creations that Serena had invented in which the designer and five of the best known on-camera women in New Orleans would prance down the runway with the Storyville Stompers Brass Band leading the way.

The show's producer, Patsy Jo Sullivan, had just completed her final pep talk to the amateur models when Corlis emitted a low groan, startling Serena, who looked at her with alarm. The broadcaster's slender form was encased in an unforgivingly skin-tight mermaid gown, every inch covered in bright green sequins. A headpiece with royal blue and green ostrich feathers perched on the WJAZ anchor's upswept brunette hair.

"What's wrong?" Serena asked anxiously. "Is the corset too tight? Can you breath?"

"No…no, that's not it," hissed Corlis who suddenly had plastered an inane smile on her face as an attractive, well-coiffed young blond woman drew near.

"Well, aren't you just a sight," the stranger said.

"Well, hello," replied Corlis. "Yes, aren't I, just? All in the name of good works, right?"

"Well, bless your heart. And as a member of the board, I can't thank you enough for participating in the fashion show and for King's sponsoring a table, and all," she said, oozing insincerity in a tone that only a true magnolia could summon at will. She waved her program while eyeing Serena in her figure-hugging copy of Allegra's equally arresting Seas of Venice sage-green, organza gown. "I saw all your names in the program when I came in. You must be Serena Antonelli of Antonelli Costume Company. Corlis's great, new friend, I hear, who just got back from Venice, am I right?"

"I've been back a couple of months," Serena replied.

Who was this woman, and why was she shooting daggers at her as well as at Corlis?

The young woman, dressed in a "look-at-me" bright yellow ensemble, opened the program in question and read aloud in a voice that took on a shrill, singsong tone that dripped with sarcasm.

"'Serena Antonelli studied under a celebrated Venetian costume designer and only recently returned from Italy.'" The intruder paused and gazed icicles at Serena over the top of the program. "I suppose that's where you met Jack Durand, the man I thought was going to be my husband—that is until he went off to that conference in Venice and ran into *you*!"

Corlis took command of the conversation and said in a brisk tone, "You're quite the little sleuth, Lauren. I figured you'd seen the story on Serena I did for WJAZ."

"I guess I missed that," Lauren snapped. "I prefer to watch your competition."

Corlis put a hand on Serena's arm and announced, "Meet Doctor Lauren Hilbert, who's a spanking, new plastic surgeon, which is probably a wise choice in medical specialties since business will undoubtedly be brisk with all the new people from Texas and California buying up the French Quarter."

Serena could only stare and try to keep her jaw from dropping. Meanwhile, Corlis turned to address Lauren again.

"Yes, this is Serena Antonelli whose company has been generous enough to provide these fabulous costumes for your event."

"I already know that, Corlis," Lauren retorted, and then her honeyed tone returned as she faced Serena. "As I said, I serve on the board of the charity sponsoring Mardi Gras Madness in May," she announced, her mouth in a tight smile as fake as the one still plastered on Corlis' lips. "I'm also doing reconstructive surgery on children who've been scarred in accidents, as well as face lifts on people like you and Corlis."

Serena inhaled deeply and tried to steady her nerves. So *this* was the woman that Jack had kept company with for years.

"Now, Lauren, let's not all turn into scratchy cats, okay?" Corlis shot back, clearly bristling with annoyance.

Ignoring her, Lauren took a step even closer to Serena and hissed under her breath, "Last I heard, your Daddy's company was about to go bankrupt…but I guess you had enough money to go gallivanting off to Venice, didn't you?

I suppose you think you can use our charity to try to drum up more business and save your pathetic family's sorry ass?"

"Lauren!" chided Corlis, cool as a mint julep, "now what would your mama say if she heard you talking trash like this?"

As for Serena, her friend's sarcasm was lost on her, for all she wanted to do was to crawl under the skirted, raised runway to her right and escape through the hotel's dumb waiter.

By this time, Lauren was dividing her glares equally between the two women. She appeared about to leave but, instead, turned around to deliver an exit line she must have been thinking about for some time.

"Trust me, sugar," she addressed Serena, "You won't see *my* krewe giving you any orders for costumes—nor will anyone else I know, if I have anything to say about it! But, on behalf of the board of directors, thank *yew* for donating your services tonight, y'hear?"

"Oh for Christmas sake, Lauren!" Corlis exclaimed ignoring the curious stares of the models nearby. Serena saw her friend's eyes narrow, as if she was going in for a killer question aimed at a hapless interviewee. "Why don't you just face the fact you and Jack were never going to make it and act like the lady your mama tried to teach you to be!"

Lauren ignored the barb.

"You know, don't you, Serena," she jeered, "that Jack will never marry you or make any sort of commitment like—God forbid—letting you actually move into his condo on Julia Street. He told me less than four months ago that he never planned to marry *anyone*!"

Corlis glanced at Serena, who couldn't help but be dumbstruck by Lauren's verbal assault. The seasoned reporter edged in front of her friend and said sweetly to the interloper in the neon yellow suit, "Well, from what I remember from the miserable times I've spent with you, Lauren Hilbert, who could forget what a train wreck you and Jack were together? I've heard that you've been complaining for months to anyone who'd listen that you didn't find a little ring box under your Christmas tree last year. Given that all of New Orleans seems to know this, I suggest you don't try to imply that Serena, here, is some kind of home-wrecker."

"I think after ten years sleeping with Jack Durand, I know the man a lot better than you do, Corlis McCullough—unless you were cheating on King behind his back."

Serena couldn't suppress a small gasp, but Corlis kept her cool and turned to address her friend.

"Didn't you just tell me, Serena, that Jack *wanted* you to move in with him on Julia Street, but you decided to wait awhile since you only met each other in February?" Corlis turned back to Lauren and added with an even bigger smile, "Look at it this way, Lauren. You've already been Queen of that old krewe you're in, so you won't be needing any gorgeous costumes, like we're wearing, any time soon. I'd say we don't really have a problem here. C'mon, Reenie...it's *show time*!"

Shaken by the venom aimed in their direction, Serena allowed Corlis to take her by the hand and haul her to the spot where the last group of models was scheduled to enter the runway.

"I think we just experienced the classic 'woman scorned' kamikaze attack," Corlis said cheerfully, giving Serena's trembling shoulders a squeeze.

"No kidding," Serena replied, taking several deep breaths to try to calm her racing heart.

"Understand, now, why Jack didn't want to marry the lady?" Corlis asked, pursing her lips in a droll smile.

"There's plenty I don't understand about the two of

them," Serena said on a shaky breath, "like why he was with her at all…or whose fault it was their relationship fell apart."

Corlis's expression became serious as she realized how deeply upset Serena was by what had just happened.

"C'mon, Serena, forget her! Jack was far more tolerant of her out-and-out bitchiness after the storm than I ever was," the broadcaster assured her in a hoarse whisper. "Just be glad that's over. *I* sure am. I hope I never lay eyes ever again on that Wicked Witch of the South."

"Sheesh…she was *really* pissed off."

"Of course she was! She's a spoiled little Dixie chick who's gotten her own way every day of her charmed life—until now. You gotta trust me on this one: Lauren Hilbert has always been a big pain in the ass, and you can quote King *and* me on that."

"If you say so," Serena murmured distractedly.

She attempted to focus on the task ahead, that of showing off the clothes to their best advantage during the fashion show, but her mind was whirling with questions.

Was Jack's former girlfriend steaming mad because she'd discovered, to her sorrow, that the man she'd loved had had an affair in Venice when they hadn't officially broken off their own long term relationship? Had she been crushed when she believed that he was just one of those guys who claimed he couldn't commit, and then discovered Jack had immediately replaced her with another woman? Even worse, maybe Lauren spoke truth: at the end of the day, Jack was the kind of guy who constitutionally *wouldn't* commit to a long-standing relationship, despite his hints of a future together once his Katrina pieces were published?

The young doctor had looked positively stricken when Corlis said Jack had asked Serena to move in with him—which wasn't quite true, of course. He'd only said he *wanted* her to, and that wasn't the same thing. Clearly, Lauren was still devastated that Jack had broken up with her, or was she merely being spiteful that she'd lost out to another female?

Serena *hated* that Lauren's vile words had so quickly eroded the wonderful feelings she'd nurtured toward Jack since they'd returned from Venice. She felt as if she were one of the trapeze artists she used to dress in Marco's Vegas show. One night, the woman stood on the platform, high above the audience, suddenly lost her nerve, and refused to leap toward her partner's outstretched hands. Could she, Serena Antonelli, still summon the courage to believe that what seemed to exist between Jack and her in Venice had been real—and would last—now that they were both back in New Orleans? Had she been lulled into thinking they'd sorted through a lot of the issues between them when, in fact, there was plenty she didn't understand about the man with whom she'd fallen so deeply in love—and had made love in the past to the woman she'd just met?

Just then, the fashion coordinator that had originally invited Serena to participate in the charity event was gesturing wildly for the costumed models to move closer to the entrance to the runway.

"C'mon! C'mon!" she urged in a hoarse whisper. "Y'all are next up! Serena, you're first, remember. Take your time and smile real big as the M.C. tells the audience all about you and Antonelli's and these gorgeous gowns you've created!"

A sound track of pounding music faded and just as quickly, the 'live' Storyville Stompers Brass Band, dressed in dark suits and ties and white captain's caps, struck up their first tune. Trembling with anxiety, Serena drew ever closer to the parted curtains she was expected to walk through. The musical group marched onto the runway first, but Serena stood, frozen where she was.

"Oh, Corlis," she choked. "I *so* don't want to do this!"

"Oh, yes you do! If I could, I'd hug you and tell you

that Jack is absolutely crazy about you and everything's gonna be fine, but we don't have time and this mermaid costume will split a gusset." She leaned close to Serena's ear and whispered fiercely, "Look here, kiddo...Lauren Hilbert's trying to put the voodoo on you, so don't let her! You just go out there and knock 'em dead, girl!"

After the fashion show, Jack was the first to stride to Serena's side with congratulations for the spectacular showing she and the other models had made as the finale to the glamor-filled event. By this time, she had donned a white pair of slacks and linen blouse, stripped her face of the theatrical make-up all the models had been required to wear, and stood like a zombie, feeling as if a truck had run over her.

"I think the performance these gals gave deserves a bottle of champagne," King proposed. "Let's take 'em to the Palm Court for a little Veuve Clicquot, what do you say?"

Corlis looked ready to party, but Serena shook her head.

"Y'all go ahead. Gus and Nick are waiting for me backstage. I've got to help them get all those costumes back to the shop and onto the mannequins before morning."

"I'll go with you," Jack offered.

"That's sweet of you," she replied quickly, "but we have a system. It'll go faster if I just go back and take care of it with them."

"You look dead on your feet, Serena," Jack said, his brow furrowed. "Let me help."

"No, really. I-I've got to get back there. Thanks for coming. I'll talk to y'all soon," and before the three of them could stop her, Serena disappeared behind the curtain where the runway ended.

Jack looked at Corlis.

"Something's wrong. The show from out here looked as if it went flawlessly. What happened back there?"

"Take a wild guess," Corlis said with a sour look. "Did you read the program? You must have seen Lauren sashaying around the tables out here, just like she did backstage. Just our luck, she's on the board of this thing." She pointed at the group's banner hung across the ballroom. "I bet that poor woman who organized the fashion show is going to get an earful."

"Because of Serena? The costumes made the entire night!" King declared loyally. "Lauren Hilbert should kiss Serena's feet!"

"You men can be so dense sometimes," Corlis said, shaking her head. "When Lauren saw the program after she arrived and put two-and-two together, what with Jack sitting out front and the costumes being from a designer who recently returned from Venice...she basically went apeshit."

"Didn't she *know* before tonight that Antonelli's was part of the fashion show? You say she's a part of this group," King protested.

"I talked with a few of the other board members right afterwards," Corlis said, ever the inquiring reporter. "Lauren just has her name on the letterhead, they told me. Too busy to get her hands dirty helping put together this fundraiser, apparently. Turns out, though, that her family gave a big chunk of change to the charity to get her a seat on the board. It was game over, though, once she caught sight of that gorgeous girlfriend of yours, Jack. And Lauren got pretty nasty. For a second, there, I thought Serena wasn't going to make it down the runway."

"God, that woman fries my oysters!" Jack exploded.

"I assume you mean Lauren," King said.

"You bet I do. What did she say to Serena?" he asked Corlis.

"Vicious crap. Serena was totally blindsided, so I did most of the talking. Trust me, I was just as much of a harridan as that witch doctor."

King said, "Tell Jack how you *really* feel about Lauren, Corlis."

His wife shot him a look. "I've been nice as pie for years around that woman as long as Jack was dating her, but now that he's not, I can speak my mind."

"As if that's unusual," King teased.

"King!" she said, and gave him a gentle punch to the jaw.

"Look, you guys," Jack interrupted, "I'm going to go find Serena."

Corlis put a restraining hand on his arm. "I wouldn't, if I were you. She's utterly exhausted and feeling pretty raw. Let her get her costumes put away and have a good night's sleep. Then, you'll have a much better chance mending your fences."

"But I didn't *do* anything!"

"Silly man! The fence you have to mend is to refute all the things Lauren insinuated you *said*… and didn't say. Like Lauren's predicting that you would never ask Serena to live with you, and, of course, telling Lauren when you broke up with her that you'd probably never get married to *anyone*."

"She said all that to Serena?"

"Yup," Corlis replied nodding up and down. "It was quite a little drama Ms. Magnolia pulled backstage. If you want to hear Lauren's exact words, I have to act out all the parts. C'mon with us to the Palm Court, Jack, and let's have us that champagne. Then I'll tell you everything."

Corlis hooked arms with her husband and their friend and steered them both out of the Hotel Monteleone's now deserted ballroom.

CHAPTER 21

All the next day between fact-checking calls and phone interviews on Part 2 of his up-coming series, Jack kept dialing Serena's cellphone—but she never picked up or called back. He tried texting her, but got no response.

At five o'clock he left the newsroom and headed for one of his favorite restaurants that also did take-out. Packages in hand, he strode across Canal Street and into the CBD. It was nearly six when he rounded the corner and confirmed that the costume mannequins were back in their windows. He pushed the bell and held up his takeout booty in front of the glass when Serena arrived at the front door.

"Gumbo from the Gumbo Shop," he announced and then studied Serena's expression. It seemed to reflect neither welcome nor rancor, but a version of neutrality that sent cold chills down his spine despite the humid weather soaking the shirt on his back as he stood on the street facing Antonelli's. Given the details Corlis had filled in for him at the Palm Court, he was glad Serena was even willing to open the door.

"I was just about to close up and go home," she said. Much to his relief, she turned toward the shop's interior and led the way. "I guess we can eat what you've brought in the cutting room at the big table in there."

"Great," he replied, closing the door and following her through the phalanx of costumed mannequins that immediately brought back memories of *Il Ballo di Carnevale*. For some reason, what he remembered most about that night was the time he'd spent looking for Serena among the masked and costumed revelers in the festooned *palazzo*, keeping a wary eye out for the predatory Stefano Fabrini.

Antonelli's front office was deserted and Serena explained over her shoulder that the rest of the staff had already departed. "Nick and Gus just went upstairs to their apartment on the third floor to make their dinner. They invited me, but I said no."

A CD with familiar Dixieland tunes was playing softly over speakers dotted throughout the warehouse. Even in the cutting room, the venue for their impromptu dinner party, he could hear the strains of "Got My Regulator Shakin'"—a tune he loved. Serena disappeared into a back room, shut off the music, and soon emerged with ceramic bowls and cutlery.

"Sit," he commanded when she placed everything on the table, "and I'll serve."

Serena perched on a stool and waited in silence for him to dish out the gumbo, its rich, chocolaty-brown roux and chicken chunks sending out an irresistible aroma. They each flanked a corner of the cutting table, now cleared of the day's work. Before Serena could reach for her soup spoon, however, Jack took her hand.

"Corlis told me everything that happened backstage last night," he began. "I'm really so sorry Lauren attacked you like that. She should have said all that stuff to me, not you."

"Like you never inviting a woman to live with you?" Serena shot back. "No wonder you were silent when the subject came up at the Duvallons that night."

"But, I *want* us to live together," Jack protested. "And I've told you that. Just that we can't do it…right now."

But Jack could see Serena was not to be mollified.

"Did Corlis repeat the other things that whack job said to me right before I was supposed to go on the runway?" demanded Serena. "That she's going tell as many krewes as she knows *not* to patronize Antonelli's Costume Company because she heard we were going bankrupt?"

"Holy crap!" Jack exploded.

Serena's gaze bored into him from across the table.

"*Jack*! How could you ever have *been* with a person who says things like that?"

"She wasn't always that bad," Jack said, deeply disturbed that Lauren would so viciously attack someone she hadn't even met before. "And I haven't been with her for a long time, actually," he defended himself, "not like I was, right after Katrina. The scene at Charity Hospital during the storm...changed her...scarred her in a way I didn't realize how bad until a couple of years later."

"I'm sick of everybody using Katrina as an excuse for bad behavior!"

Jack nodded slowly.

"You know, you've just asked a fair question, though. Why *did* I allow things between Lauren and me to go on for way too long?" He placed his spoon beside his bowl, giving himself time to think. Then he said, "This may sound like I'm using the Katrina Excuse again, but I suppose my reasons were that I was too busy at work doing all those follow-up stories about the storm, and too preoccupied with my sister Sylvia's problems." He paused again, and then gave a short laugh. "A big part of the answer is—I see *now*—that I was distracting myself from how depressed I felt about the way New Orleans was literally hung out to dry after the storm. And I used all the various diversions at my command as a reason not to call it off with Lauren when things really started to go seriously sideways. Then, four years ago, she headed off to Houston to Med school, and that provided even *more* of an excuse just to let things slide. Believe me, I'm not proud of any of that."

"You shouldn't be," Serena said quietly and took her first bite of gumbo.

They both ate in silence for a while.

Then Serena said, "Look, Jack, my first obligation is to my family, and especially to Nick and Gus not to damage the business we've all worked so hard to build up again after the storm."

"You haven't done anything to damage the business!" he protested. "In fact, you've only enhanced it!"

But Serena stubbornly shook her head.

"It's bad enough that our father has so little faith in the three of us, without your girlfriend doing her best to torpedo our company by poisoning the well with all the krewe members she knows all over town."

"*Ex*-girlfriend," Jack reminded her, tight-lipped.

"I figure I'll just have to work twice as hard, now, to overcome her disparaging us everywhere she can. God knows whatever else she plans to do to sabotage us here, but there are only so many hours in the day, so I don't think you and I can—"

Jack cut in, "You're letting her win, you know."

Serena paused and set her spoon down beside her bowl.

"Well, she has. I surrender."

Jack inhaled a deep breath. "Driving a wedge between us like this is exactly what she intended and she's succeeding—just like the terrorists succeed when they make everyone afraid to get on an airplane."

Without looking at him she asked, "Well, what about the other stuff she said?"

"About my not ever intending to marry anyone?"

Serena appeared startled.

"How did you know about that?"

"Corlis has a steel-trap memory and aptly described the hissy fit Lauren threw backstage."

"I'm not fishing for a marriage proposal, mind you," Serena blurted, "but what she said rang the old Mr. Elusive bell in my head."

"Do I seem elusive lately?" he demanded. "I've been calling you five times a day and buying tickets to fashion shows, to say nothing of bringing gumbo to your very door," he elaborated with a crooked grin. "What other proof of my serious intentions should I be demonstrating, other than ask my mother for my grandmother's diamond ring that she keeps at the bank—which I hope to do before long?"

Serena gazed across the table at him.

"'Serious intentions,' are they?" she quoted him.

He could tell she was trying not to smile.

"As serious as I can make them until my stories are published," he allowed.

"Seriously?"

"You like that word, don't you?"

"I do."

"So…?"

Serena hesitated only a split second before saying, "Soooo…come here, will you?"

Jack put down his spoon.

"Come where?"

She crooked her index finger and gestured with a nod of her head.

"In there."

"It says Ladies Room on the door."

"And inside, there's an old fashioned fainting couch for our female employees to take naps on when they're working late shifts."

"Like the sofa at the top of the costume workroom in Venice?"

"Bigger," she replied, her voice low and husky, "and a lot more comfortable. Mine's even got a velvet coverlet and a couple of pillows."

Their glances locked and their memories of the first night they made love were reflected in each other's eyes. They both stood up simultaneously and their bodies collided near the corner of the cutting table.

"I *hate* what you were subjected to last night," he whispered into her hair, and then scattered kisses everywhere, finally reaching her lips. "I've been on the receiving end of that stuff Lauren can dish out, and, man-oh-man, can it poison your spirit and dull your shine. I'm sorry, Serena, sweetheart. I am *so* sorry! I'll keep her away from you from now on, I swear!"

He gazed down at her, filled with a surging love for the woman he held in his arms. Serena's eyes were filled with tears.

"It was pretty awful," she murmured, "especially when she said I'd started an affair with you when she was still in the picture. She was right, you know."

"Now don't go taking on sins that belong to me!" he countered. "You are the last person on earth who deserved that kind of an assault. You're the sweetest, nicest, prettiest, most talented…"

"Better say 'the sexiest' or I'll kick you right out of here!" she retorted softly, swiping the moisture that had spilled down her cheek with the crook of her elbow.

For a second time since he'd met Serena, Jack tasted the salt when he kissed both eyelids. Then he placed one hand on her breast and cupped it through her sweater.

"Oh, yeah…definitely…'sexiest' makes the list."

"Those were the magic words, *signor*," she teased, kissing him back. "C'mon, then…let's finish our gumbo and head for the Ladies Room where you can whisper in my ear whatever other sweet nothings you have up your sleeve."

"How about doing all that in reverse order? There's always the microwave to heat up food in your employees' lounge."

By mid August, Jack had completed Part 2 of his Katrina anniversary piece and was working on the last section of the series that would begin running the week of

August 29th. He called King and asked if he could come over to talk to him about an aspect of the story that had begun to trouble him even more deeply than before.

"Sure, buddy. Just you?" King answered, and Jack was grateful his friend sensed this was a conversation that couldn't include Serena.

When he got to King's place on Dauphine Street, he was relieved to learn that Corlis was, in fact, still at work, which had been part of his calculations. He was warmed by the friendship that had developed between the two women, which was all the more reason he needed to speak with King alone.

He quickly brought his friend up-to-date on the important factors that would be new to the reading public and, because he trusted King implicitly, told him of his uncle's full admission on tape confirming that both Jacques and a number of his superiors had been well aware in 1982 that they were building canal walls to lower standards than had been recommended by outside engineering consultants.

Jack also outlined the statements of several other named experts who were of the opinion that what had been rebuilt in the wake of Katrina had woefully been under-engineered to less than a Category Three.

"And it was done like that for the same, damned reasons of undue influence that have plagued New Orleans, as well as Venice, Italy, for years," he concluded.

"So you've got all these folks on the record?" King reiterated.

"Some names will be named in the published pieces…and some declined to be named, but spoke on the record to me on my assurance they would be quoted as 'informed sources who wished to remain anonymous.' Uncle J is in the second classification."

"And this information has been kept water tight?"

pressed King, "because if you ever think it will be leaked as to *who* those unnamed sources *are*, you'd better prepare Serena ahead of time for these revelations."

"That's what I wanted to talk to you about. The only people who have seen and read what I've written so far are my editor and the lawyers and a very few select members of their staff—and now you."

"Hmmm...that's good, but not perfect," King said. "Why are you still trying to convince yourself that there's no need to tell Serena about all this before the pieces run?"

"You mean about the role that a 24-year-old greenhorn engineer played in the corrupt process of how some of these walls and levees were built—even though that greenhorn is my elderly uncle who has come clean to me and mightily regrets his role in the death of her family members?"

"Yup. And I assume that's why you're here. Despite all, it's still got you worried, hasn't it?"

"Yeah...a bit...but then I think, why put Serena through the pain of knowing who did it, if the basic facts about all the circumstances will be revealed, even if Jacques' name in this instance isn't disclosed publicly?"

"C'mon Jack," King replied. "Maybe you're choosing to take this path because *you* will also be spared the possibility that if Serena knew the specifics, she'd dump you."

"Jesus, King, why are you so smart?"

"Well, because we both know it might someday get out," insisted King, "and if it did—and Serena realized you'd known all this time and kept it from her—I don't know what would be worse: being devastated by the news your uncle had a hand in her brother's death, or feeling betrayed by you because you hid it from her."

"But Jacques is a protected source!" Jack said, agonizing over his dilemma between two competing loyalties. "You're married to Corlis. You know the rules I'm working under."

"You're dealing with more than journalist 'do's and don'ts' here, Jack," King reminded him gruffly. "Your source also happens to be your uncle *and* you're his namesake. The woman involved happens to be your lover! Outsiders might say the only reason you're keeping that quiet is due to special interests yourself."

Jack stared at his friend, stung by his words.

"Well, the frigging lawyers agreed that I don't have to name him!" he retorted, though he could hear the defensive tone in his voice. "*They* didn't think I was pulling rank," he added heatedly. "Why *not* let sleeping dogs lie? The odds are in my favor that Serena never has to know and never has to be hurt by all this. She even told me once that she might not even read the three-parter because she's afraid of it picking the scabs off old wounds."

"If you say so," King commented, arching an eyebrow.

"Well, at least this way, the story can still be told without ruining everybody's life. And who knows? Maybe it'll make a big enough impact that we can stop what's happening to our goddamned city!"

"That's a mighty big secret to keep, especially if you want to marry this woman—and I think it's pretty clear you do." King replied quietly. "And may I remind you, you just told *me* all about your protected source. Your wanting to go over all this again today indicates that this conflict you've been wrestling with for months is bothering you, big time. That should tell you something."

"But you're my best friend," Jack protested. "I told you because I trust you completely."

"And you don't trust Serena?"

Jack's lips clamped shut and he looked away.

"Honestly? I guess I don't trust the fact that I have no idea what she'd do if she ever found out. One thing I *do* know: I love her and I can't risk hurting her like this."

"What's *honest*, Jack," King said harshly, "is that you're not willing to risk hurting *yourself* by taking a chance you might lose her if you told her the truth." More gently he added, "Believe me, I understand. I'd feel the same way about Corlis, but I still think you should tell Serena before the story is published."

Jack remained silent absorbing King's admonitions.

Duvallon heaved a shrug and said, "But, hey, you're the guy on the hot seat this time. Your call."

"I dunno know, King. I just don't know," Jack mumbled and left without saying goodbye.

In the early morning of August 29th, 2015, as they had every year since Katrina struck New Orleans, Serena and her family met at 9 a.m. at the gates of the St. Louis Cemetery Number 3 near the outskirts of City Park. The somber little group set out for the gravesite where her grandmother, brother, sister-in-law, and the deceased couple's unborn child were buried. The newspaper that morning was already on the front porch. Serena had steeled herself to read Part 1 of Jack's story, but once she'd grabbed the paper from the top step, she took it upstairs and left it in her bedroom, the rubber band still around its folds.

Earlier in the week, Nick had been seething when their mother had told him not to bring Gus to the cemetery, or risk "heaping unpleasantness on an already upsetting day." As a result, Serena's brother hadn't uttered a word during the entire time the family began its annual pilgrimage .

Serena paused on the path that led from the cemetery's gates to the family monument her parents had erected ten years ago, once the floodwaters subsided. Her breath caught at the sight of the close proximity of another family plot with a large stone marker stamped DURAND. How had she never noticed it, she wondered? She realized, taking in the front view of the mausoleum built above the ground, that she'd never even told Jack where her brother was buried. It made her wonder, given her unsettling exchanges with Lauren Hilbert recently, how well *did* she and Jack know each other?

After each member of her family said a prayer at the raised Antonelli family tomb, they drove to Commander's Palace for their annual brunch of turtle soup and pecan-encrusted gulf fish. Serena diplomatically took a seat beside her father to allow some distance between him and his surviving son, Nick, who had immediately selected a chair at the other end of the table.

"I thought you told your mama we were finally going to get to see this Jack fellow again at brunch today?" Cosimo declared.

"You were," Serena replied, "but he called me this morning at six. He's on deadline for something he's writing for the *T-P* and wanted me to extend his apologies. It's a complicated story and he said he had to meet with the paper's lawyers one final time today."

Actually, Serena had no true idea why Jack had begged off from meeting her entire family for the first time since the day they both left from the New Orleans airport for Venice. He'd offered the excuse of having some problems with Part 3 that had required his meeting with company lawyers at the newspaper office on this anniversary of the hurricane—but something was definitely amiss.

For the first time in ages, he'd exhibited an edgy and out-of-sorts demeanor that had been prompted by nothing that he'd chosen to share with her. Even stranger had been his off-putting behavior that had followed a meeting with King on a subject he hadn't disclosed when he'd picked her up from work earlier in the week. He'd been very quiet all evening when they'd gotten back to the Julia Street flat. Then, when they went to bed, Jack seemed almost desperate to show her in a night of intense lovemaking how much he cared for her. The next morning, however, he'd suddenly grown tense and uncommunicative again.

And the irony was, Serena reflected, dipping a large, silver spoon into her turtle soup, she had told him when they'd first awakened after that wondrous night that she'd definitely decided not to build out the remaining square footage into an apartment for herself on the third floor at their costume company.

"I've thought a lot about it," she'd said, tracing a teasing finger down his perfectly straight nose, "and I've decided that I'd rather move in with you at some point—that is, if you still want a very friendly roommate."

She recalled with disquiet that he'd shifted onto his side and gazed long and hard into her eyes. Then, without responding to her proposal, he'd leaned across her pillow and kissed her lightly on the forehead before pulling away and telling her he was already late and had to get to work.

During breakfast, when she'd invited him to join her family on the 29th for brunch after they'd visited her brother's gravesite, he'd nodded his acceptance, but had immediately risen from the table and headed for the door with a terse, "Talk later." Almost at once, she'd sensed a familiar, worrisome stab in her chest and experienced the fear that Jack's sudden withdrawal had turned him back into a shadowy figure whose thoughts and feelings were being kept tightly under wraps.

Shades of the Hotel Danieli.

And since, in a recorded telephone message, he'd ultimately begged off joining her at today's important family occasion. He had spoken in such a strained and stilted way, what else could she assume but that her declaration she wanted to move in with him triggered some primal fear of intimacy and proved to be more than he wanted in his life? More than he could apparently handle when he was under so much pressure at work?

Serena had the unhappy thought that perhaps Lauren Hilbert hadn't merely responded as a woman scorned. Perhaps she had experienced the same thing that now confronted Serena—Jack's chronic inability to communicate directly about any emotional turmoil going on with him and thereby being unable to form a solid bond with a woman he cared for? Serena had been utterly baffled by this rapid sequence of events, and just as her response had been in Venice when Jack left so abruptly, all she could do was go back to her family home, dress for the day, and put one foot in front of the other.

Still, she couldn't banish a question that kept lurking in the back of her mind: was his notorious elusiveness a persistent condition that would ultimately lead to her unhappiness? Was her relationship with this man whom she loved so dearly, now, just another New Orleans version of Marco Leone?

Jack...Jack...what has happened? What's changed in your world?

Jack stared unseeing, at his computer screen in the bustling newsroom, that is, if a newsroom could be said to be bustling anymore, he reflected sourly. All around him, reporters were tapping away on their silent electronic keyboards and the only other sounds were emanating from TV screens on the wall with their volumes turned to a low murmur.

He felt numb. A leaden sensation had come over him as soon as he knew the first of his three-part series had landed on the lawns across New Orleans and popped up on the landing page of the online version of the paper. He was sure that a hammer was bound to descend on his head in response to what he'd written. It was just a matter of time.

He glanced at his watch. Brunch at Commander's would be over by now. He simply couldn't face discussing the tenth anniversary of Katrina—or what he'd written about it—with Serena or her family members. He was certain that if they read his story it was bound to bring up traumatic memories and probably prompt a desire to know who were the unnamed engineers who'd signed off on the faulty plans for the 17th Street Canal so long ago. What, they were bound to wonder, was the name of the person whose statements were framed by quotation marks?

Why had I ever thought I could keep it all a secret and live with myself?

He punched in King's number and got him on the first ring.

"Hey, Buddy," King replied when he knew who was calling him, "how're ya doin'?" After a moment's silence, and no reply from the caller, King said, "Part One was terrific, by the way. Thanks for sending me the advanced copies of the other two. They're first rate work." After another long pause he asked, "Did you tell her?"

"No," Jack answered shortly. "I plan to, but just not now. Frankly, I'm totally wiped. We just put Part Three to bed. I've got to get outta here, you know what I'm saying?"

"I get how you feel, Jack, but you're taking a big risk."

"Maybe so, but I've got to clear my mind of days dealing with fact-checkers and lawyers—and get some God-damned sleep. Can I use the cabin in Covington?"

"Key's inside the dried alligator head sitting on the front porch."

"Thanks."

And Jack hung up.

After the Antonelli's multi-course brunch at Commander's Palace, the family had gathered around the table at their home that evening for a simple meal of red beans and rice, along with an *insalata mista* and a big pitcher of sweet tea.

Serena's mother called into the living room for young Flavia to come to the table, which, surprisingly, she did. She walked into the dining room with her cellphone in her hand and tears running down her cheeks.

"Have y'all *read* the paper today?" she demanded, waving her phone where she tended to get her news from the online version of the *Times-Picayune*. She looked at Serena accusingly. "You never told us that your invisible boyfriend did the big anniversary story on ten years since the storm."

Serena quickly glanced around the table at the startled faces.

"H-he told me he was working on a big, hush-hush three-parter on the anniversary but wasn't allowed to say much about it, so I haven't either. Rules at the *T-P* and—"

Flavia interrupted, pointing to her small screen.

"Well, did he tell you that he finally tracked down the jerk engineer who, way back when, was one of the guys who signed off on plans for the Seventeenth Street Canal? It says here he did that *knowing* that the damn pilings should have been driven to at least a depth of thirty-five—and even *fifty* feet where the peat was that deep—but okayed them being sunk not very far at all!"

Nick scowled. "No wonder the damn thing collapsed in Katrina!"

Tears continued to bathe Flavia's cheeks.

"Whoever this guy was," she shouted between sobs, "he *murdered* our brother and screwed up this whole, fucking family!"

Serena's mother dropped her spoon into the bowl of red beans and rice that she was about to dish out and enfolded her youngest daughter in her arms. Cosimo sat with both fists clenched on top of the table, silent, his face ashen.

"Where's the paper?" Sarah Antonelli demanded. "I want to see exactly what it says! Did it name this person?"

Nick volunteered, "I saw it on the front porch earlier this morning when I came from the shop. It's probably still there."

"I'll get it," Serena said quickly.

She bolted upstairs, snatched the paper off the bedspread in her room, and dashed back to where her family was still gathered around the dining table. Collapsed in a chair, Flavia sunk her face in her hands. Serena sat next to her, her throat tight with tears of her own, and slowly began to read aloud.

An hour later, Serena called Jack from her bedroom on her cellphone. When he didn't pick up, she sent him a text praising his work, then adding:

> **It was hard for all of us to read your story, but at last you answered our questions about why the 17th canal failed so horribly. Flavia demanded to know who it was that signed off, but I explained what an 'anonymous source' meant and the reasons for keeping it confidential. Call when me you can…**

By the next day, when she'd had no reply from Jack, she called the landline at his office and was told he'd taken a few days off after his big three-part story "had been put to bed," the editor's assistant had told her. Puzzled by this news, she borrowed her mother's car and drove over to Julia Street.

When she emerged from the sedan's air-conditioning, the suffocating August heat bore down hard, and by the time she reached Jack's front door, she could feel her cotton shirt sticking to her back. She looked for his car parked on the street and didn't see it anywhere. Then she rang his buzzer and stepped back on the sidewalk to see if she could spot any movement in the window of his office where he always waved to her before sprinting to the intercom to buzz her in.

Nothing. Jack wasn't home and he hadn't told her where he'd gone.

She retraced her steps and got into the driver's side, turning on the ignition. For several long moments, she sat with her hands on the wheel, staring through the windshield up at Jack's flat as frigid air-conditioning blew on her face and legs. How could he just take off and disappear like this when he had to know the devastating impact his story would have on her...would have on everyone in the Antonelli family? *Why* had he gone into hiding?

She thought of calling the Duvallons to see if *they* knew where he was, and then couldn't face how demoralizing it would feel if they knew his whereabouts and she didn't.

A feeling of crushing desolation invaded her chest along with the synthetic air pouring out of the car's dashboard. The sensation was like none she'd ever experienced—except for the instant Marco died in her arms, followed by his estranged wife screaming at her the next day to get the hell out of his house.

Twenty minutes later, she somehow managed to drive home and leave the car in the family driveway. Without speaking to anyone, she immediately boarded the St. Charles Street car back to the CBD. When she got to the costume shop, Nick met her in the reception area, waving a newspaper.

"Have you seen Part Two of this thing?" he demanded. "That boyfriend of yours sure pulls no punches, I'll say that for him. There are gonna be a lot of folks around here mighty unhappy with the guy about all the stuff he's dug up. But I hope it'll do some good before the next time New Orleans gets walloped."

Serena merely waved her hand, unable to speak.

"Have you talked to him?" Nick asked, looking at her questioningly.

Shaking her head "no," she tore past him and bolted up three flights of backstairs. Gus was on the top landing, about to head downstairs. Without a greeting, Serena brushed past and disappeared into the empty flat, slamming the door and then locking it. She was betting no one could hear her crying with her head buried beneath the pillows on their double bed.

CHAPTER 22

Nick reported to her that every single customer who had come into the shop the following day was buzzing about the three-part story in *The Times-Picayune*.

Gus chimed in, "Finally, we're finding out why the damage went far beyond the power of the storm, itself—and who was ultimately responsible."

Nick agreed, adding, "It's kinda scary to learn that even all the new stuff that's been built to keep the water out might not work. What does Jack say about the reactions he's got? I bet there are people in certain quarters that want to tar and feather him. He sure played guts ball on this one."

Serena barely managed a casual shrug and continued to fiddle with her colored pencil at her drawing board. Her brother and his partner exchanged looks and left her in peace.

Later that afternoon Nick asked, "Sis, are you okay?"

"In a word: no."

"Want to talk about it?"

"Second word: no." Then she added softly. "Maybe sometime, but not today, and please don't ask me anything more about Jack."

"Uh-oh...trouble already? Jeez, and I hardly met the guy. Kinda like the Phantom of the Opera." At Serena's stricken look, Nick put an arm around her shoulder and apologized. "I'm sorry...that was a real stupid crack. I'm sad if things have gone haywire between you two."

"That, they have," Serena said, waving him off.

Despite the stifling heat that continued to bear down on New Orleans, the fall social season had already begun. Thankfully, Lauren Hilbert's negative comments at the fashion show the previous May were proving to be empty threats. Given all the positive public exposure that had flowed from the media stories and the fashion show itself, the Antonelli Costume Company had started to enjoy a huge boom in business. Both krewes and private clients were flocking to the shop. Scores of customers had ordered outfits not only because of Mardi Gras the following early spring, but also ball gowns and fancy dress items for everything from Southern Decadence over Labor Day, to Halloween, to balls that were scheduled from October through Christmas, and beyond. Meanwhile, it was Day Four and Jack's "radio silence" had been a total blackout.

Just do your work…eventually he'll let you know one way or the other what's going on and why he's pulled a disappearing act again.

But maybe this time, she'd have the guts to let *him* know she wasn't interested in hearing about it.

Jack sat in King Duvallon's flat-bottomed pirogue watching his fishing line twitch in the murky waters of Bayou Lacombe. His boat bobbed on one of several tributaries that fanned out from the main body of water and flowed near the old slave cabin his friend had restored on what was left of a family plantation property, long since carved up by post-war descendants.

The first day Jack arrived in this remote part of Covington across Lake Pontchartrain from New Orleans, he'd dove into the big double bed, pulled up an ancient quilt some ancestor of King's must have stitched, and slept a straight eighteen hours.

His body obviously had craved rest after long weeks of concentrated work, but when he awoke, his mind spun into the death spiral that had driven him to seek this isolation in the first place.

It had been a couple of days since the last of his Katrina anniversary pieces were published. There was no calling back anything he'd written. He could just imagine his office email Inbox and the howls of protest from certain quarters throughout the city from officials who only wished to be described publicly in the noblest of terms.

And Serena? Just as King had predicted, the very big secret Jack had been keeping from her weighed as heavily on his shoulders as a waterlogged cypress stump. He'd found it impossible to summon the strength to confront it—or her—right now.

An image floated through his mind of thousands of New Orleanians holding newspapers in their hands, reading what he'd written. He figured a lot of people were unhappy with Jack Durand about now. And a lot of people had questions that he didn't have the energy—or wouldn't be allowed—to answer. Absently, he watched the ripples ruffling the water from an unseen creature passing below the boat. One of the best things about coming out here, he considered silently, was that there was no cell coverage. He couldn't call anyone, and they couldn't call him.

And he'd never felt lonelier in his life.

It had been six days with no word from Jack. During this time, Serena had kept to herself at work, hunched over her drawing board in a corner of the big cutting room and slept on the fainting couch in the ladies room, figuring her family would think she was at Jack's.

By the third day of this silence, she'd moved her drafting board and drawing implements into one of the private client consulting rooms, shut the door, and posted a "Creative Frenzy - Do Not Disturb" sign on the window. Anyone who looked at her, she guessed, would know how upset she was becoming by the hour so seclusion seemed the only answer. Her makeshift office became a blessed hideaway, even though it faced the corridor that led to the enormous room where some 1500 rental costumes hung on tiers of clothing racks stacked all the way up to the warehouse's tall, tin roof.

Despite her clear request for privacy, the intercom speaker overhead announced that two potential clients had just arrived, asking for her by name. When she didn't respond, Etheline, the receptionist, buzzed her on the phone, inquiring politely if she'd heard the page. The employee hurriedly explained in hushed tones that two very well dressed women were waiting in the large conference room situated toward the front of the building.

Serena glanced down at her appointment book and sighed. She'd thought she'd have an uninterrupted few hours to do some design work, the best way she'd found to distract herself, but real, live customers took precedence. She pushed back from her drawing board where sketches of a new costume had done a reasonable job keeping her mind off a certain reporter and his latest disappearing act. She waved her thanks to the receptionist who signaled from the front door that she was on the way out to her lunch break.

At the entrance to the glass-enclosed conference room, Serena halted at the door, stunned by the sight of a young woman whom she didn't recognize sitting beside none other than Dr. Lauren Hilbert.

"Yes?" Serena asked, her heart starting to pound at the sight of the person who'd said at their last meeting that she would make it her business to dissuade her friends and fellow krewe members from patronizing Antonelli's.

Oddly, it was Lauren's companion that rose from her seat next to the conference table and extended her hand in an ostensibly friendly greeting.

"Hi!" she offered with a nervous laugh. "I'm Judy Mansfield. My friend Lauren, here, said we should come by and see about maybe ordering matching costumes? We're planning to walk with a group of our friends from Tulane days in the St. Anne Parade next year. We heard how busy you are and…well… we…we thought we should get our order in *early*."

Serena remained where she stood, thereby declining to shake the woman's hand. The visitor looked embarrassed and glanced at Lauren, apparently waiting for further instructions.

"Well, hello again, Serena," Lauren said, with a slight smile, as if they were friends—or at least acquaintances. "That costume you wore at the children's charity event? It was certainly eye-catching. I think it was called 'Venice Rising Waters' or something like that? Well, our group is thinking of marching in St. Anne's as 'New Orleans' Rising Waters'…as kind of a tribute to all those who died in Katrina, you know?"

By this time, Serena had regained her composure and gazed at the two visitors, her mind filled with all sorts of speculation, none of it good. She wanted absolutely nothing to do with Lauren Hilbert and figured the quickest way to get rid of her and this friend of hers was to quote an outrageous price and be done with them both.

"Well, you should know before we discuss anything further," Serena said in her most pleasant and professional tone, "that a costume like the one you've just described, Seas of Venice—made to order—would be *very* expensive."

"How expensive?" asked Lauren's companion with a nervous glance at her companion.

"Somewhere in the range of five-to-eight thousand dollars and up…*each*," Serena replied blandly.

Just as she thought, the young woman's eyes widened and she looked again at Lauren with alarm.

"Oh, I don't think that's anything *I* could afford on my salary," she explained with a nervous laugh.

"Well," drawled the fledgling plastic surgeon, "come to think of it, maybe Katrina's tenth anniversary being *this* year is a bit too close to do something like 'New Orleans' Rising Waters'...especially given that newspaper piece in the *Picayune* a few days ago about all the corruption and skullduggery that went on when the levees and canals were built, back in the day. I'm sure you read all about it, right, since Jack Durand *wrote* it?"

Serena could see that Lauren's friend was made uncomfortable by this turn of the conversation and had seized her purse, obviously intending to make a hasty exit.

"Look Lauren," the young woman said in a rush, "I'm way past due back at the courthouse. If it's a non-starter here, I think we'd better..."

Her sentence dangled, unfinished, as Lauren took a step closer to Serena who stood blocking the door that led out of the conference room.

"Y'know," Lauren said to the designer, "upon second thought, wearing a get-up called 'Seas of Venice' or 'Gulf's Rising Waters' or anything like that would be the height of bad taste, probably. Especially since everybody in New Orleans is kinda depressed about learning somebody at the Army Corps signed off on that faulty design of the canal walls, right? What amazes me is that Jack quoted him as an *anonymous* source when the guy is his own *uncle!*"

Silence now filled the room in the wake of Lauren's declaration that Jack's namesake relative was the person whose identity every member of the Antonelli family had been speculating about since Part 1 had landed on their doorstep. Serena felt her lips part with surprise and couldn't disguise her shocked reaction to this announcement.

By this time, Lauren's cohort looked positively ill.

"You promised you wouldn't repeat what I told you in confidence!" exclaimed the woman who'd introduced herself as Judy, looking for all the world as if she were about to be sick. "You *swore* as a sister Theta! You just said you wanted to come here because you needed to find out how much Antonelli's charges for stuff!"

However, Lauren ignored her and moved even closer to Serena, who could only stare, speechless, at the two visitors.

"Maybe this is news to *you*, Serena," Lauren said softly, "but Jack told me one time that his Uncle Jacques was an engineer with the Army Corps since back in the eighties. All the damaging stuff was probably on the public record that Jack must have dug out in his research—but just didn't want to name his uncle in person, right? And besides," she added, sending a stern look in Judy Mansfield's direction, "I have it on good authority that it's Jacques Durand's *signature* on the plans for that under-engineered Seventeenth Street Canal debacle. Just imagine how that old guy must have felt ten years ago on the morning Katrina hit and the walls broke. Or maybe he didn't care?"

Judy bolted for the door and brushed past Serena.

"Lauren, I've gotta go!" she declared harshly, "and I truly don't think I'll ever speak to you again!"

Unmoved by her sorority sister's outburst, Lauren casually picked up her handbag that she'd left on the table and slung it over her shoulder. She gazed at Serena as if she'd just realized how this information might affect her.

"Oh...that's right," she said, her voice lush with false concern. "How thoughtless of me. I remember hearing through my mama how your brother drowned in Lakeview that day when the Seventeenth Street canal buckled, did I get that right?"

"Yes. And my sister-in-law, who was pregnant," Serena murmured, wondering that this woman could either be so cruel...or so clueless...that she'd say such things to her face. She felt as if she were suddenly inside an aquarium looking at Lauren through a sheet of glass that held back a tank of water. A thousand thoughts were swimming through her brain, but she remained unable to utter another word.

Lauren continued with an innocent air, "I'm sure Jack must have warned you about all this before his story was published, didn't he?"

Serena suddenly wanted to yank the woman's velvet headband off her head and beat her to a blood pulp. Finally, she found her voice.

"Get out," she said, her fists curled by her side.

But Lauren merely continued to speak with a smug smile tracing her lips. "I mean, he must have prepared you for the shock of its being *his* own flesh-and-blood that, basically, killed your family members."

Serena suddenly heard herself screaming, "I said, *get out!* Get the hell out of here, you witch!"

It was obvious, now, that Lauren had carefully planned another frontal assault on the person she blamed for wooing Jack away from her. Some way, somehow, she'd extracted from this Judy person the information she needed to mount her attack...but how did that Nervous Nelly who just left the room know about any of this? How in the world did all the dots connect? And, journalistic ethics be *damned*, Serena seethed, how could Jack *not* have prepared her for explosive information like this? Information that always had a way of leaking out to people determined to use it to their own advantage?

Meanwhile, Lauren had sauntered past Serena and strolled toward the front door of the shop that Judy whoever-she-was had left wide open when she escaped onto the street. The unwanted visitor turned to bid farewell with a triumphant expression. Serena followed in her wake and leaned against the counter where Etheline could usually be found greeting customers as they entered the establishment.

"Well, bye-bye now, Ms. Antonelli. Sorry we couldn't order anything from you, but do accept my belated condolences for your family's loss."

This woman is a doctor? Serena thought, dumbfounded.

She remembered Jack or Corlis or someone saying that Lauren Hilbert was a true magnolia that had always gotten her own way—especially when it concerned her ability to manipulate men.

And when she couldn't?

God help the rest of the world…

For several long minutes after the two women had disappeared around the corner of the building, Serena took a series of deep breaths hoping to still the pounding in her chest. She wondered, suddenly, what the experience of Lauren's having been a nurse during the nightmare at Charity Hospital had done to her when Hurricane Katrina roared through the building filled with elderly, dying patients? How could she have become so twisted? So walled off when it came to having some empathy for the feelings of others? So incredibly messed up in her thinking and behavior?

And then Serena was struck by a startling thought.

As Rhett said to Scarlet: frankly, I don't give a damn!

She could only hope that she'd never lay eyes on that woman as long as she lived and fought hard against an overwhelming sensation that she might, indeed, be drowning in the rising tide of Lauren Hilbert's malevolence.

"Great piece of work, Jack," called a fellow reporter across the newsroom as the journalist sat down at his desk for the first time that week.

"Yeah," agreed another, two desks away, "but I'm not surprised you hot-footed it outta here as soon as we published the series. Man, the phone's been ringing off the hook. I don't envy the Inbox on your computer, pal."

His editor, John Reynolds appeared at the door of his glass-fronted office.

"Did you get some rest?"

"Slept the first day and a half. Then went fishing."

"Good." He crooked his finger, signaling Jack should come into his office. As soon as he entered the door, his boss lowered his voice. "Your girlfriend called my office the day after Part One ran and you were gone, worried something had happened to you. I had my assistant tell her you were taking a few days off after your story ran, but didn't say where or why. I guess you didn't tell her you were going out of town?" he added with a skeptical lift of his eyebrow.

"No," Jack said without explanation. After all, he'd been straight with his boss about being in love with Serena and the conflict that put him in, given the twists and turns of the Katrina anniversary series. Reynolds' expression, however, remained mildly disapproving so Jack justified his actions with a familiar excuse. "I-I needed to clear my head and besides, my cellphone didn't work in the swamp. I saw some texts from her just now. I'll answer them in a minute." He heaved a small sigh. "Have complaints been pouring in from the usual quarters?"

"Some," Reynolds acknowledged, "but so far, nobody's threatened suit."

"Last I heard, truth *is* a defense," Jack said, and returned to his desk that was piled high with papers.

The truth.

He hadn't lied to Serena, but he sure as hell hadn't told her the truth. He'd just avoided it.

He dialed her cellphone, but it went straight to voice

mail. When he didn't hear back from her within the hour, he sent a text. By four-thirty, he'd still had no reply. Just before five, he called the landline at Antonelli's Costume Company, only to be told by the receptionist on the other end that Ms. Antonelli had instructed her to "tell Jack Durand—if he should happen to call—to please not contact her again by any means whatsoever."

"You're kidding!" Jack said.

"No, I'm not. Sorry, sir," replied the receptionist, "but those were her exact words. She also said she hoped you'd respect that. Bye now."

Jack sank back in his chair, his mind considering every word he'd just heard from the young lady who'd delivered Serena's ultimatum. He thought back to the way he'd departed Venice that first time without telling her that Lauren Hilbert wasn't the real reason he'd left so hastily. He knew that in Serena's view, he'd just pulled the same act again and, even worse, disappeared for days without a word.

In his own defense, once the three-parter had closed and the lawyers finally stop pecking at his story like ducks, he was literally putting out a dial tone. He'd been so damned exhausted, he couldn't speak to *anyone*. Even Serena. But he never dreamed that she would declare she didn't wanted to see or hear from him again—ever—over something like leaving town without telling her.

A voice in his head gave him a reminder that pulled him up short.

You assumed, somehow, that dropping off the radar wouldn't be that *a big deal because you did that to Lauren many times over your years together—and she tolerated it.*

He realized, now, that in the back of his mind, he'd figured Serena might be plenty steamed and let him know in no uncertain terms that he'd better not pull that sort of trick again, but to cut him off permanently like this? *That* he didn't expect.

This was a very different situation, and you know it, Jackie boy. This story hit her in the gut, and you weren't here to console her—or level with her, as you promised.

Jack stared at his phone, deep in thought. But it had to be more than wounded pride at work here. Something else had definitely gone haywire. Ice began to invade his chest despite the steamy September weather outside his window. Had she somehow guessed who one of the anonymous sources was? Had he not stated that passage in his piece in such a careful way as to protect poor Jacques' identity? Maybe she thought Uncle Vincent was the culprit?

He quickly dialed his namesake uncle's number and got him on the third ring. After a few pleasantries he asked Jacques if he'd received any blowback from former colleagues at the Army Corps.

"Nothing so far. I think a lot of folks expected the media to be poking around since it was the tenth anniversary and all. The guilty ones want to keep as low a profile as I do. How 'bout on your end? Any fireworks at the paper?"

"Nothing terrible here," he answered carefully. "Well, just checking in. Let me know if you hear anything weird."

"Will do, son. And by the way," Jacques Durand added, "that was some amazing stuff you found out and put in the paper. Hope it does some good."

"So do I," he agreed and bid farewell, murmuring aloud to himself after he'd hung up, "and I hope the damned story hasn't permanently wrecked my life!"

"Politely tell Ms. McCullough I'm terribly sorry, but I can't come out front to see her," Serena said over the phone's office intercom to Etheline. "Just tell her that I'm tied up with a client."

"But she's been here twice, today," was the whispered response, "between covering stories for WJAZ, she said." Then Serena heard, "Wait a minute, Ms. McCullough! You can't go back there!"

"Yes, I think I can," Serena heard Corlis' determined voice declare.

The next thing she knew, the reporter was standing outside the glass-fronted door to her friend's newly declared work zone.

With a sigh, Serena opened the door and stepped aside to allow her visitor to enter. Corlis immediately closed the door and let go of her large, leather tote bag that thumped onto the floor. She shook her head.

"Okay. You're furious with Jack—I get that—but you can't just hide at work like this for the rest of your days. *Talk* to him! He sent me to tell you he wants to explain—"

"Explain what?" Serena countered, unable to keep the bitter tone out of her voice. "He belatedly wants to tell me, now, what he obviously already told *you*?"

"I'll tell you exactly what he told me *prior* to the piece being published," Corlis responded calmly. "He asked—and I gave him access—to some Freedom of Information Act material that WJAZ had in the archive. Because of what I learned reporting on Katrina ten years ago, I suspected he was looking to find out how involved both his uncles might have been in the design and maintenance of the levees and canal walls."

"He had more than *one* uncle who helped build the goddamned levees and canals?" Serena exploded.

"Well, sort of," Corlis replied. "One worked for the U.S. Army Corps and another was a retired barge captain who got himself put on the Levee Board that inspected things."

"God help me," Serena muttered. "*Two* uncles who caused this disaster!"

"I want you to duly note that Jack never confirmed with me exactly what he'd found. Given what I knew to begin with, and doing a search after his piece came out for Jacques' name in the FOI docs I'd given him, I confirmed Jacques Durand's name was, indeed, on some of the canal retrofit documents in 1982, alongside a few of the other people Jack interviewed who'd signed off on a bunch of bad stuff as well. And by the way, I have *never* said a word since to anyone else—not even to my own TV station, which I probably should have."

"Except to Jack," Serena corrected her. "You've talked everything over with *him*!"

"Well, only last night. He came to see me, very upset, asking if I'd come over and talk to you since you won't take his calls."

"I won't take his calls because, even after he'd confirmed that his own uncle was definitely involved in building that flawed project that killed my brother, he *kept* it from me!"

"Well, he knew you'd have exactly the reaction you're having now and he didn't want to lose you. And besides, the lawyers had laid down their edicts which sources should be anonymous—and Jacques Durand was one of them."

"Really?" Serena exclaimed. "But the lawyers didn't order Jack to take a powder to catch up on his shut-eye after the pieces ran and not answer any of my calls or texts for a week!"

"Yes, he took a powder without telling you he was going to," Corlis echoed, "and that was a very dumb move. I told him last night it was. But he didn't answer you because there was no cell coverage in that swamp where King's fishing cabin is, outside Covington."

"He went *fishing*?"

"Look, Serena. I know you're upset and you have every right to be, but Jack was really feeling some major stress after he filed his stories. I've been there myself. I know the feeling. He hadn't slept for a week and felt he had to get away from everything."

"And get away from *me*, because he probably felt guilty for not telling me about his uncle."

"Well he *did*," Corlis allowed. "Feel guilty, I mean. But remember that Jack's not the guy who signed those documents. He just was the one with the courage to get to the bottom of what caused the collapse of the walls."

"C'mon, Corlis! Give me some credit, here. I'd never hold him responsible for something someone else has done, even if it's his own flesh-and-blood. But not to tell *me*? Not to prepare me, given what happened to my family in Katrina? Not to protect *me*, in case it got out who Mr. Anonymous was, which it obviously *has*!"

"How did you find out?" Corlis demanded.

"What does it matter *how*? The fact is that it *did* get out. What am I going to tell my family? That I want to marry a man who wouldn't come clean about *his* family's involvement in a tragedy that has wounded the Antonellis for all time? How was *that* going to work?" she demanded. "How can I ever trust a guy who dives underground whenever bad things happen?" Her voice had begun to shake and tears rimmed her eyelids. "He didn't even have the *courtesy* to tell me he was leaving town right after the story was published. He had to know what an impact it was going to have on me and on my family and others like mine who'd lost loved ones! And then not to assume I'd be trying to get a hold of him afterward—"

Corlis cut in, protesting, "The paper's lawyers forbade Jack to tell anyone except his editor about the more explosive parts of his reporting once he'd nailed down all the facts. He couldn't risk maligning anyone *until* he could prove certain aspects, along with confirming with several other sources to back it all up. And maybe his exhaustion from all that prompted his very bad judgment to leave town without telling you, I agree! But trust me, it *does* matter how you found out. There were very few people who knew what was in the final version of the pieces that ran last week, including me! Who told *you*?"

"Take a wild guess."

"Serena, stop playing games! Tell me! We'll never be able to sort this out if you don't level with me."

Corlis was in Commando Mode and Serena could see how upset all this was making her as well. She'd come to Antonelli's to see if she could help, and Serena owed her at least an explanation.

"Okay. Here's what happened," she murmured, staring at the half-completed sketch on her drawing board. She looked up to meet Corlis' questioning gaze and described the scene when Lauren Hilbert and her sorority sister came to Antonelli's under the guise of wanting to order a costume.

"Oh, glory, not her Woman Scorned Act again!" Corlis declared with disgust. "That drama queen just never gives up, does she? Who did you say was with her?"

"I dunno. I never saw her before in my life. Judy Somebody. A Theta."

"They're the snobby ones at Tulane?"

"They were *all* kind of snobby," Serena declared unable to keep ancient resentments out of her voice. "At least the ones I knew back then. Meanwhile, Lauren delighted in telling me Jack had told *her* that the uncle he was named for worked at the Army Corp when the walls were being built. She said that *all* of New Orleans had always suspected Jacques Durand was involved in the design of the walls that failed. She was positively ghoulish, wondering how my family would react, knowing someone in *his* family guaranteed my brother and his wife's death by drowning."

"What *bullshit*, pardon my French!" Corlis exclaimed. "Lauren's hardly ever read a newspaper in her life, and she didn't just 'happen' to come here with her pal and 'happen' to know who Jack's anonymous source was. Protocol says sources' identities must be scrupulously protected—or insiders will never come forth to blow any whistles on the bad guys. Lauren must have found out from someone very high up at the *T-P* who leaked it to her and she figured what a great way to get back at you!"

"Maybe Jack was the one who told her!" Serena retorted.

Corlis stared at her.

"You don't mean that," the journalist said, her eyes flashing. "For God's sake, Serena, you've got to know Jack wouldn't do a thing like that! He's one of the most honest reporters left alive in our business, and that's saying a lot!"

"Oh, jeez," Serena apologized. "I didn't mean that."

Corlis softened. "Of course you didn't. Look, Serena, Lauren Hilbert wants to *hurt* you and Jack, and *especially* Jack for dumping her—which he did, thank you, Jesus! Look, her Daddy knows everybody in town. Maybe he found out from some *T-P* brass who's a member of his country club, or something."

"That's how it often works in New Orleans," Serena agreed bitterly.

"Well, one thing I can tell you is that Lauren got very weird after Katrina and dealing with all those deaths at Charity Hospital during the evacuation. There were rumors some of the patients were…well…speeded on their way to heaven, so to speak. It must have been a horrible experience and I have no idea if Lauren witnessed that or was even a party to it…but even so," Corlis said grimly, "now I truly think she's gone off her nut!"

"Well," Serena replied, "she succeeded in her goals to

throw me under the bus, but that still doesn't change the fact that Jack didn't warn me beforehand what he'd discovered about the link between our families. I can't *be* with a guy who does that. Maybe he loves me, but he didn't *trust* me to keep my mouth shut, however hard it would have been. Now, *I* have to keep a secret, too, from my whole family, and I won't be able to have him in my life anymore to help me *bear* knowing what I now know about his uncle!"

She would have done anything not to dissolve in tears in front of Corlis, but a wave of grief and misery had grabbed her by the throat. She buried her face in her hands, elbows on her drafting table, and wept openly.

In two strides, Corlis arrived by her side and threw her arms around her shoulders, murmuring, "Oh, sweetie...I am so sorry this has happened to the both of you. What a holy mess...but we'll think of something we can do to fix this," she assured her. "Just speak to Jack, will you? The guy is ready to jump off the Huey P. Long Bridge."

Between sobs, Serena said, "Tell him... tell him the feeling's mutual."

"Look, Serena, four heads are way better than that bitchy, scheming brain belonging to Lauren! C'mon over to our house and let's figure this out together."

"I-I can't," Serena hiccupped, a sound that practically ended in a wail. "I'm dealing with my own family's reaction to merely learning about the deficiencies in those walls, let alone keeping it secret that my boyfriend—my *former* boyfriend," she corrected herself, "is related to the people whose behavior guaranteed my brother and sister-in-law would one day drown. I've had enough drama and trauma in my life, not to put myself in the path of anything else involving Jack Durand!"

"Men!" Corlis exclaimed. "They do stupid men tricks—like Jack going into some swamp where there's no cell coverage. But have you ever considered how digging up all this stuff about the storm has affected *his* psyche? Who could have predicted that whack-job Lauren Hilbert would somehow have access to all this and then *do* something so cruel and malicious to a man she supposedly loved?"

"My thoughts, exactly," Serena managed to reply between gulps for air.

Corlis gave her shoulders another squeeze.

"Listen, Serena…guys like Jack and King don't come along very often, sweetheart. You've gotta know by now that Jack Durand is profoundly in love with you beyond anything *I* ever imagined was possible for that guy. You've got to believe me that he has your deepest interests at heart."

Serena didn't answer, her shoulders heaving. Corlis leaned closer, her voice urgent.

"Not only has he had to deal with big-time legal issues on a story like this, he's been holding his poor, repentant elderly uncle's broken life in his hands." She reached out to lift Serena's chin between her fingers and gazed somberly into her eyes. "Talk about your PTSD! Our boy Jack had a lot to contend with on this one, just as you have. A *lot*."

But Serena could only shake her head from side-to-side, tears once again beginning to slide down cheeks already sheened with moisture.

Finally she replied barely above a whisper, "Tell him I'm sorry. Tell him my heart is breaking, but I can't see how any of this can come right. Explain to him that I just can't live through the pain of trying…when the odds against us are so huge."

CHAPTER 23

Dirty dishes sat on the kitchen table where King, Corlis, and Jack had consumed the muffalettas that King had brought home from Napoleon House a few blocks from the Duvallon's place in the French Quarter. Jack had left his hero-like sandwich half eaten on his plate while listening with a grim expression to Corlis relate how Serena found out about his uncle being the unnamed source in his story.

"So Lauren had a friend come with her to Antonelli's?" he pressed. "Did Serena know her or recognize her name?"

"She'd never seen the other woman before. All she said was that it was Judy somebody."

"Do you know any Judys?" King asked Jack. He looked at his wife. "Who do *we* know named Judy?"

All three of them were silent for a few moments. Then Jack slapped the top of the table.

"Judy, the court reporter!"

"Who?" they chorused.

"Judy Mansfield! Our lawyer, Chambordeau, and the outside firm that the *T-P* brought in, hired a freelance court reporter to take verbatim notes when they were quizzing me about all my sources and fact-checking details. They had her there to transcribe every word said in the room during our conference, in case we ever got sued. By the end, she knew every single facet of all three stories in the series! Did Serena describe her to you? Kinda short? Brown, frizzy hair?"

"No, but Serena did say she was a Theta sorority sister of Lauren's. Would that about jibe with this Judy Mansfield's age bracket?"

"Absolutely," Jack replied. "Judy even mentioned that day we worked together that she'd been invited to the children's charity fashion show, but the price of the tickets was too high for her budget." The scene in the lawyers' office came back to him, clear as day. "She also hinted she'd like me to take her out afterward, but I said I had to meet y'all at the Monteleone."

"Oh, crikey!" exclaimed Corlis. "Judy probably knew about the fashion show because Lauren must have tried to get her sorority sister to buy a seat to the dinner! And this Judy character was nosing around you, Jack, because she'd probably heard you'd broken it off with Lauren and thought you were an available man."

"That's gotta be it!" King said, glancing at his wife admiringly.

"Yeah," Jack agreed. "That has to be the *connection*. For some reason, Judy Mansfield told Lauren about Jacques—although I was present when the lawyers cautioned her, as well as the rest of us, that everything we'd heard and talked about that day was not to leave the room."

"It was a juicy tidbit she couldn't resist imparting to someone. Too bad it had to be Lauren," King said sourly.

Corlis asked, "I wonder who *else* Judy or Lauren have blabbed to? Serena said that once the cat was out of the bag, Judy looked miserable. Maybe she'd just traded casual gossip with Lauren? She apparently said in front of Serena that Lauren had promised never to repeat what Judy had told her and yelled, as she was leaving, that she'd never speak to Lauren again."

"I hate to say it," King said to Jack, "but Lauren may have seen an opportunity to make trouble and grabbed it, since we already know how she's had you in her crosshairs since the day you broke up."

Jack abruptly rose from the table to make a phone call to his editor. He was under an obligation to tell him that the secret was out and the repercussions could be far worse than any misery he and Serena had endured to date.

Editor John Reynolds, three lawyers for the newspaper, and reporter Jack Durand sat at a long, mahogany conference table with a sniveling Judith Mansfield positioned at the far end, the male group serving as judge, jury, and executioners.

"You realize, don't you, Ms. Mansfield," said one of the lawyers, "that we are making some very serious accusations against you? What do you have to say? Are we right? Did you tell Dr. Lauren Hilbert and anyone else about Jacques Durand being one of the anonymous sources in Jack's Katrina story—which is in a clear violation of your well-known professional obligations?"

"Lauren just wrangled it out of me," she said tearfully. "I happened to mention I'd done a free-lance job for the *T-P* and she asked me if I'd seen Jack, here. She wanted to know every single thing about him! It was weird."

"And you said?" John Reynolds asked sternly.

"I said he'd been working on a hush-hush story and she asked 'what about' and we got to talking, and I-I *might* have mentioned that...well...that New Orleans is such a small town, even his own family was one of his sources."

"Right," Jack broke in. "And then what happened?"

"Quiet, Durand!" snapped another of the lawyers. "Let us ask the questions."

But Judy responded to Jack directly.

"Well, you know how mad she was you broke up with her! She said you'd humiliated her over Christmas when you didn't give her an engagement ring and took up with some slutty girl in Venice when you were over there."

"Oh, Jeez…"

"You know what she's like!" Judy whined. "She just kept pushing and pushing me to tell every single detail about what you were doing since you'd ended it with her."

"And that's when you told her about the details of Jack's story?" Reynolds confirmed. "That his uncle, Jacques Durand, was an unnamed source?"

Judy nodded, gulping. "I didn't mean to, honest!" She turned to Jack.

"And you have to believe me that I had no idea when she said she wanted us to go over to Antonelli's Costumes to see about getting outfitted for next year's St Anne Parade that she was going to drop a bomb on your new girlfriend. I didn't even know that that costume lady *was* the girl you'd met in Venice until later, when Lauren and I had a huge fight in Lafayette Park, down the street from the shop."

Jack's editor shook his head in disgust.

"Well, Judy," Reynolds said evenly, "here's why we asked you not to repeat anything you heard in your duties transcribing what went on between the paper's lawyers and our reporter, Jack, here. Yesterday, the newsroom received an anonymous tip that Jacques Durand was the one who signed the documents that approved the final plans for the Seventeenth Street Canal back in 1982. Of course, we, here at the paper, already *knew* that, and knew the names of some of the other engineers who'd been part of all that, but we'd decided not to publish the senior Mr. Durand's name to protect him from further harm as a whistleblower. But now that people *outside* those in this room are aware that it was Jacques Durand, our newspaper must publish that fact ourselves—or be rightly accused of protecting one of our own reporters who happens to be Jacques Durand's nephew!"

"So you see how serious this breach of confidentiality is for everyone involved here, Ms. Mansfield?" asked the lawyer who'd spoken previously.

"Yes, sir," Judy replied meekly. "Believe me, I'm sorry I ever spoke to Lauren Hilbert in my entire life! She was never very nice when we were Thetas together at Tulane."

"Ever heard of the phrase 'Loose Lips Sink Ships?'" Reynolds asked sharply.

Judy Mansfield gazed at him, bewildered.

Reynolds told her grimly, "It's a World War Two expression. Idle chatter can cost lives, or in this case, cause others to commit suicide, even. We're dealing with raw emotions here."

At the sound of the word "suicide," Judy blanched.

"Oh, God!" she moaned.

Reynolds nodded. "You, in such a position of trust, should have known better!"

Avery Chambordeau, the newspaper's in-house lawyer intervened.

"Divulging what you heard to Lauren Hilbert is not only going to cost you future work here at this newspaper and with our outside law firm," Chambordeau said, his lips pressed in a straight line, "but I have contacted both the agency that got you this assignment and have spoken with the head clerk of the family court about this matter. I suggest you train for another line of work. You may go, now, Ms. Mansfield."

Judy Mansfield remained where she was, stunned by this announcement. Meanwhile, Jack's editor turned to speak directly to him.

"And Jack, I'm afraid you'd better warn your uncle immediately that he's about to be officially 'out-ed' to the entire state of Louisiana and beyond by your own newspaper. I'll meet you downstairs and we can work together on the wording of our very brief follow-up story."

When Jack arrived at his uncle's house half an hour later, he was relieved to learn his aunt was out shopping. To his amazement, Jacques took the news of the leak and the coming public announcement in a surprisingly stoic manner.

"No one can keep a secret in this town," he said. "I've been waiting thirty-three years for this to finally come out."

"I'm sorry, Uncle J. The transcriber the lawyers used was Lauren Hilbert's sorority sister and she let it slip after Lauren pressured her to tell her what I had been doing since we split up. Lauren told—"

"Never liked that old girlfriend of yours," Jacques interrupted.

"Why are you acting so resigned about all of this?" Jack demanded as he followed his uncle through the living room and out to the screened-in back porch.

"Relieved, I'd call it," Jacques said, sinking heavily into a wooden chair. "It's real strange, but ever since that day when I told you everything while we were standing by the Seventeenth Canal wall, I feel…well, more at peace with myself, I guess you could say. It was a mighty big burden, keeping that secret all these years." Then he paused and his expression grew grave. "Does Serena Antonelli and her family know, yet, that I was the person you were writing about in your story?"

"I didn't tell her, but she found out from Lauren, who stormed into where she works and took great delight in informing her. Serena hasn't told her family, but they'll all know soon enough when the paper comes out with this update. Even before this, she stopped speaking to me."

"Who isn't speaking to you? Serena or Lauren?"

"Both, actually."

Jacques shook his head slowly from side to side, his stricken expression registering the dire estrangement that now existed between his nephew and the woman he loved.

"I want to meet with this Serena and her family," he announced quietly.

"What?" Jack asked with amazement. "Why would you want to do that?"

The older man inhaled a long breath and then answered, "To make it right between you two...and to ask for everyone's forgiveness."

Jack had a sudden vision of Serena's large clan arrayed in a circle in their family home, glaring with hatred at two generations of Jack Durands.

"Do you think that's such a great idea? They probably won't want anything to do with either one of us for the rest of eternity."

But Jacques spoke as if he hadn't heard his nephew.

"If what I did has ended your relationship with Serena Antonelli and she and her family won't give me their forgiveness, I'm done with all this."

"What do you mean...'done'?" Jack asked slowly.

"You know what I mean, son. Please arrange a meeting if you can."

Jack felt a sense of gloom descend upon the two of them more smothering than the hot, September winds that were blowing through the palmetto trees outside his uncle's screened porch.

"I can't promise anything," Jack murmured, "but I'll see if I can gather everyone in some neutral place."

Serena didn't notice Corlis until she was walking beside her a half a block from the costume shop.

"Just because you're still furious with Jack doesn't mean you can dump me as a friend," Corlis declared, keeping pace with Serena who continued to walk toward the front door of her family's business.

"I'm not dumping you. I'm…taking a break from you."

"Same as," Corlis shot back. "Look, just so you know. Jack is in terrible shape. So is his uncle. Lauren has told everyone she meets that the anonymous source was Jacques Durand and now the paper has had to print this disclosure before anyone else does to avoid being charged with protecting their reporter instead of the source."

"Well, that's nothing to do with me. At least now I don't have to keep the secret from my own family! Soon, *everybody* will know that my former boyfriend's uncle murdered my brother, his wife, and their unborn child!"

Corlis whirled on her heels.

"Now you stop that right now, Serena Antonelli! Nobody committed murder. Get your facts straight and stop punishing people who don't deserve it anymore than your family deserves to suffer from all these past sins. Jack's uncle begs to meet with you and your entire family."

"*What?*" Serena was both startled by this news and stunned by Corlis' vehement chastisement, which she knew she completely deserved. Even so, she felt defensive. "For God's sakes, why would Jacques Durant want to do that?"

"To ask for your forgiveness."

Serena stared at Corlis, shocked into silence.

"That's right," the reporter reiterated. "He and Jack want to speak to all of you."

"And why would we grant our forgiveness to Jacques Durand—or his nephew—for that matter?" she asked, feeling as if a raw wound was being poked with a sharp stick.

"Because if you do," Corlis replied with quiet intensity, "maybe everyone can escape from this terrible cycle of hurt and suffering and endless recrimination since the storm."

Serena yanked open the door to the shop and prepared to disappear inside.

Corlis asked from the threshold, "Can I come in?"

Serena heaved a defeated sigh and led the way to the glass-enclosed conference room where she had met with Lauren and Judy Mansfield that terrible afternoon. Corlis followed in her wake and shut the door.

"Look, Serena, none of this is going to be easy. Maybe you just can't find a shred of forgiveness for any of the Durands. But one thing you should know is, from what Jack tells me, Jacques Durand is borderline suicidal since the paper decided they'd have to print his name. Making it even worse, Jack also told his uncle that you still won't respond to any calls or texts and that it's caused this breach between the two of you."

"We've already been over all this," she retorted. "Jack caused the breach by taking off for Covington after the story ran."

"He knows that now," Corlis replied patiently, "but the misery will never end for you—for any of you—if you don't allow Jack and his uncle to come see you. How about this?" she proposed. "What if y'all come to our house on Dauphine Street. Nice, neutral territory for both sides."

"Not so neutral. You and King are Jack's best friends."

"Well, then," Corlis retorted, "why don't you all meet on the grassy bank next to the new Seventeenth Street Canal wall? Is *that* neutral enough for you?"

Serena allowed Corlis' angry words to sink in and took a deep breath.

"I'm sorry. I am being *such* a bitch." She reached for Corlis's hand. "You have been a wonderful friend to me through all of this. It's just I've been so...so unable to—"

Tears, as they did most days lately, sprang to Serena's eyes and she choked on her words.

"I know, sweetie," Corlis said, instantly sympathetic. "You and Jack are the walking wounded right now."

Serena gazed at her through the tears blurring her vision.

"Okay..." she said barely above a whisper. "I'll see if I can get my family to agree to hear out Jacques Durand, but I don't want Jack to come. I just couldn't handle it if he were there too."

Corlis arched an eyebrow but remained silent for a long moment. Then she said, "Aside from Jacques meeting with your family, would you also be open to a bit of woo-woo?"

Serena frowned. "Woo-woo? Do you mean voodoo?"

"No, I mean woo-woo," Corlis said with a laugh. "I have this friend, Dylan Fouché, who might be willing to help you...and Jack...prepare for what follows down the road—however the meeting between your whole family and Jack's uncle turns out."

Before Serena could protest such a strange proposal, Corlis described how her very successful real estate agent—a gay dropout from the Catholic priesthood—had a reputation as a psychic and spiritual counselor.

"Why Corlis McCullough, I am shocked that such a 'just the facts, Ma'am' news hen like you even *knows* such a character, let alone has faith in his abilities to fix something that's unfixable."

"Now, keep an open mind, Serena," Corlis cautioned with a mysterious smile. "One day I'll tell you how Dylan sorted out a big mess between King and me when odd things were happening to me within the walls of my old condo on Julia Street."

"Where Jack lives now?" Serena asked with surprise.

"The very one. Do you ever sense there are ghosts or strange entities when you've been there?

"Not a one," Serena retorted.

"Well, see?" Corlis replied. "Dylan's amazing! He cleared 'em right outta there! The guy does the same kinds of things about ancestors' angst."

"He does *what?*"

"Look," Corlis said in a rush, "it's too complicated to

explain everything right now, but you've got to trust me on this. King and I love you two guys…and for the first time, I just know that Jack has met his perfect match…and you've met yours! Please, *please* come to our place before we set up a meeting with Jack's uncle and your family," she pleaded. "Just sit down and *talk* to Dylan about how you feel over what has happened and what Jack did that's upset you so—and allow Jack to be there too."

Serena gazed through the glass wall at the reception desk and watched Etheline hand a long garment bag protecting a Marie Antoinette costume to a customer. Finally, she turned to face her friend.

"I do trust you, Corlis—and have since the first day I met you—so I guess I'll trust you about this Dylan person."

"Wonderful!" Corlis exclaimed and Serena could see relief flood her face.

"But," Serena added, raising one finger in warning, "I retain the right to get up and leave Dauphine Street at any time, if I want to. And sorry, but I just want to meet Dylan on my own. No Jack."

Corlis titled her head and regarded the other woman for a moment.

"Agreed," she said finally and with unaccustomed solemnity added, "Let's take this a step at a time…and see what happens."

Serena rang the bell near the wrought-iron gate and stood nervously on the banquette outside the Duvallons' French Quarter residence. When Corlis opened the door, Serena noted the look of surprise that flashed across her friend's features.

"Well, hello, you two. Dylan's here already."

"I brought my brother, Nick," Serena announced.

"Moral support...or riding shotgun?" Corlis asked, gazing at the slender young man with similar coloring to his sister's, standing by her side.

"Kind of both. Do you mind?"

"Of course not," Corlis replied, unlatching the iron gate and beckoning both to enter through the front door into the marble-tiled foyer. "Glad to see you, Nick. Please, come on in."

Corlis led them into the formal parlor with floor-to-ceiling windows and two elaborately carved fireplaces, spaced fifteen feet apart, which were typical in nineteenth century New Orleans sitting rooms. Sage silk drapes and an elaborate crystal chandelier hung fourteen feet above their heads.

An unusually tall man in his early forties unfolded his frame from a side chair. The reedy figure was dressed in a crisp, seersucker suit, bright yellow Brooks Brothers button-down shirt, and a solid, royal blue tie. In his lapel he sported a yellow carnation, paler than his shirt, but definitely a considered part of his sartorial ensemble.

"Meet Dylan Fouché," Corlis announced with a faint smile as if anticipating her guests' reaction to the flamboyant dresser.

Dylan greeted them cheerfully, "Ah...my next victims."

He extended a long, thin arm to shake hands first with Serena and then, Nicholas. The two men exchanged a look that told Serena that Nick and Corlis' favorite psychic may have met before through New Orleans's gay network.

"The Antonelli siblings, I take it?" Dylan said. "Good to see you both. Why don't we all sit down?"

Serena tried not to stare at Dylan's pale brown complexion, high cheekbones, mildly flared nostrils, and his generous smile that made her think of President Obama on a day when the U.S. Congress wasn't bedeviling the poor man. The "spiritual counselor" Corlis had urged them to meet this day was undoubtedly a descendant of Free People of Color that had once made up some forty percent of all blacks in New Orleans in the nineteenth century. Light-skinned descendants of slave mothers and white, plantation-owning fathers had often received excellent educations—sometimes in France—along with their all-white half-siblings, and were later emancipated when their Caucasian owners died. In the twenty-first century, men and women with Dylan's heritage tended to make up the majority of middleclass African-Americans in this most southern of cities.

By this time, Dylan had taken a seat on the pale, green, silk-covered sofa and patted the cushion next to him, indicating that Serena should sit beside him. Nick took the chair Dylan had just vacated. Corlis selected the *chaise lounge* on the far side of the room.

"I don't know what our hostess, here, has told you about me," Dylan began with an easy smile, "but what I thought we might try to do today is talk a bit about the subject of ancestral clearing."

"*What?*" Serena blurted, beating her brother's similar response by a nanosecond.

Dylan laughed and glanced at his hostess again.

"I guess you didn't dare tell them about this *special* stuff I do, did you?"

"It was hard enough to get them here as it was," Corlis replied dryly.

"Well," Dylan continued, focusing his attention on the visitors, "what I do with my clients isn't *all* 'woo-woo' as Corlis likes to call it, but can involve a fairly new field in science. DNA researchers are the ones who have formulated this new view of the building blocks of life. It's the field of 'epi-genetics,' along with what's now labeled 'epi-genomes'—-substances that can attach to the genes and change them."

"Epi-what?" Nick repeated.

"Epigenetics. 'Epi' is Greek for 'above,' as in "above the genes.' Kinda like a light switch, turning a bulb on and off. Have any of you heard about the work of John Newton?"

Nick and Serena nodded in the negative.

"Well, John Newton is a spiritual teacher who coined the term 'ancestral clearing.' And then there's stem cell biologist, Dr. Bruce Lipton, who started out at the National Institutes of Health and then went to Stanford and now he's—"

"Hold on, there," interrupted Nick. "I don't see what Lipton or the other guy you mentioned, or what *you* are saying about DNA and ancestral clearing—whatever *that* is—has to do with anything that brought us here."

"Well, Dr. Lipton was one of the first to study under a microscope how DNA can be altered, and—"

"I thought DNA determined everything about a person, period," Serena interjected.

"That's what we *all* thought until about a decade or so ago," Dylan nodded. "Now, this isn't something I'm just making up! You can read about it on the government's NIH site. There's a great monograph on the relevance of Epigenetics to PTSD by a Dr. Rachel Yehuda. It basically talks about environmental influences—physical *and* emotional, like experiencing Katrina—altering the way the genes express themselves."

"Wow," breathed Serena. "That's pretty amazing to hear. The storm altered our genetic make-up somehow?"

"And, wouldn't you agree that most of us who went through the hurricane and its aftermath have been affected to greater or milder degrees by Post Traumatic Stress Disorder, yes?"

"Well...I don't know about that," Nick replied quickly.

"I wasn't even here for the storm," Serena chimed in.

"But you were here within the first year afterward, am I right? You went through some of the awful stuff that followed trying to put this city back together again?"

"Yes, but—"

"Well, there's a connection. Just hear me out."

Serena and Nick exchanged looks and then nodded their agreement to listen to what Dylan had to say.

"There are scientists like Bruce Lipton who now believe that—in addition to the strands of DNA we're born with—the matter *surrounding* DNA within the cell also plays a role in what happens during our lifetimes to our minds and bodies."

"Gosh, really?" Nick said, sounding intrigued.

Dylan nodded eagerly. "State-of-the-art thinking currently is that we're not only the sum total of our genetic make-up at birth, but that those genes can be changed after we're born…*altered* in various ways, and to varying degrees, by *stress*."

"Stress gets blamed for just about everything, these days," Serena retorted skeptically.

"Well," drawled Dylan, "we know that accumulated stress…in other words, the sum total of many things that have happened in our lives—positive and negative—have produced chemical reactions in our bodies. Say, a happy marriage. Or a bitter divorce…or a death. Maybe even a hurricane," he added with causal emphasis. "Changes in body chemistry that, in turn, may actually alter a person's genes in specific ways."

"You mean body chemicals like adrenaline when a person nearly has a car accident, or that serotonin stuff, when somebody wins a marathon?" Nick asked, his interest obviously piqued by such a theory. "You and this Lipton character are saying that those hormones, or whatever they are, can put a notch on a gene or chromosome somehow and it acts differently after that happens?"

"You're pretty close, there!" Dylan complimented him. To Serena he explained, "I'm sure you both have heard about the fight-or-flight response when a person is threatened by a tiger in the jungle, right?"

Serena nodded with a shrug.

"Well, now there are crazy folks like me who believe that the terror and adrenaline that might have scared your *ancestor* in the jungle could have changed his or her given set of DNA. Then—as altered—that set of DNA could be handed down through the family line to…say…someone like you two."

"You mean past traumas could change the *next* person's DNA?" Serena asked incredulously. "How?"

"Good question," Dylan said with an admiring nod. "Traumas as distant as an ancestor fighting in the Civil War or in Vietnam or being locked up in a concentration camp in World War II, for instance, could have prompted that fight-or-flight response which, in turn, produces chemicals in the body like adrenaline and cortisol—which are known as stress hormones. Are you with me so far?" he asked parenthetically.

His listeners both nodded, giving him their rapt attention, now.

"These chemicals surrounding the DNA in the cells contain proteins—those *epi*genes I mentioned before. Remember, now that the Greek *epi* means the word 'above.' So epigenes are substances above and beyond the genes that *attach* to the DNA, thereby changing or mutating a gene that is subsequently handed down to the next generation in its altered form."

"Holy Mother!" Nick said on a low breath. "That's a terrifying thought."

"Exactly," Dylan agreed with enthusiasm. "Traumas like Katrina that happened in *our* lives, along with the traumas that may have occurred in the lives of our forebears, can, we now think, imprint themselves on DNA and change it—and then can be *inherited* by those born after us, just like my kinky hair got handed down to me, or Serena's dark brown eyes to her."

"Wow," breathed Serena. "It sounds like you're saying that not only might we be trying to cope with the aftermath of what happened during Katrina—but we might *also* be wrestling with terrible things that occurred in our family line, way back when—and not even know it?"

"And probably piling on to make everything seem even worse," Nick added glumly.

"That's the idea," Dylan replied. "PTSD—Post Traumatic Stress Disorder—may reach farther back than merely one bad thing, like the aftermath of Katrina, for those who experienced it. Family traumas from the past might actually exacerbate a trauma like a hurricane or being in a war zone for *some* folks."

Serena pointed her index finger at Dylan, her brow furrowed in concentration.

"So are you saying that for some people, PTSD may affect them worse than others because of an *accumulated* amount of stress, past and present, affecting their DNA?"

Dylan nodded, adding, "In some cases, I happen to think it could."

"How depressing is *that*?" Nick exclaimed.

"But not all cases, mind you," Dylan cautioned. "There's the unknown factor of *resiliency*. Some of us have it and some don't and we don't really know why that is."

"Like with Mama," Serena murmured, adding, "though how can anyone truly recover from the loss of all those family members at once?"

"Ah, but what if there's an *antidote* to some of these stress hormones, or a way of better coping with the PTSD that often accompanies them?" Dylan suggested.

Serena and Nick both shot him looks of incredulity.

"A magic psychic bullet?" Nick scoffed.

"Nah. Something that's been practiced by certain extraordinary people over the centuries."

"Who? When?" Serena demanded curiously.

"Oh, folks like Nelson Mandela, Martin Luther King, Gandhi…Christ. These folks mastered the art of *forgiveness,*" Dylan said quietly. "And before you two charge out of the room, let me tell you what I mean."

CHAPTER 24

"Forgiveness?" Serena repeated, incensed. "That's you're idea of an *antidote*? I don't think that's quite applicable in this case," she added with frosty reserve, recalling silently how Corlis had proposed the preposterous idea that Jacques Durand wanted to meet in person to ask for her forgiveness for the unforgiveable.

For his part, Nick's expression had grown thoughtful. He turned to Serena and said, "Remember when Pope John Paul the Second met with the man who'd attempted to assassinate him? The pope came to see the guy in his prison cell and said he forgave him. I could never understand that, but it was pretty amazing."

"And do you remember," Dylan interjected, "that the prisoner was eventually pardoned and thirty-three years later, he arrived at the Vatican to put roses on the pope's tomb when he died?"

"I'd forgotten that…" murmured Serena.

Dylan said, "Science has proven in the lab, now, that a feeling of true forgiveness—as well as practices like meditation—can produce certain physiological reactions in the human body, reactions that can prompt different behavior in humans than what went before."

Nicholas and Serena both still looked unconvinced.

"So that's what you're asking us to do?" said Nick. "Forgive a man like Jacques Durand who *knowingly* put his signature on a plan to build a canal whose walls weren't engineered to be as strong as the experts said they should be? Forgiveness is gonna trigger some magic hormones in me and my mama's body that'll make things all better?"

"Not *all* better, but it might improve the terrible situation you're facing right now," Dylan replied with a faint shrug.

Serena stood up and began pacing in front of one of the two fireplaces.

"And just how do you suggest I forgive his nephew, Jack, a man I thought I trusted completely…a man I even thought I might spend the rest of my life with, who didn't *tell* me he was writing a story about his own uncle whose actions directly resulted in the death of our brother!"

Serena not only saw but also felt Dylan's look of deep compassion, but even it couldn't stem the flood of anger that washed over her for the hundredth time. Fouché might be able to forgive certain things in his life, but he hadn't suffered a loss on a scale like that of her family.

"Granted that forgiveness at first seems impossible," Dylan agreed, "but try to think of times when *you* hurt someone…maybe not as badly as you feel hurt by Jack or his uncle. But remember the situations where you behaved in such a way you knew to be wrong or unethical, but you never owned up to it publicly because you never got caught?"

Serena was struck by a sudden vision of Marco Leone's wife at the moment she'd realized her husband had died in Serena's arms. The older woman had immediately begun asking questions of the staff about her husband's relationship with the costume designer. Serena was chagrined to admit to herself that all her friends in the cast lied for her—except one person.

Dylan, as if he were reading Serena's mind, asked hypothetically, "Wouldn't you have felt so much better if the injured party said he or she honestly forgave you your transgression and allowed you to pass out of the prison of your own guilt?"

Serena turned her back on Dylan and her brother, fighting off an avalanche of recriminations about the way Marco's wife eventually discovered that the father of her children had been living for two years with a woman a third his age in his Las Vegas condo. A disaffected seamstress on Serena's staff had asked to speak to Marco's wife privately, and—bam! Mrs. Leone had suddenly barged through the door of Marco's home while Serena was in the act of packing her bag to leave town.

Mrs. Leone had said dreadful and totally accurate things to Serena that day. Ever since, she'd tried to justify her illicit affair with a married man by pointing to Marco and his wife's dysfunctional relationship and the fact she and her children had not been living in the same city as Marco for years. But if Serena were truly honest with herself, she realized with a flash of insight, she'd hurt the Leone family, no matter how much she'd denied it to herself all this time.

Shafts of steamy September light were pouring through the tall windows in the front parlor on Dauphine Street. Serena walked past Corlis sitting on the *chaise lounge* and stood near the sill, gazing out at the enclosed courtyard with its fountain splashing water that glistened in the hot sunshine outside.

What if, thought Serena bleakly, Mrs. Leone had her own view about why her marriage had broken down? If Marco had had an affair with Serena, perhaps there had been other women in Mr. and Mrs. Leone's early marriage that had destroyed the trust between husband and wife?

The silence in the room lengthened and Serena sensed that her brother was staring at her back, probably wondering why she'd stood up so abruptly and walked away from them. She had never told him or anyone in her family about her affair with Marco, which certainly indicated she was ashamed of what she'd done.

There was no escaping it: her behavior had wounded Mrs. Leone…just as Jack had hurt her by *his* actions. That horrific afternoon in Las Vegas, Serena had grabbed her suitcases and bolted out the door, refusing to answer the woman's accusations. And for damn sure, she'd never listened to Mrs. Leone's side of the story, just as she hadn't given Jack a chance to explain why he'd never revealed his suspicions about the role his uncle played in the canal wall failures. Feeling righteous, she'd refused even to talk to him when he'd come back from King's cabin in Covington after his story ran in the newspaper. She'd ducked him, just like she'd ducked an ugly confrontation with Mrs. Leone.

Serena turned and faced Dylan who remained sitting quietly on the satin settee.

"So?" drawled the erstwhile real estate agent when she'd remained silent, unsure what to say next. "What do you think about this idea of ancestral clearing by means of forgiveness? Willing to give it a try?"

Serena inhaled a deep breath. Briefly, she wondered how many generations of Antonelli women had transgressions they'd never owned up to? Finally, she made a decision.

"Jack is not his uncle," she said in a low voice, "and *Jack's* actions did not result in the death of our brother Coz and his wife and baby. Corlis has told me a bit about the legal constraints that both the paper and standard journalistic ethics place on reporters regarding safeguarding their sources. Maybe he had other reasons—other than cowardice or protecting his uncle—for remaining silent, as he did. At least, I should hear him out."

"Good girl," Dylan said softly. "I think you understand that there *are* ways to call a halt to all this misery between people who, at heart, love each other very much."

Nick spoke up.

"You know...I-I've treated my father with very little respect and have felt tremendous anger in response to how nasty he's always been about having a gay son like me. If I were religious—and believe me, I am not—I'd have to say I have not lived up to the 'Honor Thy Father' bit, but then neither has he showed me one bit of compassion or respect."

Dylan nodded. "That one I understand very well, Nick," he said, craning his neck for a quick, playful whiff of the carnation in his boutonniere. "But I'd better point out that forgiveness is kinda a one-way street. You have to decide to forgive, regardless of how the other side reacts. If you don't initiate the process of forgiveness from your end, the continued bad feelings you harbor toward your father end up poisoning *you* without regard to whether *he* forgives you for being gay—or not."

Nick shook his head. "Forgiving the guy seems impossible, but trying to run a business with him as a partner is killing me! God only knows what it's been doing to my DNA," he joked.

Dylan smiled faintly. "Exactly. So for starters, maybe just try telling yourself that, at least, you can forgive a man of his generation and religious upbringing for not *understanding* your world, and leave it at that for a while."

Nicholas nodded and Serena could tell he was mulling over Dylan's suggestion.

"Sounds like *we* have to be the ones to reverse that old adage: 'the sins of the father shall be visited on his son'" Nick replied, heaving a sigh. "Otherwise, I 'spect the vicious stuff just keeps repeating and repeating."

"You got it!" Dylan said, grinning as he stood up, indicating their conversations were coming to a close. "That's what ancestral clearing is all about. And when you change your *thinking* about something—like going from hatred to forgiveness, for example—you kinda rewire your brain's reactions. Hopefully, that means you're not going to suffer from so much stress on that particular subject, which can relieve PTSD symptoms sometimes. I promise you, a little direct forgiveness goes a long way toward clearing up a lot of this psychic ca-ca that's handed down and then revived with each generation."

Serena crossed the room and put a hand on her brother's shoulder.

"I suggest, however, Nick, that we don't go into much detail with Mama and Daddy or Flavia about this little woo-woo session we're having here today," she said wryly. "And we definitely shouldn't mention the idea of 'ancestral clearing.' The part about DNA and trauma, though, sounds okay, doesn't it, bro?"

Nick looked at her and then broke into a grin.

"Agreed. How about we have a session where we see if Dylan can help the family work though all this stuff about Jack's articles, or—"

"...or the pain will never end," Serena completed his sentence.

Nick nodded. "Maybe we should just call it a plain, ole' family meeting with Dylan here, as a neutral third party. It might do some good to get everyone concerned in the same room and deal honestly with what we've learned since Jack's revelations came out, just like we did when all of us finally admitted that Mama's drinking was killing us, including her."

Serena cast a look of gratitude at Corlis and said, "I've changed my mind. I think Jack as well as his uncles should be there, too. And I second the notion that we definitely don't have the skill to handle this on our own."

Nick asked his sister, "Is it really okay with you to include Jack?"

"It's worth a shot," she replied with a shrug. "It may not solve everything between Jack and me, but at least we might not have to cross to the opposite street if we meet now and then."

Dylan asked Corlis, "What *if* they all came here, to this house? Neutral ground, you know?"

"That would be fine with King and me," Corlis agreed,

"...that is, if you two can get everyone to show up" she added, addressing Serena and Nick.

Nick answered for them both.

"One way or the other, we'll get the Antonellis here, won't we, sis?"

But will Jack and his uncles be willing to face them all? Serena wondered silently.

As if Corlis as well as Dylan could now read Serena's thoughts, WJAZ's anchorwoman volunteered in her no-nonsense style, "And I'll do my best to deliver at least two of the Durands. How about tomorrow, five o'clock?"

The bomb had been dropped. That week, the newspaper published the revelation that reporter Jack Durand's uncle, among other sources cited, had been one of the whistleblowers. It had been the senior Durand who maintained that undue influence in the oil industry and politics had produced ill-advised decisions made by the U.S. Army Corps of Engineers, decisions that ultimately resulted in Hurricane Katrina's catastrophic flooding of the city of New Orleans. Also in the short, follow-up article, the self-same Jacques Durand was identified as having placed his signature, among other engineers, on the final plans for the 17th Street Canal walls back in the early eighties. This was due in part, he was quoted as saying, to pressures he claimed were placed on then-junior engineers by higher-ups in the chain-of-command.

On the same day the news story appeared, Vincent Durand called Jack's father in an absolute fury.

"I never want to see my nephew again as long as I live!" he announced to his brother. "And believe me, I will *never* attend a Durand Sunday family dinner if that little bastard is sitting at the table!"

The retired barge captain and former member of the New Orleans Levee Board continued to scream over the phone that Jack had cast shame on the entire Durand family. Jack's mother said that her husband, George Durand, Jr., refused to disclose whether he or his younger brother hung up the phone first.

Turning over these events in his mind, Jack rested his hands on the steering wheel of his car parked in the Duvallons' courtyard and stared at the splashing fountain near the paving stones that led to the front door. King must have moved his Jaguar to a parking lot somewhere else in the French Quarter because an unknown vehicle Jack assumed was owned by the Antonellis already occupied the spot next to where he'd pulled in minutes before.

"You coming, son?" asked Jacques, his hand on the passenger door handle. "Or are you chickening out?"

Jack pulled his thoughts back to the present and met his uncle's gaze.

"I'm coming," he replied, "but I have a feeling this could turn out to be a total disaster."

Just then, the front door opened and King stood blocking the view into his three-story house, its broad wrought iron balcony looming above their heads.

"C'mon in, you two," King called. "The party's already started."

Just as Jack feared, the first few minutes were unbearably awkward when he and Jacques entered the large parlor with its set of double fireplaces. His gaze immediately sought Serena's who was sitting next to her brother Nick on the small settee facing the second fireplace fifteen feet away. Jack noted that the two siblings held hands for mutual support, he figured. Both studiously avoided any glances in Jack's direction.

His Uncle Jacques remained standing near the marble mantel nearest the windows that faced the courtyard where they'd just entered. Turning away from Serena, Jack sat down in one of the chairs left vacant when Corlis and King quietly excused themselves and went upstairs.

Dylan Fouché, the man Corlis had explained in her email would "facilitate" this summit meeting between the Durands and Antonellis, appeared totally at ease in his seersucker suit, pale blue Oxford shirt and pink tie, with a matching pink carnation in the buttonhole of his lapel. He took his place next to Jacques and then calmly explained that he had been asked to help "clear away—or at least reduce—any feelings of anger and hurt that had been caused not only by the newspaper series, but by events like Hurricane Katrina that were out of the control of everyone in this room."

Serena's parents, Cosimo and Sarah, stared stonily at the wall behind the two men, while their youngest daughter, Flavia, twisted her fingers unceasingly in her lap.

"To start us off," Dylan suggested with friendly glances in all directions, "I want to bring you up-to-date about what the medical world knows about PTSD: Post Traumatic Stress Disorder, which I think may play a role here."

He swiftly repeated the information he'd shared earlier with Serena and Nick about the new science of epigenetics and how it related physiologically to people experiencing traumatic events like war or witnessing a murder or…"going through destructive storms—and all that comes with it before, during and after."

"You a doctor?" Cosimo Antonelli challenged the African-American guiding the discussion. "Serena told me you were a dropout from a seminary someplace and now you sell houses to lotsa gays in the Quarter."

"Dad!" Serena protested and looked at Nick for support, but her brother merely shook his head as if his father's rudeness was par for the course.

Dylan, however, appeared unfazed by the senior Antonelli's obvious hostility.

"Oh, I am definitely an equal opportunity real estate agent. I happily sell homes to anyone who has the money to buy them, sir. In my spare time, I do family mediation…and other work…as my brand of 'give back' to the community."

"If you're just some house hustler, why should we listen to you about this PTSD stuff—which I think is mostly an excuse for not just getting on with life?"

"Good question," Dylan replied pleasantly. "No, I'm not an MD or a shrink, but I *am* a student of several experts in the field of post-traumatic problems and can, perhaps, explain in layman's terms various forms of PTSD some of you may still be experiencing—along with the latest research in helping people cope." He gazed directly at Cosimo. "Plus, I cost a lot less than going to the Ochsner Clinic or someplace, 'cause I do this work for free."

"Why the hell do you do *that*?" he sneered.

"Glutton for punishment, I guess," Dylan said lightly. "Now then, I think Jacques Durand wants to say something first and then please feel free to ask me any questions you want."

Jacques, who had remained standing took a step toward the senior Antonellis and nervously cleared his throat.

"I-I know that my nephew's articles brought back some terrible memories for y'all." He paused as if gathering his courage, and then continued. "'Cause those three stories in the *Picayune* sure did for me, too. Like Dylan just said, it's kinda this PTSD thing, I think. Reading what he wrote made me feel as if Katrina hit me all over again."

"Yeah, yeah…it's all about *you*, you bastard!" Cosimo spat.

Jacques grew silent and Jack wondered if his uncle would simply throw in the towel and walk out. To his surprise, the retired engineer merely nodded as if he accepted this verbal abuse as his due, but would not be deterred from what he'd come here to say to the Antonellis.

"Reliving Katrina because of the anniversary last month affects all of us, I 'spect, in different ways, but I came here today ready for your anger and blame—both of which I deserve. Even so, I want to tell you how sorry I am for everything that happened to your family…and to ask…to ask for your forgiveness for not…for not having the strength of character to stand up to my superior officers thirty-three years ago."

"So it's all the Corps fault, is it?" Cosimo scoffed.

"Partly it is," Jacques countered, "but *I* could have made a different choice."

"Well, for God's sake, why *didn't* you?" Cosimo shouted, shaking his fist. "If you had, my namesake son wouldn't have died and we wouldn't have to be in this stupid meeting!"

Jacques raised his chin and took a step toward his accuser.

"I was twenty-four-years old and a new father with a wife and a mortgage for my bungalow in the Lower Garden District that I could barely afford. It's no excuse, but maybe it explains why I signed those documents, along with a bunch of other junior engineers."

"It sure *is* no excuse!" Cosimo shouted.

"I know," Jacques agreed, the deep lines carved on his face reflecting his misery. "As the project was being readied for construction, it got real nasty. They threatened my job in '82 if I didn't sign off on a set of engineering specifications for the Seventeenth Street Canal retrofit that everybody involved knew weren't what the outside consultants said that they should have been. I told my commander that the walls could fail if we ever got a storm again like Hurricane Betsy was in '65. But Cosimo is right," he addressed his listeners. "I signed anyway." To Serena's mother he said softly, "It's *my* fault your son and daughter-in-law and their baby died August 29th, 2005, and I would do anything to have that not be so."

"And my mother died of a heart attack the same week!" Cosimo exclaimed, his fists clenched. "She had it when they tried to evacuate her from the nursing home and they couldn't save her."

A sob escaped from Sarah. Jack winced at the stricken looks that invaded the expressions of every person in the room. Serena's mother stuffed her fist in her mouth and began to cry softly. Cosimo stared straight ahead, making no move to comfort her. Meanwhile, Jacques stoically continued.

"Back in eighty-two, I was a young, wet-behind-the-ears engineer who was scared to death of the higher ups and too weak to stand up to them. I was a coward and a fool and I'm deeply sorry for what I did—and for everything that happened to your family and others like you as a result."

"I don't need to hear this!" exclaimed Cosimo, but his wife put a surprisingly strong, restraining hand on his arm to prevent him from bolting from his seat.

Jacques turned to address Nicholas, Flavia, and Serena.

"A decade ago, when I saw the news reports about the monster storm they were calling Katrina bearing down on New Orleans, I literally got down on my knees and prayed this wasn't the one that would break the wall," Jacques said, his voice choking. "But the wall broke anyway—and so did all those other ones." Tears had begun to stream from his eyes. "God help us, but eighty-seven percent of all the water that flooded New Orleans was the result of the failures of these canals and levees that the Corps had built."

He stretched out his right arm and clasped the mantelpiece with a look of desperation that signaled to Jack his uncle was close to pitching forward onto the carpet. A grief-stricken look etching his features, Jacques addressed Serena directly.

"I am so sorry for that weakness. If I could go back in time and tell my commander to go to hell—and me, not sign off on those specs, no matter what they did to me—I'd do it in a heartbeat! Nothing is worth what I've been through and what my actions put y'all through." Jacques' chin sunk to his chest, his voice barely above a whisper. "I am so sorry I am Jack's uncle and have brought all this pain and sorrow back into your life and your family's lives. My nephew loves you so much, Serena. I can see that so clear, now...and because of *me*—"

Jacques' shoulders began to heave and he brought the hand not clutching the mantel to his face to hide the anguish he could no longer suppress. "I don't expect you to forgive me, but please...*please* don't blame Jack—"

"I forgive you, Jacques," Serena intervened with quiet intensity as she rose from her chair. "I can't speak for the others in this room, but I *do* forgive you." She took the few steps to reach his side, and embraced the man's hunched and trembling shoulders. "It must have been terrible living with this secret all these years. I know," she added, "because I've lived with a few secrets myself."

Jacques let go of the mantel and put both arms around Serena, his forehead resting on her shoulder. Jack felt he, too, might not be able to keep the tears rimming his eyes from streaming down his cheeks. He knew perfectly well the secret Serena referred to...and that he was the only person she'd trusted enough to tell about her affair with Marco Leone.

We all have sins for which we need forgiveness...he reminded himself.

Much to Jack's shock, Serena released his uncle and turned toward where he was sitting on the far side of the room. She approached his chair with an air of melancholy that twisted his gut.

"And please forgive *me*, Jack, for refusing to talk to you all these weeks. I can only imagine how tough it must have been for you to learn that your uncle was among those who signed those documents to build the same walls that ultimately failed in Lakeview."

"It was," he admitted hoarsely.

"And that as the honest reporter that you are, you couldn't avoid revealing the role the U.S. Army Corps and your uncle had played in the anniversary story—whatever would happen afterward—even if it eventually meant that I'd blame you and your uncle for the death of four members of my family...which I *did*."

Jack could only stare into the pools of her dark brown eyes that had so captured his heart the first time he'd held her gaze. He stood up from his chair and reached for her hands, but before he could touch her, she swiftly stepped back.

"Your uncle's mistakes aren't yours, Jack, and I ask your forgiveness for the way I've behaved about a lot of things lately. You, more than anyone in this room, know that I have apologies to make to some other people as well."

Her expression told him that number one on her list was Mrs. Marco Leone, though whether she'd do so in person or find other ways in which to make her amends was anybody's guess.

Jack pulled a resisting Serena into his arms and held her trembling body against his chest. His chin on the top of her head, he could feel her finally relax against him. He sighed with relief when she raised her arms and wrapped them around his waist.

To his amazement, the rest of her family—except for

Cosimo Antonelli—rose from their seats and moved toward the forlorn figure standing near the fireplace. Over Serena's shoulder Jack watched them, one by one embrace his uncle.

After a few moments, Jack released Serena from the bear hold he had her in and led her back to join the family circle. Cosimo, however, had remained seated, his head bowed. Dylan stood beside the patriarch of the Antonelli clan and placed a hand lightly on his shoulder.

"Peace be with you all," he said in quiet benediction.

And still Cosimo said nothing, but at least he didn't storm out of the room, Jack thought with a hopeful glance at Serena. In response, she turned a tearful face inches from his and then kissed him on both cheeks.

"Peace be with you, Jack," she whispered. "Peace...and love...but we still have a few hurdles to get over, don't you agree?"

"We do?" he replied, his heart taking a nosedive once again.

"We *do*," she repeated firmly. "And it scares me that you don't seem to know what they are. Let's take a walk by the river, okay?"

"I have to drive my uncle home first."

"Meet you down by the aquarium in half an hour?" Serena suggested.

"Not at my place?" he asked.

"Not a chance."

Serena was the first to leave the Duvallon house on Dauphine and swiftly walked down Ursulines Street past Royal, and turned right on Decatur. She stopped at Café du Monde for a *café au lait*-to-go and sat on a bench that overlooked Jackson Square, a wide expanse of parkland that was dominated at the other end by the three spires of St. Louis Cathedral. After a few minutes mulling over the things she still had to say to Jack, she crossed the trolley tracks to the Riverwalk paralleling the sharp curve in the Mississippi that had given early New Orleans its name as the Crescent City.

By the time she reached the Audubon Aquarium of the Americas, as it was advertised to the tourists, she spotted Jack already sitting on a bench that faced the river. A paddleboat was tied up nearby that doubled as a floating casino, its patrons already streaming up the gangway for a night of wagering. The sun was low in the sky and yet the autumn heat was only now starting to diminish a few degrees as dusk was coming on.

Gazing at the slow moving water near the shore, Serena suddenly thought of the canals of Venice and wondered what the weather was like there now? Probably still hot, too, she mused, but most likely not as humid. She could feel the stickiness starting to gather on her back, but the warm surroundings would prompt her to make what she had to say to Jack short and…well… maybe not so sweet.

Before she could begin, Jack spoke first.

"Hey…hi. I saved a spot for you," he said, patting the seat beside him. He paused and awkwardness lay thick between them like the high humidity reflected at the water's edge. "First of all," he said finally, "I'm really grateful that Corlis found that Dylan guy to help us with all this."

"Apparently she and King had some major blow up that he guided them through before they got married."

"Hmmm…King never told me that Dylan was involved."

"Well," Serena said, "it's been my experience that men tend to keep a lot of secrets to themselves about important stuff and how they…really feel. And that's what I want to talk about."

Jack's gaze searched hers, but she could see there was a wary look in his eye.

"I thought—after what happened this afternoon—"

"Look, Jack," she cut him off, "I was very moved by what happened at the Duvallons earlier, but as far as you and I are concerned, I have to tell you that I just can't be with a guy who keeps a lot of secrets that relate *directly* to me and doesn't let me in on what's really going on with him. With *you*, I mean. Like you did in Venice and again, when the Katrina story was published."

"But I thought you understood, now, that the paper insisted—"

"I *do* understand, but at some point—when it involves *us*—you have to trust the woman you say you love," she retorted heatedly. "You're not in the C.I.A., for God's sake, you're a journalist at a newspaper that only publishes three days a week! You have to trust I have both our best interests at heart and would never do or say anything to others that would harm either one of us. If you can't tell me who your sources are, okay. But on absolutely everything else, you have to be *straight* with me, Jack. Straight with *me*!"

Her last words had become close to an anguished cry and Serena turned away on the bench, willing herself not to get teary. After a few moments' silence, Jack spoke first.

"I will after this," he said, reaching over to lay a hand on her shoulder. "Whatever you ask me from here on out, Serena, I swear to you, I'll tell you the truth."

"How do I know that?" she demanded, looking over her shoulder. She shifted her weight with a shrug that caused Jack's hand to slip to his side. "In two important instances, when I asked you multiple times to tell me straight out what was going on with you, you avoided coming clean. Then you disappeared into the swamp for a week with absolutely no word when you *had* to know how tough it would be for me to read your stories! How can I trust that you won't do that again when the going gets rough?"

Jack looked at her for a long moment and then said quietly, "You'll just have to because I'm not the same guy anymore. I should have told you I was going to King's place to crash, and I'll never go into radio silence like that again. You'll just have to take a big ole' leap of faith, screw up your courage, and trust me—Jack Durand—that I've finally learned my lesson. It's simple as that."

"It's *not* simple with you!" she retorted.

"Well, we're getting there, don't you think? You've shown me in so many ways that I *can* trust you…so it feels…different from the ten years before I met you. I have to get used to that, I guess."

Despite her resolve, her eyes filled and she stared at him mutely.

"Serena," he said gently, "it's like what Dylan said. We both probably have some raw nerves, given everything that's happened to us individually in the last decade. We have these automatic reactions that can probably be chalked up to the fight-or-flight thing he explained to us. We two just have to begin laying down *new* experiences with each other to erase the bad ones. Rewire our *brains*, I guess you could say. We have to remind each other that you're not Lauren and I'm not Marco and keep the truth clearly in mind that we love each very much, remembering that we *only* have good intentions toward one another."

"I don't know," she replied doubtfully. "I'm just exhausted from it all. I think I'll just go back to the shop and sleep on the couch at Gus and Nick's. I don't want to talk to anybody for a while. Even you."

Jack cast her an odd look.

"That's exactly how *I* felt when I finally filed my stories at the paper and took off for King's cabin in Covington. I didn't even want to talk to you, and look how *that* turned out. So I think…you should come home with me."

Silenced by this, Serena stood up from the bench and stared at the slow moving river. Then she turned to him and murmured, "Touché."

The squeals of children punctuated the silence that grew between them as a gaggle of youngsters emerged from a side door of the aquarium, their tour of the underwater world concluded. Jack rose from the bench to stand beside her. He reached for her hand.

"How about some gumbo, *Signorina* Antonelli? I've got some in the fridge. I could steam some rice and spoon-feed you while you're taking a little rest and we won't talk at all. We're much closer to Julia Street than Antonelli's Costumes, way up there on Lafayette," he added, his look beseeching.

Serena turned to meet his gaze, her melancholy expression transformed by the faintest of smiles.

"And if I'm too tired to go home after the gumbo, do you promise to sleep on top of the covers like we did the first night we were together at *Ca'Arco Antico*?"

"I'll try, darling, but let me be real straight with you," he said, his words gently mocking her earlier ones, "I can't promise."

"I didn't think so."

"Hey, look at it this way," Jack said, "I'm telling you how I *really* feel."

"Well, *Giovanni*…" she drawled, her smile broadening, "that sounds like a very good start to a wonderful friendship."

"And if, tomorrow, I ask my mother to get my grandmother's ring out of the bank vault? What do you say?"

Serena's eyes widened and her lips parted in surprise. Then, without answering, she stood on tiptoe, slipped her arms around his waist, and kissed him in a slow, languid fashion that signaled she'd be sleeping in Jack's quarters on Julia Street this night—and most likely for many nights to come.

Under the covers, of course.

EPILOGUE

Venice, Italy May

"I checked the tide chart," Jack said, waving his cellphone in one hand. The wind whipping around their water taxi prompted him to lean closer to the other three passengers in order to be heard. "No *acqua alta* expected the entire time we're in Venice, thank you, Jesus!"

The waters of the Grand Canal splashing against the hull of their boat threw off diamonds into the clear, bright sunshine of early May. Mardi Gras and Carnival were mere memories both in New Orleans and *La Serenissima,* and spring had clearly come to northern Italy.

"Oooooh, and it's *warm* but no humidity!" exclaimed Corlis excitedly, stretching her arms out as if to embrace both sides of the canal and the sun pouring down on the travelers, late of Louisiana.

King Duvallon reached over and bestowed a bear hug and then a kiss on his wife's neck.

"Aren't you glad we were invited on the honeymoon?" he said, chucking her under her chin and then kissing her again properly.

"And aren't you glad the wedding is behind us?" Serena added, her arms around the waist of her husband of less than two weeks.

The foursome laughed, mostly with relief.

The nuptials joining the Durand and Antonelli families had been held at St. Louis Cathedral some eight months after the tenth anniversary of Hurricane Katrina. The traditional Catholic ceremony was followed by a reception upstairs in the Gold Room at Arnaud's, the tin-ceilinged

Grand Dame of Creole dining in New Orleans since 1918. Wedding preparations had required feats of navigation that rivaled any regatta ever held on the Venetian Lagoon. This included persuading Arnaud's French-centric chef to create *papardelle con scampi* as part of the menu, one of the late Serena d'Este Antonelli's most famous family dishes.

In the end, Serena's father Cosimo IV walked his eldest daughter down the aisle toward the groom waiting expectantly beside the altar. In Jack's view, this was a minor miracle, given the fact that Coz Antonelli had barely exchanged two words with his prospective son-in-law since Jack's story had been published and the couple's engagement announced at Thanksgiving.

The composition of the wedding party, alone, gave Serena's father "heartburn," he'd declared. It had numbered the firebrand preservationist, Kingsbury Duvallon, as Jack's best man. The elder Antonelli was none too pleased, either, that his gay son's partner Gus LeMoyne, along with Nick himself, and that "whacky real estate agent, Dylan Fouché," all served as ushers.

To Coz's utter disbelief, even Jack's whistleblower uncle, Jacques Durand, handed out the order-of-service pamphlets at the back of the cathedral, and later escorted Jack's sister, "that animal nut, Marielle Claiborne," down the aisle as a bridesmaid.

To the wedding planners' relief, Coz appeared mollified somewhat when his reclusive daughter Flavia was also asked to be a bridesmaid, even if it was alongside of Jack's other sister Sylvia—whom the senior Antonelli had heard "had been a druggie." It had been his wife, Sarah, who pointed out that the young woman was "currently sober, just like I am, you'll be happy to know," she remarked with some asperity.

And damned if Sarah K. Antonelli didn't wax over the moon that her Kingsbury cousin's daughter-in-law—"that hell-raiser newswoman, Corlis McCullough"—was given the role of Serena's Matron-of-Honor.

Adding to Cosimo's shock and consternation, however, the wedding received much more media attention than even WJAZ's anchorwoman expected.

Unbeknownst to any attendees, including the reporters Jack and Corlis themselves, the April 20th nuptials coincided with an announcement that was leaked earlier that day on the Internet. The three-part Katrina anniversary series in the *Times-Picayune* by Jack Durand had garnered the environmental journalist his second Pulitzer Prize.

Every TV station and radio outlet, plus a multitude of correspondents from area print media clustered outside the church waiting to shove microphones into Jack's face minutes after he and Serena had been declared husband-and-wife.

For their part, both were well aware that the joy of that day had been dampened when Jack's other uncle, Vincent Durand, and his wife had not even deigned to reply to the heartfelt invitation to bear witness to the two families having mostly healed their breach.

"Look at it this way," Serena had said a week before the wedding, trying to cheer up her fiancé, "The group that committed to our team is pretty darn great! Let's be grateful for progress, if not perfection…"

Listed on the "Grateful Ledger," as Serena dubbed it, Vincent's grown children—Jack's cousins Michael and Mary Lou—came in force to the wedding *and* the reception, a decision that helped salve the wounds, especially for Jack's father and mother.

In fact, the tentative feelings between the two families seemed to evaporate in the wake of the obvious joy shining in the eyes of the bride and groom when they'd turned to face the congregation at the end of the nuptial mass. Among the wedding party and their guests that April afternoon, a feeling began to percolate that all the pain of reliving the events of Katrina that Jack had chronicled in his newspaper series had been somewhat assuaged by a city's citizens finally understanding a great deal more about what had happened in August of 2005.

This sunny day in May, all the drama of Serena and Jack's wedding seemed as distant as Venice was from New Orleans. The recent bride lifted her face and reveled in the warmth and the freshness in the Adriatic Sea air. She gazed off the bow of the boat and soaked in the beauty of the buildings on either side of the canal and the gondolas gliding by. Then, Serena had a sudden, sobering thought: how many generations beyond her own would be able to exult in the magnificence of the city—to say nothing of delighting in the charms of New Orleans, for that matter—before the water pushed landward one day, never to recede? Would people on Planet Earth *ever* be willing to grapple with the undiminished threat of rising waters in both cities, come hurricane season and the annual *acqua alta*?

With pure force of will, she banished the awful images of Venice and the Crescent City languishing below sea level by turning to absorb the sight of her dearest friends, their arms around each other, gazing, awestruck as she was, at their stunning surroundings. Serena and Jack couldn't imagine a return to Venice without Corlis and King. The bridal couple had surprised them at the end of the wedding reception at Arnaud's with a note saying there would be two round-trip tickets to the Marco Polo Airport in their names, funded with Jack's ten thousand dollars in Pulitzer prize money.

"Without you two…and a little of Dylan Fouché's woo-woo, or voodoo, or whatever we want to call it," Serena had declared, raising the last glass of champagne left in the last bottle that joyous evening, "…we'd never have made it to this happy day."

And so, the foursome had arrived in the most romantic city in the world on a lovely spring afternoon, heading for a secret destination that only Jack knew.

Serena pointed as their boat plied its way past the tiny side canal that ended at the door to her former guesthouse, *Ca'Arco Antico*.

Jack also gestured toward the narrow alleyway. "Let's hear it for the *Canaletto* Room!" he said, with his thumbs up, prompting all four to cheer lustily.

They soon passed the *palazzo* where *Il Ballo di Carnevale* had been held that frigid night in February a little more than a year earlier. A few minutes later, Serena clapped her hands as they passed the *San Tomà vaporetto* stop.

"There's the landing that led me through sleet and snow to the costume shop," she declared for her friends' benefit, describing the privilege it had been to learn more of her craft "from the finest designer and seamstresses in the industry."

"Where are you taking us now?" Corlis demanded of Jack.

"You'll see," he said with a smug smile and leaned to whisper something into their water taxi driver's left ear. Then he turned to address his fellow passengers. "We're almost there."

Serena linked arms with Corlis and the two women peered out at the Peggy Guggenheim Museum just passing by. Then the boat's engine slowed to a low throb, and the magnificent, domed, *Basilica di Santa Maria della Salute* came into view on their right.

"Ooooh," breathed Serena. "The Gratitude Church!" She turned to Corlis and briefly explained about the devastating seventeenth century plague and the survivors who built the magnificent baroque edifice to demonstrate their thanksgiving for having been spared.

Jack smiled down at his bride.

"I brought Serena here in the moonlight on one of our first evenings in Venice."

Serena rose on tiptoes and kissed him on the cheek.

"And believe me, my friends," she said to Corlis and King, "gratitude is certainly what I feel right now. Thank you for coming with us on this sentimental journey to...*where?*" She turned toward her husband once more, adding, "He's kept everything a secret about this honeymoon from me, too!"

Jack merely smiled as the water taxi headed straight for a magnificent, russet hued *palazzo* with Gothic arches and pale plaster tracery around its many windows. The huge building fronted the Grand Canal and rose out of the water in the shadow of the looming basilica. The boat bumped gently against a wooden dock leading to a short stairway and small deck that allowed access to the arched loggia in front of them. A discreet brass plaque on one wall announced the Centurion Palace Hotel where inside, the original interior had been replaced with a wildly modern and colorful design scheme and a staff that seemed primed to meet their every need.

"Jack...this is incredible!" exclaimed Corlis, her sweeping glance taking in the eclectic mix of modern and antique surroundings. "How did you ever find this place?"

"Allegra Benedetti suggested it," he replied and then he pointed across the marble lobby with its futuristic, curved white leather settees. Creamy marble Corinthian columns stood sentry in this atrium where a sole figure stood waving a bouquet of flowers in their direction.

"Oh! Oh wow...Allegra!" Serena cried. She rushed across the space separating them to fling her arms around the woman whose skill and kindness had done so much to help Antonelli's Costumes regain its footing in New Orleans.

Allegra stepped back and handed Serena a long-stemmed collection of deep red roses mixed with white baby's breath.

"I couldn't come to your wedding, so I wanted you to have these immediately upon your arrival," she said, smiling greetings to Serena's companions who had advanced across the lobby to say hello. "Welcome, all of you, back to *Venezia* where the sun is finally shining and it's lovely and warm!" Allegra's declaration got a laugh from all four visitors. "Everyone at the shop and from the *Il Ballo* crew can't wait to see you all."

"And they will," Jack announced, "when they come tomorrow night to our *second* wedding reception on the terrace, just out there," he added, gesturing through the windows."

"You're kidding?" Serena exclaimed with a stunned expression. "All my Italian friends will be here?"

"Yep," Jack said with a satisfied expression, and then added, "Even the Italian Stallion."

"Who?" asked Corlis curiously.

King gave his wife's shoulders a squeeze. "Tell you later. Don't want to spoil Jack's dream trip," he said, ribbing his lifelong friend.

Allegra said, "Well, I just wanted to be here to greet you when you arrived, but I know you must be tired from your long journey. *A domani sera*! Until seven o'clock, tomorrow night, yes? *Arrivederci, carissimi.*"

The quartet soon checked in at the front desk and was escorted to their rooms on either end of a long corridor whose décor was equally *avante garde*, in contrast to the antiquity of the building's exterior.

Jack held back in the hallway until the porter had deposited their luggage inside their assigned chamber and received his tip. Then he waited until the man had turned the corner to return to the elevator.

"I'm not completely certain I can do this, but I'll try if you're game, Mrs. Antonelli-Durand."

"Try what?" Serena replied, confused.

"*This*. Ooof!" Jack huffed as he scooped one arm under his wife's knees and lifted Serena against his chest.

"You already attempted this on Julia Street," she protested, laughing.

"But this…is Venice," he said between gasps for air. "Worth a second attempt."

He managed to stagger across the threshold into their suite and covered the twenty or so steps to the broad bed without dropping his bride. There, he placed her as gently as he could manage atop the mattress of the modern, king-sized bed.

"Whee! Much better this time," Serena complimented him as Jack collapsed beside her.

After they stopped laughing, they lay shoulder-to-shoulder, hands clasped at their sides. They gazed at the carved wood ceiling with its verdigris patina that Serena wagered aloud was at least fifteen feet above their heads. The soaring walls of their room were painted a burnt umber with matching velvet drapes and tailored valances that framed the spectacular view of the Grand Canal and the famed Gritti Palace Hotel across the water. A massive, carved marble fireplace, almost large enough for them both to walk into, faced the bed that was festooned with pumpkin-hued velvet cushions contrasting smartly with the cream colored coverlet.

"Oh, Jack…you are amazing," she smiled at him, her arms cradling her head. "I can't believe you've arranged all this."

Jack rose from the bed, shut and locked the door to the corridor, and shrugged off his jacket. Then he slowly began unbuttoning his shirt. With one knee on the coverlet, he leaned close to her ear and whispered, "Shall I show you just *how* amazing I can be?"

"On top...or beneath the covers?" she teased.

"After a long soak in that big, marble tub in there," he said with a nod toward the stylish bathroom they could see through the doorway, "why don't I let *you* decide?"

"What a great way to start a marriage," Serena said softly, holding her arms wide, her love for this man filling the elegant chamber far beyond her fingertips. "But forget taking a bath!" she pronounced, reaching upward to pull him to her. "Come here, *Giovanni, il mio amore…*"

AUTHOR'S NOTE & ACKNOWLEDGEMENTS

There are many names on my list of people who guided me through the necessary stages creating this newly imagined tale of two cities—Venice and New Orleans. And what an incredible adventure writing *That Winter in Venice* turned out to be!

The best bit of luck in the middle of the process was in the person of Cheryl Popp, a journalist and public relations specialist who wanted to "tag along" on my third junket to Venice and write about it for *Marin Magazine*. "Girls On The Loose" we certainly were, dashing on and off the *vaporetto*, checking off entries on our long, individual 'To Do' lists for the magazine stories she wrote and the book I was researching. What *really* happened the night of the Venetian ball on February 14, 2015, could make another novel…and I treasure the wonderful time we had in Italy as traveling pals. Cheryl's friend, DJ Puffert—who spends half the year in *La Serenissima* and the other half in Sausalito, California—armed us with valuable travel tips and a list of local contacts and restaurants in Venice that kept us well fed and provided me with delicious Venetian fare with which to feed my fictional characters.

When I first had the idea to set a novel in two cities dealing with rising water and climate change, I never dreamed I would eventually attend a genuine masked *Carnevale* ball in the *Palazzo Pisani Moretta* in the dead of winter and dance till 4a.m. Nor did I anticipate listening to Vivaldi played exquisitely by candlelight on ancient instruments, or sleeping in a *palazzetto* within a stone's throw of one of my favorite churches in all the world—the *Basilica di Santa Maria della Salute*, the Basilica of St. Mary of Health—which I called "The Gratitude Church" in the novel.

Early in the research, I had the great good fortune to interview and "shadow" Antonia Sautter, a legendary costume designer who also creates exquisite modern clothing and accessories for Atelier Antonia Sautter in the San Marco district. Not only did she generously allow me to visit her rental establishment where some 1500 costumes await the next customer, she also permitted me to spend an invaluable afternoon at her workshop where magnificent attire denoting several past centuries is constructed. What a visual feast to see that second-floor "inner sanctum" overlooking the roofs of Venice that was filled with magnificent fabrics and mannequins dressed in silk and satin gowns in various stages of completion and staffed by a small battalion of talented seamstresses. They and Mrs. Sautter's other staff were incredibly helpful to this author and I thank them, too. You can find images of the workshop, clothes, and costumes on:
 www.pinterest.com/cijiware.

And, about that ball! For the last two decades Antonia Sautter has also produced the incredible *Il Ballo del Doge*, an evening of spectacular entertainment, food, wine, and a magical Renaissance ambiance that must be experienced to be believed. You can see videos of previous balls (and even buy tickets for next year's event) at www.ilballodeldoge.com. Mrs. Sautter's making it possible for me to attend as her guest so I could experience the event first hand was a gift I can never repay, other than to confirm that it was one of those way-beyond-a-bucket-list experiences that I will cherish for the rest of my life.

On two of my three trips to Venice, I was welcomed to the magnificent *Palazzo Alverà* overlooking the Grand Canal by Contessa Ketty Alverà, my guide to all things that are "genuine Venetian." During the winter trip in 2015, she hosted a magical dinner and, the following day, personally escorted us to see Venetian artisans that create everything from gilt-covered, carved lion bookends to handmade linens, to perfumes to leather goods to fanciful masks, all to swoon over. "Nothing made in China!" she declared fiercely, with a sweep of her hand toward the street sign, *Salizzada S. Samuele,* whose shops sold only authentic Venetian products. Clearly, *La Contessa* is a champion of the beauty, history, and artistic talent of the true Venice that is fighting to survive in a global economy.

I must also thank Ketty's cousin, the Contessa Anna da Schio, who was our hostess for ten days at the *Palazzetto da Schio*, a tucked-away guesthouse in the *Dorsoduro* section of Venice adjacent to the aforementioned *Basilica di Santa Maria della Salute*. Each apartment featured family antiques and came complete with Wi-Fi and a cellular phone, which made life for a journalist and author immeasurably simpler. Situated on a small canal known as the *Rio della Fornace* and a stone's throw from the Peggy Guggenheim Museum, we were welcomed like members of the family and will forever be grateful for the experience of staying there and gaining an appreciation in some small measure of the daily life of modern Venetians. You can view the rooms we stayed in at http://www.palazzettodaschio.it/.

Among the scores of interviews I conducted for this novel, Mario Belloni, mask maker extraordinaire in his shop *Ca'Macana Venezia* was a charming host and a master of the ancient art of disguise. His workshop (where visitors can take classes) bedazzles the eye, and the history of his art is referenced several times in my story. You can see the listings of classes and the location of his shop at www.camacana.com .

My friend Wenke Thoman opened the door to visiting the Fortuny showroom on the island of *Giudecca*. We had a wonderful interview with General Manager Giuseppe Ianni who, when we asked if we could see the factory next door, said with a sad smile, "I am so sorry, but we don't allow visitors in there. Not even my wife knows the secret process [used in the manufacture of the fabrics]." To make up for this, he took us behind the building to see the magnificent private gardens.

Equally welcoming and helpful to this project was Francesco Nassivera, antiquarian and a fund of wisdom about Venice and its fine and decorative arts. His shop, *Campiello Ca'Zen* in the *San Polo* district is not to be missed. He was kind enough to walk us around the corner to *Atelier Pietro Longhi* to meet costume designer Francesco Briggi and his partner, Raffaele Dessi. The firm specializes in creating authentic historical costumes for the general public and museum displays around the world.

Another source of helpful information about the daily life of modern Venetians were our hosts at the second guesthouse we stayed, *Ca'Arco Antico*, which became my heroine's home for the two months she lived as a high-level assistant to the fictional costumer Allegra Benedetti. My hosts Antonella, Lorenza, Gianfranco, and Marco have my deepest appreciation for a lovely stay in the *Canaletto* room and for answering the questions I peppered them with every day of my visit there.

My American friend and antiques expert, Tom Rotella, has Italian roots and pointed me toward a number of aspects in Venice that proved valuable. That he gifted me with his mother's beautiful opal and emerald ring purchased in *La Serenissima* many years ago has been a treasured bonus.

As part of my mission to understand the similarities between Venice and New Orleans, I also made several "refresher" trips to the Big Easy (many natives scoff at that designation, but others love the sound of it, as do I).

Over the years, I have acquired my share of "throw beads" during the St. Anne Parade on the morning of Fat Tuesday; attended a Mardi Gras ball in all its finery (made in China and locally as well); listened to incredible Louis Armstrong tunes, among many jazz greats, at Preservation Hall and at clubs along Frenchman's Street; and have even slept on a "fainting couch" on Dauphine Street in the French Quarter in my writer pal, Michael Llewellyn's former apartment (that served as King and Corlis's abode both in *Midnight on Julia Street* and its stand-alone sequel, *That Winter in Venice*). Michael also generously sent me his list of parallels that exist between New Orleans and Venice which he gave me permission to use in the novel and that formed the basis for the Prologue that I created to "set the stage" for the story that would follow. Gratitude, big time, is owed this dear friend.

On my latest sojourn to NOLA in May of 2014, I ate my fill of incredible chicken and Andouille sausage gumbo at The Gumbo Shop in New Orleans' French Quarter, swooned over Oysters Rockefeller at Galatoire's, along with biting into the best po'boy sandwich in creation at Liuzza's on Bienville. For these and many other wonderful and/or unforgettable experiences, I not only have Mr. Llewellyn to thank but also local pals that include: Samara Poche, who leant me an apartment in 2014 for two weeks in the heart of the French Quarter; Leslie Perrin and Chuck Ransdell, who, among many kindnesses over the years, escorted me to a charity event in support of historic preservation in the FQ; Lee Pryor and Julie Smith, who are an amazing and reliable source of the latest intelligence about their beloved city.

Since Katrina, I made three very different tours in the Crescent City that were tremendously helpful in creating the background canvas for this work. The first included a visit to the Mardi Gras World float-building workshops. My behind-the-scenes view was made possible by one of the partners, Barry Kern of the celebrated Kern Studios where the Louis Armstrong statue at the New Orleans airport was constructed.

The second tour sent me to Southern Costume Company in the Central Business District, the "CBD," where I spent a few days with owner Wingate Jones and saw thousands of costumes the company supplies to the public as well as for some sixty "krewes"—or clubs—that sponsor parades during the Mardi Gras season in New Orleans.

At the costume shop I also met Clara Diaz, a multi-talented designer who demonstrated the intricacies of "building" a mermaid outfit covered in emerald green sequins with a hidden handle so the wearer wouldn't trip over her heavy fish tail!

The third tour in the spring following Hurricane Katrina was far more sobering. New Orleans friends of longstanding, Lee Pryor and his wife, mystery novelist Julie Smith, took me to see the Post-Katrina Ninth Ward where we drove down many mortally wounded and deserted streets and stared out the car windows, fighting tears as each block unfolded. I felt the same overwhelming wave of sadness when I stood next to the rebuilt 17th Street Canal that rises above the remaining and newly constructed houses, as well as still-empty lots in Lakeview, one of several neighborhoods backing up on Lake Pontchartrain that suffered heavy losses when the levees and canal walls failed in 2005.

I could not have begun to grasp the realities of post-Katrina life in Louisiana without picking the brain of environmental journalist Mark Schleifstein of NOLA.com | The *Times-Picayune*. One of the great reporters still working at a newspaper, he virtually predicted Katrina in print several years before it happened in a piece called "The Big One" written with John McQuaid. In 2006, Mark's subsequent stories were among those honored with Public Service and Breaking News Pulitzer Prizes for Katrina coverage. This hardworking journalist was incredibly generous with his time and expertise to a fellow *former* journalist trying to understand what it was like to cover a disaster like Hurricane Katrina. A long lunch at Herbsaint in the CBD early in the research sent me off and running after the story of the 17th Street Canal in particular and the repercussions of its failure on two fictional families. He is another "source" I owe, big time. Nevertheless, any mistakes or misinterpretations of his words and writings, as well as of the vast data that exists about the storm, rest squarely on my shoulders.

One of the best books giving a full account of Hurricane Katrina and its aftermath is Dr. Ivor van Heerden's *The Storm* (written with Mike Bryan). This is a harrowing read and one that every American should take the trouble to absorb. Former deputy director of the now shuttered LSU Hurricane Center, Dr. van Heerden subsequently had a "set-to" with the administration at Louisiana State University as a result of his unflinching reports about the U.S. Army Corps of Engineering's responsibility for the levee and canal wall failures. LSU's "questionable behavior" involved alleged retaliation, including van Heerden's firing for fear his remarks would jeopardize the school's federal funding. Subsequently, a judge found van Heerdan's assertions of wrongful termination were "undisputed" in the documents related to the professor's suit that was finally settled in his favor in 2013. Dr. van Heerden now resides in the Chesapeake Bay area but maintains his ties with New Orleans through www.levees.org where he and his fellow crusaders fight for safer protection for this water-ringed city.

Orphans of Katrina by Karen O'Toole about the massive effort to rescue the animals abandoned or stranded in the storm is a book that breaks your heart and a story that suggested the fictional character of Marielle Durand Claiborne. If you're an animal lover, you can learn more at www.orphansofkatrina.com

Much of the foundation of the New Orleans sections of *That Winter in Venice* was laid pre-Katrina during my research for *Midnight on Julia Street* (first published in 1999; revised edition, 2011), and so I extend repeated thank yous to New Orleanians Jeannette Bell, Bill Borah, Patricia Gay, Paul Neveski, William D and Sally K. Reeves, Britton Tice and the gang at Garden District Bookshop, along with the authors of the books listed below.

From my base in California, I must thank my "Ciji's Beta Readers" who are brave enough to scan early drafts of my work: Diane Barr, Ellie Cabot, Carol Kavalaris, Diane Natt, Joy Ware, Marilee Zdenek, and most especially New Orleans native, public relations expert and dear friend, Gaynell Rogers. Betas, too, in a sense were certain pals who heard me yak about this novel often enough to *feel* as if they'd read one draft or another: Jola Anderson, Linda Bucklin, Pat Boddy, Chris Butler, Janet Chapman, Phoebe Fielding, EV Gilbreath, Alison Harris, Bonnie MacLaird, Cindy Mason, Deb and Larry Mindel, Linda Ojeda, Dean Stolber, Susan Wintersteen, Millie Zinman, and my dear friend of longstanding, author Cynthia Wright.

I am also deeply indebted to Kim Ostrom-Cates (pen name: Ella Marsh Chase) who is not only a sublimely talented novelist but also a very skilled editor. I am so grateful for her candid editorial wisdom, copyediting, friendship, and for worshipping that special breed of dog as much as I do: our beloved Cavalier King Charles Spaniels.

The novel is dedicated to two friends who are both consummate professionals in their fields: the aforementioned Cheryl Popp, and Carol Kavalaris, my dog walking pal, the perfect neighbor, and a woman who runs a global enterprise called ArcusStone™. This limestone product, with the proper sealant applied underneath, can make an historic building look "antique" but still be watertight. What are the chances of living across the street from the one person I've ever met that knows how to fix a leaky palazzo? ("Serendipity One Million!") Carol's guidance and practical advice provided a crucial "plot point" just when I needed it and I will be forever grateful to her for helping me figure out how to deal with stemming the *acqua alta* that threatened to cancel my fictional *Il Ballo di Carnevale*! And without the help of my cousins, Eve Forester Rossi and her husband Marino who live in Florence, my university-vintage Italian employed in the novel might be completely comical. Let us hope I instituted their "suggested changes" in decent form. If not, it's my fault and *le mie scuse più profonde*!

As with every book I write, I am deeply grateful for the love and support of my husband of nearly four decades, Tony Cook, who has always encouraged my "gallivanting around the world." We've got one more to go in the Four Season Quartet project—*That Spring in Paris*—a work-in-progress that is likely to provide a few more interesting adventures. My much-loved son and daughter-in-law, Jamie Ware Billett and Dr. Teal Eich—New Yorkers, now—provided welcome respites to and from several trips to Venice and will probably do the same on the next one as we head for France!

And, finally, a posthumous thank-you and bon voyage to Ensign Aubrey, my dear, sweet fourteen-year-old Cavalier King Charles Spaniel who loyally laid under my desk until I wrote "The End" on this one. As for Venice and New Orleans, let us pray measures are taken in time to prevent a similar epitaph...

For anyone wishing to explore more about this "tale of two cities," here follows a partial bibliography culled from the many books I consulted for this effort:

VENICE:

Venice: A New History by Thomas F. Madden
Venice: The Biography of a City by Christopher Hibbert
The City of Falling Angels by John Berendt
Carnival Masks of Venice: A Photographic Essay by J.C. Brown
Save Venice, Inc: Four Decades of Restoration in Venice edited by Melissa Conn, et al
The Costume Designer's Handbook by Rosemary Ingham and Liz Covey

I read nearly a dozen photography and large format books on Carnival in Venice, including one I purchased and dreamed over some twenty-five years ago:

Carnival in Venice by Shirley and David Rowen, published by Harry N. Abrams, Inc.

NEW ORLEANS:

The Storm by Ivor van Heerden and Mike Bryan
1 Dead in Attic by Chris Rose
Rising Tide: The Great Mississippi Flood of 1927 and How It Changed America by John M. Barry
New Orleans: Elegance and Decadence by Richard Sexton and Randolph Delehanty;
New Orleans Interiors by Mary Louise Christovich, photography by N. Jane Iseley
The Free People of Color of New Orleans by Mary Gehman;
The Second Battle of New Orleans: A History of the Vieux Carrè Riverfront Expressway Controversy by William E. Borah and Richard O. Baumback Jr.
The French Quarter by Herbert Asbury.

Treating Trauma - Survivors with PTSD by Rachel Yehuda, Ph.D
"The Big One," Times-Picayune archive, by Mark Schleifstein and John McQuaid.

Numerous accounts about Hurricane Katrina and its aftermath are available online from the archives of the *Times-Picayune*; the U.S. Geologic Survey; the U.S. Army Corps of Engineering; *The New York Times*, and a number of ad hoc blogs and newsletters from various interest groups that sprang up in the wake of the storm. All make for compelling reading.

CIJI's "WOO-WOO" LIBRARY:

The Biology of Belief by Dr. Bruce Lipton
Epigentics by Lyle Armstrong
Ancestral Clearing — 5 audio tapes by John Newton

If intrigued to explore this field further, simply type "Epigenetics" into a search engine and see what turns up.

Ciji Ware
Sausalito, California

Visit Ciji at:
http://www.cijiware.com

Facebook:
http://www.facebook.com/CijiWareNovelist

Images of the author's researches can be seen at:
http://www.pinterest.com/cijiware/that-winter-in-venice/

The Four Seasons Quartet — Book 1
That Summer in Cornwall

Meredith Champlin, the newly appointed guardian of an unruly "Beverly Hills brat," decamps from her settled existence in Wyoming with her charge and her Welsh Corgi to spend the summer with her English relatives at Barton Hall, a shabby-chic castle perched on the remote cliffs of UK's West Country.

Meredith's summer escape gets even more complicated when former British Army Lieutenant Sebastian Pryce, veteran of a bomb-sniffing K9 squad in Afghanistan, proposes they join forces to found the Barton Hall Canine Obedience Academy, along with signing her up for his volunteer rough-and-ready Cornwall Search and Rescue Team.

Even with an assist from a novice search dog named T-Rex, the odds seem long that a mere three months in the land of Meredith's Cornish ancestors can transform her troubled ward into a happier child, heal the wounds suffered by her soldier-turned-significant-other, and save the Barton-Teague estate from pending disaster.

Available at online retailers or through cijiware.com.

"Ware again proves she can intertwine fact and fiction to create an entertaining and harmonious whole." — *Publishers Weekly*

The Four Seasons Quartet — Book 2
That Autumn in Edinburgh

Can memories of a tragic, eighteenth century love triangle be passed down through a descendant's DNA?

When Fiona Fraser's mercurial boss dispatches the American designer to Edinburgh to create a Scottish Home Furnishings Collection, the chemistry deepens instantly when she and tartan manufacturer Alex Maxwell discover their ancestral bonds to the star-crossed lovers Thomas Fraser—the "Lost Lieutenant"—and Jane Maxwell, the flamboyant 4th Duchess of Gordon who died in 1812.

From the cobbled streets of Edinburgh's Royal Mile to the tartan and cashmere mills of the Scottish border country, the modern lovers grapple with the imminent threat of financial ruin to their respective firms, along with ancient wounds echoing down through time...and a heartbreaking mystery, hidden for more than two centuries, that will dictate Alex and Fiona's own destinies...

Available at online retailers or through cijiware.com.

"A deep, complex novel exploring love, betrayal, healing, and renewal in the human heart." — *Affaire de Coeur*

"Vibrant and exciting..." — *Literary Times*

Midnight on Julia Street — the prequel to
That Winter in Venice

If you enjoyed meeting Kingsbury Duvallon and Corlis McCullough in *That Winter in Venice*, you will love reading their own story in *Midnight on Julia Street*, a novel of scandal that transcends time in the Big Easy.

The sultry streets of pre-Katrina New Orleans, the glamorous Garden District, derelict riverfront cotton warehouses, and gritty back alleys come alive in this time-slip novel of a feisty reporter who inexplicably glides between the nineteenth century and the modern world. A long-forgotten drama of blackmail, swindles, and a love affair that is still changing lives leaves Corlis and King wondering if their burgeoning, unholy attraction will render them pawns in a matrix of mystery and deceit.

Available at online retailers or through cijiware.com.

"Vibrant and exciting…an intriguing plot full of rich characters that I couldn't wait to see what happened." — *Literary Times*

"Wonderful storyteller, Ciji Ware is in rare form with this intriguing and terrific novel." — *RT Book Reviews*

ABOUT THE AUTHOR

Ciji Ware is the *New York Times* and *USA Today* bestselling author of nine novels, a novella, and two nonfiction works. She is the daughter, niece, and descendant of writers, so writing fiction is just part of the "family business." She has been honored with the Dorothy Parker Award of Excellence and a *Romantic Times* Award for Best Fictionalized Biography for *Island of the Swans*, and in 2012, was shortlisted in the prestigious WILLA (Cather) Literary Award for *A Race to Splendor*.

An Emmy-award winning television producer, former radio and TV on-air broadcaster for ABC in Los Angeles, as well as print and online journalist, Ware received a BA in History from Harvard University and has the distinction of being the first woman graduate of Harvard College to serve as the President of the Harvard Alumni Association, Worldwide. As a result of Ware's first novel, *Island of the Swans*, she was made a Fellow of the Society of Antiquaries of Scotland (FSA Scot), and in 2015 was named to the "Martha's Vineyard Writers-in-Residence" program—both honors she treasures. The author lives in the San Francisco Bay Area and can be contacted through her agent, Celeste Fine at Sterling Lord Literistic, or at http://www.cijiware.com

Any notes of grammatical or formatting errors are most appreciated. If you spot any of these pesky devils, please send them to Ciji at Ciji@cijiware.com. We will gather them together and make the corrections, enrolling you among our honored "Ciji Beta Readers!"

Made in the USA
San Bernardino, CA
20 May 2016